GORDITA CONSPIRACY

LYLE CHRISTIE

This book is dedicated to all who have faced

adversity in terms of health, work, relationships,

or even a really disgusting public restroom, and

now desperately need a FUCKING literary, if not

FUCKING literal, break from this crazy thing we call

life.

•Please excuse the use of profanity and be warned
that there will be more to follow, as well as some
traditional humor, bathroom humor, and a goodly
amount of spirited sexual encounters, though it
will all be delivered tastefully and with the intent of
conveying a deep, rewarding, and soulful catharsis.

GORDITA CONSPIRACY

MANTASY INC.

WWW.LYLECHRISTIE.COM

LYLE@LYLECHRISTIE.COM

BOOK DESIGN AND LAYOUT: CHRISTOPHER IMLAY

COVER DESIGN: CHRISTOPHER IMLAY & LYLE CHRISTIE

EDITORS: RUTH A. BRIGHT • CHRIS COOPER • ARIA PEARSON • KATHERINE GUNDLING

PROOFREADERS: MATT ZEEMAN • KRIS CHRISTIE • MATT THOMAS

FIRST PUBLISHED IN 2013

REVISED IN 2020

ISBN-13: 978-1-949386-19-6

CHAPTER ONE-PROLOGUE: **Stranger on a Plane** — 9

CHAPTER TWO: **A Sort of Homecoming** — 16

CHAPTER THREE: **The Long and Winding Road** — 35

CHAPTER FOUR: **The Nightcap** — 53

CHAPTER FIVE: **Mile High Club Provisional Membership** — 65

CHAPTER SIX: **Road Trip** — 88

CHAPTER SEVEN: **The Great Exodus** — 105

CHAPTER EIGHT: **Colleagues with Benefits** — 120

CHAPTER NINE: **Pink Pig: the Little Jeep that Could** — 139

CHAPTER TEN: **Istanbul not constantinople** — 154

CHAPTER ELEVEN: **Saturday Night Fever** — 174

CHAPTER TWELVE: **Staying Alive** — 190

CHAPTER THIRTEEN: **First Class Idiot** — 213

CHAPTER FOURTEEN: **Flying the Friendlier Skies** — 230

CHAPTER FIFTEEN: **A Room with a View** — 248

CHAPTER SIXTEEN: **Dead Men Don't Wear Jogging Shorts** — 269

CHAPTER SEVENTEEN: **The Linen Gorilla** — 289

CHAPTER EIGHTEEN: **Mall Rats** — 306

CHAPTER NINETEEN: **Boys Will be Boys** — 326

CHAPTER TWENTY: **Are You There, God, it's Me, Tag** — 360

CHAPTER TWENTY-ONE: **Smokey and the Bandit** — 379

CHAPTER TWENTY-TWO: **The Oddest Couple** — 393

CHAPTER TWENTY-THREE: **The Desert Fox** — 409

CHAPTER TWENTY-FOUR: **The Oasis in the Oasis** — 430

CHAPTER TWENTY-FIVE: **The Flight of the Phoenix** — 455

CHAPTER TWENTY-SIX: **A Walk in the Clouds** — 471

CHAPTER TWENTY-SEVEN: **Cannonball Run 4**   **496**

CHAPTER TWENTY-EIGHT: **Two Tickets to Paradise**   **514**

CHAPTER TWENTY-NINE: **Blond Ambition**   **530**

CHAPTER THIRTY: **A Kind of Homecoming**   **548**

Mr. Pickles   **552**

Acknowledgements   **554**

Origin of the Mantasy Genre   **557**

About the Author   **561**

BOOK THREE IN THE

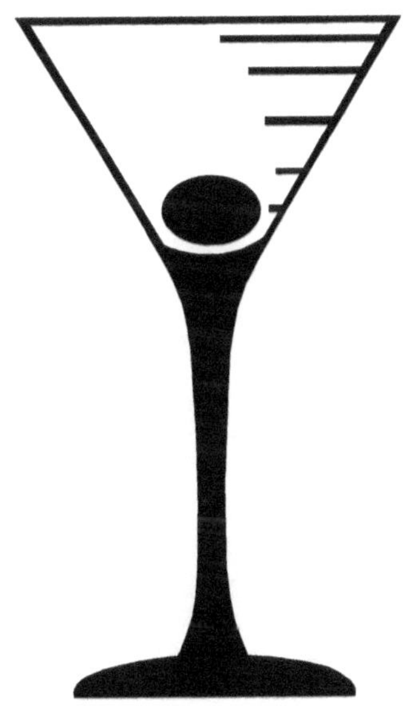

MANTASY SERIES

CHAPTER ONE: PROLOGUE
Stranger on a Plane

Virgin flight 442 from Frankfurt Germany was on final approach to San Francisco International Airport, and, up in first class, the flight attendant, a beautiful and shapely brunette named Amber, was making her final walk-through of the cabin. She checked to make sure that everyone was properly buckled in, but she saved her last stop for her new favorite passenger. His name was Klaus, and he was romance novel cover hot with his chiseled jaw, shaggy blond hair, and muscular frame. He was also particularly charming, and he and Amber had been flirting with each other since the very first moment he walked in to the first class compartment. She smiled as she arrived at his seat, and he, of course, smiled back at her as he pointed down at his seat belt buckle.

"Am I properly buckled in?" he asked, his English excellent though clearly flavored by his German accent.

"I'd better check."

She leaned over and purposefully dangled her enticing cleavage in front of his eyes as she reached down and checked the buckle before moving her hand past it and giving his groin a playful squeeze. Klaus was already sporting a semi, and Amber appeared to be fairly impressed.

"Oh, well now! Everything seems to be just fine here," she said, before looking around the cabin to make sure none of the other flight attendants were nearby.

At that point she lowered her voice and leaned in close to Klaus.

"So, when you finish up with your business, let's go out for that drink," Amber said, with a flirtatious smile.

Klaus found himself feeling pretty damn excited by Amber's spicy comment, though, strangely, it was her rather outgoing nature, not her beauty, that he found to be her most alluring quality.

"Yeah, though I might be running a little late depending on how things go," he said.

"Better late than never, and, in case you need a little motivation, you'll have this," Amber said, as she picked up his iPhone, activated the camera, then knelt down out of view of the other passengers.

Klaus was curious what she had in mind and couldn't believe his eyes when she undid her two top buttons, slid her shirt open to reveal one of her breasts, then smiled and snapped a quick selfie. Finished, she put his phone down, buttoned up her shirt, and leaned in and gave him a quick kiss.

"I'll see you tonight," she said, as she stood up.

"Or perhaps even sooner," he responded.

She headed back towards the front of the plane, and Klaus couldn't help but watch her every step, as her tight fitting uniform made quite a show of her stunning figure. Sure, Klaus tended to garner more than his fair amount of female attention, but his busy work schedule and frequent travel made it nearly impossible for him to meet someone as charming and alluring as Amber. He was, therefore, definitely going to do his best to finish up his business and make it out for a drink with her tonight.

Once she disappeared from view, he turned his gaze out the window and saw that the weather was clear and sunny, and it was looking to be a lovely day in the San Francisco Bay Area. As the large jet descended, he heard and felt the thump of the landing gear being deployed, and, not long after that, the nose of the jet flared up, and they dropped smoothly onto the runway. They taxied to the terminal, and, when the jet came to rest, all of the passengers prepared to disembark. Klaus reached up and grabbed his carry-on bag from the overhead compartment then joined the slow procession for the exit door. There, he came across Amber and the other flight attendant, who were both making sure to personally say goodbye to each and every one of the first class passengers.

"Until tonight," he said, as he nodded and smiled.

She smiled back and gave him a little wink, which inspired him to pick up his pace and pass the other people ahead of him as he made his way up the jetway. Now, that he had some enticing plans for the evening, he was even more determined to finish his work in a timely manner. He arrived at customs and flashed his diplomatic passport, and it allowed him to bypass the usual security checkpoint, and he was soon at baggage claim. His suitcase came onto the carousel, and he grabbed it and texted the person who was picking him up to tell him that he was headed outside to wait at the curb. A minute later, a white Audi S4 pulled over in front of him, and the driver, a well dressed, clean cut Arabic looking man, popped the trunk release. Klaus went to the back of the car and placed his luggage beside a black leather attaché case then closed the trunk and walked around and slid into the passenger seat.

"Welcome to San Francisco, Klaus," the man said, with an obvious British accent as he held out his hand to shake.

"Good to see you, Gareth," he said, as they completed the gesture.

"How was your flight?" Gareth asked.

"Excellent, as I managed to score a date with a lovely flight attendant."

"Bloody hell, mate! I had to spend at least a month is this city before I met an eligible woman, and you fucking met one before you even put your feet on the ground."

"Perhaps you should go to the gym more often."

"I don't think they have a machine that will make me look like you."

"Yeah, they do, it's called a bench press."

The two of them shared a laugh as Gareth turned onto the access road that skirted the airport and led to the location of many of the support businesses such as catering, air freight, and aircraft maintenance. Traffic was unusually light, and it wasn't long before Gareth turned in to the parking lot of an unmarked warehouse and parked beside a silver BMW M4.

"All right, mate, this is where I get off," Gareth said.

"Yeah, but, unfortunately, I won't be getting off until later," Klaus said, as he pulled out his phone and brought up the picture of Amber.

It was an obvious attempt to rub it in his friend's face, and it worked exactly as planned.

"You bloody ass! Does she happen to have a twin sister?"

"If she does, I'll call you and tell you how it went—with both of them."

The two of them shared another laugh, then they stepped out of the car and walked around to the back.

"All right then, my friend, everything you need is in the attaché case, and I obviously don't need to tell you that it will be a lot easier for everyone involved if it happens to look like an accident."

"Yes, I understand."

"Good, then I'll be going and let you get to it, so you can finish up and get to that date tonight. Cheers," he said, as they shook hands.

"Cheers," he said, with a smile.

Gareth pulled a key fob out of his pocket, hit the unlock button, and went over and took a seat in the BMW M4. It started with a deep throaty grumble, then he gave a final wave as he headed out of the parking lot. Klaus waved back then popped the trunk of the Audi and opened the attaché case to see there was a silenced 9mm Glock pistol and four magazines. He picked up the Glock, slid in a magazine and chambered a round, then placed it back in the case and closed the trunk. It was time to get to work, so he casually strolled around and slid in behind the wheel then pulled out his phone, made a call, and patiently waited for three rings for the person on the other end to answer.

"Hello, Klaus, I take it you've arrived," the person said.

"Yes, so everything is in motion," he responded.

"Excellent, and I would say good luck, but I know you don't believe in that kind of thing," he said, with a chuckle.

Klaus was notorious for his very German-like belief that success always depended upon proper planning and execution.

"No, I definitely do not," Klaus said, also chuckling.

"Well then, call me when it's done."

"I will," he said, just before ending the call.

He opened the picture app on his phone and had another look at Amber, and couldn't help but get excited at the thought of seeing her later tonight. Unfortunately, he had a job to do first, so he swiped his finger back to the left to reveal a picture of the man he would soon see in person. He'd, of course, already memorized his face and various details, but Klaus was a perfectionist and thought it wise to have yet another look. Satisfied he would be completely able to recognize him, he closed the app and placed the phone down in the car's center console. He instinctively had a look around his surroundings and, seeing no suspicious persons or vehicles in the vicinity, started the car and drove out of the parking lot. He left the frontage road and merged onto the 101 freeway heading north towards San Francisco, though his final destination would be on the other side of the Golden Gate Bridge, specifically the beautiful little town of Sausalito, where he had one simple objective: kill Tag Finn.

CHAPTER TWO
A Sort of Homecoming

It was nine fifteen on a Saturday morning when I arrived home and entered my houseboat for the first time in almost a month. I had forgotten to take out the garbage before departing on my last job, and my place smelled faintly of the last meal I had cooked. I believe it was a breakfast consisting of eggs and chicken apple sausages, and it certainly smelled better then than now. Still, it was nice to be home, but I was missing the warm weather of the Caribbean and the excitement and female companionship I'd had on my European adventure. Oh well, life moves on I suppose. I put my things down at the foot of the stairs and strolled into the kitchen and made a pot of coffee. While it brewed, I took out the garbage, opened some windows, and soon the heavenly aroma of coffee was wafting across the kitchen on the bay breeze. The brew cycle finished, and it was time to walk over and pour myself a cup. Unfortunately, the half and half had soured, so I had to open up a carton of almond milk that I kept around for just these kinds of emergencies. It wasn't as good as my usual cup, but it would do the job and get my morning moving, so that I could make the most of the twenty-four hours before I started my next job.

The first and most important chore was to unpack the case of Soft Taco Island premium rum I had acquired during my travels. Each precious bottle was carefully encased in bubble wrap and stored in a wooden case, and it took a good five minutes before I could free all the bottles and move them behind my bar. With the alcohol stashed in its new home, I strolled back to the kitchen to sort through the pile of mail that my neighbor had left on the breakfast table. As usual, I discovered only bills, but at least I could afford to pay them for once, as the last month of work had been particularly lucrative. Speaking of which, I needed to go to my bank and make a deposit that was going to make my banker shit his pants when he saw the amount. When I had left three plus weeks ago, I was in dire jeopardy of losing my home, but now I was worth in excess of a hundred and fifty million dollars. Money may not buy happiness, but it sure as hell made misery more bearable. Of course, I wasn't exactly miserable at the moment, quite the opposite, in fact, though my recent wealth came with a lot of strings attached and a hell of a new client and requisite back story.

It all started with an exciting adventure in the Caribbean, where I rescued a damsel in distress and went up against a French arms dealer in order to sabotage the largest terrorist attack since nine eleven. The arms dealer got away in the end, and my next job entailed chasing him down in Europe and bringing him back into the loving arms of the Central Intelligence Agency—the caveat being I was paid more than a hundred and fifty million dollars in valuable gems left over from the failed arms deal. I got my man, but, things were far more complicated than I could have ever imagined and the entire affair, from start to finish, had been cleverly orchestrated by a secret society. Unlike the Illuminati, who had a cool and menacing name, my puppeteers were simply called the Topless Agenda. They were a collection of some of the most powerful people across the globe, and their esteemed ranks included politicians, wealthy industrialists, royal families, and of course lots of old money. They might have a silly name, but they were a very serious group of people with very serious plans, and everything thus far was just a prelude to the real prize—a new and exciting assignment whose success lay solely in my humble hands.

Five years ago I went on my last assignment for the CIA's Special Activities Division. The mission had entailed smuggling a brilliant scientist out of Iran. His name was Farid Ardeshir, and he was the head of their rapidly growing nuclear program, but he desperately wanted to escape to a better life in America, and America, in turn, was more than happy to take him into their loving arms. As is the case with most special operations, things didn't go exactly according to plan, and, when Iranian agents showed up in Istanbul, the mission orders changed for the worse. Rather than risk the scientist falling back into enemy hands, the people in charge of the operation ordered me to kill the scientist and send his body to the bottom of the Aegean Sea in an old fishing boat. As far as the official record was concerned, I completed my mission then, completely disenchanted with government work, resigned from the Agency and returned home to Northern California and became a private investigator.

Somehow, the Topless Agenda knew the real story—that the supposedly dead scientist was, in fact, currently alive and living large under a new identity in the United Arab Emirates, and, more importantly, had discovered the Holy Grail of the modern age—the secret to making cold fusion work. Cold fusion had been the bugaboo of the scientific community since electrochemists Martin Fleischmann and Stanley Pons believed they had discovered it back in 1989. Unfortunately, further research showed that they were incapable of replicating their findings, and cold fusion, or low energy nuclear reaction, was believed to be technically impossible. If Farid could indeed make it work, then it would become the biggest energy boom since crude oil, and the Topless Agenda believed, rightly so, that his discovery was going to forever change energy production, and in turn, the fate of the entire world. Thus, they desperately wanted to bring him back to the west, but, they needed me because I was the only person in the world Ardeshir would theoretically trust after the whole CIA debacle.

So, there I sat at my breakfast table, my mind spinning as I pondered the thought that I was about to head halfway across the world on yet another exciting job. It was certainly hard to believe that a month ago I was an underpaid private investigator, yet now held the solution to world's energy problems in my very existence. The immortal words of Ferris Bueller suddenly came to mind: life moves pretty fast, and, if you don't stop and take a look once in a while, you might miss it. Well, I had been missing it and living a bit like Ferris's best friend Cameron, though my hiding place wasn't my bed, but rather my daily mundane existence. Those times were over, however, and I certainly wasn't missing anything anymore.

I took another sip of coffee and felt that familiar pressure in my lower abdomen and realized that my favorite morning beverage was doing its job. Ah—to be home and alone with my porcelain mistress. I missed her simple lines, comfortable white plastic seat, and I longed for her gentle embrace. I refilled my cup, grabbed my book from my bag, and entered the greatest, though least appreciated, sanctuary of humankind. There, I sat upon the porcelain throne, put my cup on the sink beside me, and opened my book to the folded piece of toilet paper that served as my bookmark—an item that told the story of where I obviously did most of my reading. I took another sip of coffee and was about to initiate the release sequence when I remembered that my iPhone was in my pants pocket. Shit. With my luck, every friend, relative, telemarketer, and scam artist would start calling in the next five seconds. I reached down, dug my iPhone out of my pants pocket, then set it on the sink next to my coffee and gave it a stern warning.

"OK, fucker, right now I need some alone time, and you are my filter to keep out the world. Do me this little favor, and I'll get you that new ballistic glass screen protector we've been talking about," I said, aloud.

I took another sip, opened my book, then felt the gentle release of my bowels. It was almost bittersweet as I said goodbye to my most recent meal of pork chops, broccoli, and scalloped potatoes. It had been delicious and served me well, so now, I sincerely hoped it would enjoy its new existence at the waste processing plant at the other end of Sausalito. Parting was such sweet sorrow yet a necessary evil of the cycle of life. I took another sip of coffee then turned my attention back to my book and skimmed the pages until finding the spot where I had left off. I started reading, but only made it to the next page when my phone rang.

"Goddammit! You promised!"

Who the hell would be calling now? I looked at the number and saw that it was from the 510 area code. That was the East Bay, and I only knew a couple people over there, and none of their names had popped up on the screen.

"Oh shit!" I said, just before hitting the answer button.

"Hello, Tag Finn Investigations."

"Yeah hello, it's me—Estelle. Is it a good time to talk? You're not taking a shit or anything are you?"

Estelle. Wow. I hadn't seen or talked to her since our time together on Soft Taco Island three weeks ago. She was the chief purser on a mega yacht that I'd traveled on in the Caribbean, and we'd had a short though amazing relationship. Unfortunately, we parted ways when I flew off to Europe to chase down the French arms dealer Babineux, and she had left for a visit home and apparently hooked up with her ex-fiancée and was re-engaged.

"Of course not."

"You sure? Because I thought I heard an echo."

"I'm in the kitchen."

"You don't have to lie. Remember, we talked about all this. Going to the bathroom is a completely natural part of life. I really thought you had made some progress."

"I don't want to talk about it."

She laughed.

"I imagine you didn't call just to talk about my bathroom issues."

"No, I wanted to tell you what I'm up to."

"I heard about you and the ex. I guess I should say congratulations."

"Thanks, but I was hoping we could get together for coffee and talk in person."

"Sure, but I leave tomorrow on a new job."

"With Lux?"

She was of course referring to Lux Vonde, the woman I had rescued back on Soft Taco Island. I had also cheated on Estelle by engaging in some amazing nostalgic beach sex with Lux. It wasn't exactly textbook adultery, however, because Estelle and I had only been together a couple days, and Lux and I had been past lovers who were never actually able to make love and, therefore, felt that we needed to do so in order to have proper closure.

"No, I'm a lone wolf on this one. When do you want to meet?"

"How about right now? I'm outside your place."

Not again! She had to be fucking with me. The last time I took a call on the crapper, it had been from the woman who hired me for the Soft Taco Island job. She too had been outside on my front porch, and unfortunately for me, I had told Estelle about that little incident, so it appeared she was doing her own cruel reenactment.

"You're not serious are you?"

"Yep, I'm here on the South Forty Pier. You gave me your address—remember?"

"OK fine, I'm taking a shit. I'll let you in when I'm finished Goddamn it."

"No hurry, take your time. It's a beautiful morning."

I finished up, washed my hands, gave a little spritz of air freshener, then nervously walked to the door. It seemed as though a lifetime had passed since I'd last seen Estelle, and I was feeling this reunion might be a little—awkward. When we had first met, I'd had sex with two women in two days, and she had called me a man-whore. In the week since parting ways, that number had more than doubled, so I suppose I really was a bit of a man-whore now, though I hadn't been before the entire Soft Taco Island adventure began. I could only imagine that the gods of sexual intercourse had decided to reward me with dubious amounts of female companionship because my cheating ex-girlfriend had inadvertently ushered in several months of abstinence.

I opened the door, and there stood Estelle looking even more beautiful than I remembered, and it was a little painful to think that she was officially off the market. She smiled and hugged me, and, with her lovely breasts pressing against my chest and the scent of her hair tugging at my olfactory receptors, blood was starting to flood into my gentleman region. She brought her head around and kissed me, and, while she didn't throw in any tongue action, it was still very friendly and not doing much to deter my emerging semi.

"Goddammit. You're just as beautiful as I remembered."

"Were you hoping I had gotten uglier?"

"Kind of—when I heard you were engaged."

She laughed.

"Are you going to invite me in?"

"Yeah, sorry, come on in to chez man-whore."

She stepped inside, and I closed the door and motioned for her to head towards the kitchen, which was on the other side of the house. She was a few steps ahead, and I noticed that she was wearing some rather lovely black stretch pants. They were extremely flattering to her figure, but then she probably could have made a brown paper bag look good. Interestingly, I had only ever seen her in four outfits: a white sailor uniform, exercise clothes, a bikini, and a stunning red dress. Apparently, she looked amazing in everything—though I wish I could add my bed to the top of that list.

"Coffee?"

"Love some," she said.

I poured her a cup and added some almond milk, and we sat at the counter.

"So, what's your new and exciting case?" she asked.

"Sorry can't give out any details, but I can say it's a big deal."

"Are you working for the CIA again?"

"Not exactly. It's almost worse if you can believe it."

"Ah, the exciting life of a private investigator."

"If only. Do you know that up until a month ago, my cases were all adultery and lost pets."

"Bullshit."

"Seriously."

"Well, I suppose there's nothing wrong with finding someone's lost pet. It's actually kind of sweet."

"Yeah—but adultery is definitely not."

"How ironic. Coming from a man-whore that is."

"I see being engaged hasn't killed your sense of humor."

"Or my hunger. Do you want to get a late breakfast?"

"Sure."

We decided to go to my local diner, so I took a quick shower, and we left my houseboat and headed up to the parking lot, where I hit the unlock button on my key fob. The lights of my beloved Subaru WRX STi flashed twice, and Estelle paused in mid stride and appeared to be a little taken aback, for she gave me a questioning smile.

"What? You're not impressed by the Silver Hornet?" I asked.

"Did you add the spoiler and hood scoop?"

"Fuck no, this motherfucker came that way!"

"So, what's with the nickname?"

It's an homage to Inspector Clouseau's car in the movie *The Revenge of the Pink Panther*, but, unlike his car, which was a pice of shit, this is a fucking sweet ass ride!"

"It looks like something out of *The Fast and Furious* franchise."

"Yeah, because it is, though sadly it goes rather unappreciated by my smug fellow Marin residents, who prefer name brand cars such as Audi, Porsche, Mercedes, and BMW. Unlike their overpriced fancy pants rides, this beast is Japanese and has a whopping three hundred and five horsepower and two hundred and ninety pounds of torque."

"I think I could live with the enormous spoiler and hood scoop with those numbers."

"Indeed you could, now climb aboard m'lady."

We reached the restaurant to find it was fairly crowded, but we soon got a booth along the side wall, and Nancy, the owner, who was also my favorite waitress, stopped by to take our order. She was a lovely thirty something who I'd helped out with an ugly divorce a few years back, and we'd been good friends ever since. I introduced Estelle then ordered a Denver omelet with cheese. Estelle ordered some girly vegetable omelet with a side of fruit instead of hash browns, which was a typical chick maneuver, but it was probably decisions like that which accounted for the fact that women generally outlived men. Nancy returned with our coffee and a couple of waters and looked a little uncomfortable.

"What's up? Difficult customers? Do you need me to kill them?"

"Not exactly. It's your ex, Melanie. She's out on the patio with Yacht Club Guy."

"No way."

"Way."

Melanie had dumped me for a wealthy yacht club guy — right after getting together with him on his yacht, and sadly, the following months had been particularly devoid of female companionship. Then, three weeks ago, I was hired for the Soft Taco Island job by a stunningly beautiful woman named Bridgette Vandenberg, and we had the incredible luck of running into Melanie while we were out shopping in Sausalito. Needless to say, Melanie was not thrilled to meet Bridgette, and today she would see me with Estelle! That's two beautiful women in less than a month — awesome! While it might seem petty to revel over such trivial matters, anyone who has ever been dumped knows the effect it has on your self-esteem, and why any subsequent revenge brings so much joy. Now, three weeks and five incredible women later, my life was finally on a dramatic upswing.

"What's the big deal with your ex?" Estelle asked.

"She's a fucking bitch," Nancy said.

"Fucking being the operative word. She had sex with the new guy on his yacht then called me right afterward to break up."

"That's cold, and I can only imagine that event precipitated you turning into a man-whore."

"Man-whore? Tag? No way," Nancy said, looking a little surprised.

"I'm not really a man-whore—I've just had a sudden run of good luck with the ladies."

"More than luck," Estelle said.

Nancy eyed me suspiciously before leaving and returning a few minutes later with our food. She mumbled man-whore and laughed to herself as she left to check on one of her other tables.

"Thanks for sharing my nickname. Now, I'll never hear the end of it."

"You reap what you sew."

"And apparently sew all I see."

She frowned and grumbled as she finished the last strawberry in her fruit bowl. Soon thereafter, Nancy dropped off the check, and, just as I put down my card, Melanie and

Yacht Club Guy came walking by on their way out of the restaurant. She froze when she saw me with Estelle, and the shocked look on her face brought me more joy than any night of lovemaking I had endured with the cheating bitch.

"Hello, Melanie."

"Um, hello, Tag."

"I'm Estelle, Tag's fiancé," Estelle said, holding up her hand with the engagement ring clearly visible in front of Melanie's face.

Melanie shook her hand timidly, as though she were touching a leper.

"Nice to meet you, and might I say that's a beautiful ring," Melanie said, in a surprised tone.

"Thanks, it's Tiffany!" Estelle said.

"Yeah—I noticed."

Even I knew about the significance of having a Tiffany ring. It was expensive and an obvious measure of how much a man cared for a woman—or at least how much he was willing to spend. Melanie, therefore, was officially in abject shock as she pondered how in the hell I may have purchased something so expensive and, better still, believed that I was engaged. Fucking awesome. Life could be so good at times. Yacht Club Guy cleared his throat and dug into the front pocket of his Dockers for his key fob, which was obviously his signal to Melanie that he was ready to leave. She gave a halfhearted smile then said goodbye as she followed her smug paramour out the door.

"Thanks! That was awesome!" I said.

"It's the least I could do considering she turned you into a man-whore."

We left the restaurant, and Estelle asked for a little tour of Marin County, as she had inexplicably rarely travelled here in her time growing up across the bay. I decided to start with coffee in Mill Valley, a quaint little town which was nestled in a redwood forest at the base of nearby Mount Tamalpais. It was once the fabled home of musicians, artists, and writers, but now was populated by accountants, attorneys, and doctors, all of whom were there for its scenic tree-lined streets, lack of crime, and top tier public school system. We arrived in the little downtown to find it bustling with locals and tourists, and we had to head off onto a little side street to find a parking space.

"Where to?" Estelle asked, as we exited the car and stepped onto the sidewalk.

"Corporate coffee chain, local coffee chain, or local coffee shop totally unassociated with any kind of chain?" I asked.

"Which is the best?"

"They're all good."

"OK, let's go with the middle."

"Equator it is!"

We walked downtown and entered Equator to find a fairly long line, but it went quickly, and soon we were out enjoying our java and walking around town. We did a loop of the square then walked up past the theater before circling the block and heading back down to the car.

"This place is beautiful. I can't believe I never came over here," she said.

"Yeah, but our next stop is going to be the top of Mount Tamalpais, and you're going to shit your pants when you see the view."

"Is it as good as the view we had from the parasailing rig?"

Estelle and I had made a dramatic exit from Soft Taco Island in a parasailing rig and ended up having the best airborne makeout session of all time.

"Yeah, but I doubt it'll be as much fun."

"You never know."

Hearing Estelle utter those words now felt as though she were shooting an arrow straight up my ass and right through my heart, so I tried to ignore them for the moment. Instead, I focused on navigating the winding road that took us up past a bevy of spectacular homes and to the official beginning of the Mount Tamalpais State Park. From there on out, our journey was even more treacherous, as we had an endless parade of extreme curves populated by bicyclists, tourists, and the occasional bus.

We finally reached the west peak parking lot and found a space and began the short trek to the very top of the majestic mountain. It was one of the tallest peaks in Marin County and afforded a spectacular three hundred and sixty degree view of the bay area that included everything from Point Reyes and Sonoma to the Farallon Islands and hills of the East Bay and Santa Cruz. We arrived at the fire watch station then ventured down a small path to the southern-most patch of rock and sat arm in arm—the experience making me feel unusually sentimental for the time we had spent together in the Caribbean. It also made me think about her fiancé, who I imagined was, in all likelihood, better marriage material than me considering the crazy and rapidly evolving state of my love life at the moment. Still, I secretly hoped the fucker was boring as all hell and had a beer belly and bad facial hair. Was that petty? Absolutely, but a coping mechanism was for coping after all.

We continued to sit and enjoy the view and each other's company until the sound of footsteps somewhere off behind us interrupted the usual quiet that existed around sunset on the mountain. I looked west over my shoulder towards the setting sun and spied a blond man using his phone to take pictures from the other side of the peak. We were between him and a pretty spectacular view, so it made sense we happened to be in his foreground. I turned back around and continued to enjoy the view with Estelle, when, on a whim, I decided to turn back around to take another look, but the man had apparently disappeared. Strange. People usually stayed up here until sunset, but perhaps he was German and had to keep to an especially efficient pre-planned travel itinerary. Vacation for me was about not having a schedule, so I could never understand people who spent hours planning how they were going to relax. Maybe they should have spent that time relaxing so that they would have enough energy left over for their busy vacation.

Soon, the sun dipped down behind the other side of the mountain, and the temperature dropped dramatically. Estelle said she was cold, so we got up and started walking towards the car. The path wound around the mountain and back into the warm rays of the remaining sunlight, and it gave us a spectacular view of the ridgeline to the north. The fog was rolling in from the ocean, but it could go no further than the mountain, and it made it look as though we were standing at the edge of the world. It was at times like this that I really appreciated how lucky I was to live in Northern California.

"I can't believe I've never been up here before," she said.

"In high school, we used to come up here every Friday."

"You're lucky. In the East Bay, we used to go down to People's Park to watch hippies have sex in the bushes."

"I think I'd take the mountain over that."

"Me too."

We continued on and reached the parking lot to find out that we were the last remaining car and therefore had the mountain to ourselves. If this had been Soft Taco Island, we would have downed some rum and probably had an impromptu hump session on the little ledge that bordered the parking lot. Instead, we got in the car and headed back along the ridge road. At the intersection, a car turned in behind us that had come from the other part of the mountain where they filmed all the car commercials. Apparently, tourists and car companies all loved the same scenic stretch of highway. The car in question turned out to be a white Audi S4, which was about as common in Marin County as a Ford F-150 pickup was in the American heartland. I looked at the driver in my rearview mirror and saw that he was blond and might very well have been the same guy who had been taking pictures back on the peak, though that would have been one hell of a coincidence. I decided to have a little fun and go a little faster than usual, but the Audi managed to stay right on my bumper. Perhaps he was indeed German, as they took driving very seriously and tended to be fairly competent behind the wheel. I upped the ante a bit more and hit the gas, and, once again, my new friend managed to stay within a few car lengths. It appeared that we were pretty closely matched in driving skill, and our cars were also pretty similar—both had comparable performance and all wheel drive. The biggest difference between the two was that my Subaru definitely lacked the amenities of its German counterpart, though it cost about forty thousand dollars less. We continued on for nearly a mile and had a pretty fun drive down the mountain until my Audi friend had his fill and slowed down and fell back out of view. Up ahead was a major intersection known as Four Corners, and I suddenly had an excellent idea.

"What are you doing for dinner?"

"I don't know. Where are you taking me?"

"I've got just the place."

CHAPTER THREE
The Long and Winding Road

I turned right and continued on Panoramic Highway until merging onto highway 1, which was a two lane road that wound west down along the side of a treacherous canyon until reaching Muir Beach. It was a fairly short though dangerous piece of highway that always seemed to have roadwork going on to repair a section that had been washed away during the last storm. The Audi had also decided to go this direction, which wasn't too unusual, considering we were heading to the only bar and restaurant in the entire area. It was called the Pelican Inn and supposedly was an honest to goodness British Inn that had been transported over from England. The story is that it was disassembled piece by piece and reassembled over here. God only knew for sure, but I wouldn't have cared if it had been built in Arkansas, as it was a cool little place with seemingly authentic

British charm, good food, beer, and usually attracted an interesting international crowd of people on the weekends.

The Inn came up on the left, and it was hard to miss with its black and white facade and Tudor style architecture standing in stark contrast to the lush green valley of Muir Beach. I pulled in to the crowded little parking lot just in time to snag a space from a departing blond family of four, who I would bet good money were Scandinavians or southern Californians judging by their fair hair and obvious tan skin. It's strange, but Scandinavians all seemed to tan very easily for people from the upper latitudes. We Scotch Irish people were from a similar climate, but we burned like potato chips—or crisps, as they would say in the old country.

"Cool looking place," Estelle said.

"Wait until you see inside."

We walked around to the entrance on the southern side of the building and ventured through the quaint little wood and stained glass door. Immediately inside, resided a tiny hostess stand while beyond and off to our right was the crowded dining room that even had a fireplace with special seating for the lucky few who got there early. To the left, and more importantly, was the bar, which was purposefully a little dark, and its wood paneled walls made it look like a set piece from *The Lord of The Rings* minus, of course, a brooding Ranger and his small band of hobbits. We made our way into the small crowded space to find it alive with the sound of lute music and dialects from every corner of the world, but we were lucky, and a couple decided to leave at that moment, allowing us to take their table.

"Beer or wine?" I asked Estelle.

"Beer. What kind do they have?"

"Lots, but I usually go for a Guinness or a Newcastle."

"Guinness, I guess."

"Ay, for strength," I said, with an exaggerated Irish accent.

She looked at me with a puzzled expression, so I guess she hadn't ever seen the Guinness poster, which I suppose made sense, considering she had spent the last few years living and working aboard a yacht in the Caribbean, where rum was the preferred alcohol of choice. I went to the bar and saw my favorite bartender. His name was Tim, and he was one of those lifelong surfer types who enjoyed the quiet calm existence of Muir Beach, and he had worked here so long that they eventually made him the innkeeper, where he, in my humble opinion, had the coolest job on earth. It afforded him a free beautiful place to live and all the food and beer he could ever want.

"Hey, Finn, who's the girl?"

"She's kind of an ex."

"That's sad. How did you fuck it up?"

"Long story."

"So, she's single?" he asked, sounding more than a little interested.

"No, unfortunately, she's engaged."

"Shit."

"Tell me about it."

"So, two Guinnesses to drown your sorrows?"

"Oh yeah, and you might as well start a tab."

Tim carefully poured two perfect Guinnesses, then I took them and rejoined Estelle, who had started up a conversation with a French couple sitting to our immediate left. I laughed quietly to myself when I saw that the guy was wearing yellow pants and a turquoise sweater. Only a pop star or a Frenchman could, or would, pull off that kind of outfit. I took a sip of my beer and turned my gaze around the rest of the ol' bar and saw that it was a typical Saturday night, and the place was crowded with all manner of tourists, both domestic and foreign. Estelle finally took notice of her beer and held it up so we could toast.

"What shall we toast to?" she asked.

"Friendship," I said, in an ever so subtly patronizing tone.

She smiled a little sadly before taking a drink and inadvertently giving herself a Guinness mustache. I would have liked to lick it off, but those days were long gone. Just then, I felt a rush of cold air and looked over to see the front door open, and in walked a man that I thought might be the driver of the Audi. I had only seen him from afar and through a windshield, so, now, being able to see him up close and in person, made me suspect that my suspicion was correct, and he was indeed German. Of course, it didn't hurt that he looked like the poster boy for the Aryan race with his blond hair, blue eyes, and six foot plus frame that made it obvious he spent some serious time in the gym. There was also something in his bearing that hinted at a hardcore military background, and I wouldn't have been surprised to learn that he had been a member of the KSK, or Kommando Spezialkräfte, Germany's elite special operations unit. Those guys were bad motherfuckers and, like my German tourist here, generally looked like bad motherfuckers. He managed to score a table across from us in the corner, and I noticed he had a smartphone, so perhaps he was indeed the same tourist who had been up on the mountain. I turned my attention away from him and back over to Tim, who had been practically tethered to the small bar by a long line of customers but was now finally free to venture out to pick up empty glasses and stop by our table, where he obviously wanted to get a closer look at Estelle.

"Nice to meet you, I'm Tim."

"I'm Estelle, it's nice to meet you too."

He looked at her left hand, saw the enormous diamond ring, and frowned.

"Ah—that's sad."

"What?" she asked.

"That you're off the market."

Estelle smiled and held up her ring finger.

"Oh, are you referring to this little thing?"

"Yeah, it's probably worth more than my car."

"Well, honestly, I find it a little gaudy and would prefer something more subtle and vintage."

I had a feeling her response made Tim like her even more, because it definitely made me like her more.

"You obviously have good taste. Speaking of which, are you guys going to order anything to eat?" Tim asked.

"Yeah, I'm starving," Estelle said.

"Normally we have a separate menu for the bar, but I've brought you restaurant menus, so feel free to order whatever you want."

"Thanks," Estelle said, as she took a menu and started scanning through the various items.

I did the same, and, after a few moments of indecision, we both decided on the roast chicken with mashed potatoes and vegetables. Tim took the menus and left to put in our order, and I had a look around at our fellow patrons and couldn't help but wonder if they would get jealous when, and if, they saw that we managed to get nonstandard meals. The bar menu was a lot smaller and only included items like fish and chips, shepherds pie, or a cheese plate, so a chicken dinner would be highly coveted—which was yet more proof that it was always worthwhile to know your bartender. We also ordered another round of beers, which had the unintended effect of inspiring Estelle to tell me the details of her upcoming wedding. It was tough to stomach, and it was all I could do not to pull out my iPhone and secretly play solitaire under the table. Somehow, I just wasn't all that interested in her new life with her old boyfriend.

She was talking about which of her friends and family she invited and which ones she left out to save money, and my mind started wandering back to the unknown tourist. It was odd that we kept crossing paths, and it suddenly gave me an idea, and I told Estelle that I had to leave to use the bathroom. I walked towards the baño but made a last minute detour to the right and went out the door to the parking lot. I started at one end and worked my way to the other before I found the Audi off in the corner. I glanced around to make sure I was alone then used the light app on my iPhone to shine it into the interior of the car but found nothing of interest other than a coffee cup and an empty energy bar wrapper. He was probably just a tourist, but my intuition and recent foray back into the exciting world of espionage was making me a little paranoid.

I put my iPhone away and decided I might as well pee, so I walked over to the edge of the parking lot where the foliage was thicker. Sure, I could have gone back inside to the bathroom, but there was something particularly satisfying about peeing in nature, and I'm not sure if it was the fresh smell of the outdoors or some primal desire to mark my territory, but soon a steady stream was flowing into the bushes. Watching my urine glow in the ambient light from the Inn, I realized that it looked vaguely like a poor man's lightsaber. I made a humming sound as I completed a few figure eights before steadying it back down to a straight stream. I was close to finishing and, as often happens during the course of urinating, realized I needed to let loose a fart that had been simmering in the background for some time. I hadn't had a moment away from Estelle until now, and I was finally able to free myself of its building pressure. I relaxed my sphincter and let it loose and was pleasantly surprised by the thunderous sound in the quiet solitude of Muir Beach. With my well run dry, I gave my manitude an obligatory shake, zipped up, and took a moment to enjoy the beautiful night sky. It was incredibly peaceful out here, and I envied the lucky few who got to live in this oceanside community. I was about to turn and head back in when the door of the car I was standing in front of opened and the interior lights turned on. Oh, for fuck's sake.

I turned to look at the car and noticed that it was a brand new Mercedes, and a pretty woman was smiling at me from inside. She was holding a phone to her head, so I imagined she had come out here to make or take a call, and I was really hoping she hadn't seen my little lightsaber re-enactment or heard the fart. That's when I noticed that her window was down. Lovely.

"Nice fart, Skywalker," she said.

"Yeah, unfortunately the force is so strong in me that it sometimes slips out in unexpected ways."

"No shit—well, hopefully no shit—if you catch my meaning."

I smiled at her joke in spite of the fact that I was feeling particularly embarrassed as I turned and walked back to the front door, desperately hoping she wouldn't be following me back inside anytime soon. I sat down with Estelle and was happy to be back in the warmth of the Inn and far from my little parking lot performance.

"What took you so long?" she asked.

"I took the scenic route."

She raised an eyebrow and gave me a disapproving look, obviously thinking my answer was a little strange. I grabbed my beer and took a long sip, hoping to forget the last five minutes, but a sudden sweep of cold air came rushing in, which signified that someone had just entered the Inn. I looked over to see that it was the woman from the Mercedes, and she was smiling at me as she walked over to the bar. She spoke with Tim, and shortly thereafter he handed her a beer and she came over to our table and set it down in front of me.

"Here's a beer to thank you for the laugh. That was the funniest thing I've seen all week," she said.

"You're welcome."

"What was so funny?" Estelle asked the woman.

"You'll have to ask Skywalker here," she said before turning and walking towards the dining room on the other side of the building.

"Now, what the hell did you do?" Estelle asked.

"Nothing really. Just a little lightsaber demonstration in the parking lot."

"That sounds to me as though you were man-whoring again."

"No, far from it, I'm afraid."

Before Estelle could probe me for any further details, Tim arrived with our dinner, and we ate, drank, and got very merry. Afterward, we moved over to the dartboard and played a few games with a nice Irish couple. They won the first game, so we bought them a round of Guinness, but Estelle and I stepped up our efforts in the second, and it was the Irish who bought the next. The evening continued on in the same merry way until we decided it was time to get going, and I went to the bar to pay our bill. Tim looked a little uncomfortable as he handed it over, as he knew that I was usually strapped for cash.

"I put two of your beers on the house," he said.

"Thanks, but money is not a problem at the moment."

"I'm serious—it's OK."

"I'm serious too."

I slapped my new ATM credit card on the bar and slid it over. When he handed it back, I added the cost of the two beers to his tip. San Francisco might be two percent below the national average of twenty percent, but I was going to do my part to make sure Marin County stayed in the top ten. Tim looked at the tip and practically crapped his pants.

"Dude—I can't accept this."

"Dude—trust me, it's not a problem. But I do have a way for you to earn it."

"How? And don't say hand job."

"No, but I do have a different job in mind."

"What is it?"

"See that guy over there—the one who looks German?"

"Yeah, and having already talked to him, I'm pretty sure he is German. What about him?"

"I think he's been following Estelle and me."

"Oh, is he a jilted ex-husband from some divorce case you worked on?"

"Not that I know about, though it could have something to do with my latest job."

"Which is?"

"Not divorce, but fairly complicated."

"So why would the guy be following you?"

"Not sure yet, but that's why I was hoping you might be able to tell me something about him."

"I don't know shit, except that he likes Paulaner Hefe-Weizen."

"Has he already paid his bill?"

"Yeah, he paid it hours ago and has been nursing the same beer ever since, which is kind of weird since Germans are usually bigger drinkers."

"Yeah, usually they are, and that means I might actually be correct in believing he's been following us."

"Why is that?"

"It's a typical field agent move. When you're following someone, you need to be able to leave at a moments notice, so you pay your check right away."

"I guess someone was paying attention in spy school."

"Yeah, when I wasn't passing little love notes to the super hot female trainees."

I went back and joined Estelle, who was talking animatedly with the Irish couple about her upcoming wedding. The woman gave me a big smile and congratulated me on buying such a beautiful ring, and it was suddenly a little awkward. Estelle decided it would be easiest not to explain the reality of our situation and instead threw her arms around me and kissed me. I wasn't sure if it was the booze, some latent feelings, or some excellent improvisational acting, but it certainly wasn't making it any easier on my libido. Every touch reminded me more and more of the amazing time we had spent together back on Soft Taco Island. I therefore decided to focus my sexual energy on darts, and we played a final grudge match with the people of the Emerald Isle then said good night before making a brief stop at the bar to talk to Tim.

"It was nice meeting you, Estelle, and please feel free to come by again—especially if you don't end up getting married," he said.

"Nice try," I said, as I herded her out the door.

We walked to the car, and I kept a keen eye out for the German, but no one followed. We got in, and I fired up the beast, turned on the heat, and let it warm up before pulling out and making a right turn onto highway 1 for the winding drive back over the hill. We had made it about halfway up to the summit when I looked in the rearview mirror and saw headlights quickly gaining on us. Whoever was in that car was driving like a maniac, because they were getting closer in spite of the fact that I was going at a pretty decent pace.

"Do you get carsick?" I asked.

"No, I can even read in the car."

"Good, because it's going to be puke city in a minute."

Estelle looked at me nervously as I downshifted and brought the turbo charger screaming to life—the added power sending the back end out slightly before the all wheel drive traction control pulled it back into place. I hit the next corner even faster and had to use both sides of the road in order to steer the proper apex and not fly through the thin metal barrier that separated us from certain death.

"That was a lot less than a minute," Estelle said, angrily.

"Sorry, I'm just trying to see how serious the German is."

"What German?"

"The one who has been following us around all day—and is most certainly the same asshole who is chasing us up the mountain at the moment."

"Why in the hell would a German be following us, let alone chasing us up this mountain?"

"Assuming he doesn't know I'm smuggling a load of wiener schnitzel in the trunk, it probably has something to do with my latest job."

We crested the hill and started the descent down into Tam Valley, and it wasn't exactly the perfect place to lose a tail. The turns were tight, and we had nothing but dead end streets until we got lower into the valley. We came out of a long switchback onto a short straight, and our pursuer managed to accelerate right up to our bumper, where I could now see that it was indeed the Audi S4. It raced forward and gave us a solid bump that sent the back end of the Subaru sliding out, but I corrected and brought the car back in line. I hit the next turn hard, but the Audi managed to stay right on our bumper, and, on the next straight, it accelerated and hit us again. I corrected and kept us on our side of the yellow line, and we barely missed an old truck coming from the other direction. Fuck, I needed a game plan, as our German friend was out for blood, but I didn't currently have any I could spare.

I thought about the route ahead and remembered a perfect spot along the salt marsh inlet—assuming we could just stay alive long enough to make it there. Knowing your surroundings was a crucial tool in surviving out in the field, so I would always spend hours studying the maps and memorizing the topography of a location long before I ever put my actual feet on the ground. It gave me a distinct advantage when, and if, I needed to get the hell out of Dodge. At the moment, I was thankfully on my home turf, and, as I knew these roads like the back of my penis, it was time to use that knowledge to get this sour *kraut* off our ass.

"You OK?" I asked Estelle, curious how she was holding up in the middle of all this unexpected excitement.

"Of course. Practically every one of our dates has ended up in some kind of chase."

Unfortunately, that was a fairly accurate statement, as back on Soft Taco Island we'd experienced at least three harrowing chases—two in cars and one on foot. I turned my attention back to the road in front of us just in time to round the final turn that brought us into the more densely populated section of Tam Valley. I knew we had a brief straightaway followed by a tight right turn, so I powered out of the corner and shifted quickly up through the gears before slamming on the brakes and making a hard right turn off the main road. The engine screamed as we raced up the small street then made a tight left that sent us skidding onto the next street. This one took us to the other side of the valley, and I used my knowledge of the local area to gain precious seconds before turning onto Tennessee Valley Road and roaring through the gentle curves that led to a tight section where the highway skirted the canal. Now that the German had fallen behind, I hit the brakes at the entrance to Mill Valley's only cemetery then quickly backed up into its driveway and turned off the lights to wait for my prey.

The white Audi came roaring by moments later, and I pulled out and followed but kept the headlights off. It was kind of like driving blindfolded, but I knew this particular stretch of highway, so it was just a matter of keeping just far enough away to stay out of the glow of his tail lights until we rounded the turn and approached the place where the road wound closest to the estuary. I hit the gas and slammed into the right rear fender of the Audi, and the impact sent it flying off the embankment and down into the water below. It was close to low tide, so he would be able to get out of the car without drowning, but I didn't really care, considering that he had just spent the last ten minutes trying to kill us.

I pulled off to the right into a church parking lot, dialed

911, and told the Highway Patrol dispatcher that a lunatic nearly ran us off the road then crashed into the estuary. Five minutes later, a patrol car, a Sheriff, an ambulance, and a fire truck were on the scene. The CHP officer happened to be a friend that I had met several years back while I was teaching an advanced firearms course to the local department. We became friends and often met for coffee or beers, so we could talk shit and hopefully encounter members of the opposite sex. He emerged from his patrol car and smiled and shook his head when he recognized me.

"What the fuck did you do now, Finn?"

"Not much, other than avoid being killed by a fucking crazy German."

"So, then he lost control and plunged into the drink?"

"Yeah, though he might have had a little help."

"Well, everybody hates a tourist. Now, more importantly—are you going to introduce me to your friend?" he asked, as he turned his attention to Estelle.

I introduced Estelle to Officer Sean Haverly, and he was of course pretty excited to meet her, in spite of the fact that he obviously spied the engagement ring on her left hand. It wasn't every day you ran into a woman as attractive as Estelle out on the streets of Marin County. Sure, we had plenty of beautiful trophy wife MILF types running around, but Estelle was in a league all by herself, and I was guessing it was making Sean's dull night on the highway a hell of a lot more interesting.

"So, what's the real story?"

"This is going to sound a little weird, but the asshole in the car has been following us all day and then tried to kill us on our way back home from the Pelican Inn."

"Ex-client?"

"Nope."

"Scorned girlfriend?"

"Nope."

"Scorned boyfriend?"

"Not this time. He's a total stranger."

The firemen and paramedics returned from the car.

"The car's empty," the lead one said, to Sean.

"Weird."

"Germans are sneaky," I said.

"And decent swimmers. Oh well, I'll have it hauled out and call you if we find anything interesting. You two might as well get going."

"Thanks. Have fun tonight."

"You too," he said, with a wry smile.

We got in the car and headed for Highway 1 then merged into the mild nighttime traffic and onto 101, where we got on the freeway for the short drive to Sausalito. Three turns later, we pulled into the parking lot of my marina and found an open space between two BMW's—an event which was practically a statistical certainty in Marin County and second only to the likelihood of parking between two Priuses.

"Nightcap?" I asked.

"You bet your ass. Goddammit, Finn—is it ever boring hanging out with you?"

"Sometimes I wish it were."

CHAPTER FOUR
The Nightcap

The docks were mostly quiet except for the sound of people's televisions. Everyone seemed to have flat screens and surround systems these days, so it was no wonder that some ambient noise spilled into the tranquility of the night. We arrived at my place, and I checked the locks for signs of a break-in. It stood to reason that if we were followed around then my house might also have been a target. The locks looked untouched and showed no sign of tampering, so I entered the alarm code, and we went into the kitchen and took a seat at the counter.

"Rum?" I asked.

"Hell yeah."

I brought out a bottle of Soft Taco Island Rum and poured us each a glass. It was a welcome respite from our exciting drive over the mountain, and I took a long sip and felt the tension ease from my body.

"So, what in the hell does your latest job have to do with

that German asshole?" Estelle asked.

"No idea, but I think it's a bad omen this is going to be a tough couple of weeks."

"And you can't tell me anything about it?"

"Sadly, no."

"So, who is it this time? The President of the United States?"

"No, but it's a group of people with comparable stature if you can believe it—though I can't imagine who would be crazy enough to fuck with these fuckers."

"Well, powerful people almost always have enemies."

"Apparently so."

I grabbed the bottle, and we moved into the living room, and I built a fire in the fireplace and joined Estelle on the couch. It would have been a pretty romantic little scene had we not just experienced a potentially deadly car chase—or been under the ominous specter of the fact that my beautiful guest was engaged to another man. I picked up the remote control and brought up Pandora on my Apple TV then chose a mellow indie rock station. With music filling the air, I grabbed the bottle of rum and returned to the couch to refill our glasses, but I was rudely interrupted by the sound of farts blaring from my iPhone. Shit, that was the ringtone I assigned to my friend Sean, and I had chosen it in order to give him a little shit about his propensity for always having gas. It seemed like a funny idea until you were sitting in a quiet cafe or perhaps on a couch beside your former lover.

"Perhaps you need to go potty," Estelle said, patronizingly.

"It's my fucking phone," I said, pulling it out of my pocket and holding it up so that she could see that I wasn't the culprit.

Fucking Sean—it seemed a little soon for him to have found out anything, so the fucker was probably just calling to get Estelle's phone number. I begrudgingly hit the answer button.

"What do you want?"

"Fuck you. I'm calling with news. It turns out the Audi is registered to a foreign corporation based in Dubai called Vanity Endeavors. Ring any bells?"

"Nope, probably just a front for some other mysterious asshole corporation."

"Oh well, I'll call if I learn anything more. Estelle still with you?"

"Yep."

"Maybe I should come by."

"I don't have any donuts."

"You have something better."

"Good night, Sean," I said,

"Good night, Finn," he said, with a laugh as he hung up.

I couldn't blame him for trying, as it was in our nature to seek out attractive members of the opposite sex. I put down my iPhone and turned my attention back to Estelle, and we continued to talk and drink rum, though every second made me remember how much I enjoyed her company. It certainly wasn't helping that I was looking at her through some pretty serious rum goggles—which, combined with the emotional quotient, was making it a hell of a lot harder to keep Tag Junior from swelling up and making a scene in my pants. Around eleven-thirty, she glanced at her watch and looked a little concerned.

"Do you need to get back to your future hubby?" I asked.

"No, he's visiting his family in Los Angeles."

"Are you OK to drive?"

"Not even close. I'm going to need to spend the night."

Gulp.

"Is that really a good idea?"

"It's a better idea than driving, and you never know—it might be fun."

"I'm sure it could be fun, but I don't think your fiancé would be too thrilled."

"It's just a friendly sleepover. Don't be such a pussy."

"What about clothes for tomorrow?" I asked.

"I have an extra outfit in my purse."

"Thinking ahead, I see."

"Always."

We stood, and I led Estelle upstairs to the guest room.

"Is this where Bridgette slept?" she asked.

She was referring to the beautiful woman who had hired me for the Soft Taco Island job, and, while Bridgette might have started the night in the guest room, she definitely ended it in my bedroom—with a bang.

"Technically, no."

"Then I guess it will do. Which bathroom should I use?"

I showed her to the guest bathroom, got her a fresh towel

from the linen closet, then said good night before heading to my room. There, I took a well needed piss, brushed my teeth, and took a shower. Clean and fresh I at last slid into my bed and realized it was good to be home—even more so because I had one of those memory foam mattresses that perfectly adhered to my body, and I had missed its soothing embrace after almost a month away. I looked at the clock and saw that it was twelve forty then turned off the light, lay back, and listened to the sound of running water from the guest bathroom. Estelle was taking a shower, and the thought of her on the other side of the wall soaping up her naked body was not exactly putting me to sleep. Fuck. Sleepovers could be fun, but not if they gave you a world class case of blue balls. The water turned off about five minutes later, and three and half minutes after that there was a knock at my door. It opened, and Estelle stood there with the moonlight reflecting off the bay behind her, and it made her glow like an angel.

"You asleep?"

"Not even close."

"Mind if I join you."

"Yes and no."

"Good enough."

She walked in and padded across the floor wearing only her thong underwear and a thin camisole top that did very little to conceal her pokey nipples. I tried not to stare, but I unintentionally slipped into man-mode and ended up having a nice long heathy look at them before she slid into bed and wrapped her leg and arm across my body.

"This feels a lot better," she said.

"Yes it does, but that's the problem."

"Oh take a man pill, we're just snuggling."

"Yeah, but you're going to be snuggling up against my boner any second."

"Maybe you should masturbate."

"On your breasts?" I joked.

"Would that be cheating?"

"Not to an enlightened forward thinking culture."

"Then get to it."

"Obviously you're kidding."

"I'm not."

"Oh."

We lay there without speaking, and I spent the time trying desperately to clear my mind of sexual thoughts. Unfortunately, trying not to think about sex is essentially the same as thinking about sex—a pursuit made all the more difficult by the fact that one of Estelle's breasts had slipped out of her top, inadvertently allowing me to see one of her nipples. I quickly averted my gaze, but it was too late, for the image was burned into my consciousness, and soon, my second brain was springing to life, becoming fully inflated and straining against my pajama bottoms. Estelle accidentally brushed her hand against it and giggled.

"Wow, I guess you weren't kidding."

"Nope."

"Will it keep you from sleeping?"

"Only if I try to sleep on my stomach."

I gazed out the skylight above my bed and saw the moon just coming into view, and it was déjà fucking vu. It had been almost a month ago that Bridgette had crept into my room under a very similar moon, and we'd spent a hell of a night together. Actually, it had been my first sex in almost two months since breaking up with Melanie, so I had been particularly vulnerable. Tonight, I wasn't exactly starved for sex, but I was suffering from a phenomena that occurred at the other end of the sexual appetite spectrum.

A friend had once described sexual appetite as it relates to Newton's first law of motion, which states that an object at rest tends to stay at rest while an object in motion tends to stay in motion. It made perfect sense, as libido seemed to work the same way. If you were single, or at rest for a long enough time, you got used to not having sex. If you got into a relationship, you became accustomed to the regular sex and wanted to stay in motion, so to speak. Studies even showed that regular sex increased the production of testosterone and, in turn, sexual appetite, thus backing up the Newtonian theory of sex drive. Interestingly, masturbation did not affect the production of testosterone, so a single man whacking away like a mad woodsman would not affect his testosterone level and would, therefore, be somewhat content to continue without sex—and remain at rest.

At the moment, I was fully in motion having just gotten back from a wild adventure in Europe, where I'd met some incredible women and had gotten to know them in the biblical sense. Testosterone was likely flowing out of my body as easily as the breath from my lungs, and I wouldn't be surprised to find out that climate scientists were currently tracking my testosterone emissions from space for fear they might be affecting global warming. So, there I lay in my humble bed beside a beautiful half naked woman, all the while feeling utterly helpless in the face of my growing desire.

"That thing looks painful. If you're not willing to whack off, then maybe we should have sex—for medicinal purposes," Estelle said.

"You have no idea how badly I want to do that—but we can't."

"Why? I'm not married yet."

"It's not fair to your future husband. I wouldn't want you to do that to me if the situation were reversed."

"I wouldn't do that to you if the situation were reversed."

"That doesn't make any sense."

Estelle reached under the blanket and guided my manchild out of its cotton prison, and she began to gently caress it as though it were a purring kitten sitting in her lap.

"Look, Tag, this might be the last thing I do as a single woman. Can't you grant me this one final pre-marriage wish?"

"I want it more than anything I've ever wanted in my life, but it just seems wrong."

The bed was aglow in moonlight, and my manhood was standing at full mast as I stole another quick glance at her nipple. Fuck. It was still peeking out from under her flimsy top, and I felt my hand began to move completely of its own accord towards her breasts until my fingers were gently gliding over their baby soft curves. I traced a path up and over each nipple and sprung them to life as though I had depressed the top of a ball point pen. The cat was officially out of the bag, and my dick was out of my pants, and there was nowhere left to go except deeper into the great inferno of hell. Dante had a special place for adulterers on the second ring, and Estelle and I were well on our way to cozying up for a nice double date with the fabled lovers Francesca and Paolo.

Both of our hearts were beating hard in our chests as we stared into each other's eyes, both of us desperately wanting the other but neither of us willing make the first move. Estelle found her courage first and started moving closer until her lips were touching mine. Our kiss started out delicate and exploratory but quickly raged out of control when we opened our mouths and touched tongues. Our lips became entangled in a furious embrace, our tongues twisting hungrily to gain the advantage in a battle that had no losers. The world around us receded, and we found ourselves immersed in our own private fold in time where our personal big bang was only moments away.

I broke from her lips just long enough to slide off her top and take hold of her breasts then lean down and encircle each nipple with my tongue. She gasped in pleasure then abruptly proceeded to take off my pajama bottoms, using her foot to slide them down with the practiced efficiency of a mountain climber ascending a jagged peak. She took off my shirt next, and, now, with me properly naked, she abruptly dropped her mouth onto my painfully hard member and used the formidable presence of her lips and tongue to bring me to the edge of climax in mere seconds. I narrowly avoided release by sliding backwards and away from her powerful efforts.

"Sweet Lord, woman! You're playing with sweet hot man-fire here, and nearly set this entire room ablaze!"

"Oh, sorry, I got caught up in the moment," she said.

"No need to apologize. I generally live for moments like those."

I eased Estelle back onto the bed, pulled off her underwear, then gently pressed her legs open and ran my hands up her thighs and all the way to her breasts. Sweet mother of God how I missed touching her body. I suddenly felt the very real need to kiss her, and, as I leaned forward, my hard member inadvertently pressed against her wet essence and caused her to let out a little moan of pleasure. I brought my lips to hers and lingered only long enough to touch tongues before moving down and kissing her neck, nipples, and then stomach with my goal being to prolong the journey to her great divide, so that I could enjoy every inch of her supple flesh. I finally dropped down the final stretch then pressed my tongue deep into her essence, and she threw her head back and gripped the sheets with both hands. I moved teasingly upward and at last brought my tongue to her clitoris, where I did circles and gradually increased the speed and pressure. Her face became flushed with color, and her chests was rising and falling rapidly with each breath as she started losing herself to the growing pleasure. Her hips flexed involuntarily, and I used the moment to slip my hands around and take hold of her buttocks, so that I could pull her pelvis to my mouth and make her clitoris a prisoner to every whim of my tongue. Her back arched, and her entire body started shaking as I forced her mercilessly headlong into the throws of sweet climax. I held on tight, as though to a bucking bronco, and continued to deliver pleasure that brought on cries of ecstasy so loud that they were surely echoing across Richardson Bay and filling the ears of the smug residents of Tiburon.

She came to rest when I at last released her clitoris from my mouth, and she urgently pulled me up and guided my throbbing member all the way in to her essence, which was still pulsing with orgasmic aftershocks. I began sliding in and out at a slow luxurious pace, and she reached up and ran her hands through my hair then guided my mouth down to her breasts, where I ran my tongue over each of her nipples to make damn sure they stayed taught and elongated.

I pulled back, and we shared of look of wanting desire that was an unspoken cue to increase our efforts. Our hips were now pounding together at a furious pace, and that meant we were well past Newton's first law and into his third, which stated that for every action there was an equal and opposite reaction. I was pressing in, Estelle was pressing back, and the end result was pure unadulterated pleasure. Time and the world around us disappeared from our perception, and we were the only two people in existence as we rode on the edge of bliss, lost in the mental purgatory between arousal and release. Estelle began to cry out, and I joined in, pouring my entire being into a great final burst of energy until both of us were lost to climax. With our gaze firmly locked upon one another, we continued on until our bodies were completely spent, and we at last came to rest and lay silently with our breathing the only sound except for the distant fog horn on Alcatraz. We stayed in that moment without speaking a word until I could no longer hold back my voice.

"Are you really sure you want to marry that guy?" I asked.

"No, I'm not. In fact, I'm as confused as hell at the moment."

CHAPTER FIVE
A Talk in the Clouds

I awoke around seven and noticed that Estelle was already awake and sitting over by the window, where she was wearing my bathrobe and enjoying a cup of coffee as she watched the marine life frolic outside on Richardson Bay. She saw that I was awake, smiled, and pointed at the cup of coffee sitting next to me on the nightstand.

"Well good morning to you too," I said, as I sat up and took my first sip of the heavenly elixir.

"Morning, sunshine. How did you sleep?" she asked.

"Pretty good after all that excellent cardio last night. How do you like the view?"

"Amazing—did you know your neighbor has a giant fucking cat?"

I laughed.

"Yeah, that's Mr. Pickles. I had to rescue that little fucker last month."

"Rescue? From where? The pet food section at

Walmart?"

"Not exactly."

She walked over and sat beside me on the bed, and the robe fell open to reveal her lovely breasts.

"Hungry?"

"I am now."

"I mean for food."

"Exactly—man food."

"I'm talking about real food."

She closed her robe, and I sighed to myself as I wondered if that was the last time I would see her lovely bosoms. With a hint of sorrow filling my thoughts, I got up and went into the bathroom while Estelle headed next door to the guest room. Thankfully, she was well aware of my predilection to having the bathroom to myself during my morning movement, so I knew I didn't need to take the precaution of closing and locking the door. I sat on the throne, took another sip of coffee, then took a moment to think about shit—and I wasn't referring to the actual shit that was about to fill my beloved commode. Instead, I was referring to the shit that was taking place in my life— namely, the unexpected appearance of Estelle and that fucking German assassin. Sure, I was at least happy to see Estelle, but who in the hell was this mysterious German, and what did he want with me or, more likely, the Topless Agenda? It was definitely time to give Senator Matheson or Daniel Vandenberg a call. Oh well, I'd deal with that later, as right now it was time to focus on my dump. I took another sip of coffee, but, as I prepared for release, Estelle suddenly came walking into the room.

"Mother of goats!" I yelled practically falling off the toilet.

"Relax. I just needed some toilet paper."

There were two rolls stacked off to the left of my toilet, and I grabbed one and threw it over.

"Thanks," she said, as she caught it one handed.

"You do know what you've done?" I responded.

"Let me guess. I've ruined your dump?"

"Definitely, but it's worse than that."

"Seriously? Because from the smell of things, you haven't even started it yet."

"True, but it doesn't matter, because interrupting me, even in the opening stages, is enough to be a great harbinger of doom."

"Anyone ever tell you that you can be a drama queen?"

"Only when it comes to matters of the toilet, and now you should know that it is entirely likely that something terrible is going to happen to me today."

"Well, if something terrible does indeed happen to you, then I will make it up to you with the most amazing blowjob you could ever imagine."

"Before or after you're married."

"Doesn't matter. I'll do it either way."

"OK, but I can imagine a pretty fucking amazing blowjob."

"Good, now enjoy the rest of your dump," she said, as

she left.

I downed the last sip of coffee and did my best to relax and let loose my bounty. It came with some trepidation, but soon I was done and stepping into the shower, where I hoped the hot water would help me relax. I emerged five minutes later feeling refreshed and clean then got dressed, packed my bag, and headed downstairs to join Estelle. She had on a fresh outfit and looked as beautiful as ever, and, better still, she was in my kitchen cooking scrambled eggs. I grabbed some plates, and we dished up breakfast and moved to the dining room table, where we were bathed in the soft diffused light of a typically foggy Sausalito morning. We ate in relative silence and hardly spoke a word, and the only sounds were our silverware scraping the plates and the cries of the nearby seagulls.

"So, when do you leave?" Estelle asked, after she took her last bite and turned to me, looking a bit uncomfortable.

"My flight's at noon."

"When do you get back?"

"Hopefully a week if all goes well. When is your big day?"

"Saturday."

"So, only six days away. Shit, I'm really sorry for interfering with your life like this."

"There's nothing to be sorry about. I was the one who came knocking on your door."

"I suppose, but I can't help feeling a little guilty."

"Don't. This is what I thought I needed to do in order to make sure I was making the right decision."

"Did it help?"

"Not so much."

Shit, I would have been happy as all hell if Estelle didn't get married, but, I also didn't want to be the home wrecker who thwarted her potential nuptial bliss. Either I was the lucky asshole who stole the girl or the lonely miserable asshole who didn't, and either outcome still seemed to make me an asshole. Estelle was looking at me, and I got the impression she knew what I was thinking.

"Don't worry. If I somehow decide not to get married, it would be because of me, not you."

We cleared the dishes and cleaned up the kitchen, then I grabbed my things and met her at the front door, so that we could walk out together. The sun was just starting to burn through the morning fog, and it looked as though it was going to be a clear beautiful winter day in Northern California. It was therefore kind of a bummer that I was heading off to the Middle East, but the weather would likely be even nicer where I was going. We reached the parking lot and stopped at her car, which turned out to be a white BMW M2.

"This is a seriously sweet fucking ride for someone who grew up in Berkeley. Honestly, I figured you for a Prius."

"Fuck no, though the fiancé thinks this car is too sporty and wants me to sell it and buy a Prius."

"I'd say that's all the reason you need to cancel the wedding."

"Yeah, I'd have to agree."

We stood there for an awkward moment with neither of us sure what to say next.

"Well, I suppose I should be going," she said, breaking the tension.

"Yeah, me too."

We hugged, then exchanged a final kiss, and it abruptly grew in intensity until we were fully making out with our lips locked together and our hands wandering all over each other's bodies. This unintentional flareup of passion started sending copious amounts of blood flowing into my man parts that quickly awakened the flesh dragon. Estelle could obviously feel it pressing against her body, because she reached down and started stroking it until it reached its full potential. I therefore decided to match her enthusiasm and slipped one hand into her pants and the other into her shirt, the former delivering some strategic clitoral stimulation, and the latter making sure her nipples didn't feel left out in the cold. We continued on, every second driving us farther into the madness of lust with the public setting being the only thing keeping us from making sweet love right there in the parking lot. She abruptly stopped and pulled away, leaving my member painfully hard and pressing angrily against the fabric of my pants.

"Whoa, sorry. I didn't mean for that to get so out of control," she said.

"Me neither."

Another quiet awkward moment ensued until Estelle once again broke the silence.

"Fuck, this is really hard."

"Yes, as is my penis, but it's OK. I spent all of my youth and at least half of my adult life dealing with blue balls, so I'll be able to soldier on."

She laughed and punched me in the arm.

"I'm serious, asshole."

"I know, and aside from this serious boner, I'm seriously sad to see you leave right now."

"And I'm seriously sad to leave."

"This all seems so crazy when you think about the fact that we've only known each other for a little over two weeks but..."

"I know, it feels a lot longer," she said.

"Yeah..."

"Oh well, I should be going."

"Yeah—so—good luck with the whole wedding thing."

"Yeah, and good luck with your latest mysterious job and that fucking German."

"Thanks, I'm probably going to need it."

We hugged, then she let go of me and smiled, though her expression grew noticeably sad as she turned and walked to her car. I stood at my door, my eyes never leaving her until she gave me a final wave as she drove out of my parking lot and disappeared from view—and perhaps even my life. Shit, I hated saying goodbye to Estelle, and it was even harder knowing that the next time I saw her she would likely be another man's wife. I put my bags in the trunk of my Subaru WRX STi then took a minute to regard my silver beauty.

"Ahhh, my sweet Silver Hornet, it was all likely thanks to you that we survived our little encounter with the German last night," I said, as I patted the enormous rear spoiler.

My attention was suddenly drawn to my neighbor Stephanie who had just arrived at the parking lot. She was attractive, probably around forty, and tended to dress in form fitting clothing that showed off her rather impressive figure. She and her fellow workout junkie husband Robert lived two houseboats over, and both of those fuckers seemed to take an unusual interest in my daily life. I'm not sure if they were particularly nosey or just bored with their idyllic yuppy existence, but I got the impression they were attempting to live vicariously through me by observing my various travails. Case in point being the fact that she decided to walk right up to me and smile as she gazed down at the very obvious boner that was still pressing against the front of my pants

"Wow, you really do love that car, don't you?" she said.

"I do, but you'll be happy to know that this boner came from a woman."

"It looks pretty serious, so it's probably a good idea to deal with it before you get on the road."

"Oh, is that a roundabout offer of sex?"

"Yeah, though it was hardly roundabout."

"Well then, my place, your place, or the back of the Silver Hornet?"

We had a quiet moment where we stared at each other, and I had the feeling it was a challenge to see who would blink first. Before she could answer, however, her husband Robert came driving in, and I wasn't entirely sure but I think Stephanie might have looked a little disappointed.

"Nice boner, Finn," Robert said.

"Thanks, your wife gave it to me."

"Yeah, right."

She climbed into her husband's car and gave me a peculiar smile as they drove away. With my embarrassing public boner debacle officially at an end, I decided to give the Silver Hornet a quick once-over, as I hadn't had a chance since our dramatic car chase. I checked the front and rear bumpers, curious how much damage they had taken from that fucking Audi, but, thankfully, the polyurethane material had absorbed most of the impacts, and all that remained where some scuff marks on the paint. Oh well, I'd deal with them when I returned home.

I climbed inside then hit the start button and felt my heart race ever so slightly as the engine roared to life. I gave it a few gentle revs then put it in gear and headed to highway 101 to begin the thirty minute drive to the San Francisco Airport's private air terminal. City traffic was light, but I still took Sunset Avenue instead of 19th and reached my destination a full five minutes ahead of schedule. The Vandenberg Jet, a beautiful converted Boeing

777, sat parked in its usual spot while a number of ground crew prepared it for its long voyage to Dubai. I grabbed my things, locked the car, and headed for the jet's forward hatch. As I arrived at the bottom of the stairs, Brett, one of the plane's regular pilots, appeared at the doorway with his skin as tan as ever and his teeth still blindingly white.

"Hey, Finn, how was your visit home?"

"Short but sweet, as I received an unexpected visit from Estelle."

"How did that go?"

"Great, except for the fact that she's about to get married to her fucking former fiancé."

"Ouch."

"Yeah, ouch indeed, but on the bright side, you'll be happy to hear that I've brought you a present."

"Let me guess—it's either whitening toothpaste or tanning oil."

"Nope, it's a book about the naval academy."

Brett, aside from always being tan and having inhumanly white teeth, was also a graduate of the United States Naval Academy, and it was his third most annoying obsession.

"Oh, you shouldn't have," he responded sarcastically.

"Don't worry, I didn't. So, how's Yvonne? Did you two have fun in San Francisco last night?"

"Yeah, we did, actually."

"It must be nice to be able to work with your girlfriend."

"Yeah, and it makes it a hell of a lot easier to hump."

Brett's girlfriend Yvonne had been on the Vandenberg

yacht while a lovely woman named Tiffany had worked on the plane, but, due to romantic entanglements, the two had switched positions. In the corporate world, this kind of partner and job swapping would have likely gotten all of them sent to HR and fired, but they were lucky to work for an eccentric pair of billionaire twin brothers. I walked through the main salon and on to my cabin, which resided near the rear of the plane. It was my home away from home, and everything looked as it had the day before with the exception being that they had changed the sheets and brought in fresh towels. I stowed my things then headed out to the main salon to wait for takeoff by spending my time browsing through the latest copy of Wired magazine. I quickly learned that things were still moving ahead at the speed of thought in the nerdisphere, and the movers and shakers of the digital age were creating new technology faster than the world could possibly figure out how to use it. I heard talking coming from the front of the plane and looked up to see two of the Topless Agenda's key members making their way to the main salon. In front was the esteemed Senator Douglass Matheson and behind him was the billionaire industrialist Daniel Vandenberg,

"Afternoon, boys. Didn't know the Illuminati would be joining me on the flight," I said, as I put down the magazine and stood up to greet them.

"We wanted to meet with you personally to go over some last minute details."

We all shook hands and sat down, and, soon thereafter,

Brett came over the intercom and told us to put on our seat belts and prepare for takeoff. We all strapped in and waited as the large jet made its way out to the runway and got in line behind a 747 that was just taking off. A moment later, the two 110,000 horsepower engines throttled up, and the entire plane vibrated until the brakes were released, and the behemoth started tearing down the runway. Within seconds we were airborne and climbing into the sky, with each of us held firmly in place by the substantial g forces. Through my window I could see the East Bay, and I imagined Estelle down there somewhere, sitting in traffic in that white BMW. All of a sudden, I heard the starboard engine spool down, and the plane bucked slightly, before leveling off. A second later, Brett came over the intercom to inform us that the number two engine had overheated on takeoff and had to be shut down. Consequently, we would be returning and making an emergency landing back at SFO. Lovely.

"Ever had any trouble with your Jet before?" I asked Daniel.

"Never."

Jets were actually highly maintained and crashes incredibly rare, so it was therefore pretty fucking unusual to have an emergency like this suddenly spring up. My thoughts, of course, turned to two key events, the first being the fact that I had been followed and almost killed by a German the previous day, while the second was Estelle's interruption of my morning dump. Either one or both of those events were, I suspect, related to the cause of this potentially catastrophic situation. I looked around the cabin and noticed Senator Matheson looking particularly concerned as he used the sleeve of his shirt to wipe the perspiration from his forehead.

"This might be a good time to tell you guys about something," I said.

"What would that be?" Matheson asked gravely.

"Yesterday, I was nearly killed by a German tourist."

"Why in the hell would a fucking German tourist try to kill you?"

"Well, he was posing as a tourist, but in reality he was more likely an assassin."

"And why are you telling us this now?"

"Because I think it's related to our current predicament. It turned out that the kraut's car was registered to a company in Dubai, the very place we're headed at the moment. That's way too much of a coincidence, so I think it's possible that our little air emergency here is an intentional attempt to kill me, or potentially even all of us, which could also mean that someone knows about this operation and is trying to thwart it."

"Can we talk about this later—assuming we all survive?" Vandenberg asked.

Matheson leaned back in his chair and looked troubled as he thought about my news. He abruptly turned to me and was about to say something when we heard the port engine spool down.

"Fuck! That doesn't sound good," Vandenberg said.

"I should have taken my own jet," Matheson responded.

"Maybe we all should have," I added.

Brett's voice came over the intercom saying that we had also lost the number one engine and should prepare for an even more extreme emergency landing. There was nothing quite as terrifying as being in a noisy jet when it suddenly stopped making noise—especially when you were several thousand feet in the air. We had lost both engines and were now nothing more than a glorified glider, which meant the only power would be coming from one of the generators that kept the flight controls functioning. We were therefore in a very similar position to Air Transat flight 236, which had lost power over the Atlantic Ocean back in 2001 and had to glide in for an emergency landing in the Azores. Everyone had survived that landing, so I was praying that we would be just as lucky. What I wouldn't give for a parachute right about now, but sadly all I had was a Senator and a billionaire, and neither would be very useful in a crash landing.

I looked out the window and saw South San Francisco off to our left and the water below coming up a lot faster than I'd ever experienced. Suddenly, the number two engine came back on line, and the plane's descent slowed ever so slightly. Maybe this would have a happy ending after all. We sat and calmly waited for the worst or best to occur. It turned out to be the best, as the plane dropped down and made a hard, though successful landing on the runway. We had to come in faster than usual, so now our fate fell on the skill of our pilots and especially the brakes, which were already straining against the mass of the large jet, as they only had the aid of one of its reverse thrusters. I gazed out my window to see the terminal racing by, and I was starting to wonder if we were ever going to stop in time. At last, the big plane started to slow down and finally came to rest only feet from the end of the runway, where I could already hear the sirens blaring from the fire trucks and emergency personnel who were racing up the tarmac. We unbuckled and made our way to the front of the plane to find Tatyana, Wendy, Yvonne, and Brett all looking surprisingly calm, considering we had all just survived a crash landing on a jumbo jet. They had even been so thoughtful as to have the door open and the emergency slide inflated and ready to go.

"Dubai sure looks a hell of a lot like South San Francisco," I said.

"With enough oil money, you can apparently build anything these days," Tatyana said.

"If you two are done making your jokes, it's about time we vacate the jet," Brett interrupted.

"In all seriousness, nice job, guys! And Brett, I'll never make fun of your white teeth and excessive tan again."

"I highly doubt that."

"Yeah, you're probably right—but good job either way. I owe you all a fancy dinner and a night on the town."

"I'll hold you to that pledge," Tatyana said.

"Come on, we better exit and let them clear the plane," Brett said.

Everyone waited their turn then jumped on the slide, and it actually ended up being pretty fun and something I'd always wanted to do—without the crash landing part, of course. An EMT approached us to make sure we were all OK, then we were herded onto a plus sized golf cart and driven over to the terminal and ushered into a private lounge. An airport official arrived soon thereafter and had a private meeting with Matheson. Upon finishing up, the man left, and our esteemed Senator came over to give us the latest news.

"They're going to transport all our luggage over here, and in the meanwhile, we should use the time to regroup and plan our next move, so I'm thinking we should probably take this conversation to a more private area."

The three of us moved over to the bar on the other side of the room, and Matheson grabbed each of us a shot of whiskey. We clinked our glasses and drank the shots. Normally, I never drank during the day but surviving my first plane crash was a special occasion.

"Finn, based on what you told us, and what happened today, I think you're right, and we have to assume that this operation has somehow been compromised."

"And that means that someone knows about the Topless Agenda, which also means it might have a leak," I said.

"Yeah, though I find that to be utterly impossible, as all of our members are beyond reproach."

"Hopefully, anyway."

"Well—to be safe, I think that from here on out, we only communicate with each other."

"And continue on with the mission?" I asked.

"Absolutely, which means putting you on a commercial flight and getting you to Dubai as quickly as possible. If someone is trying to sabotage this operation, then we need to try and stay a step ahead."

"Oh well, I guess I'm back to the dismal existence of flying commercial," I said, a little sadly.

"First class is not exactly dismal," Matheson responded.

"Well, if you're correct then I'll be sure to use the Topless Agenda as my travel agency from here on out," I said.

Matheson frowned at my childish enthusiasm as he poured himself another drink. Obviously he had never flown coach and was therefore bewildered by my excitement to get bumped up to the front of the plane. He picked up his phone, and two and a half minutes later I had a first class ticket booked on an Emirates Air flight to Dubai. Fifteen minutes later, our luggage arrived, and it was time to prepare to leave for my flight. I joined Tatyana, Wendy, Yvonne, and Brett on the other end of the lounge and could see that the stress from earlier was starting to show on their faces. Sure, three of them were former Navy pilots, but I imagine the lack of ejection seats and parachutes took all the fun out of a crash landing.

"You continuing on your own?" Tatyana asked.

"Yeah, sadly."

"Too bad, I was looking forward to another flight together," she said.

"Me too. Maybe we'll see each other on the return flight if all goes well."

The two of us had shared a hell of a shower aboard the Vandenberg jet a while back, so I definitely was a little bummed we wouldn't be flying together. She gave me a hug and a kiss, then Brett came forward, and we shook hands.

"Good luck and remember to brush," he said.

"Yeah, and floss—only the teeth I want to keep."

"I'm Tag, by the way," I said, to Wendy, who I had yet to officially meet.

She was, of course, beautiful, but, unlike the other Vandenberg employees I had met thus far, was a redhead, and she sported a scant few freckles, which, combined with her blue eyes and full lips, made her look like the consummate all American girl that you'd expect to see on the cover of a Sports Illustrated swimsuit edition.

"Nice to meet you. It's too bad we haven't had a chance to get to know each other better," she said, her voice belying a charming Southern accent.

"Well, hopefully another time—preferably when we don't have any engine trouble."

Last up was Yvonne, and we shared a hug that ended when Matheson intervened and led me away from the others, so that he could subtly slip a flash drive into my hand.

"Everything you need to know is on there. Study it on the plane then destroy its contents before you land."

It sounded a little like an intro line from a Mission Impossible movie, and I had to smile.

"It won't self destruct on its own in five seconds?" I asked.

"No. So you'll have to get creative. Maybe soak it in your martini or something."

"That I can do, though I have a related question. What about my gun? Will I have any trouble checking it in?"

"No. Leave it in your checked luggage, and I'll take care of the rest."

I said my final goodbyes, shook hands with Matheson and Vandenberg, then joined the airport security guy, who had been patiently waiting to take me to my gate. I grabbed my carry-on bag and my laptop, and we boarded a golf cart and headed off to the international terminal. They took me past security and brought me right to the boarding ramp, where I bypassed the passengers waiting in line and walked directly onto the plane. I made a left and found the flight attendants lined up and looking very official as they awaited the arrival of the first class passengers. They were all female, pretty, and wearing a beige uniform with a red hat that had a cream colored silken scarf hanging down from the right side, obviously intended to be evocative of a veil, which would give passengers a little foreshadowing of exotic Arabia. I showed them my ticket, and the nearest one, a pretty brunette with olive skin and dark almond eyes, led me down the left hand side of the plane to my seat.

"Welcome aboard Emirates Air, Mr. Finn. My name is Asma, and I will be your primary flight attendant for the journey to Dubai," she said.

"Good to know, though please call me Tag or Finn. No Mr. is necessary."

"Finn it is. Now, is there anything you would like before we take off?" she asked, her lovely dark eyes coming alive.

"You mean right now? While we're still on the ground?"

"Of course."

"Sorry, I'm still adapting to life in first class."

"Is this your first time?"

"Yep, I'm a virgin. It's officially my first time in first."

"Then I shall have to make sure your first time is as special as possible."

"Thank you, Asma, and it makes me wish all my first times were with you."

She gave me a flirtatious smile then moved on while I put my laptop and small carry on bag on the floor and settled into the spacious first class seat. It was more like a living room recliner, and the instruction manual showed that it apparently converted into my own private cabin when I was ready to go to bed. I'd read that Emirates Air's first class accommodations were amongst the best in the world, and now I'd have to agree—even more so, after having spent the majority of my life in one of those shitty seats back in coach, where I was invariably squeezed between an irritable alcoholic and someone with a hacking cough. The former would eventually fall asleep, but the latter was the real problem, because he or she would cough for the entire flight, and, since commercial airlines saved fuel by recirculating most of the air, the sick person would end up spreading their germs to the entire compartment. This explained why everyone in coach had a tendency to get sick on long flights, and it made me wonder why people even went on vacation to somewhere exotic if they arrived with a cold or the flu and ended up spending their time in bed.

The rest of the first class passengers began arriving, and in my immediate section I saw a pretty Asian woman, a wealthy looking couple with their teenage daughter, five guys in suits, and, directly behind me, was another suit, though he had an attractive woman with him who was either his associate or his girlfriend. He ordered a scotch the minute he sat down while his female companion ordered a mineral water, which was a much wiser decision when it came to long distance commercial travel. The mucous membranes tended to dry out in the thin air and drinking plenty of water counteracted that fact and made it much less likely to pick up one of the many viruses circulating through the plane's air conditioning system.

Asma came along again, and I ordered a mineral water as well. In coach, they wouldn't even offer you a pillow at this stage of a flight, let alone a beverage, and a moment later I was enjoying my sparkling water as the Airbus A380 disconnected from the jetway, backed up, then began taxiing out to the runway. This was also my first experience with the goliath of the skies, and the brochure said it had a cocktail lounge on the lower level that I hoped to check out later after I was good and hydrated. The massive plane rolled onto the runway, applied its brakes, and waited for takeoff.

A minute or so passed, then the engines started spooling up, making the massive jet vibrate until the brakes released, and it started accelerating rapidly down the runway. The airport and its outer buildings sped by faster and faster, and the g forces pushed me back in my seat as I settled in for my second, and hopefully successful, takeoff of the day. The big jet left terra firma and climbed up into the mostly clear San Francisco skies, and I looked out my window to see that we were passing over Colma, the city just south of San Francisco. It was an interesting, if not slightly morbid place, where its dead residents outnumbered its live ones by a thousand to one. I suppose San Francisco needed somewhere to bury its many residents, and this made Colma a veritable metropolis for the dearly departed.

The jet leveled off at its cruising altitude of thirty five thousand feet, and the ride was surprisingly quiet and smooth, with the mammoth size of the plane making it hard to believe that we were actually flying. The fasten seat belt sign turned off, but I chose to keep mine on out of habit and the fear of random turbulence. Of course, it felt a little silly to be so cautious, considering all the mischief I had gotten up to on the Vandenberg private jet, but I was back to flying commercial and, therefore, taking the proper precautions.

Asma arrived and took my lunch order and, instead of the run of the mill gruel that I had gotten back in coach, I now chose chicken pesto pasta and a spinach salad on the side. Fifteen minutes later, the food arrived, and I dug in and enjoyed the best commercial airline meal I'd ever tasted. Full as a tic and with my blood sugar well into normal levels, I pulled out my laptop and inserted the flash drive that Matheson had given me. A second later, the icon popped up on my screen, and I double clicked it with more than a little trepidation. The file was in PDF format, and the first page showed a present day image of Farid Ardeshir. Judging by the shallow depth of field, the photo was obviously taken from a distance with a telephoto lens, but it was clearly the man I remembered. It was strange to see my old friend again and looking at his face instantly took me back five years to Tehran, Iran, and the unusual circumstances of our first meeting.

CHAPTER SIX
Road Trip

Tehran Iran, 2013 — five years earlier.

It was nine a.m. in the morning local time, and I was taking my morning dump and reading my book *Persian Pilgrimages: Journeys Across Iran.* I had already spent a lot of time on the internet researching Iran, but I liked to have as much knowledge as possible about any place where I had an assignment. Iran had never been on my list of travel itineraries because of its Islamic revolution in 1979, so now I was engaged in a bit of a crash course on its history and customs. I had, of course, been to its neighbors Iraq and Afghanistan in the service but never to Iran, which was actually too bad, for it was a veritable treasure trove of history. It was also the origin of many of our modern day sciences such as algebra and medicine, the latter having been explored in great detail by a fellow named Avicenna, who is generally thought to be the father of modern medicine.

Currently, however, Iran was considered to be a third world country and a menace to peace in the Middle East, which was why I was here on a joint operation with the Mossad code named operation Eagle Feather.

The objective was to help one of Iran's most brilliant nuclear scientists escape to the decadent West, thereby crippling their nuclear program while enhancing ours. His name was Farid Ardeshir, and he was thirty-four years old, a shade over six feet tall, good looking, unmarried, and according to his file, hoped to meet a blond, big breasted American woman when he reached the United States and started his new life. He was also a gifted linguist, fluent in Persian, Arabic, French, German, and English, with the last having been particularly useful, as he had earned his PhD at Stanford University. Today, I would be meeting him in the steam room of his gym, where he would don his new identity, and we'd slip out the back door, get into a non-descript sedan, and drive north to meet up with a Mossad agent before crossing the border into Turkey. The first leg of the trip was fairly straightforward and would take about eleven hours if all went well.

I put down my book, flushed, then took a shower before getting dressed and taking my things down to the car. It was towards the end of summer, but the morning air was still cool, crisp, and dry, because Tehran sat about three thousand nine hundred feet above sea level. By afternoon, however, it might climb to as high as a hundred degrees Fahrenheit, but I personally found it to be a rather comfortable climate and not just because of the temperate weather. The main reason was because I had a long existing allergy to dust mites, but the little fuckers didn't generally live above three thousand feet, and that meant my sinuses were celebrating sweet relief, and I could smell all the nuances of the city, whether it was the restaurants, car exhaust, or the local flora and fauna.

Farid's gym was an upscale place about a half mile from the hotel, and the local traffic was light, although slightly chaotic with few drivers adhering to the rules of the road. The city soon transitioned from taller buildings to two and three story structures, and I had a clear view of the distant Alborz mountains, the pinnacle of which was Mount Damavand. It was an eighteen thousand, five hundred and fifty foot extinct volcano, which resided about fifty miles northeast of the city. It's funny, I'd always assumed Iran was a flat desert country, but it was quite the contrary with plenty of mountainous terrain and all manner of climates, from arid in the south to subtropical up where it bordered the Caspian Sea. The capital, Tehran, was kind of mixed climate-wise, and tended to be warmer in the southern desert districts and cooler in the higher northern parts of the city.

At the moment I was in the temperate though crowded middle and luckily managed to find parking along the back street, though I desperately hoped that the sign beside my car didn't translate as tow away zone. There were plenty of other cars, so odds were on my side that I had parked wisely. I walked two blocks away before turning and heading to the street that bordered the front of the gym. My roundabout route was so that I could do some reconnaissance and spot any security teams that might be watching Farid. Up on my left, and across the street from the gym's front entrance, I spotted a white Mercedes with two men in the front. They were obviously from MOIS, or Iran's Ministry of Intelligence and National Security, and both sported bushy mustaches, sunglasses, and menacing glares, so, if they were trying to be subtle, it wasn't working.

As I reached the entrance to the gym, I spotted a second car with two more security men parked about half way down the block on my side of the street. Shitters, Farid was obviously an important man, and that wasn't going to make my job any easier. I entered the double doors to the gym and handed the front desk guy a guest pass from my hotel. He was a young, buff, twenty-something with a serious tan and the signature acne of a roider. He grunted something indiscernible then pointed me towards the main workout floor. The place turned out to be modern and as nice as any gym back home, with the only obvious difference being that it was all male. Apparently, women either went to different gyms or came at different times, and I had to admit that the lack of women in tight exercise clothing here was definitely another point for the West.

I stepped onto a treadmill and did about ten minutes of moderate cardio to warm up then moved over to the leg press before finishing up on the free weights. I doubt the

Agency would have been happy that I was taking all this extra time to workout, but I had spent the last eighteen hours on a plane and desperately needed the exercise. It also added to my cover, as what kind of pussy would go to a gym just to use the steam room?

Finished and feeling the welcome fatigue of a decent workout, I did a little recon of the back door where we would be exiting. It was a typical steel reinforced double door that unfortunately had been chained closed and padlocked, probably to keep people from letting their friends in through the back. So much for fire safety in Iran. I looked around to make sure I was alone then slid out my lockpick tools and quickly set to work on my tiny case hardened foe. It took all of five seconds to get the tumblers in sequence before it clicked open, but I left it unlocked and still looped through the chain so that it appeared to be holding it in place. Step one was complete.

I headed into the locker area and found the steam room in the back left corner near the showers. I grabbed a towel and headed in, hopeful that I wouldn't be waiting too long in the intolerable heat and humidity. It was soothing for a short period of time, but, if I stayed too long I'd come out feeling like an over cooked stalk of asparagus. The room was empty except for a man lying on the top bench with a towel over his head, and a slang term for a person of Arabic decent came to mind, but I kept it to myself for two reasons. The first was that it would be fairly rude to say it to a complete stranger, and the second was that it would be inaccurate, as Persians weren't Arabic. A lot of people grouped them in with the Arabs, but they were, in fact, Aryans of Indo-European origin. The man stirred and peaked out at me from under his towel for a moment before speaking.

"Hello, white devil, you smell of fornication and god-lessness."

Believe it or not, that was the code phrase I was hoping to hear, which meant it was time to respond in kind.

"Yes I do, and soon you too will know the soft center of the infidel."

He sat up and smiled as he held out his hand.

"Nice to meet you, I'm Farid."

"I'm Tag, I hear you like big tits," I said, as I shook his hand.

"Of course. You don't?"

"I like all tits. Big and small."

His look turned serious.

"Is everything ready?"

"Yep, the car's out back, and I have your new clothes, identity, and phone right here in my gym bag."

It was important that Farid leave everything behind for fear that they might have some kind of tracking sensor in either his clothing or his phone.

"You ready to give up this decadent eastern lifestyle?"

"You bet your sweet ass."

We left the steam room and headed for the showers for the big transformation. Farid had a full beard, but he would be shaving it off as the first step of disguising his appearance. We reconvened at the sinks five minutes later, and he smiled and rubbed his chin as he looked at his face, which was now as smooth as a baby's bottom.

"How do I look?" he asked.

"Clean and ready to motor boat."

"What does that mean?"

"You place your face between a woman's breasts and wiggle your head back and forth while making a motorboat sound. It's much more effective without facial hair," I said, as I mimicked the motion.

He laughed out loud then rubbed his smooth new face again as he smiled in the mirror.

"Perhaps when I find a big breasted woman in America, I can try this motor boating thing."

"Do or do not. There is no try," I said, in my best Yoda voice.

Farid laughed again.

"Yes, good point, Master Yoda, so I will do this motor boating," he said, the do done in a Yoda voice.

We finished getting dressed and headed for the back door, where I had a quick look around to make sure we weren't being watched. With the way clear, we stepped outside, and I reached back inside and relocked the chain before closing the door, thus covering our tracks. The car was right where I parked it and thankfully hadn't been towed or ticketed, which was hopefully an omen of good things to come. We loaded our bags in the trunk then took a seat in the car, with Farid at the wheel. He was accustomed to the local roads and traffic and would therefore allow us to blend in better, so it made sense for him to take the first shift.

"Road trip!" I said.

He looked at me curiously.

"I've never heard that phrase either."

"Well then, time to learn it, because it's kind of a tradition in America and the subject of endless books and movies."

"OK, then let's get this fucking road trip on the road!" he exclaimed excitedly, throwing up his arms.

"That's the spirit."

He started the car, and off we went, heading west on Azadi Street, passing the University of Tehran, where scores of college students were milling about between classes. After a couple more turns, we were on the Tehran Qazvin Highway and doing a little over a hundred and twenty kilometers an hour which was about seventy-four. Right now, the MOIS Agents were hopefully still sitting out in front of the gym, waiting for Farid and glaring at passersby with their menacing stares. Eventually they would go in and look for him, and his disappearance would bring about a nationwide alert, so it was imperative to gain as much distance as possible. Their initial search would focus on the city, and, specifically, the airport, which was the reason we were in a car. It would eventually expand to the entire country, but, if all went well, we'd be long gone and already across the border in Turkey.

The traffic was light at this time of day, and it allowed us to make good time, and, better still, gave me a brief respite from the stress of the mission to enjoy a little sightseeing. Off to the left there were agricultural fields while off to the right there were grassy golden mountains, and it reminded me of the drive along California's central valley between San Francisco and Los Angeles. It was an interesting phenomena to think of my long lost home that I hadn't seen in years, though it made sense, because our minds always looked for familiarity.

A little over an hour and a half later, we were entering the city of Qazvin, and the road was becoming more congested, but Farid drove like the local he was and hit the horn and waved an arm here and there as the need arose. On the other edge of town, a police car sat parked on a side street with two officers inside that appeared to be watching traffic. Farid looked at me nervously, and both of us held our breath as we passed it. A little ways down the road, he checked the rearview mirror then relaxed and smiled.

"They weren't the least bit interested in us."

"That's good news and means one of two things. Either they didn't recognize you sans the beard or they haven't put out a nationwide alert for you yet," I said.

"Good to know, but I have a more pressing problem—namely the fact that I'm starving. How about you?" he asked.

"Now that you mention it, I realize I'm also starving."

I hadn't eaten since breakfast and managed to get a pretty decent sweat on at the gym. Generally it was important to eat protein within a one-hour window of working out in order for the muscles to begin rebuilding, but I was an hour behind schedule and hungry as hell.

"Where should we eat?" I asked.

"There's a great falafel place on the other side of Qazvin."

"Perfect, falafels give me incredible gas."

"Me too," he said, smiling.

"Then I'll guess we'll be hot boxing it."

"What does that mean?" he asked.

"It's just another silly American expression, and one you'll understand in about two hours."

The highway wound north to the fringe of the city then back west, and we exited off to our right and drove to a small restaurant about a hundred yards off the main road. It looked nice enough on the exterior, but once we entered the building, I had a little trepidation. I wouldn't say that it looked dingy, but it wouldn't be a stretch to imagine Gordon Ramsey filming one of his Kitchen Nightmares episodes here, where he would most certainly end up delivering one of his profanity laden tirades to the owner and staff.

"Trust me, the food is excellent," Farid said, sensing my unease.

"OK, but my life is in your hands."

We went up to the counter, and Farid ordered us falafel

plates with hummus, salad, and a side of their famous rice with berries and saffron. I had to admit that, in spite of my initial reservations, everything smelled and looked delicious. We took a seat at a window table, and the owner brought us over silverware and cups of black tea. He returned a few minutes later with our plates of food, and Farid and I dug in like starving hyenas, abstaining from speech until our plates were empty. I leaned back in my seat hoping to take a little of the pressure off my stomach and saw Farid do the same.

"So, what is your life like back in America?"

"Well, my job doesn't actually allow me to spend much time there at the moment, sadly."

"So you live like James Bond? New places and new women every week?"

"Well—new places at least. A few women—not exactly Bond girls."

He laughed.

"Do you plan on getting married and having a family?" he asked.

"I certainly would like to someday, as I'm not getting any younger."

"Yeah I understand—that's why I'm doing all this. I want to raise my future children in a free society where they can be or do whatever they please."

"You won't miss Iran?"

"Afraid not. The greatest time in my life was when I was doing my PhD at Stanford."

"Yeah, I read that in your file. You know, I went to college there as well, which is probably part of the reason why they sent me—figured we'd have some common ground."

"No way! When were you there?"

"99 to 2003."

"Holy shit, I started my doctorate in 2002!"

"Fucking over achiever! I was only just finishing my bachelors."

"What would you expect from a boy from a strict Muslim country. No womanizing or alcohol—all I had as a youth were my studies."

"Very sad, my friend."

"Indeed."

"What the hell brought you back here?"

"My father had died, and my mother needed me. Now that she's passed away, I have no ties here anymore."

"That's kind of sad."

"Yes it is, but it frees me up to pursue other things," he said, holding up his hands, the gesture meant to imply two formidable breasts.

"Everyone needs a dream," I responded.

I was just taking the last sip of tea when a group of young college age girls walked in and sat at the next table. Farid glanced over at them then turned back and smiled at me. I took a quick look at the girls and instantly understood why he was smiling. The girl facing him was particularly attractive and a bit on the chesty side, which was evident even under her headscarf and traditional dress. Ample breasts were ample breasts regardless of how you tried to hide them.

"Are you sure you really want to go to America?" I asked.

"Yes, especially if large breasts are the rule rather than the exception," he said.

"It certainly is in Southern California."

"Then perhaps that is where I will live."

We finished our tea, then I told him I needed to pee before we hit the road. Farid pointed towards the far end of the restaurant, and I headed back and entered the bathroom to find that it had stalls, and each housed a hole in the floor with two rectangular foot holds. My hotel had been fairly westernized, so this was my first experience with the usual squat toilets of Iran, but, thankfully, I was just peeing. Interestingly, many Iranian men supposedly squatted down to pee, which seemed like too much work in my opinion. Standing and peeing was the hallmark of being a man and the trade-off for needing more time than a woman to drop a deuce. And, least of all, standing made it that much easier to control flatulence, which could be pretty common during urination. I stepped into the left stall, not bothering to close the door, unzipped and let loose a mighty stream of urine. The gracious restaurant owner had refilled my glass about eighteen times, and now I was emptying a bladder that felt about eighteen times larger than it should. I was at least halfway to empty, or half full if I was a urinating optimist, when I heard the door open behind me.

"American or European?" I heard someone say.

I turned my head and glanced over my shoulder to see two Iranian policemen standing behind me, and my urine instantly stopped flowing.

"Excuse me?" I asked.

The one on the left was the first to speak. He was a serious looking middle-aged man with a well-trimmed beard and the yellowed teeth of a life long smoking habit.

"You are standing, so you have to be one or the other."

Wonderful, he was observant but hopefully not too curious.

"You guessed it. I'm American, but then you obviously already know that because I responded in English."

"Yes, so what brings you to Iran? Searching for more weapons of mass destruction?" he asked.

Even better—he was a comedian, and he and his young partner shared a laugh at his little quip.

"Afraid not. I'm just a photojournalist doing a piece on Iran's ancient ruins."

"Interesting. Which ones?"

"Lots of them."

"Such as."

God bless the Internet and the research I had done before going on this assignment. Since I was posing as a photojournalist, I had done a lot of reading up on Iran's storied history and related ruins.

"Mostly ancient Persian. Places like Shushtar, Passagard and Persepolis."

"Ah, Persepolis, which Alexander The Great pillaged

and burned to the ground. Another of the many western leaders who have invaded our lands."

"Truly a shame."

"Yes," he said, taking a moment to think.

"Where do you plan to go next?" he asked.

"South to Bishapur."

He gave his partner a look then turned back to me.

"I hope you don't mind if I check your tourist visa."

"Not at all. Do you mind if I finish peeing first?"

"Go ahead. Assuming our presence doesn't hinder your flow."

It sounded like a challenge, so I turned back and looked towards the hole in the floor and tried my best, but the urine wouldn't come.

"Oh, are you shy?" he asked sarcastically.

"Not usually, but then men in America rarely stare at each other while they are holding their penises."

"That's not what I've heard."

The two of them laughed again. Hardy, har, har. What a couple of shitbags.

"Do you mind waiting outside?" I asked.

"Yes, we do."

Oh well, might as well make them feel at home. I was lucky enough to feel a nice fart coming on, and I let it out slowly, making it rumble and sound like a series of backfires from a car's exhaust. Middle Eastern food tended to give me terrible gas, so it was unlikely that it would smell particularly good to someone other than myself. I heard both of them backing up, obviously searching for clean air, and I couldn't help but laugh. The brief respite gave me the inspiration I needed, and a steady flow of urine finally started pouring into the hole in the floor. I finished and was giving Tag Junior a gentle final shake when Mr. Chatty told me to hurry up. Fuck him — some things a man must do at his own pace. I zipped up, adjusted my pants, and finally turned to face my antagonists, who both smiled smugly, as they were apparently enjoying accosting a westerner in such an awkward and usually private place. At least now I could get a more detailed look at the assholes. Mr. Chatty was heavy set, carrying a little extra weight in his mid section while his subordinate was a bit younger, fitter, and obviously hadn't been spending his down time scarfing down *zoolbias* and *bamiyehs*, which were the Iranian equivalent of donuts.

"Do you make it a habit to roust tourists in bathrooms?" I asked as I handed him my visa.

"Depends on the tourist," he said, looking at my visa and frowning.

It wasn't a forgery, so if he found any problem, he was just being an asshole.

"I think you should come with us. I'd like to verify your visa status at the station."

"And why is that?"

"Because I said so."

This was not a good development, and I was going to need to either talk or fight my way out of it — hopefully the former.

"Honestly, guys, I'm on a tight timeline with my editor back in New York. How about I buy you lunch, and we part as friends, the end result being that we're improving American and Iranian relations."

His expression hardened in spite of the fact that I thought I was being particularly amenable.

"You will do as you're told," he said, testily.

"I'm just trying to be friendly."

"Turn around and place your hands on your head," he said.

"I'm sorry, but I really don't have time for this."

"I don't care what you have time for."

"Look, this is only going to go down one of two ways. The easy way, where you leave me in peace, or the hard way, where I leave you in pieces."

"You Americans like to talk tough, but, when it comes down to it, you are a bunch of overprivileged pussies who spend your time driving your Teslas and Priuses between your mansions and your country clubs."

"Honestly, you're misinformed, as I have a condo, and I drive a Subaru to my country club."

"Enough! It's time to go to the station and see if we might quiet that big mouth of yours," Mr. Chatty said, as he pulled out his handcuffs and started to walk in my direction.

Why did people always have to choose the hard way?

CHAPTER SEVEN
The Great Exodus

Everyone looks back at particular moments in their life and wishes they had done certain things differently, and I had a feeling the Iranian police officers standing in front of me would most likely feel that way about the next sixteen and a half seconds that would unfold in this small and otherwise lackluster bathroom. I turned my back to the two men, giving them the false impression that I was going to acquiesce, but it was all a ploy. In reality, it was just a way to get them to lower their guard, so that I could inflict some very purposeful damage to their bodies and, in turn, their egos.

Unfortunately, I had two armed opponents and therefore needed to take each man out of the fight as quickly as possible, and that would entail affecting airflow, blood flow, and nerve functioning. First on my radar was Mr. Chatty, who was just coming into attack range. I glanced over my shoulder to judge the distance then lashed out with a very hard, low back kick to his groin that doubled him over. I quickly turned and grabbed his head and delivered knees to his face until he went limp, and I was able to toss him aside. His junior officer reacted by going for his holstered pistol, so I used my longest weapon, namely my leg, to front kick him in the stomach and send him sprawling back against the wall. It stalled his efforts, but he was soon back to trying to reach for his pistol. I was faster, however, and closed the distance and swung a right elbow strike at his head while I took hold of his weapon hand with my left. The blow stunned him, and I reached down and used both hands to twist his pistol back towards his center until he released his grip. The weapon was officially free, and I used it like a club and struck him in the temple then hooked it around the back of his neck and delivered a knee into his midsection that buckled him over. His next destination was going to be the floor, and, as he was already halfway there, it was easy to leverage his right arm up and flip him head over heals to land on his back. He recovered surprisingly quickly and rolled over and got up to his feet, looking particularly angry as he charged me and attempted a tackle. He rammed his shoulder into my stomach and nearly knocked the wind from my lungs as he pushed me backwards into the wall. It showed a lot of resolve, but it was a risky move because it exposed his head and allowed me to deliver two simultaneous chops to each side of his neck. The chop was the consummate martial arts movie move, and had been used by everyone from the cartoon character Fred Flintstone to James Bond. It therefore seemed a little silly to the layperson, but in actual use was quite effective—especially when done properly. This meant hitting with the bottom inside corner of the palm in order to transfer a lot of energy into a smaller point of impact. It could be used to great effect on soft tissue all over the body, but in this instance it was directed at the sides of the neck in order to enact the very fancy sounding baroreflex, which occurred when trauma to the carotid artery confused the brain into misinterpreting the blood pressure and made the unlucky victim pass out. As expected, he went unconscious, but, as the effects were temporary, I applied an inverted blood choke just to make sure Sleeping Beauty stayed out of the rest of the fight.

At the six second mark I heard a noise and hazarded a glance behind me and saw that Chatty was suddenly coherent and reaching for his gun. I quickly dragged Sleeping Beauty around to form a human shield in order to take away any chance of Mr. Chatty shooting me—unless, of course, he wanted to shoot his partner as well. He was caught in a moment of indecision, and it gave me the opportunity to shove his comatose friend onto him and knock both of them to the ground. His gun hand was trapped with his gun pointed harmlessly off to the side, and I came forward and stepped on his wrist just hard enough to make him cry out in pain. He released the pistol, and, now that I had both of their guns, I leaned down and held the guns in front of Mr. Chatty's face.

"You chose the hard way, my friend," I said.

"No, don't kill me. I have a family!"

"Don't worry, I have no intention of killing you. I don't

want you to ever forget the day a pussy American photojournalist taught you some manners in a restaurant bathroom. I think it'll be an important lesson in helping you become a better ambassador to the next batch of tourists who manage to visit this beautiful country. So, listen closely and repeat after me. You get more flies with sugar than you do salt." I said.

"I don't understand."

"You will in time. Now say it."

"You get more sugar with flies and salt," he said.

"No, you get more flies with sugar *than* you do salt."

"You get more flies with sugar than salt."

"Close enough."

He thought a moment then smiled nervously.

"I think I understand."

"Good, now don't forget it!" I said, as I leaned down and pistol whipped him hard in the temple, sending him into a dreamy sleep.

I stood up to take a look at my handiwork and realized I'd been particularly lucky, if you could call getting cornered by two policemen in a bathroom lucky. Still, I had managed to avoid a long and potentially lethal physical confrontation that could have attracted unwanted attention, and, worst case scenario, more police. The question now was what to do with officer Chatty and his rookie partner. I decided on the simple approach and dragged Mr. Chatty over to a stall, placed him over the hole facing away from the door, then lowered his pants around his ankles and leaned him against the wall, so that he would stay upright. Finished, I set his friend up in the next stall over then stood back to check my work. The two policemen looked liked a couple of close friends sharing a double dump and appeared to be so peaceful in their current state that it made me almost feel a little guilty—almost. Trouble temporarily averted, I washed my hands and left the bathroom to find Farid talking animatedly with the girls, though he looked up and paused when he saw the concern in my expression.

"Did you have a bad time in the bathroom? I assure you it wasn't from the food here."

"No, no problem with the food—yet. My problem was with the police. I take it you didn't see them go in after me."

"No, I was—um—busy talking," he said, looking guilty as he nodded towards the girls.

"Oh, well I'm glad to see you had my back—not!"

"Shit, I'm sorry, are you OK?"

"Yeah, but it's probably best if we get as far away from here as we can, so, let's roll, Cinderella!"

Farid said goodbye to the girls, and we headed out to the car and were soon back on the highway, where he looked particularly tense as he checked the rearview mirror every few minutes.

"Don't worry. We should have at least an hour before they wake up. Plus, I told them we were headed southwest towards Bishapur."

We drove another quiet hour through the beautiful Iranian countryside without incident, and Farid finally started to relax.

"So, what's the plan?" he asked.

"Pretty straightforward. We drive to Urmia and meet up with a Mossad Agent who will help us cross the border to Turkey. After that, we board a boat in Istanbul then motor out into the Aegean Sea and rendezvous with the submarine Ohio. From there, it's a brief trip to the Sigonella Naval Air Station on Naples, where we'll catch a plane to the land of blond hair and plentiful bosoms."

The next four hours passed without incident, but all that changed at the beginning of hour five when all hell broke loose—in the car that is. The falafels, or *fried explosive devices* as I came to know them, were finally starting to do their job, and a great exodus of gas was waiting to exit my backdoor. To be nice, I reached over and rolled down my window.

"What's wrong? Are you getting sleepy?" Farid asked.

"No, I'm fine, but you probably don't want to do any deep breathing exercises."

"Why—what's the prob..."

Suddenly his eyes started to glaze over, and he immediately rolled down his own window and fanned the air around his head.

"Oh my God! You fucker!" he said.

"Sorry, falafels have always had this effect on me."

"They have this effect on everyone," he said, as a smile formed on his lips.

"Really?"

"Oh yes!"

That's when I realized he had just returned fire.

"Sweet Mother of God! Your butthole is a cauldron of evil!" I said.

"What do you mean? I think it is a den of joyful goodness!"

"Yeah, if goodness smelled like three day-old diarrhea and burnt butt hair."

"Hardly, my butthole is as hairless and smooth as a baby's."

"Yeah, because that fart just burned it all off."

I fanned the air and attempted to drive the fart towards him while he did the same, the result being that it was left in a kind of holding pattern in the center of the car. Both of us started laughing, and the experience was feeling more like the innocent fun of hanging out with my friends back in college, and it made the moment oddly comforting. Working in the intelligence business was, by its secretive nature, a fairly lonely existence, and it was rare to bond with a total stranger, least of all, over flatulence. Still, I never saw James Bond fanning farts in his Aston Martin, but then he was generally in the company of beautiful women.

Several farts and many laughs later, we were almost halfway to Urmia, and it was time for a necessary bathroom stop. I was desperately hoping that Farid would perhaps take a dump and lose some of his mojo, which would de-escalate our war of the bungholes and allow me to breath a little easier. We exited the highway and crossed over to the other side and pulled in to the nearest gas station.

"I can pump the gas if you want to go first," I said.

"Thanks, I'll be right back."

I went around and started pumping the gas and took a moment to look around at the countryside. The flora and fauna reminded me a lot of the American Southwest, specifically New Mexico, which made sense, considering we were pretty close in terms of latitude and elevation. It was strange how places even thousands of miles apart on different continents could look similar, and it was at moments like this that you could really visualize that the landmasses of the earth used to be one giant super continent called Pangaea. We really had to be thankful for tectonic plates and oceans, as I couldn't even imagine how turbulent and fucked up the world would be if all the countries were side by side. Farid appeared a moment later, looking relieved although not as relieved as I would have liked. He obviously hadn't dropped the deuce I'd hoped for, because no man could have emptied his bowels in that little amount of time.

"No dumpage?" I asked.

He smiled.

"Afraid not, my friend, but I wouldn't have gone either way, as I absolutely detest public restrooms, and I'm serious when I say I would rather shit in a fucking bucket."

"I would agree, as long as that bucket is nowhere near a public restroom."

I ventured inside to the bathroom and once again opted to stand as I emptied about three cups of tea then washed my hands and returned to find Farid looking tense. He motioned to the car on the other side of the pumps, and I saw that it was a Police cruiser. Fuckinzee. It was a Mercedes and a hell of a lot faster than the nondescript piece of shit we were driving, so, if it came down to a chase, we would be greatly outmatched.

"Anything I should know?"

"I've been listening to the police radio chatter and heard that there's an alert out for us, and they have a description of our car."

"Oh shit fuckers! I guess that means one point for the MOIS."

"Yeah, but fortunately for us, our guy here hasn't noticed us yet."

The policeman walked inside while Farid and I got into the car and looked at each other.

"Well? What now?" Farid asked.

"We need to get off the main highway until we can find a different car. Do you have any friends or colleagues out here?"

"I have a colleague in Sanjun-rud."

"Is it far away?"

"No, it's the next town, and I think she might be willing to help us."

I was picking up on a distinct discomfort in Farid's tone—one I recognized to generally be derived from interactions with the opposite sex.

"Wait a minute—did you by chance have more than a friendly relationship with this female colleague?"

"Yeah," he said, uncomfortably.

"And how did it end?"

"Badly, but she's no friend of the establishment."

"Have you heard the expression that hell hath no fury like a woman scorned?"

Farid considered my words and looked legitimately worried as he turned onto the frontage road and drove northwest, where we thankfully didn't see another car, let alone a police cruiser. About a mile from Zanjan-rud, we came over a slight rise and, just ahead, saw the remnants of a departing dust storm. In its wake lay a massive pile up of cars that had obviously collided during the temporary loss of visibility, and Farid and I both stared at the horror of the scene before our eyes.

"What do we do?" he asked.

"My CIA handbook would say to keep going, but the PJ in me feels like we need to stop and help."

"What's a PJ?" Farid asked.

"Parajumper. I used to be in a special operations unit that specialized in rescuing people and, if necessary, provide emergency medical help."

"How the hell did you end up in the CIA?"

"I guess they figured I'd be equally good at hurting people."

"Are you?" Farid asked a little nervously.

"I'd like to think I'm not, but the two Iranian policemen back at that falafel restaurant would probably disagree."

We continued to drive closer and saw that a number of cars and a large fuel truck had collided, and now the center of the highway was blocked by a massive tangle of smoking metal. There weren't any ambulances or safety vehicles in sight, so the victims were, for the moment, on their own.

"Fuck, we're the only ones around. We have to help them," I said.

"Absolutely."

Farid pulled the car over to the side of the road, and we got out and were instantly bombarded by the sound of men, women, and children crying and calling for help. A fuel truck lay on its side at the center of the accident, and the smell of petrol permeated the air as a steady flow of gasoline was pouring from a ruptured valve and slowly engulfing the cars in a vast lake. It was only a matter of time before it ignited, and the entire place became a raging inferno.

"Any idea what we should do first?" Farid asked.

"Normally, we'd isolate any neck and back injuries, but the risk of them burning to death takes precedent, so we need to get everyone out and the hell away from the vehicles."

We raced into the midst of the accident, and the smoke, screams, and carnage made me feel as though I were back on the battlefield. I hadn't had to use my medical training much since leaving the Air Force, but it would definitely come in handy today. Farid and I spread out, going car to car, finding and helping people get free of their mangled automobiles. My first task was helping an old man out of his pickup truck, but the door was jammed, so I lifted him up over the sill and dragged him a safe distance away to where I created an improvised triage station. Next was a young couple in a sedan, and the woman was only semi-conscious as her husband tended to her by pressing his hand to a gash on her head. Unfortunately, they were both in shock and oblivious to the growing danger of their situation. I checked the woman first and suspected she might have suffered a mild concussion, but thankfully there was minimal bleeding and no sign of secondary symptoms such as nausea or vomiting. The man, on the other hand, had a leg injury, the severity of which was impossible to tell in the car. I helped them get out of the vehicle then carried the woman while the husband limped alongside holding onto my shoulder for support until we reached the triage area.

I made sure they were comfortable then rejoined Farid, where the two of us continued our search and managed to extricate what appeared to be the entirety of the victims. We paused to catch our breath but heard a cry for help, and the two of us ran over to discover a sedan that we had missed, because it was wedged between another car and the fuel truck. The car's roof had been smashed down leaving only a thin opening, and inside was a woman, a little girl, and a baby boy who was strapped into a child seat in the back. The doors were obviously too damaged to open, and we needed a tool like the Jaws of Life but had nothing but our bare hands. Farid and I looked at each other and knew full well that we were their only hope. We therefore set about trying to pull up on the roof to create an opening, but it wasn't long before I could smell smoke, and I looked up to see that flames were starting to rise from the front of the car.

"We're running out of time. This entire place is going to ignite and catch fire any second," I said.

"How are we going to get them out?"

"I'm going to check the truck for a tire iron or anything that might help us pry up the roof."

I went to the toppled truck and kicked out the front windshield in order to rummage through the cab. Under the seat I found a massive tire iron, and I returned to the car to find the flames growing ever higher. I jammed the sharp end of the tire iron into the crack between the door and the roof, and Farid and I combined our strength and pushed down on the opposite end and forced a small section to bend upwards. A few more tries and we had a good-sized space, but it still wasn't large enough for a person.

"I have an idea," I said, taking the tire iron and running around to the trunk.

I managed to pop it open then rummaged around until thankfully finding the jack. Without the Jaws of Life, this was the most powerful tool we were going to find. I brought it over to the hole Farid and I had created then started cranking. In a matter of seconds, the roof started to creak and bend upward, and we finally had a big enough opening to reach in and pull the woman out of the wreckage. Half-way out, she started screaming, obviously for her children, but Farid managed to console her until she finally relented, and we pulled her free. With the mother clear of the car, I had room to reach across and get a hold of the little girl in the front seat, lift her out, and hand her to her mother. The flames were growing higher and practically burning my face, and I realized we only had seconds before this became a raging inferno. I desperately tried to reach the baby in the back seat, but I was too big to fit any farther through the opening.

"I'm thinner. I think I can reach him," Farid said.

A man in an emergency services uniform appeared and tried to lead the mother and her daughter to safety, but she wouldn't leave without her son. Farid spoke to her briefly, and she begrudgingly left with the man.

"I take it that you told her we would get her son out of the car."

"Yes, in fact I promised."

"Well then, you better get your heroic ass in that car and get that little fucker out of there pronto!"

The engine compartment of the car was now completely in flames as Farid slid into the front seat, disappearing into a cloud of smoke before reappearing a moment later with the baby boy in his arms. He handed him through the opening then followed just behind, coughing and retching from the smoke. We ran as fast as we could, but, when we were only about thirty feet from the car, a great blast of heat and concussive force knocked all of us to the ground. I lay there for a short time, recovering from the blast until more rescue workers arrived. They helped us up, and Farid carried the baby over to the mother, who gratefully took hold of him with tears of joy tracing paths down her soot laden cheeks. A paramedic led Farid and me back towards one of the waiting ambulances and gave us a quick exam, but, aside from the layer of soot that now coated both of us from head to toe, we were basically fine, so they turned their attention to the more needy people.

The arriving fireman started spraying water on the flames, and it sent up a massive cloud of smoke and steam that made it look like hell on earth. Unfortunately, the growing number of rescue workers and, more importantly, policeman on the scene were making me realize that our own personal hell was just coming into fruition. We needed to get the fuck out of here, and our only hope of a clean getaway now lay in the chaos of the moment. Judging by Farid's face, he was thinking the same thing as we stood up and started moving calmly towards the edge of the crash scene. We stayed at the fringe of the activity and passed through the lines of firemen to finally come out of the maelstrom to find a gaggle of policemen surrounding our car. They all slowly turned their attention to us, then the closest one spoke something in Persian.

"What's going on?" I whispered to Farid.

"Don't worry. You might be a man of action, but I'm a man of words. I can totally talk our way out of this," he said, confidently."

CHAPTER EIGHT
Colleagues with Benefits

Two and a half minutes later, Farid and I were handcuffed and sitting in the back of a Mercedes police cruiser. The upside was that it was more comfortable than any other car I been in since arriving in Iran, but the downside was that it might very well end up being the last comfortable car I was in before my premature demise.

"Great talking, Farid! At least you're good at science," I said.

"I'm sorry that I'm not more versed in the ways of deception and subterfuge," he said, sarcastically.

"Yeah, me too."

The trunk behind us opened, and some items were placed in it before it was slammed shut. The person who closed it walked around to the front and took a seat and proceeded to turn around and look at us with a rather stern expression on his face.

"Hello officer, is there perhaps a chance you might take us to the local bus station?" I asked.

He didn't answer and, instead, turned back around and started driving northwest towards Zanjan-rud, where he was presumably taking us to the local police station. Meanwhile, more emergency vehicles came racing past from the other direction, and chatter from the police radio filled the car. It wasn't the most enjoyable drive, and it was made even less enjoyable, considering we were handcuffed in the back of a police car and likely heading off to be tortured, imprisoned, and potentially executed, but I suppose that was the downside of being a spy.

We entered the city and soon came upon a large building that was bustling with police, but our driver, instead of stopping, continued past and made a right turn at the next block. This wasn't a good omen, as it meant we were likely being taken into the custody of the local Iranian Secret Service office. We had a chance of escape with the local police, but a government installation would have much tighter security. We continued on for another half mile then turned left onto another street, where our driver inexplicably pulled to the side of the road in front of a bus stop then turned around to address us.

"I assume you were joking about the bus stop, so, if you have another destination, now is the time to tell me," he said, in surprisingly passable English.

"Are you serious?" I asked.

"Yes, now, where can I take you?"

"Are you a cop or a cab?"

"Cop, but right now you may think of me as a cab," he said.

"I'm sorry if I'm having a hard time understanding you but…"

"Look, I know that you two are wanted because of an altercation with a couple of policeman."

Sweet salty nuts sacks! We finally had some good luck! The police were unaware that I was trying to spirit away one of their most gifted nuclear scientists!

"Yeah, and I'll have you know that those officers attacked me without any provocation in a restaurant bathroom. I was only defending myself," I said, which was kind of true.

"You don't need to tell me anything else about the matter, because I already know about those two officers and their well-known history of questionable behavior."

"So, that's why you're letting us go?" I asked.

"No, the real reason that I'm not taking you to jail is because you risked your lives and your freedom to save a bunch of strangers, three of them being my wife, daughter, and son whom you pulled from that burning car. They were coming to meet me for lunch when they got caught in that accident, so again—where do you want me to take you?"

Holy shit. If I ever had a time to believe in Karma, this was it.

"But, won't you get into trouble?" I asked.

"No, because the same dangerous men who managed to knock out a couple of policemen at a restaurant also managed to overpower me and get away, so, where to?" he asked.

"Well?" I asked Farid.

"Take us to Nabovat Street," Farid said.

The police officer pulled back into traffic and, about five minutes later, pulled over and stopped. He exited the car and came around to the back door and let us out before removing our handcuffs.

"Your things are in the trunk," he said, as he opened it, allowing Farid and me to grab our items before stepping up onto the sidewalk.

The man looked at us a moment, and tears appeared in the corners of his eyes as he began to speak.

"I will never be able to adequately repay you, so this is the best I can do at the moment. Also, I suggest you leave the country as soon as possible. Good luck, and may Allah be with you," he said, before he hugged each of us then got into his car and drove away, leaving Farid and me standing there in awe at our incredible fortune.

"I didn't see that coming," I said.

"Me neither."

"So, your colleague lives here?"

"No, two streets over. I wanted to be safe in case that policeman had a change of heart."

"Nice! Now you're utilizing proper deception and subterfuge and acting like a real spy."

"Hopefully the effects are temporary."

We grabbed our things and walked two streets over and stopped in front of a nice, though small, house.

"It looks like she's home," Farid said, pointing at the Mercedes parked at the curb.

We continued up to the front door, and Farid looked at me nervously as he reached out and knocked. A moment later the door opened, and there stood the perfect picture of exotic Iranian beauty. The woman before us had smooth olive skin, large inquisitive brown eyes, and dark lustrous hair that fell well past her shoulders. She also had a spectacular figure that was toned yet curvaceous, and her generous bustline strained against the fabric of her tight body hugging black dress. Unfortunately, she was scowling and apparently not very happy to see us, or, more likely, Farid, so I decided I better take the initiative.

"Hello," I said, cheerfully.

She looked at me for a mere second before turning back to Farid.

"Hello, Farid," she said, curtly.

"Hello, Afshid."

"Aside from losing the beard, you look like shit," she said, before turning her attention back to me.

"And you are?"

"Finn, Tag Finn. It's nice to meet you," I said.

"And you are obviously American."

"Correct, I'm an infidel."

She smiled, but it disappeared when her gaze returned

to Farid.

"What do you want?"

"I kind of need a favor."

"You seriously have the gall to ask for a favor after the way you disappeared and never called?"

"I'm sorry about that but..."

"But nothing, you are a—what is the English word for it? Ah, yes—an asshole."

"We really need your help—it's life or death," I said, interrupting.

She stood there simmering for a time before finally inviting us to come inside her home.

"Why don't you clean up, and then we'll talk."

"That would be great," I said.

"Farid, you can use the guest bathroom. Mr. Finn, you can use mine. Farid will show you where it is—he's been there before."

Farid led me down the hall and pointed to the right, and I entered a rather neat and tidy bedroom, whose only furnishings were a kingsize bed, an Eames chair with a matching ottoman, and a floor to ceiling bookcase that took up an entire wall. I did a quick inventory of the shelves and saw that she was clearly an intellectual with the subject matter ranging from Plato to Thoreau to some more contemporary fun fiction such as Tom Robbins and Barbara Kingsolver. I gazed at the rest of the room and saw on one wall a number of family pictures neatly arranged in black frames, while on the wall opposite the bed was a lone piece of artwork by the Iranian artist Samira Alikhanzadeh. I'd actually heard of her and therefore knew about her predilection for using acrylic paint, found images, and mirrors, as well as the fact that her work was often seen as exploring the search for identity in modern Iran. Afshid's particular painting featured a combination of an image of a Persian rug blended with a black and white picture of a woman lost in a moment of thoughtful sadness, and it made me wonder if perhaps Afshid too felt it hard to find her identity in this culture. Clearly, her taste in art and literature showed that she was a complex and interesting person, though I couldn't help but wonder why she would let me, a complete stranger into such an intimate space. I suppose it was just more proof of how angry she was with fucking Farid.

I put my bag down on the floor and entered the bathroom and finally had a good look at myself in the mirror. I really did look like hell. My face, arms, and clothes were covered in soot, and, worse still, I smelled like gasoline and charred rubber. I stripped down and left my clothes in a heap on the floor then turned on the taps and stepped into the shower. When the water was hot enough, I slid under the flow and let out a long sigh of relief then applied shampoo and lathered up with soap, all the while using the moment to try and process the events of the last few hours. I hadn't encountered a scene like that since I left Afghanistan, and it brought on a surge of emotions that had been dormant for quite some time. I didn't suffer from any extreme post traumatic stress disorder, but I still had a hard time forgetting the faces of the many wounded soldiers I went out to save. Many of them lived, but some of them died, and I'd forever carry the legacy of their death on my conscience.

I closed my eyes, took a few deep breaths, and leaned my head under the stream of water and tried to let my traumatic memories pour from my mind and join the soap and water as it left my body and flowed down the drain. It helped, and I felt noticeably better as I turned off the water, though I discovered that I didn't have a towel. Oh well, at least I was clean. I set about whisking the water off my body but stopped when I heard a knock at the door followed by Afshid's voice.

"Tag? May I come in?" she asked.

"Absolutely, but you should know that…"

Before I could finish warning her about my state of undress, she stepped inside and immediately froze when she saw that I was naked and in plain view.

"Oh, I'm sorry. I was just bringing you a towel and didn't realize you were—um—naked," she said.

"It's OK. We're all adults here."

"Yes, and I should have known better," she said, as she tossed me the towel and looked particularly embarrassed as she tried to avert her eyes.

I unfolded it and went to wrap it around my waist and let out a little laugh when I noticed her sneaking a peak at my gentleman region. She also laughed, and it suddenly felt like an awkward sitcom moment.

"I'm sorry if my eyes have a tendency to wander, but it's been awhile since I've been in the presence of a naked man," she said.

"I would think a woman as beautiful as you would have men lined up out the door just dying to show you their goodies."

"I'm afraid that's not the case. My independent nature makes dating in my culture a bit more difficult, and, unfortunately for me, one of the few men I have connected with is your friend Farid."

"Well then, you should come to America, where I can guarantee you'll have a date every night of the week—preferably with me."

She blushed and gave me a flirtatious smile.

"Perhaps I should visit America."

"Perhaps you should move there."

She smiled again.

"Something to think about," she said, as she grabbed my pile of soiled clothes and left.

Now that I was alone, I dried off and got dressed before grabbing my things and heading out to the living room. I took a seat on the couch and, a minute later, was joined by Farid, who was looking a hell of a lot better. He took a seat on the nearby chair while Afshid arrived a moment later and asked if we would like some tea. Farid and I both said yes, and she excused herself and walked out of the room, whereupon my eyes unintentionally fell on the sweet curves of her backside. It was a lovely, and, combined with all the other attributes of my hostess, made me wish I had the time to get to know her better.

"Dude, you might be Iran's most brilliant nuclear physicist, but you are a dumbass when it comes to the ladies. What the hell were you thinking when you disappeared?" I asked.

"It's a long story."

"And one where you majorly fucked up," I said, quietly.

Afshid suddenly appeared in the doorway to the kitchen, carrying the tray with our tea.

"Thank you for the sentiments, Tag. At least someone appreciates me," she said.

Apparently she also had exceptional hearing to go with her other assets. She placed the tray on the coffee table, and her backside hovered before my eyes for a brief though wonderful moment before she took a seat beside me and proceeded to hand us each a cup of tea.

"Thank you, it's delicious," I said, after taking a sip.

"You're welcome. Now, before you ask for this favor—do you mind telling me why you two looked like hell when you arrived?"

"Car accident," I said.

"Are you OK?" she asked, looking concerned.

"Yeah, we're fine. Thankfully, we weren't involved. We just stopped to help after a dust storm caused a massive pileup on the highway."

"Farid too?"

"Asshole here risked his life to rescue a baby from a

burning car."

"I'm impressed."

"You should be—he was a real hero today."

"It was a team effort," he said.

Afshid took another sip of tea then turned to Farid.

"So, why are you here? What could you possibly need from me?" she asked.

"To borrow a car."

She laughed out loud.

"Oh, but of course," she said.

"I'm serious," Farid said, tensely.

"I'm afraid he's telling the truth. You see, I'm here to help Asshole escape from the country, and we just lost our ride back at the car accident. We only have a small window of opportunity before they expand the search and eventually capture us, which, as you probably know, means we'll most likely be executed."

"Well, probably not me, I'm too important—but Finn for sure," Farid said.

Afshid looked at Farid for a moment then turned back to me before she spoke.

"I'll loan you a car—but only because of you, Tag. Honestly, I could care less what happens to Asshole."

"Thank you," I said.

"So, Tag, you are a guest in my home. Would you like to eat while I finish washing your clothes?"

"Absolutely," I said at the exact moment that Farid said no.

"Don't we need to keep moving?" he asked.

"I'm afraid that my favorite shirt is in the laundry, and, besides, I learned in the service that you always rest and eat when you can, but, more importantly, I learned from James Bond that you never turned down the offer of a beautiful woman."

Farid rolled his eyes and leaned back on the couch as Afshid got up and headed into the kitchen."

"Need any help?" I asked.

"Absolutely. You can slice up the vegetables."

I joined her in the kitchen and stood on the other side of the center island and watched as she made a wonderful smelling marinade then placed in a couple of plump look-ing chicken breasts. She sprinkled on a little salt and pep-per then took a moment to talk, leaning forward with her hands on the counter, the gesture inadvertently pressing her breasts together and emphasizing her enticing cleav-age.

"I hope you like chicken," she said.

"I do—especially the white meat. I'm a bit of a breast man," I responded.

She smiled at my double entendre and made no effort to change her position, thus pushing the sexual tension meter up to about DEFCON 1.

"Well then, let's put you to work, breast man," she said, as she placed an onion and a green pepper on the chopping block in front of me.

"So, have you ever had home cooked Persian food?" she

asked.

"Never. I've only ever eaten it in restaurants."

"Well, I think you're going to enjoy it."

I knew I was going to enjoy it, but mainly because I enjoyed the chef. It wasn't often in my line of work that I met such a beautiful and interesting woman, so I was happy to be in Afshid's company and serve as her prep chef. To that end, I cut up the onion and bell pepper, all the while watching as my hostess prepared a rice dish called Adass Polo, which was basically rice mixed with lentils and various spices. It smelled amazing, though I couldn't help but feel a little wary at the thought of another bout of gas when the lentils kicked in. At least Farid and I would be alone in a car and miles away from our incredibly attractive chef.

As is often the case, cooking with someone was an ideal way to get to know them, and I learned all about my charming hostess. She was a professor of Philosophy and had met Farid when she invited him to be a guest lecturer at her university. Apparently, Quantum Mechanics was revealing new theories about life and the universe, and Afshid wanted to broaden her budding young student's horizons. One thing led to another, and the two academics ended up having dinner, and later, a night of passion, after which Farid dropped the ball and disappeared, which was truly a bad move in my opinion.

All of the prep work was officially finished, so Afshid reached into a cupboard and pulled out a bottle of wine and three glasses.

"I thought alcohol was illegal in Iran," I said.

"Oh it is, though mostly for Muslims, but the rest of us manage to brew our own or smuggle it in—as is the case with this bottle."

"Wow, I had no idea," I said, pleasantly surprised.

"Yes, and were it not for alcohol, how else would I have ended up in bed with Farid?"

"You know I can hear you!" Farid said, from the living room.

"Yes, I do, now why don't we go join Asshole and enjoy a glass while dinner finishes cooking."

We went back into the living room and joined Farid, who was sitting on the couch and looked mildly annoyed as he pretended to read a magazine. Afshid refilled our glasses and poured another for Farid, then we held them up to toast.

"To new friends," she said, looking at me.

We clinked glasses, and I had a sip of wine and found it was surprisingly good and a welcome respite from an otherwise difficult day. Afshid too had a sip then looked at me with her full lips parting to form a warm smile that made my pulse race and my mind swirl with impure musings. Sweet fire in my loins! She was smart, sexy, and everything a sane man could want in a woman, so it of course made perfect sense that I would meet her while I was on the run in a foreign country—and therefore, in no place to pursue any kind of real relationship. Even worse, I was evading a clever enemy and risking the possibility of a premature death, let alone ejaculation, but that's how my life seemed to work out lately.

A timer sounded from the kitchen signifying that dinner was ready, so we adjourned to the dining room, and Afshid graciously served up the meal. It took two trips, and, when she was done and seated, we held before our eyes a delicious looking feast—the aroma as lovely as the view.

"To Afshid, for making one of the first home cooked meals I've had in a long time. Oh, and to Farid, who made one of the greatest mistakes in his life by letting her get away."

"Well, thank you, Tag," she said, tilting her glass towards me.

Afshid's dark eyes twinkled, and her lips parted into another warm smile as we set about eating and talking until our plates were empty. After the meal, silence settled over the table, and I shared a look with my hostess that seemed to reflect my sadness that our time together was about to come to an end.

"That was absolutely amazing," I said.

"Yes, that was a lovely meal, but I imagine we'd better be going," Farid said.

"I'm afraid that Asshole is correct."

Afshid stood up and began clearing the dishes from the table, and I joined in the effort and brought my plate to the sink, where I stayed and helped pass the dishes to her, which she rinsed and placed in her dishwasher. Once we finished, we joined Farid and began the rather gloomy task of heading out to her driveway. She opened the driver's side door of her silver Mercedes and grabbed something out of the center console.

"I imagine we can arrange to have the car returned from Turkey," Farid said.

Afshid laughed.

"Don't bother."

Farid look confused.

"I don't understand. This is a very expensive car," he said.

"I'm not giving you my Mercedes. I'm giving you my other car, the one that belonged to my mother," she said, as she held up the object she'd grabbed from her car.

It was a garage door opener, and a subtle smile appeared on her lips as she pressed the button.

The door rattled on its tracks as it slid slowly up towards the ceiling to reveal a small baby shit pink jeep. On closer inspection, it appeared to be some kind of Suzuki, which made sense, considering the fact that Suzuki had a manufacturing plant in Tehran. I wasn't exactly thrilled about driving around in what looked like a little pink pig, but it was all we had at the moment. Of course, I should feel lucky, as it might be handy to have off-road capability in the event that things get a little hairy at the border, and we need to leave the main highway. She threw me the keys to the jeep, and I sat down in the driver's seat and turned the key, curious if it would even start. The little engine coughed to life and remained idling dutifully as I backed out of the garage and onto the driveway, where I stepped from of the jeep and held out my arms as I addressed Farid and Afshid.

"I hereby christen this vehicle the Pink Pig!" I proclaimed.

"And I hereby officially approve of that name," Farid said.

At that point, we both turned our attention to Afshid.

"Thank you for everything," Farid said, as he went to hug her.

She cut him off by offering up her hand instead, making it very clear she was still angry about how he terminated their relationship. Farid obviously still didn't understand the whole concept of hell having no fury like a woman scorned, but I suspect this little exchange would help him on his way to enlightenment. They shook hands then it was my turn to say goodbye, so I stepped forward, feeling genuinely sad having to end our time together so soon after meeting.

"Thank you for everything. Maybe someday, I can return the favor and cook for you," I said.

"I'd like that. Now have a safe journey—and be sure to get the asshole here to his exciting new life in the West," she said, as she hugged me.

"I'll try."

Before letting go, she leaned in and kissed me, and Farid looked as shocked as I felt, and I couldn't help but wonder if it was a small parting jab at her ex-lover. Either way, I was happy to take the hit and soon felt a familiar tingling below my waist that was a sure sign that Tag Junior would be up for a much longer visit with my new lady friend. We parted, and I climbed into the driver's seat and looked at Afshid one last time before waving and pulling out of the driveway and heading back towards the main highway.

"Dude, I seriously don't understand why you would fuck that up," I said.

"I know—she's beautiful, smart, sexy as hell—but I just have this thing for blondes."

"A brunette in the hand is worth more than a blond bush."

Farid adjusted his seat back slightly and put his right foot up on the dash, before leaning back and smiling.

"How long do you think it will be before the lentils kick in?" he asked.

"Not long enough."

I made the final turn onto the freeway, and twenty-seven seconds later, the little jeep topped out at about seventy-five miles per hour, which was about twenty more than I expected or wanted, but at least we would make good time. I took one last look in the rearview mirror and sighed to myself as I thought about the lovely Afshid. She was quite a woman, and it would be nice, although unlikely that I might see her again someday. Sadly, people in my profession didn't get a lot of time to forge any kind of lasting or meaningful relationships. Perhaps, after this mission, I would take some time off and get a little rest and relaxation and spend some quality time with a member of the opposite sex. Sadly, it was more likely that I'd just end up drinking some beer and watching a movie before waking up the next day to go on my next assignment. The life of a spy was not as glamorous as the movies made it out to be, and I sighed to myself as I turned my attention back to the long lonely road ahead.

CHAPTER NINE
Pink Pig: the Little Jeep that Could

It was getting late in the day, and we were driving along the southern end of Lake Urmia only about a half hour from our destination. Off to our right was the lake, or, more accurately, a vast stretch of dried salt in between us and the actual shoreline, which was several hundred yards farther out. Farid explained that the lake had been steadily evaporating for years, and Iranians had been rallying for the government to step up and save this precious wildlife sanctuary. Sadly, it appeared that little was being done, and, as the water level dropped, it left old boats rotting like corpses on the now dry edges of the lake. I was just thinking about how beautiful this place must have been when Farid rudely interrupted my moment of reflection by letting loose his first lentil based assault. I thought falafels were bad, but now I was truly experiencing the full force of his vast methane production potential.

"Oh many pardons, my friend," he said.

"Fuck you. Do you know there's an actual cloud hovering around you?"

Farid wafted the air and fanned it towards me while I desperately tried to get my window down. It was one of those old fashioned manual cranks and time and weather had made it particularly difficult to rotate. After a few turns, it finally loosened up a bit and down went the window. It ended up being kind of a futile effort, however, as it now sucked the fart across the car and past my face as it made its way out the window, with my only consolation being that it was at least leaving the jeep. The late afternoon air was now buffeting my face, and, while it might have been a nuisance, it was my lifeline of survival from Farid's flatulence. Suddenly, another avenue of respite arrived when I felt a subtle gurgling in my stomach and realized that my gas was kicking in, and I would at least be able to retaliate in kind. I rolled up my window and smiled as I prepared to add a taste of my own seasoning to the stew, which would make the air in the car a little more bearable for me and a lot less bearable for Farid.

"Why are you smiling?" he asked.

"Do you really need to ask?"

"Oh shit."

"Oh, I wouldn't go that far."

A great explosion of air came from my anus, and now it was Farid who was rolling down his window and leaning out for fresh air. It was hard to believe that we were only in the opening salvo of our little war, and, if this madness kept up, we'd be driving with the windows down the entire trip for fear of acute methane poisoning. Twenty painful minutes later, the sun was setting, and the light was slipping away as we pulled into the ancient city of Urmia with a vast trail of methane likely swirling in the air currents behind the little jeep.

Our contact would be waiting at a safe house on the northern end of town, which inadvertently allowed us a brief tour of the ancient city. Urmia, which basically meant water town because of the surrounding rivers, had been a center for learning, agriculture, and a whole lot of trouble, as various peoples and empires sought to occupy its lands since around 2000 BC. At the moment, it was one of Iran's tenth largest cities, but it was fairly quiet at this hour, and we encountered very little traffic as we drove past the downtown area and into the more suburban neighborhoods. Two turns and one roundabout later, we pulled up to a nondescript house, and I beeped the horn twice.

"I hope our Mossad friend doesn't mind a little flatulence," Farid said, with a laugh.

"All men secretly love farts."

The front door of the house opened, and a figure carrying a small overnight bag emerged and walked across the dark front yard and over to the passenger door of the jeep.

"You two swingers want to party?" the visitor asked.

That was the correct code phrase, but the person

speaking the words obviously was a she and not a he, so a flatulence friendly fellow passenger was not looking very likely. Of course, she might be the outgoing tomboy type who grew up with three brothers, in which case, we'd have a three way flatulence extravaganza.

"You know it! We are just two wild and crazy guys," I responded, reciting the proper response phrase, which was taken from a now ancient episode of the television show Saturday Night Live.

"Well now, Dr. Ardeshir—are you ready for a wonderful decadent life in the West?"

"Indeed, I am," he said, opening the door.

The light came on in the jeep and revealed, to my utter surprise, that our contact was not just female but intoxicatingly beautiful. Sweet lord of covert operations! She had hypnotically bright blue eyes, silky long brown hair and lovely smooth olive skin. Fuck—so much for a flatulence friendly contact. Even if she were the rugged tomboy type, there was no way in hell I was going to break the fart barrier in the tiny air space of the Pink Pig. The next few hours were therefore going to be a little painful, and I imagined that Farid was also feeling the same unease. Regardless, he smiled and offered to get in the back, but she declined and told him to stay where he was because of his height and longer legs. She threw her bag into the back seat and climbed aboard, sliding through the small opening, where I quickly realized that she also had a lovely figure. She plopped down in the middle and smiled as she leaned forward.

"I'm Ayala, it's nice to meet you both," she said.

"Nice to meet you too, and I'm Finn, Tag Finn," I said.

I could now see that she was even more beautiful than I already thought, and I found myself imagining her in various states of undress. It certainly didn't help that my sharp vision and male brain had already unintentionally allowed me to discern from her underwear lines that she favored a thong. It was a bit unprofessional to take note of a cooperating agent's assets, but, sadly, it was just one of the pitfalls of being a male of the species. I was definitely excited about our new fellow passenger, but I couldn't imagine why in the hell fate would put a woman like Ayala on an assignment that entailed riding around in a jeep with two gaseous idiots like Farid and me.

Suddenly there was a subtle pain in my stomach, and I looked over at Farid, and we shared a glance that let me know that he was feeling equally gassy. The next twelve hours were going to be especially difficult now that we had just welcomed a female aboard the lentil express. This was no longer a fart friendly operation, but, if Farid and I could hold in our gas and not explode in the next two hours, we would pass into Turkey, and he'd at last be a free man with a new life. I put the jeep in gear, and we left the quiet city of Urmia and headed into the gentle rolling hills of northern Iran and towards the border, which was a mere ten miles to the west. The windows were still down and Ayala leaned forward so she could be heard over the noise of the wind.

"Any reason you have the windows down?"

"No," I lied.

Farid and I looked at each other nervously then closed our windows. I was back on the manual hand crank, and it took a hell of a lot more effort to roll it up, and each turn was a delicate balance between muscling the handle and holding back a great outburst of flatulence. Once the windows were up, the car was a lot quieter, and now we could hear the tiny Suzuki's motor straining with all its might. It wasn't exactly a comforting sound, but the Japanese had a knack for building small, reliable engines. I recited a silent prayer for the little Jeep to last another day then turned my attention to our new guest.

"So, what's the plan for the border," I asked.

"Since the authorities have an alert out for you, it's plan B."

"What's plan B?" Farid asked.

"I'll drive across while you two walk. They'll be looking for two men but not a woman. Then we'll meet on the other side about a half mile north of the border."

"Lovely night for a walk in the open air," I said, to Farid, who smiled back at me.

"Indeed."

"You two look a little uncomfortable. Is there something I should know."

I laughed and almost farted, but thankfully kept my sphincter locked shut by wedging it against the vinyl seat.

"Have you ever eaten falafels and lentils in the same day?" I asked.

She leaned back and laughed out loud.

"Now I understand why you had the windows down. Please don't let me be the source of your discomfort. Fart away if you have to. I've been trained to withstand all manner of torture."

"Not this kind of torture, I'm afraid."

Man could evolve only so far, and farting was hardwired into our brains. Still, I made it a rule never to do it around a new female companion for at least the first month or two if I could help it. After that point, however, practicality eventually won out—usually from both sides of the biological spectrum—and farts started flying. Since this mission was only going to last a few days at most, we'd hopefully never have to cross the fart barrier, so I, therefore decided it was time to focus my thoughts on the mission rather than my beautiful companion, and that started with a time check. I looked at my watch and realized it was a little after nine and well after dark, and all was going perfectly according to plan. The lights of the border were now visible in the distance, and there was nothing between us but open space and a smattering of rural dwellings. About a quarter mile down the road, Ayala leaned forward and told me to turn right at an old farmhouse. I slowed down, made the turn, and we bumped along on a dirt road, but the little Jeep's suspension did its best to handle the holes and ruts. We passed another house, though this one was well-lit, and I kept a close eye on the windows for any people. Ayala was watching me in the rearview mirror and placed a comforting hand on my shoulder.

"Don't worry, this road gets a fair amount of traffic from the locals, so no one is going to give us a second look," she said.

Oddly, I enjoyed the brief, though innocent touch, but soon I was back to focusing on the road, where I had to constantly swerve to one side or the other in order to avoid a ruthless procession of bone jarring potholes. At just under a mile according to our odometer, Ayala told me to stop the Jeep.

"There is a path here that leads to the border. After you cross over, continue following it for about a half mile due west until you reach the road on the Turkish side. I'll be waiting there, but if you don't arrive by midnight, I will assume you have been killed or captured. Good luck."

"Then, either way, I suppose we'll be seeing you on the other side," I said.

I meant it as a wacky double entendre, with the other side referring literally to the other side of the border, and, figuratively, to the afterlife if we didn't survive, but no one seemed to get it, so I suspect it was more of an American thing—or perhaps, more likely, my own peculiar thing. Farid and I headed off into the dark Iranian night, the air crisp and a little cool for summer, but a welcome respite after having spent the first part of the day huffing farts in the Pink Pig. The path left the road and soon skirted a lovely little creek, where the only sound beyond the trickling water was the chorus of frogs and crickets. Unfortunately, this was a covert border crossing, so we didn't have the luxury of using flashlights and instead had to navigate using only the tiny slivers of moonlight that made it through the trees. This made the going slow, and we only managed a few unhindered steps before stumbling over the next root or rock that dotted the path.

"This brings back some memories," I said.

"Oh, have you made many border crossings in the middle of the night?"

"A few, but I'm referring to a night in Afghanistan when I rescued a downed helicopter pilot up in the mountains."

"I assume by your presence here that you were successful?"

"Yeah—but just barely."

"Should I find that reassuring?"

"Mostly—but I did get shot."

"Well—as long as it was only you."

The path eventually left the creek and headed into an open grass covered hill, where the partial moon was illuminating the surroundings with monochromatic light and making it look more like an alien planet. The path soon came to a road, and I decided to pause and take a look at my GPS.

"Almost home," I said.

I felt a sudden building pressure in my abdomen and realized I was still holding back all the gas from the lentils. I leaned slightly onto one leg and let loose a long powerful blast of gas, and immediately felt better.

"That's all you've got? The mere ramblings of a child," Farid said, just before ripping a much louder, longer fart.

"That was just the opening band," I said, before letting loose another, slightly louder fart.

Farid suddenly placed his hand on my shoulder.

"Wait, did you hear that?"

"Of course, everybody in a hundred mile radius probably heard it."

"No, not your fart. I think I heard something else."

I listened and realized I could hear a vehicle rapidly approaching from down the hill.

"Who do you think it is?" Farid asked.

"I want to believe it's a local farmer, but I have a bad feeling it's probably an Iranian border patrol. Either way, we need to find a place to hide."

"Yeah, but where?"

The area was pretty much devoid of cover except for a large rocky outcropping on the other side of the road.

"Let's get our asses behind that rock," I said.

I could see the headlights now, and it would only be seconds before they were on us. We sprinted and dove behind the rocks just as the vehicle arrived, and the entire area was suddenly ablaze with light. The vehicle drew closer and suddenly stopped no more than twenty feet away, and I was really, really, really hoping that they hadn't seen us. I leaned out to take a peek at our new arrival and discovered that it was indeed an Iranian border patrol, and, shortly thereafter, two men got out of the truck and began walking towards our rock. Shit monkeys. I continued to watch and listen, and, as they drew closer, I could hear them speaking.

"What are they talking about?" I asked Farid.

"I believe they are stopping to go to the bathroom."

"Seriously?"

"Yeah."

"Well, I suppose it is the only real landmark in the near vicinity, so what man wouldn't pee on it?"

The two men walked over to the other side of our rock, and we heard two zippers followed by the sound of urine trickling like a mountain brook. A moment later one of them farted, and they both laughed. Then, there was another fart, and, judging by the difference in tone, was probably the other guy. Farts often had distinctive sound signatures depending on the physiology of the farter, and I always suspected that people's anuses were like musical instruments and, therefore, had a unique resonance and tone depending on the farter's anatomical makeup. Perhaps in our primordial past before speech, we communicated with our anuses. It was certainly a possibility, considering the fact that people studying gorillas in the wild often found them by listening for their insanely loud flatulence.

The peeing came to an end, and we heard them zip up and then walk back to their vehicle. Their truck started a moment later, and I breathed a sweet sigh of relief when they continued on their way along the road that skirted the border. A second later Farid farted again, and it enveloped us in a great cloud of methane.

"Sweet mother of God. My eyes are starting to water."

"Tears of joy, my friend—tears of joy," Farid said.

"Come on, let's get the hell out of your fart."

We continued on down into a ravine and came upon a wide slow moving river, which bisected the valley floor and, along with a barbed wire fence, created both a natural and man-made barrier between the two countries. This wasn't the wet season, however, so the low water level inadvertently provided the perfect way to simply crawl under the fence. We made our way across the riverbed by going from rock to rock before finding a spot with enough room for us to shimmy under the fence and emerge on lovely Turkish soil.

"Better get all your gas out now, as we'll be back with that hot Mossad agent in about fifteen minutes."

A quarter mile later, the trail reached the road, and that meant we had arrived at our designated meeting spot.

"Where's our girl?" Farid asked.

"No idea—she should have gotten here first. I guess we'll just have to wait."

We found a fallen tree just off the road and sat down and listened as the sounds of nature returned and filled the formerly quiet night. Tiny animals foraged, insects buzzed, and the wind rustled gently through the trees and grass. Back in my early martial arts training, my eclectic karate teacher taught me how to blend into my environment and read the signs and, more importantly, the sounds. A quiet forest or jungle meant that something or someone foreign was nearby or had just passed through, while a noisy one meant exactly the opposite. The goal, therefore, was to become a part of your surroundings and blend so perfectly that even the wild creatures around you accepted your presence. This came in especially handy during my years in special operations, where I spent a lot of time out in forests and jungles. There, the idea was to was to master my surroundings in order to make it a hell of a lot easier to master my enemy.

Ten minutes of silence, and we were so completely in tune with the world around us that a fox came out of the brush and gave us a brief sniff before moving on down the road. A moment after he passed, Farid passed gas. It wasn't exactly a peaceful sound and odds were pretty good that any nearby animals were already scurrying for their little lives. In ancient times Farid could have fed an entire village by hunting with his mighty anus. He would have walked onto a grassy plain, farted and, shortly thereafter, hundreds of animals would have been dead at his feet. Larger animals like buffalo or deer might have needed two farts, but, either way, dinner would have been served.

"I used to think I was a pretty good farter until I met you," I said.

"What can I say? I excel at everything I do, and farting is just an extension of my greatness."

"Yeah, or your diet. Sweet Lord, I would have thought that your digestive system would have adapted to Middle Eastern food by now."

"No one is above the power of the falafel."

"Or the lentil, apparently."

"Yes, true, the lentil is its equally cunning cousin."

"Yeah, and let's hope both of those fuckers are behind us so we can survive the coming hours in the jeep."

Headlights appeared about a quarter mile away, and Farid and I slipped back into the trees to wait. A moment later, the vehicle drove past, and we could see it was an old pickup truck most likely being driven by one of the local farmers. A second pair of headlights appeared a minute later, though this time, the vehicle stopped about twenty feet from our hiding place. The brights flashed twice, so we knew it was our girl. Well—hopefully, but we wouldn't know for sure until we got up close and personal. Farid and I ventured out of our hiding spot and around to the passenger side of the little jeep and thankfully saw Ayala sitting behind the wheel.

"Sorry for the wait, but the border was slow, because a fucking truck in front of me got stopped and searched."

"No problem, we were having a wonderful romantic night, farting under the stars," I said.

"And talking about farting as well," Farid added.

"Well, both of those are probably romantic for guys," Ayala said.

Farid hopped in back, then I took up residence in the passenger seat and buckled up as Ayala put the jeep in gear and turned around and headed back towards the main highway. A mile on the bumpy dirt road in the little jeep, and I was happy to hit the smooth pavement of the highway, where we were soon moving along at our usual seventy-five miles per hour and pushing the little jeep's engine to its limits.

"So, where do we spend my first night of freedom?"

"We'll have to pick a spot, though I'd like to gain as much distance from the border as possible before your country figures out where the hell you've gone."

"Such a pessimist! We're in Turkey! What could possibly happen now?" Farid asked.

CHAPTER TEN
Istanbul not Constantinople

I was happy to admit that Farid's optimism was apparently justified, for we spent his first night of freedom in relative peace in a little hotel room in the city of Yüksekova. It wasn't luxurious, but it was home for a few restful hours until the next morning when we traveled north across Turkey towards the storied city of Istanbul, the former eastern capital of the Holy Roman Empire and gateway where east truly met west. There, we would be staying at a hotel near the harbor then leave the following morning on a Spanish registered fishing vessel named the *Gordita*. So far, it was appearing as though Operation Eagle Feather was going exactly according to plan, and the little pink Suzuki was still chugging along, bless its tiny little four-cylinder heart.

We could see our destination only a few miles off in the distance, while off to our left was the lovely Aegean Sea. I was at the wheel, Ayala was riding shotgun, and Farid was stretched across the back seat, where he was napping but thankfully not farting. Actually things had been unusually quiet in the flatulence department since joining up with our beautiful Mossad agent Ayala, as there was nothing like having a woman around to keep the men's sillier habits in check.

It was about noon, and being close to the water meant more humidity, but the day was still young, and the temperature was a very comfortable seventy-two degrees. The windows were down, this time for pure enjoyment rather than the fear of farts, and the car was awash with fresh sea air. I felt eyes on me and looked over and shared a smile with Ayala, and it was yet another bonding moment in our long and thankfully uneventful drive. Sure, we were on an important covert operation, but we ended up spending the time telling each other about our lives before and during government intelligence service. Oddly, our backgrounds were fairly similar, though I had done college before the military, while she had done the exact opposite due to Israel's conscription policy. Then we had both entered the spy game and lived the solitary life of someone who had to keep a lot of secrets. I enjoyed her company and found it especially nice to have someone who could actually empathize with my unusual life. Our road trip, therefore, proved to be one long cathartic conversation about the eccentricities of our career choice and eventually broached the question that we all lived with every day—namely, where does your life of service to your country end and your personal life begin? Sadly, neither of us had yet managed to find an adequate answer to that question.

We finally entered the city proper, and, as we passed a number of restaurants, the car filled with savory scents that caused a grumbling in my stomach. I glanced at my watch to see were approaching lunchtime and decided to check in with the group.

"Anybody hungry?" I asked.

"Starving, but don't worry—I know of a nice little restaurant near the hotel where we're staying, and, even better, it sits right on the water and has a spectacular view."

"Sounds nice," I lied.

I had always lived by my father's credo that restaurants on the water usually charged for the view rather than the food, but I would be willing to give Ayala the benefit of the doubt—especially since the Agency was paying the bill. We traveled deeper into the city of Istanbul and navigated the warren of roads, people, and obstacles until reaching Kennedy Avenue, named, of course, after President John F. Kennedy. It seemed oddly ironic to have a street named after a western leader, considering the city had been renamed in honor of it being taken back by the eastern powers, and it made me wonder if the peculiarly named avenue was a kind of consolation prize for the west having lost the city. Either way, I'm sure John F. Kennedy would have been proud to be its namesake, for it was a beautiful stretch of road that ran right along the water and offered a spectacular view of the

Bosphoros Strait.

"That's our hotel just up ahead," Ayala said.

"Sweet Bilbo Baggins's ball sack!"

The place was magnificent, painted a brilliant white, and at least four stories tall and, with its ornate eighteenth century style architecture, looked more like a royal residence than a hotel. We pulled into the small parking area and snagged one of two available spaces then grabbed our things and headed for the front door. The lobby carried on the same theme of grandeur with fine mosaic tiled floors, Persian rugs, and stately artworks on each wall. In the center of the room was a plaque that revealed our hotel had originally been an Ottoman mansion. This was certainly an unusual choice for the Agency, which tended to favor more modest accommodations for people like me. Sure, they would put case officers up in the nicest hotels, but agents on black ops usually stayed in the dives, so quaint and luxurious were rarely terms to describe one of my travel itineraries. In fact, it was a running joke amongst many of my fellow operators that we all shared the world's worst travel agency—namely, the CIA. We continued on to the counter to find the front desk person was a man somewhere in his early thirties with the doughy physique of someone who apparently didn't like to exercise.

"Welcome to the Dersaalet Hotel. How may I help you?" he asked with a sincere smile.

"We have a reservation under the name Emad," Ayala said.

He fiddled with the computer then handed us an envelope with three keys in it.

"You have a master suite on the top floor. Do you need help with your luggage?"

"We're fine, thank you," I said.

A bellhop in his early twenties, standing near the elevator had overheard and sadly turned his gaze back to the front door. Ayala, whose bag was hardly bigger than her purse saw his expression and spoke up.

"I could use some help."

The young man smiled and quickly came to her side and picked up the tiny bag and led us all to the elevator.

"Hello, I am Seref. Please do not hesitate to call if you need anything," he said, in excellent English.

He was a shade under six foot, had brown hair, and took an instant liking to Ayala—as any sane man, boy, or person with a pulse would. She was looking particularly good in tight black stretch pants and an equally tight white cotton shirt that told the tale of her mountainous bosom region with exacting detail. I could understand, as I too had been admiring that bit of real estate myself for the last day and a half and would have loved to have taken a walk in those hills, but, sadly, I was adhering closely to Agency protocol, which frowned on hanky panky during a joint black op. Of course, they would have personally undressed me and put on my condom if I were about to bed an enemy dignitary's wife, but such were the ironies of a life in the clandestine services.

The elevator, one of those old fashioned models with a manual sliding metal screen door, stopped and dinged upon reaching the top floor. Seref slid open the door and motioned for Ayala to walk ahead. It was the polite and gentlemanly thing to do, yet I suspect it was also a potentially strategic move to get a better view of her lovely backside. My suspicions were immediately confirmed as not only Seref, but Farid and I also proceeded to stare in rapt attention at the visage of her swaying taught buttocks. Every step became a gift from God, and it was the kind of view that filled a man's waking thoughts and haunted him in his dreams. The view was so good, in fact, that the three of us were caught completely unaware when she suddenly stopped at the door to our room and we piled into each other in an inglorious heap of male idiocy. Seref, with his professional pride slightly diminished, managed to free himself from the tangle and open the door and graciously invite everyone into the suite. Ayala went first, allowing Farid and me to follow a moment later.

Stepping inside, I could see it certainly wasn't the worst place I had ever stayed and was, in fact, a lot nicer and more spacious than I could have ever imagined—least of all on a covert operation. The suite was large and lavishly adorned with Persian rugs, Ottoman artworks, and the main lounge area had two large plush couches and a comfy looking chair. On one end of the room there was a stately fireplace, and above it hung a painting of the Ottoman leader, Sultan Selim III. He was dressed in a plush orange robe with a white leopard fur collar, and his expression was one of disdain as though he knew that one day two infidels and a Jew would be standing and admiring his visage. Opposite his majesty were three bedrooms, which meant everyone got their own bed—sadly. Seref seemed to like this fact, as it meant that Ayala was potentially single. He carried her bag to the room on the left before returning to the living room, where she walked him to the door and gave him a generous tip. He smiled and quietly slipped out, his libido likely in full swing as his balls shouted out in joy at the rapid growth of their lanky friend in the middle.

"I must say—this place is beautiful!" Ayala said, as she took a seat on one of the couches.

The sunlight was coming through the window behind her made her glow like an angel, and I found myself so entranced by her beauty that I couldn't keep from blurting out a cheesy compliment.

"Yeah, but it's nowhere near as beautiful as one of its current occupants," I said, as I sat down across from her.

Ayala smiled and was about to respond, but Farid interrupted.

"Thank you, I appreciate your kind words," he said.

"While you're a good looking man and a fine farter, I'm afraid I was referring to Ayala when I said beautiful."

"Well, thank you, Finn. You're not so bad yourself," she responded.

Farid, who had been at the window gazing out at the view of the harbor, walked over and sat beside me and made a chopping motion with his hand.

"Do you know what this is?" he asked.

"You karate chopping one of your farts in half?"

"No, it's actually me cutting through the sexual tension."

"Between you and me?" I asked.

"No, obviously between you and Ayala. Now, seriously, I've been in a car with you two for the last twenty-four hours, and, honestly, I've never felt so much sexual tension. Why don't you two do us all a favor and just kiss and get it over with."

"Farid, Seriously, we're professionals and, therefore, well above any temptations of the flesh."

Farid looked skeptical as he stared at me with his arms crossed over his chest, as he obviously knew that I was completely full of shit.

"Anyone ready for lunch?" I asked, in hopes of steering the conversation away from Farid's awkward attempt at matchmaking.

"Before or after you two have sex?"

"Before," Ayala said, getting up and walking towards the door.

Farid smiled and patted me on the shoulder.

"You can thank me later," he said.

We headed back downstairs and out to the bustling boulevard, where Ayala put her arm through mine, and we started walking the half block towards the restaurant. Farid was beside us and looked over and smiled smugly.

"Ah, love is in the air!" he said.

"Clearly, you're unfamiliar with the spy game. You see—this public display of affection is simply a part of our cleverly conceived cover."

"Which is?"

"Obviously, we're posing as a couple."

"So where do I fit in?"

"You're my awkward best friend who is so terrible with the ladies that I let you tag along on my dates in the hope that you might one day go on one of your own."

"No one would believe that, because I am way too charming and good looking."

Ayala cleared her throat to get our attention.

"Boys, isn't it about time we enjoyed this lovely afternoon?"

Ayala was correct, as it was a pleasant seventy plus degrees outside, and it was nice to walk after having been in a car for the majority of the last twenty-four hours. Of course, it was also nice because I was walking arm in arm with Ayala and feeling more like a tourist than a spy at the moment. Soon, however, my training came into play, and I started scanning our surroundings to see if anyone was particularly interested in the three of us. First on my threat radar was a man in a rumpled suit at an outdoor cafe a short distance away. He was smoking a cigarette and had a newspaper in his hand, but his eyes were clearly focused in our direction. Next on my threat radar was a young man at the bus stop. He was probably in his middle twenties and also watching us very closely. I was getting a little nervous and started moving my hand towards my gun when it dawned on me that I was misreading the situation. Understanding body language was an important part of my job, and, as realization dawned, I quietly laughed to myself. Few people outside of psychologists or professional bodyguards knew that aggression and lust could look almost identical, and telling the two apart was a matter of context. Having usually operated alone, it took a moment for my knowledge to override my paranoia, so that I could see the reason behind all this attention was the result of having an unusually attractive person at my side—and I wasn't referring to Farid. Ayala was the obvious source, which meant I could relax, lower my hand back to my side, and continue walking and enjoying this rare moment of joyful intimacy with a member of the opposite sex.

Up on the right was a yellow awning with the name Shafaa Halal Restaurant. It was written in English, so it stood to reason that they must get a few infidels through their door. We went inside to find the place fairly crowded with late lunch diners, and, as the vast majority appeared to be locals, the food was probably good. You could dupe unwary tourists, but keeping a local following required a decent menu. A very pretty girl, a little on the plump side, warmly greeted us from the hostess stand at the front.

"Welcome to Shafaa Halal," she said, in accented English.

"Thank you, it's good to be here," I responded.

"Ah, just as I thought, you're American!" she said.

"Yeah, how'd you guess?"

"Your beautiful blue eyes, of course."

"Not my powerful buttocks and biceps?" I joked.

"No, but I did notice them," she said, with a flirtatious smile, as she stepped out from behind the hostess stand and gave me a thorough appraisal that ended with a look at my backside.

Now that she was completely in view, I could she that was indeed plump, but a lovely healthy plump, carrying her weight in all the right places—mainly her ample breasts and well-rounded backside. Her shirt was low-cut, tight, and it gave more than a hint of the great mounds of flesh that beckoned below its collar. She was a tall order of feminine charm and had those dark mischievous eyes that beckoned in a way that made schoolboy's pants feel unusually tight in the crotch. She grabbed three menus, then showed us to a window table that looked out over the water.

"Can I start you off with anything?" she asked, as she leaned towards me, the move bringing her breasts to hover only inches from my face.

The term motor boating came to mind, but I instead asked for water, as I doubted that my present company, Farid excluded, would have found it very funny or appropriate. She left us, and we perused our menus, but Farid, however, was scoping the nearby table, which was occupied by a bevy of beautiful blond women. Judging by their complexion and hair color, they were likely Scandinavian, and Farid couldn't help but stare unabashedly—a hungry longing in his eyes like that of a starving lion. He really did have a thing for blondes, though in this case he was justified. They were uniquely beautiful with their Nordic, almost elfin bone structure, light blue eyes, and shampoo commercial quality blond hair. It was rare to see this many similarly attractive looking people this far from their Nordic home, so it was my educated guess that they were in town for some kind of modeling shoot. Whatever the reason for their presence didn't matter to Farid, for he was lost in his own private universe of amorous abandon and remained so even after our waiter appeared to take our order.

"Hello, I am Kartal. Would you like to start with any kind of appetizer?"

"I believe we'd like to go straight to the main meal," Ayala said.

"Very well, and for you sir," the waiter asked, looking to Farid, who was sitting closest.

Farid stared up at him blankly, as he had yet to look at his menu.

"Um—what?" Farid asked.

Ayala, sensing Farid's attention was otherwise engaged, ordered for the entire table by choosing salad and Tavuc Durum, the latter being chicken wraps with lettuce, to-mato, onions, and some kind of yogurt sauce. We had been eating a lot of lamb, which was practically the national meat of Turkey, and so we were ready for a change. Our waiter departed then, only minutes later, returned with the three salads, which were a refreshing blend of mixed greens and semi-sweet pickled carrots and cabbage. They were also served with a small loaf of bread, which was not too surprising, as every meal in Turkey thus far had come with some kind of bread. Clearly, Dr. Atkins, of the now fading Atkins diet fad, was not of Turkish decent and would have been turning over in his meaty grave if he had faced so many carbs. I was a serial omnivore, however, and never went in for fad diets and was therefore perfectly happy with the abundance of bread. I loved it, and it loved me.

Our main course arrived, and I dug in and enjoyed the chicken wraps—so much so, that I had to make a point of commending Ayala on her excellent meal choice. We soon emptied our plates, then the waiter came and cleared our table, giving us a moment to quietly digest and reflect on lunch. Farid groaned, stood up, and excused himself and walked towards the bathroom, which coincidentally took him past the gaggle of blonds. He delivered a casual smile to the girls then continued on to the bathroom. A moment later, he reappeared and stopped at the girl's table, where I was damn well sure that he was delivering some of his best lines. He was a good looking guy and clearly a ladies man, and I couldn't help but fear what consequences a decadent life in the West might bring. He would be a veritable fox in the henhouse. Suddenly, laughter erupted from the table, and, a moment later, one of the girls whispered in Farid's ear. He kissed her hand, then turned and walked back to us with his smile so big that it could barely be contained by his jaw.

"What the hell was all that about?" I asked.

"Nothing—just made a little date for later and guess what?" he asked, barely able to contain his excitement.

"What?"

"They're models, and they're all staying at our hotel!"

Farid was glowing, and I suspected the heat emanating from the growing excitement of his penile region was probably enough to melt a glacier.

"Well, don't forget that we're under cover at the moment."

"Yes! And if all goes well, I might end up under their covers tonight."

"I hate to tell you this, sex machine, but the number one rule when you're out in the field is that you don't trust anyone. Think of those models as clever temptations to lead you astray from the path to your new life in America. You must remain strong and not succumb to the pleasures of the flesh."

"I'm thinking I could really use a little succumbing at the moment."

"Maybe you should work one off in the bathroom."

"Come on, we're in the historic city of Istanbul, and it's my first night of freedom."

"And it could easily be your last."

"I seriously doubt those women pose any threat."

I looked over at the girls then back to Farid.

"Your mother and I will have to discuss this. Honey,

what are your thoughts?" I asked Ayala.

She looked over at Farid and could see the yearning in his expression and relented.

"It's just one night," she said.

"Yes!" Farid exclaimed, as he smiled.

I had an uneasy feeling about Farid's date, but I was hoping it was just a little indigestion, or perhaps the rumblings of an afternoon dump. A half an hour later, we were back in our hotel room, and Ayala and I were sacked out on the couches. It was nice to have some time to decompress after two long days on the road, and now the sounds of Istanbul were slowly fading out of my awareness as I slipped into a well deserved nap.

I awoke an hour or so later when I was startled by a mild nightmare in which I had been stuck in a public restroom without any toilet paper. I had decided, for some unknown reason, to try and climb into the next stall in hopes of finding some quilted two-ply salvation, but my foot slipped, and I fell into the toilet. It sent a blast of ice cold shit water up my leg, and it caused me to literally jump awake. Ayala was reading across from me and asked if I was all right. I told her it was just an old war dream and abstained from telling her any of the real details, as I considered it prudent to leave my whole bathroom neurosis out of our relationship for the moment.

I sat up and looked at my watch to see that we were approaching the dinner hour, which meant our Persian Casanova would soon be heading off to meet with his models. As if on cue, Farid's door opened, and he came strolling into the room wearing black dress pants and a stylish silky black shirt. He looked freshly showered and smelled as though he had just lost a fight with a Drakkar Noir fragrance model. Thankfully none of us smoked, for, if he had been within ten feet of an open flame, there was a pretty good chance he would have set the entire room ablaze.

"Somebody wants to get laid tonight," I said.

"Who wouldn't?"

"Good point."

"The ladies are waiting."

"Well look here, swinger. If you really want to risk your life for a night with a gaggle of models, then we'll have to set some ground rules. First, no leaving the hotel. Second, you have to have your new cell phone on you at all times, because I'm going to randomly call you just to make sure that you're OK."

"No problem."

"Also, we'll need to know what room you'll be in."

"Now, you two really are acting like my parents."

"Yep, and we're only being cautious because we love you."

"Fine, dad. It's just down the hall—room sixteen."

"OK, go have your fun, but don't sprain your dick. Try and save something for America."

Farid gave us an enthusiastic wave, then exited the suite, prompting Ayala to look over at me with a conspiratorial smile.

"I guess it's just the two of us for dinner," she said.

At just after seven Ayala walked out of her room and stood before me, looking beautifully stunning in a black form fitting summer dress and Roman style sandals. She was wearing makeup consisting of red lipstick and a touch of eye shadow, and her hair, which I'd only seen in a ponytail, was styled and hung all the way down to her tempting cleavage. I was already attracted to her, but seeing her looking so sultry and sexy, made it pretty clear I was aboard the Boner Express on my way to Bonerville.

"How do I look?" she asked.

"Shit. What's the rule on premature ejaculation on a joint covert operation?"

"It's highly frowned upon," she said, with a smile.

"Well then, I guess I'll just have to make a point of looking away from you every couple of minutes until my excitement subsides."

"Maybe we'll both have to."

I stood up, and we headed downstairs and back to the Shafaa Halal restaurant. It was a warm night, and we walked arm in arm along the street until entering the restaurant, which was now aglow with lovely flickering candlelight. The place was crowded, but, after a short wait, we managed to get the same table from earlier and had the same view, only now we could see the lights of the harbor and the various vessels plying the busy Bosphorus waterway. Again, Ayala ordered for us, and soon we were enjoying yet another exotic Turkish meal, which started with a lovely salad called a Coban Salatasi. Salad was apparently one of the staples of the Turkish diet, and this one consisted of tomatoes, cucumbers, onions, green peppers, and parsley. After that, came a round of Raki, a Turkish aniseed based alcoholic beverage, which some people diluted with water, but we had straight over ice. It was 40% alcohol, which meant we had a pretty good buzz on by the time the beef kabobs arrived. They were delicious and, combined with the liquor, made for one of the least likely, though most enjoyable, dinner dates I'd had in years. We talked, ate, and partook of an amazing evening, finishing up with a baklava for desert and another round of Raki. Sated and thoroughly buzzed, we decided we should pay the check and take an after dinner walk to clear our heads.

"Should we call Farid?" I asked.

"Nah, let him have fun."

We exited the restaurant and walked through the throngs of people until eventually making a right turn and heading out to a quiet pier that afforded a spectacular view of the water and the lights on the other side of the Bosphorus. It was a ridiculously romantic spot, and we stood at the railing and held hands until Ayala turned and looked into my eyes.

"Well? Are we going to kiss and prove Farid right?" she asked.

I didn't necessarily want to prove Farid right, but I desperately wanted to kiss Ayala, and sometimes a man had to swallow his pride for the greater good. I leaned forward and, for the first time in my life, kissed an agent of the Mossad. Her lips were soft, warm, and still tasted of the sweet Raki we had drunk only minutes earlier. Her mouth opened shortly thereafter, and I followed suit and brought my tongue to hers in a great collision of interagency cooperation. My heart started to pound, and I felt a surging tide of blood flowing south into my manhood—the result being that I was now lost to my growing desire. I instinctively reached out and took her into my arms and felt her melt into my body—all the sexual tension and feelings of attraction between us funneling into direct action. As I momentarily broke free to kiss her neck, she slid her hand down my chest and gave an already hard Tag Junior and exploratory squeeze.

"Should I be worried about this thing going off?" she joked, her words a reference to my earlier comment about premature ejaculation.

"Hopefully not, but don't worry, I'll warn you before it does," I said, as I reached up, slid my hands under her shirt, and took hold of her breasts.

I ran my fingertips over her hard nipples, and she let out a soft little moan of pleasure then pulled me back to her lips, so that we continue to entwine our tongues. As our kisses became more passionate, she began stroking my manhood, and it inspired me to slip my right hand down into her pants, so that I could make delicate circles of her clitoris. We were both now getting ever closer to release, so it was only a matter of time before practicality overruled lust, and we paused to consider how best to proceed.

"Are you thinking what I'm thinking?" I asked.

"Yeah, assuming you're thinking that we should get back to the hotel and finish what we've started."

"That's exactly what I'm thinking."

"Oh, such a shame—I'm thinking something completely different," came a voice from behind us.

CHAPTER ELEVEN
Saturday Night Fever

Ayala and I turned to see three men standing between us and the street. The man in the middle, obviously the person in charge, was probably in his middle fifties, wore a grey business suit, and stared at us with a cold calculating cruelty in his eyes that existed in stern contrast to the smile on his face. His two bearded henchmen also had cold eyes but seemed to lack their boss's intelligence, and I'd seen plenty like them during the course of my unusual career. They were enforcers, or, more accurately, thugs, with basic thug sensibilities, and they were the type of men who took pleasure in other people's pain. Tell them to kill and they killed, without a second thought or remorse, and it wasn't very reassuring to see that these two had the bonus of being well-armed with silenced 9mm SIG Sauers. To complete their portrait of menace, they even had distinctive bad guy marks—thug one's being a large mole on his cheek, and thug two's being an obligatory scar on his forehead.

"I see we have Mole and Scar, so who the fuck are you?" I asked, looking at the man in charge.

Of course, I was lying, for I had studied his file in great detail before taking on this assignment and already knew that the man between Mole and Scar was Ebrahim Mahdi, a brilliant senior chief of Iran's Ministry of Intelligence and National Security, and therefore not a person to underestimate.

"I imagine you probably already know the answer to that question, Mr. Finn, but either way, it's none of your concern," he said.

Fuck, that fucker somehow knew my name, which meant that he was every bit as good at his job as I'd been led to believe.

"I don't know—you know my name, and you're pointing guns at us. That seems to demand a certain amount of concern."

"I don't give a shit, now be quiet and place your hands on top of your heads."

Ayala and I looked at each other then did as instructed while the two underlings came over and expertly searched us and took our weapons before walking back to stand beside Mahdi.

"All right then. Where is Farid?"

"How should I know?"

"Yeah, how should the man who brought him all the way

from Tehran know?"

Suddenly, the sound of a large group of people talking on the street caught Mahdi's attention, and he looked over his shoulder then turned back around to quietly speak to his men before returning his cold gaze back to us.

"I believe we should follow your earlier suggestion and take this discussion back to your hotel, so we can have a little more privacy."

"We can talk all you want, but it'll be useless. Farid is long gone—thousands of miles from here. You're too late."

"We'll see. Now, start walking."

We walked past Mahdi, and Scar and Mole reached out and gave us an unfriendly push as they herded us back towards the street.

"If you make any attempt to escape, the woman gets the first bullet."

"Ahh—ladies first. You're a real gentleman," I responded.

Mole hit me in the back of the head, and, while It wasn't a particularly hard hit, I suspected that it was intended to be more of a psychological blow to show us who was in charge at the moment. That's fine, I would pay Mole back later with a real punch—to his face. We joined the crowd and moved with the flow, and no one paid any attention to the three thugs leading the couple down the street. I had to say that the walk back wasn't nearly as romantic with the looming threat of death walking just a few steps behind. Life sure could change quickly.

Just after we crossed the final street, there was a break in the foot traffic, and I turned my head slightly left then right in order to use my peripheral vision to get a good idea of the position of our adversaries. They were staying just out of arm's reach, which was a smart move on their part, because it meant we couldn't get close enough to grab one of their weapons before the other could shoot us. Oh well, I'd just have to wait for an opening. People all made mistakes, and now it was a matter of waiting for them to make one. We entered our hotel lobby and walked past Seref the valet, and he smiled at Ayala. He seemed to sense her unease, however, and his expression changed to concern, but I hoped he didn't do anything stupid, as there was no need to drag an innocent into this mess. We crowded into the elevator, and I thought it might be a good time to make a move except the close proximity would make collateral damage too likely and, therefore, an unnecessary risk for the moment.

"What floor?" Mahdi asked.

"You don't know?" I responded.

Mole punched me in the stomach, but I was ready for just such a dick move and tensed my muscles and exhaled at the moment of impact thereby lessening the blow and taking all the steam out of the gesture. It hurt a little, but it was probably a lot more painful to Mole's ego.

"Top floor," I said without the slightest hint of discomfort.

Scar pressed the fourth floor button, and we started

climbing, though now the rickety mechanical sounds of the elevator were more pronounced with a full load of passengers. Riding in a crowded elevator with strangers could be uncomfortable, but standing alongside hostile foreign agents in such a tight space was an entirely worse experience. We were shoulder to shoulder, and I could literally smell the last twenty-four hours of food, coffee, and cigarettes on their clothes and in their breath. They had been in hot pursuit, living on the go and unable to partake of the usual daily niceties, first and foremost being sleeping, bathing, or brushing their teeth. While unpleasant, it gave me some real insight into their emotional and physical state. Their exhaustion meant they would act impulsively and be more likely to make mistakes. Perfect.

We reached the top floor, and Scar opened the door, bringing in the sweet relief of fresh air to dilute the foul smelling stench of our companions. Mole pushed us ahead, herding us down the hall and past room sixteen, where I hoped Farid would stay put until Ayala and I figured a way out of this mess. We reached our door, and Mahdi told me to open it. I told him I didn't have a key, and Mole hit me in the head—again. He definitely had a mean streak, but I planned to knock that out of him when I got the chance.

"Still can't find your key?" Mahdi asked.

Mole hit me yet again.

"Oh wait, here it is—in my pocket. Imagine that," I said.

"Yes, imagine that. Now, hurry up and open the door."

I unlocked the door, and we all walked into the living

room, and Mahdi told us to take a seat on the couch while he sat opposite us in the chair with Mole and Scar standing at his sides like a couple of obedient guard dogs.

"So, anyone for coffee?" I asked.

"No."

"Tea?"

"No."

"Board game?"

"No."

"How about truth or dare?"

"Sure, truth—tell me where Farid is."

"Was that a joke—coming from the Terror of Tehran? I'm impressed."

Mahdi sincerely smiled, for I had made a direct reference to one of his lesser know titles, and that implied that he was good enough at his job that an agent of the CIA would know, not only his existence, but his favored alias.

"Ahh—you flatter me, but look, friend—we don't have a lot of time here, so things are going to get ugly very quickly, and I assume you know that we will start with the woman."

"Still the consummate gentleman."

"Always."

"Is it OK if I go to the bathroom?"

"No."

"What if I shit my pants?"

"Then you shit your pants."

Fuck, I needed some time to think, and Mahdi wasn't giving me a lot of options. I was hoping a bathroom trip might give me a little window of opportunity, but he obviously wanted to keep the situation fully locked down. Suddenly, there was a knock at the door, and I prayed that it wasn't Farid. It was unlikely, however, as he had a key, and I doubted that he had already tired of partying with the models. The person knocked again then we heard a voice. It was Seref.

"Get rid of him," Mahdi said.

Ayala stood up, and Mole followed her and took up residence just behind the door. She opened it a crack and spoke to Seref.

"Hello," Ayala said.

"Um—hello. I couldn't help noticing that you looked a little uncomfortable just now as you entered the hotel. Is everything OK?"

"Oh yes, we're just hanging out with some old friends."

"They didn't look like friends."

Ayala peered back inside at Mahdi, and he nodded for Mole to be ready to take care of the young man. The goon cocked his pistol, and stared menacingly at Ayala, who turned back to Seref and tried her best to dissuade him from any further concern.

"I appreciate you coming to check on me, but everything is just fine. I really should get back to our company. Good night."

Just as she attempted to close the door, Seref charged in but paused when he took in the scene.

"What the…"

Before he could finish his sentence, Mole grabbed him and threw him against the wall and punched him in the stomach. Seref was young and fit, however, and immediately came back, shoving Mole and almost knocking him off his feet. Mole became enraged and bared his teeth as he pointed his gun at the young man's head. Fortunately, Mahdi spoke up, and his calm authoritative voice placated his angry henchman.

"Enough, bring them over here."

Mole dragged them over to the couch and forced them to take a seat beside me, then Mahdi turned his undivided attention to Seref.

"Young man—what is your name?"

"Seref."

"And you're the valet?"

"Yes, sir."

"You obviously know these people and, therefore, know what their friend looks like."

"Not really, I only saw him for a minute when they checked in."

"You're lying."

"I'm not," he said, nervously.

"Face it, you Middle Eastern folks all kind of look alike," I interjected just to annoy our unwelcome guests.

"Be quiet!" Mahdi growled, before turning his attention back to the valet.

"Well, Seref, any idea where their friend might be?"

Seref looked at me, and I nodded my head back and

forth very subtly, hoping he would understand that it was best if he pretended to feign ignorance. Seref nervously looked back to Mahdi.

"No idea. I assumed he was in the room," he said.

"Again, I think you are lying."

"No, sir."

"Strike the woman," Mahdi said, to Mole.

He stepped over and hauled back his hand and struck Ayala just above her ear with his pistol. It must have hurt, but she gave no reaction, as she was obviously a professional, and trained to deal with assholes of this magnitude. Unfortunately, I couldn't say the same for Seref, as he was an innocent civilian in this situation and therefore the weak link.

"Hit her again," Mahdi said, without the slightest hint of emotion.

Mole brought back his hand to hit Ayala, but Seref held up his hand.

"Wait! Stop! I know where he is!"

"Don't tell them anything," Ayala said.

Seref's eyes darted nervously back and forth between me, Mahdi, and Ayala.

"He's out at a club."

"Which one?"

"I'm not sure."

"Hit her again," Mahdi said.

Before Mole could swing, Seref spoke up.

"Club Reina."

"Where is it?"

"It sits right on the water about four blocks to the east."

"See that wasn't so hard. All right, Simin—hit the woman."

"I did what you said. Why hit her?"

"To teach you a lesson, young man."

Mole pulled back his hand and swung, but I reached out at the last second and caught it, stopping the gun barrel only inches from Ayala's head. She could have easily blocked it herself but was too proud not to take the hit. I, on the other hand, was not too proud, nor was I going to stand for another senseless act of violence.

"I think he's learned his lesson, so there's no need to hit her again," I said.

Mole glared at me angrily as we engaged in a subtle version of tug of war, our hands locked together like the horns of two battling rams. Overcome by rage, he ripped the gun free and pointed it directly at my head, his finger twitching as it rested on the trigger. Luckily for me, Mahdi's phone rang, and he signaled for Mole to stand down. Mahdi turned away and spoke quietly on his phone for a few moments before hitting the end button and turning back towards the group.

"All right, I'm going to the club with Ali and Paniz. You two stay here and keep an eye on the three of them. Don't do anything until I call."

Mahdi turned and hurried out the door, leaving behind a very tense five-some.

"I guess we have some time to kill, so why not try some more truth or dare," I suggested.

"OK, fine—dare. Now, why don't you dare me to put a bullet in your head," Mole said, sharing a laugh with Scar.

It wasn't exactly the kind of game spirit I was looking for, but it would do for the moment.

"OK, Mole, you said dare, but I'm thinking you might be missing the point of the game, so I'm going to come up with one of my own dares for you, and, just so you know, it's more fun if it's sexual in nature."

He looked mildly confused as I took a moment to try and think of what I could say that would get the strongest reaction.

"OK, I've got it!" I said.

Ayala looked at me nervously, obviously worried I was about to make our situation even worse, but what could be worse than waiting to be killed by a couple of assholes?

"You know, Mole, I'm really good at reading people, and I see your whole tough guy facade as an attempt to try and hide your real self—your soft caring self."

"Bullshit, I'm an asshole."

"It's true, he is an asshole, and that's what I like about him," Scar said.

"Yeah, he is, on the outside, but it's a known fact that a lot of people who act out in a particularly violent and aggressive manner are often doing so in response to anger they feel with themselves when their actions conflict with their inner self."

"What the hell are you talking about?" Mole asked in an annoyed tone.

"I think that deep down inside you have different feelings—different desires—desires which are perhaps frowned upon in your culture, and I think that you, my repressed friend, might be secretly attracted to men."

"What did you just say?" he asked.

"Come now, Mole, I've seen the way you look at Scar, and it's a lot more than friendship. There was a real longing in your eyes, so, in that spirit, I'm daring you to come out of your dark Iranian closet right now by proudly kissing him."

His face started to redden with anger, so I had definitely struck a nerve.

"Dude, you already said dare, so there's no backing out. Now, come on, Mole, be the you that you've wanted to be, and then we'll all hug and have a good cry."

His anger finally became too much for him to control, and he moved towards me and pointed his pistol at my head. Scar, who was quietly watching our little exchange, spoke up.

"No Simin, you heard Mahdi! We are to wait!"

"I don't care. This asshole is asking for it."

"He's just trying to provoke you into doing something stupid."

"Yeah, so maybe you should listen to your boyfriend," I said, with as big a smile as I could muster.

"I am going to wipe that shitty smile off your stupid American face."

"Simin!"

Scar's attempts to calm down Mole failed, for I had finally gotten him exactly where I wanted him—up close and angry. It would, of course, have been a lot more convenient if I had been standing, but life was all about adapting to whatever situations you encountered, which meant I had to work with the current orientation if I wanted to take his gun out of his thuggish little hands and use it to remove him and his friend from the party. The pistol was now directly in my face with the barrel of the 9mm pointing ominously between my eyes.

"Seriously now? No kiss for Scar? Are you really going to continue denying your true feelings?"

"Shut the fuck up!"

"Come on, I felt the way you got a little more handsy than necessary when you searched me for weapons out on the pier," I said, goading Mole into action.

It worked, and he pulled back the pistol and prepared to slam it against my head, but he hadn't counted on me being ready and catching it mere inches before it impacted. Even better was that it was no longer pointed at my head, nor at Ayala's, which meant I could attempt to take it away. I immediately twisted it back towards his body, aware that his finger was trapped in the trigger guard, and the motion broke it with an ugly snapping sound that sent him down onto his knees screaming in agony. I pulled the pistol free, stood up, and moved away from the couch in order to make myself less of an easy target for Scar, who was luckily still coming to terms with the events unfolding before his eyes. He was therefore caught completely unawares as I leveled the pistol at his head.

"Forget about it, Scar! There's no need to die today," I said.

"I'm not the one who's going to die," he said, as he raised his pistol to shoot.

I fired first and put two bullets in his head—one on each side of his scar with the final effect looking a bit like a morbid division symbol. A sudden simple mathematical formula came to mind. One asshole's forehead divided by two bullets and a really bad decision equaled one dead asshole. This just left the Mole, who was still on his knees and holding his broken finger with his other hand as he looked up at me with terror in his eyes.

"It's not very fun being on this end of the gun, is it?"

He didn't answer and instead just continued to stare.

"I believe I owe you something," I said, slamming the pistol into his jaw.

He fell backwards but struggled back up onto his knees then held his hands out in front of his face.

"Wait, don't kill me! I can help you."

Ayala stepped forward and kicked him square in the face, knocking him back to the floor.

"We don't need your help," she said.

He squinted up at us, his eyes watering as blood started to seep from his nose.

"No, please!" he pleaded.

"Don't worry, we're leaving you alive, so that Mahdi can take care of you himself."

He looked confused for a moment until the realization set in that his boss might not be too happy with his job performance. Ebrahim Mahdi was not exactly the type of man to forgive failure, so killing the Mole would be too merciful in my opinion. His boss's punishment would be far worse than a quick death by bullet.

"Nighty night," I said.

"Wait!" he screamed.

I smiled and punched him in the jaw as hard as I could, and the blow knocked him out cold. Ayala grabbed the sashes from the curtains on the nearest window, and we trussed up the Mole and left him on the floor of the living room. Seref, who had been quietly watching the events unfold, stood up and joined us looking a bit unnerved, which was not unexpected, considering he had likely just witnessed his first homicide—albeit justified.

"Who are you people?"

"We're the good guys."

"Who are they?"

"The bad guys."

"What happens now?"

"Don't worry about it. You were never here, so, go downstairs, forget about the whole thing, and let the morning crew deal with it. By then we'll be long gone," Ayala said, as she walked him to the door.

He paused and turned back.

"But..."

"You're obviously still in shock, but remember, Seref, you were a hero tonight, and you saved us all, now, where did you say that club is?" she asked.

"It's just up the street, and it's called Club Reina—You can't miss it."

She kissed him on the cheek, ushered him out the door, then turned back to me.

"I think he'll be OK," she said.

"Good—you up for some dancing?" I asked.

"Absolutely, but I better check in with my people and give them an update."

Ayala pulled out her phone and made a call while I started getting our things together. By the time she was done, I had everything packed and sitting by the door.

"All right, I'm ready," she said.

"Good, let's go save that fucker."

CHAPTER TWELVE
Staying Alive

We took the elevator downstairs and headed out through the lobby and past Seref, who was still looking a bit shaken. I gave him a reassuring nod, then we walked out to the car, loaded up, and merged into traffic. Club Reina was four blocks away, and, just as Seref said, it was hard to miss with its neon sign and loud dance music spilling out onto the street. We pulled to the side of the road to survey the scene and saw that it had a long line of people waiting to get admitted by the rather large and intimidating looking doorman, so it was obviously a popular place.

"Fuck, I hope this nightclub isn't like the ones I used to go to in college."

"Why?"

"They generally only let the hot girls in, in which case you might end up having to go in on your own."

"You never know, the doorman might be gay."

"Unlikely. Take a look," I said, pointing out a group of

scantily dressed young women giggling as the doorman motioned them inside.

"Let's drive by the front and get a closer look," Ayala said.

I pulled back out into traffic, and, just as we passed the front of the club, I spied Mahdi and two of his thugs only a couple people back from the front of the line.

"At least Mahdi and his goons still haven't gotten inside," I said.

"Yeah, and perhaps there is a fire exit or back door that we could use to bypass security."

"Good idea. Let's have a look around back."

We continued past the club then pulled into the alley that bordered its far side and parked and exited the jeep to do a little recon. There was a large outdoor area in the very back of the club that extended out over the water but, like the front, had several security guys keeping careful watch for gatecrashers like us. I looked back up the alley and saw a fire escape along the side of the building and had a thought.

"If not in, maybe up," I said, taking Ayala by the hand and leading her directly underneath the ladder.

I lifted her onto my shoulders and held her aloft while she grabbed the bottom rung of the fire escape ladder and slid it down to the street. She started climbing, and I followed right behind her and quickly discovered that I had a perfect view up her dress, specifically her lovely backside which was being nicely bisected by her black thong underwear. She must have realized the awkward nature of our positions, because she paused to look down at me.

"How's the view?" she asked.

"Spectacular! Can you see my boner from up there?"

"No, but I thought I heard something hitting the rungs of the ladder."

"Yeah, it's like having a baseball card in the spokes of your bike."

We continued up to the second floor and found an open window, and, inside, spied an empty office with rather swanky accoutrements and a futon. Odds were pretty good it belonged to the club manager, and he used it to provide some real VIP treatment to his favorite female guests. We stepped inside then moved to the door and listened for a moment before opening it to find a deserted hallway. We slipped out and followed it to the stairs, but, halfway down, ran into a man and woman on their way up. She was pretty and dressed in a rather revealing evening dress while he looked every bit the cliché of the typical sleazy nightclub manager with his perfectly disheveled hair, tight dress slacks, and partially unbuttoned silk shirt that showed off his hairy, swarthy chest. Both of them stopped to look at us, and he immediately gave us an intimidating glare, though it wasn't nearly as intimidating as his musky cologne, which was so thick and pervasive that it was making my eyes water. He said something in Turkish, but we just stared, so he tried again in a new language that both Ayala and I spoke fluently—namely English.

"This area is only for staff," he said.

Ayala shuffled past me and stood only one stair above the fragrant philanderer, whose eyes were instantly drawn to her striking beauty. It certainly helped that she was wearing a tight dress, and it's plunging neckline was making an excellent show of her cleavage, which was hovering like forbidden fruit just in front of his eyes.

"I'm sorry—my friend and I were just looking for the bathroom," she said.

The manager's demeanor changed, and he smiled and took hold of Ayala's hand and introduced himself.

"I see—well, I'm Mustafa, and it's very nice to meet you, and, for your information, this is my club."

"I'm Katarina—it's nice to meet you too, and might I say you have an amazing place here."

"Thank you."

The woman beside him cleared her throat and nudged him, signifying she was ready to move on, probably to the futon we had passed on the way in.

"I'm sorry, but Mustafa is busy at the moment, so you'll find the bathrooms downstairs in the main hallway just beyond the dance floor," she said, a bit curtly.

"Well, thank you," Ayala responded.

The girl dragged Mustafa up the stairs, but he paused to deliver some final words.

"Um, perhaps I can come find you later."

"Sure, I'll be in the bar," Ayala said, with a suggestive little smile.

The woman gave Ayala a spiteful glare, but Mustafa

smiled dreamily before turning and continuing up the stairs. He had completely forgotten about the fact that we were trespassing, which proved yet again that there was nothing quite as effective as a beautiful woman to cloud a man's judgment. This was probably the reason why so many female spies were often more effective than their male counterparts. The penis was a powerful tool of manipulation when placed in the right hands—namely, a woman's, and this fact made me wonder about the relationship between men and women in society in general, or more specifically if men were unknowingly the puppets while the women were secretly the puppet masters.

We continued down the stairs and into a crowded lounge area. The music wasn't very loud, so this was obviously one of the side rooms where people could converse away from the heart pounding bass of the dance floor. We moved through the crowd and looked for Farid and his gaggle of blondes but saw only an endless parade of unfamiliar faces. Ayala motioned towards the door, and we moved into a crowded hallway that led to the main dance floor. I felt like a salmon swimming upstream to spawn, but instead of traversing rushing torrents of water or hungry bears, I had to navigate through drunken club goers. They moved in a slow but effective crawl, and Ayala and I had to wade through a sea of flesh scented with sweat and every imaginable perfume and cologne before at last reaching the main dance floor. It turned out to be as crowded as the hallway, and every square inch was occupied by undulating people—all of them moving in time to the lights and music in a perfect display of controlled chaos. Ayala, looking a bit worried, leaned in close so that she could be heard over the music.

"It's not going to be easy to find Farid in this mess," she said.

"Yeah, it's going to be a real motherfucker, but at least it's going to be just as hard if not harder for Mahdi and his men, as they don't exactly seem like the type to frequent nightclubs."

"Let's hope so."

We needed a better vantage point, so Ayala and I made our way to an elevated section off to the side of the dance floor and took over a spot by the railing that had just been vacated by a young couple. There, we began surveying the crowd, which was no small task, as humans had a natural tendency to have their attention be drawn to bright colors, movement, or unusual shapes. Therefore, finding someone in a crowd like this took training and discipline, and I began by methodically searching the room, breaking it down into a grid, and then visually combing each zone before moving on to the next.

Only a short time into the task, Ayala tapped me on the arm and pointed to the far right corner, and there was Farid dancing his heart out and looking like the dark hub of a wheel of bouncing blond hair. At last, he had achieved his ultimate dream, though it was tragic that a number of his countrymen were currently conspiring to take it all away.

Ayala and I moved down to the dance floor and were only ten feet away when Farid suddenly turned and walked off, probably heading to the bar or the bathroom. We followed and had to squeeze past person after person until reaching the main hallway, where the sound of music diminished and the crowd thinned enough that we could see Farid a little ways ahead. The bar was the other direction, so he was definitely headed to the bathroom.

We picked up our pace in hopes of closing the distance, but we paused when two figures stepped out from an alcove in front of us and began following him. Lovely, the thugs had made it in after all, though there was no sign of Mahdi, so he was probably hanging back to patiently wait for his loyal servants to serve up the scientist. After a left turn into the next hallway, the crowd thinned drastically, and the only people around were a young woman talking on her phone and a couple quietly arguing. Farid entered the bathroom with the thugs only a few steps behind, and I had to wonder why it was that Iranian men had such a penchant for interrupting people during their precious bathroom time.

"I guess we should talk strategy before we go busting in there," I said.

"Yeah, any thoughts?"

"Well, as it's the men's room, it might make sense for me to initially go in alone, but if things get out of control and I need some help, I'll scream like a motherfucker."

"Good, I'll hold off until I hear you scream."

I slipped through the door and silently entered the bathroom, hoping to keep my presence unknown in order to maintain the element of surprise. Fortunately, the bathroom was L shaped, and Farid and Mahdi's men were somewhere out of view around the corner. I silently slipped closer and could hear a discussion being spoken in Persian, but I didn't need to understand the language to know that it didn't sound friendly. Several tense words were exchanged, then Farid suddenly responded in English.

"Fuck off! I'm never going back!" he yelled.

"Already speaking the language of the infidels, I see. Well there's no point, as you are not going to America. You're coming home, Farid," the man said, in surprisingly passable English.

"Never! I will die first!"

I heard a grunt, which was probably the wind being knocked out of Farid. Things were getting ugly, so it was time to step in and lend a hand to my new friend. I leaned around the corner and stole a quick glance and saw that one thug was only a few steps away from me and watching as the other thug held Farid up against the wall between two of the urinals. Neither man had his pistol out, but that made sense, as Farid was far too valuable of an asset to risk killing. Sure, they might rough him up, maybe even torture him when they got him home, but murder would be strictly out of the question for Iran's most brilliant nuclear scientist.

My first obstacle would therefore be the closest guy,

who I suspect was supposed to be watching the door, but he was obviously too interested in the action. That was fine with me, because his lack of vigilance would give me an excellent opportunity to take him down nice and quietly. I crept silently forward to my target then slipped my left arm around his throat and simultaneously placed my right hand over his mouth. This kept him from screaming and alerting his friend while I dragged him around the corner and out of view. He struggled and kicked out with his legs, but I was lucky that he was in panic mode and unable to form a coherent defense. The proper first step to deal with a headlock was usually to turn your head and create a little space, as it kept you from passing out and bought you the precious time you needed to deliver a strike to either the groin or eyes. Unfortunately for the thug, the human body's most natural response could sometimes be the worst defense, and he was only focused on trying to pull my arm free of his neck. Only a few seconds passed before the lack of blood flow to his brain made him go slack in my arms. He wasn't dead, but he'd be out until well after we were long gone. I gave him a quick search and found both a gun and a syringe, the latter probably filled with some kind of sedative to make it easier to get Farid quietly out of the club. I pocketed both then pulled out my gun and slithered around the corner to take care of the final asshole.

"Come! It is time to go," the thug said, to Farid.

He went to grab him, but Farid knocked his hands away, and squared off like a cornered animal ready to fight for his life.

"Paniz, get over here and help me!" the thug yelled.

"Go fuck yourself, Ali, and while you're at it, step the fuck away from my friend," I said.

I had remembered Mahdi saying that he would take Paniz and Ali to the club, so it was safe to assume, by process of elimination, that the remaining thug was Ali. He and Farid turned to look at me, and both were surprised, though Farid's expression quickly transformed into relief. Ali, however, did not look the least bit relieved, and, as expected, he tried to reach for his gun.

"Don't even think about it, falafel face, or the first bullet is going to part your balls and make you a dickless asshole!" I said, as I aimed the pistol down at his groin.

I'm not sure he understood exactly what I had just said, but it was clear enough that he removed his hand from his coat and gazed at me wearily.

"Alrighty then, Farid, would you go take Ali's gun?" I asked.

"Gladly," Farid said.

Farid slid Ali's pistol out of his shoulder holster and started walking back in my direction.

"*Tule saag!*" Ali snarled.

Farid stopped, casually turned around, and walked back to Ali.

"Excuse me? What was that?" he asked.

"I said *tule saag.*"

"Oh, that's what I thought," Farid said, before suddenly throwing a lightening fast right cross to Ali's jaw that knocked him out cold.

Farid turned back around and walked over and joined me.

"What the fuck did he just call you?" I asked.

"The son of a dog, and no one calls my mother a dog."

"And get's away it, apparently."

"Definitely not," Farid said, as he smiled and hugged me.

"I take it you're happy to sec me."

"Yes, but how in the hell did you find me?" he asked.

"It was easy—I just followed the trail of your cologne to this club."

"Hey, go ahead and make your jokes, but how else would the ladies find me in the dark?"

"They could probably use your farts, but I suppose it's probably a little bit safer and a lot more romantic to use your cologne. Now, we'd best get going, as our plans have changed, and we're leaving tonight."

"Can I take the models?"

"Normally I'd say yes, but there just isn't enough room for all of us in the submarine."

We walked out and joined a relieved looking Ayala and headed for the exit. Unfortunately, it entailed walking back across the dance floor, which made our progress slow. I did a visual sweep of the crowd and managed to spot Mahdi up on the upper balcony, where he stood with his arms crossed in front of his chest as he watched us navigate the throngs of people. He wasn't the type of person who failed often, or at all, and I had an uneasy feeling that we'd probably meet again someday. I brought my hand up to my head and gave him a little salute. He returned the gesture, a resolute look on his face as he conceded his defeat. We were winning at the moment, though I wanted to maintain our lead by gaining as much distance as possible. We continued on to the front, and Farid looked back and stole one last glance at his precious group of Nordic models before we exited the club and reached the relative quiet of the street.

"I'm sorry I left the hotel," Farid said.

"No problem, as you bought us some precious time that made everything work out for the better."

"What do we do now?"

"Go to the boat and get the fuck out of Turkey."

We got in the Jeep and drove the quarter mile to the marina where the fishing boat was moored then parked in the mostly deserted lot. We had a good look around the place to make sure we weren't under surveillance then stepped out and unloaded our things. As we were getting ready to say goodbye to Ayala, her phone rang, and she looked at the screen then walked a few steps away and spoke in Hebrew. Farid and I waited and couldn't help but hear the tone of her voice becoming increasingly tense, and, like my recent experience in the bathroom, I didn't need to speak the language in order to know that the speaker didn't sound very happy. She was also pacing back and forth, and, when she signed off, she took an unusually long time before joining us.

"What's up?" I asked.

"I need to speak with you—alone."

"OK."

We walked until we were well out of range of Farid, then Ayala stopped and held my hands as she gazed into my eyes.

"I have bad news," she said.

"What is it?"

She stood there and looked conflicted as she considered her words, and it was starting to make me nervous.

"Unfortunately, we have new orders."

"Which are?"

"To terminate Farid."

"Are you fucking kidding me?"

"No. They believe the situation has apparently become too hot, and it would be best to terminate him rather than let him fall back into Iranian hands."

"That's bullshit. We're in the fucking clear!"

"I told them all this, but it didn't change their opinion."

"Fuck the Mossad. I work for the Agency, and I'm not going to do it."

"I'm afraid both of our countries are in agreement, and I was given explicit instructions to relay these new orders to you."

"Fuck the orders! I'll say I never got them!"

"If you don't do it, then they will expect me to finish the job."

"Are you seriously going to be able to kill Farid?"

"No, but, if we don't, someone else will."

I took a moment to try and clear my head, but my mind was racing, and my heart was feeling as though it might beat out of my chest.

"And just when in the fuck do they expect me to do this?"

"On the *Gordita*. A bullet to the head. Make it fast and painless then send his body down with the boat in the middle of the Aegean. From there on out, you are to follow the original plan and rendezvous with your submarine."

"You realize that if I can make it to the submarine, so can he."

"I know, and, as I said, I told them all of this, but they responded by saying that only you would be allowed to board the submarine, and, if you had not discharged your duty by that time, then Farid would be dealt with in a much less desirable manner."

I took a second and rubbed my head, which had started to ache.

"I'm pretty sure I've reached an all time low in my professional life," I said.

"Me too."

Farid, who had been waiting patiently, called out.

"What's up? Are you two going to have sex or what?" he yelled from across the parking lot.

Ayala and I looked at each other, but neither of us wanted to speak. After a time she let out a pained sigh.

"All right then, I guess this is where we part ways," she said, sadly.

"Yeah, and I do the dirty work."

"I'm sorry."

She hugged me and started crying, and, after a time, she lifted her head and kissed me. It was a brief respite from the misery and anger that now coursed through my body, and I didn't want to let go of her and face my new reality. At long last, it was obvious we could postpone the inevitable no longer, and we let go of each other and walked back to the Jeep to join Farid. He looked puzzled when he saw our expressions, and it made me feel even worse.

"What's wrong with you two?"

"Nothing, I'm just sad that I have to leave you guys. I've done my part, and now Tag will take you the rest of the way," Ayala said.

"I understand, but it's no reason to be sad. We can all get together again later. Who knows? Maybe we can all go to Disneyland or something," he said, trying to cheer us up.

"Yes, that would be nice," Ayala said, wiping the tears from her cheeks.

She hugged Farid, then I walked her to the jeep, and we shared a hug and a kiss.

"This is not how I saw this day coming to an end," I said.

"Me neither."

An awkward moment ensued with neither of us sure what to say.

"Well, good luck. Perhaps we'll meet again one day," she said.

"Yeah, hopefully after we've left government service," I

added.

"Yeah," she said, as she gave me a parting kiss then climbed into the Jeep.

I closed the door, and she mouthed the word sorry then gave me a final sad wave as she drove out of the parking lot. I continued to watch until she was completely out of view then turned back around to see Farid smiling.

"I guess it's just the two of us again," he said, as he suddenly shifted his hips a little to the left and let out a massive fart.

"Phew! I've been holding onto that one all night," he said.

"It smells like it."

It was a nice distraction, and I had a little laugh as I picked up my things and started walking down the gangplank. We followed the main dock, and, at the end, came upon the *Gordita*, a sixty foot fishing boat that didn't have any fishing equipment, as she was only intended to perform one last trip before meeting her sad demise on the dark waters of the Aegean. We climbed aboard and entered the main salon to find it dark, dank, and smelling of fish and diesel. I flipped the switch on the wall, and the room's built in teak furniture was bathed in the warm yellow glow of the twelve volt lighting. I put my things down then ventured into the pilothouse and started the old engine, which coughed to life after only a few turns. As it warmed up, I went to the deck to make sure water was cycling through the engine and saw a nice stream pouring from the stern exhaust port. She might have been past her prime, but the *Gordita* would serve us well on her final voyage.

Farid undid the lines, then I steered her out of the harbor and into the main shipping lane that would take us out to the Aegean Sea. We had a ways to go, so I told falafel boy to relax and take a nap while I took the first shift. It might have seemed like a nice gesture, but avoiding talking and bonding was actually an easier way to deal with my growing guilt. I instead focused on the task at hand, which was getting us away from the city of Istanbul, and, fortunately for me, the vessel had been equipped with Satellite Navigation, so it would be easy to find our way across the Aegean and eventually rendezvous with the Submarine.

We also had to contend with traffic, but, while the Bosphorus Strait was one of the busiest shipping routes in the world, the late hour meant that we had little ship and boat traffic. Still, I did a quick sweep with the radar, and, seeing that all was clear, decided to use the down time to bring up the chart and scan the coastline ahead. We would eventually have Turkey on our left and Greece on our right, and I found the area I was looking for and programmed the coordinates into the GPS. Next, I picked up my phone and made a call and, soon thereafter, had my new alternative plan in place. Surviving in the field was all about adapting to changing situations and overcoming obstacles, and I was hoping my efforts would achieve both of those ends.

With my work done for the moment, I did another quick radar scan then went below to check on Farid. He was asleep in the main salon and snoring lightly, as he was obviously drained from the excitement of the night. The world certainly wasn't a fair place, and I would miss my new friend, but now I had a difficult job to do. I returned to the pilothouse, leaned back, put my feet up, and settled into the captain's chair, where I gazed out at the dark horizon and felt the slow rise and fall of the *Gordita* as it plowed through the waves.

At three AM, I throttled back the engines and checked the GPS. We were right on target, and, a minute later, Farid appeared, looking sleepy and sporting a mild case of bed head.

"Why are we stopped?"

"A slight change of plans."

Navigation lights appeared off the starboard bow and continued to move closer until a spotlight flashed twice. I used the *Gordita's* spotlight and returned the signal.

"Is that the submarine?"

"No, it's plan B."

"I don't understand. I thought we were meeting up with an American submarine."

"I am, but you're not."

Farid noticed the pistol in my hand and looked at me nervously.

"Why? What's happened?"

"I have some good news and bad news. Now, first, the bad news, which is that the powers that be have decided that it's easier to terminate you rather than let you fall back into enemy hands."

"That doesn't make any sense—we're home free," Farid said.

"I wholeheartedly agree."

"So, then what's the gun for?"

"You."

Farid suddenly looked as though he might shit his pants.

"Wait! You're going to kill me?" he asked nervously.

"No, jackass, it's part of the good news, which is that I'm not going to kill you."

"Did anyone ever tell you that you're not very good at expressing yourself?"

"No, and for your information, the gun is for your protection!" I said, as I handed him the pistol.

It didn't seem to offer him any consolation, for he stared at me with his face still locked in a state of confusion.

"This is crazy," he said.

"I know, but it's just a precaution."

"Not the gun. I'm talking about all of this."

Farid rubbed his forehead with his free hand and took a moment to gaze out at the dark sea.

"Fuck," he muttered under his breath.

"I know. It's stupid and clearly a sign that the people in charge are a bunch of extremely stupid amoral assholes."

"I thought my countrymen were bad."

"Apparently, they're all bad, and I'm really sorry—which is why I've arranged to have that boat take you to Greece, where you will meet a contact of mine. She'll make you a new passport and all the requisite documents to create a new identity."

"But, I want to go to America."

"I'm sorry—you can't. You have to go somewhere else, preferably not Europe, then disappear. No one can know you're alive."

"After everything we went through, I…"

"I know—believe me. But, I'll cover your tracks and make it look as though you died on this old fishing boat. You'll be free to make a new start anywhere you want."

"Yeah, except America and Europe—which leaves?"

"Somewhere. It's a big world."

Farid tried to be stoic, but I could see the confusion and despair behind his dark eyes. We both turned and looked out the window to see the other vessel come motoring out of the darkness and up alongside the *Gordita*. It was about seventy feet long and appeared to be a fishing boat—in looks, anyway. In practical use, it was more of a cargo ship that specialized in transporting people and unusual items. We went out on the deck, and the crew members from the other vessel threw lines across, and Farid and I used them to tie the two boats together. With everything secure, I went to the rail and met with the other boat's captain, a man named Aleksander. He was a dashing figure and kind of looked like an olive skinned version of Errol Flynn with his good looks, athletic frame, and unruly dark hair that hung just past his ears. His country of origin was officially Greece, but he operated all over the Mediterranean, where he did special jobs for everyone from smugglers and criminals to people like me. We'd crossed paths on several jobs over the years, and I considered him to be trustworthy in spite of his somewhat dubious profession.

"I was surprised to get your call on such short notice, Finn," he said, in his Greek accented English.

"I was even more surprised you were in the area."

"Well, the fishing is better up here near the Bosphorus."

"So you were up here fishing?" I asked skeptically.

"Yes, but for what you wouldn't believe," he said, with a mischievous smile.

"That's OK, I'm guessing it's better that I don't know."

"Thus, the beauty of our friendship. So, is the passenger ready?"

"As ready as can be expected," I said.

"This is my old friend Aleksander."

Farid stepped closer and offered his hand.

"Nice to meet you. I'm..."

"Farts McGee," I said, interrupting Farid to make sure he didn't give out his name.

"Nice to meet you as well, Farts. I assume you have the money?" he asked Farid.

"No, I do," I said, pulling out an envelope and handing it over.

Aleksander didn't bother to count it and, instead, just slid it into the pocket of his jacket.

"Pleasure doing business, Finn. Now, if you don't mind, I'm going to get my vessel ready to sail."

Aleksander left us alone, and I led Farid back into the main salon and pulled out another envelope that I had prepared just for him. All covert operations had emergency money, and I was using all of mine on Farid.

"Here's a care package. It contains $50,000 and all the information on the person you'll meet up with in Greece. It should be enough to get you anywhere you want to go."

Farid stared blankly as he tried to understand what was happening. He had already given up his life as he knew it, and now it was all changing yet again.

"I have to get going. If I'm late to meet the sub they might get suspicious," I said, leading him out to the rail.

He hugged me, then stepped across to the deck of the other boat and stood there, looking back at me the way a loyal dog would watch its owner as he or she left home.

"Will I ever see you again?" he asked.

"Unlikely, and if you do—it means something went very wrong and you should run like hell."

I felt like shit, and obviously Farid could see the misery on my face. I didn't like the way this assignment had ended up, and I was having major doubts about my job and, in turn, my life.

"Be well, my friend, and perhaps you should get out of this line of work, settle down, and have a proper life," Farid said.

"I'll definitely think about it, and I hope you find your blond, big breasted soulmate."

I untied the lines, and the vessel backed off and slowly

turned around while Farid moved to the stern and waved. I waved back and said a final silent goodbye to my friend as he motored away, hopefully to a better life. An hour and a half later, I scuttled the *Gordita* and moved onto a small grey Zodiac raft where I watched, a little sadly, as the once proud vessel slipped beneath the dark waters of the Aegean. I made my rendezvous with the Submarine *Ohio*, and, within twenty-four hours of landing on American soil, I followed my new friend's advice and resigned from the CIA and decided to settle down to a quiet life as a private investigator in my beloved Northern California. Life was for the living, and it was about time I started living for myself.

CHAPTER THIRTEEN
First Class Idiot

Present Day.

It seemed as though a lifetime had passed since I had last seen Farid, and I was still lost in thought, my mind a world away, when Asma appeared.

"Would you like anything more to drink," she asked.

I was still in the hydrating stage, so I asked for another mineral water, and she opened a bottle and refilled my glass before moving on to the other passengers. I took a sip and looked around at my accoutrements. This wasn't exactly the Vandenberg jet, but it was a lot nicer than any other commercial flight I had ever experienced. I put down my water and went back to reading Farid's dossier, which was unbelievably detailed—the only fact left out thus far being whether or not his penis hung to the left or the right. My old friend had certainly moved up in the world and had a new name and a new title. He was now the esteemed Dr.

Suleiman Zuhair, the head of the nuclear energy program of the United Arab Emirates, a progressive union of states that inhabited the southeastern corner of the Arabian Peninsula. Formed on December 2nd, 1971, the UAE, was a federation of seven Emirates composed of descendants of the influential Bani Yas tribes of southern Arabia. Dubai, the second largest state, specifically made its foray into the international scene starting in the early 1800s when its ruler, Sheikh Maktoum, transformed the formerly sleepy port town of merchants, traders, and pearl divers into a safe haven for international trade and a place of peace and security. Today, it joined its neighboring state Abu Dhabi as one of the two most influential provinces of the Emirates.

Farid was currently working directly under Sheikh Hamza, who was the current Minister of Energy, and more importantly, the third son of the constitutional monarch of Dubai. Hamza was, therefore, in the royal bloodline, but he was still a few places too low in the family to ever become the constitutional monarch. If Farid really had discovered cold fusion, then he would be Hamza's most likely avenue of gaining the political and financial importance he needed to bypass his brothers and ascend to the throne. Money meant power, even in royal families.

So, Farid's prestigious job title was going to make getting to the fucker pretty fucking difficult, but there were even worse potential obstacles impeding my chances of success on this mission. The UAE was a nation built on the money from its oil reserves, but the price of oil was at an all time low, and, coupled with a number of major countries vowing to move away from oil, the powers that be had been steadily pushing the country towards a new economy based on tourism and international business, and, if all went well, cold fusion. Cold fusion would be today what oil had been back in the nineteen fifties, and it would put them back on the map and guarantee the prosperity of their country for generations to come. Hamza, in turn, would become the most important man in the country, let alone the world, and Farid would be his veritable golden goose — something he would devote a lot of resources to protect.

To that end, Hamza was lucky that the UAE had hired Academi, the American security company formerly known as Blackwater, as an extra measure of protection against terrorism and the possibility of flare-ups of unrest that were taking place all across the Middle East. Academi was also the same company the US had used in Iraq, and all of its employees were highly trained former special operations soldiers who were very good at their job. Unfortunately, these same people were also part of the security contingent that guarded Farid twenty-four hours a day.

I scrolled down to the next page and read more details about Farid's daily life. His job came with a lot of perks, and he was living large with plenty of money, a Bentley Turbo, and a beautiful home in Dubai. He was still unmarried but, true to form, was usually only seen in the company of blondes while frequenting the local bars, restaurants, and nightclubs. He was living like a prince, but in a gilded cage, and he would therefore be nearly impossible to contact. I had to get past all the security, somehow convince him to leave his exorbitant lifestyle, and then get him the hell out of the country, which meant I had a daunting, if not impossible, task ahead.

I closed the file and rubbed my temples. What did I do to deserve this? I had lived a nice, quiet, low-key existence always helping those in need and staying well below the radar of my former life. Shit—maybe it was time for a drink. I looked at my watch and saw that it was three thirty p.m., Pacific Standard Time, but that would be changing rapidly as we flew into the sun. I did some quick calculations and realized that it was well after midnight in Europe. Fuck it. I hit the page button on the armrest of my chair and soon the lovely Asma appeared.

"How can I help you?"

"I'm thinking about having a drink, but I don't want to get too hammered."

"How about a glass of red wine?"

"Fan-fucking-tastic idea!"

"Would you like to see the wine list?"

"I'm not a snob. Anything red that you recommend will be fine."

She returned a moment later and placed the glass of wine on my tray table, and I thanked her and took a sip. Not bad—not bad at all. I closed my laptop, leaned back in my chair, and relaxed and thought about the morning. Holy shit. I had been in my first plane crash, which was pretty ironic, considering I had spent a large part of my adult life in planes in combat zones and never had a single problem. That was definitely one to take off my bucket list. I downed the last of the wine in one gulp then reclined my seat, closed my eyes, and felt the strain of the day's events slip from my awareness as I drifted off to enjoy a well-deserved nap.

Two hours later I awoke to the smell of food, but it wasn't the terrible smell I usually associated with airline cuisine. Instead, it smelled like a proper restaurant, and I looked around to see my fellow passengers dining on everything from steak and lobster to pasta carbonara. Asma, seeing that I was awake brought me a menu.

"How's the steak?" I asked.

"Delicious. It's grass-fed filet mignon."

Sweet. Grass-fed meat contained CLA, or conjugated linoleic acid to someone with an MD or PhD, and diets high in these wondrous fatty acids had been shown in studies to reduce the potential for cancers such as skin, liver, colon, and breast by eighty percent. Even better, those fats were more easily turned into lean muscle mass rather than center body chub, so, ultimately, it meant steak without guilt, and it didn't get any better than that.

"I'll take it."

"For your side?"

"Baked potato and asparagus if you have it. I don't mind fragrant pee."

"And to drink?"

"Another glass of that wine, please."

Asma headed off to the kitchen, so I decided to stand up and stretch my legs while I waited for dinner. I took a quick walk around the first class cabin and saw that it was at full capacity, and every luxury seat was filled with a well-dressed, important looking person. In the last row behind me, I passed a man dressed in a suit and keffiyeh, the latter being the typical Arab headdress. We made eye contact, and I nodded and said hello, but he responded with only a contemptuous glare. I nicknamed him Mr. Friendly and moved on to the other side of the plane, where I came upon a strikingly beautiful woman. She had long silky blond hair, the cheekbones of a nordic goddess, and some of the lightest blue eyes I had ever seen. She also had quite a figure beneath her white button up shirt and short, dark grey business skirt. But, beyond all that, she had that healthy glow that came from an active lifestyle, and it transcended her more obvious physical features to make her downright vivacious.

She was also very likely more than just a pretty face, considering the stack of legal papers off to the side of her seat, which hinted that she was a high powered attorney and, therefore, likely way out of my league. I had met many women like her back at Stanford, and, even then, they were already looking for more upwardly mobile partners, and us lowly psych majors didn't stand a chance against the many business and computer science nerds trolling the dating scene. I turned my gaze to her plate and noticed that she, like me, had ordered the filet mignon, and she appeared to be enjoying it.

"How's the steak?" I asked.

"Excellent."

"And it's from grass-fed cows. I assume you know about the health benefits of grass-fed animal products?"

"I do. They have a better ratio of omega 3 to omega 6 fatty acids, and they're high in the cancer fighting compound conjugated linoleic acid, or, for short, CLA."

"Holy shit! I'm impressed. You certainly know your meat."

"I take my health very seriously, so nothing gets past my lips that isn't grass-fed."

"Then, I suppose I should tell you that nothing gets past my lips—that isn't grass."

She stared at me questioningly, one eyebrow raised as she scrutinized me.

"Wow," she finally said.

"What? Was that more creepy than funny?" I asked.

Clearly, I was still feeling a little punchy having survived that crash landing this morning.

"Considering you just hinted, in a roundabout way, that I should be comfortable with you putting your dick in my mouth—I'd say the answer is yes."

"Shit—sorry, obviously I hadn't thought that one

through before I said it to a complete stranger."

"Which technically makes you a creepy shitbag."

"I think it's technically more a case of a guy trying to be a funny shitbag, but, as he was feeling a little off having survived his first plane crash this morning, inadvertently came across as a creepy shitbag."

"Which makes you a shitbag nonetheless."

"Well then, I can see my work here is done. Enjoy your steak. This shitbag is going back to his seat to have a good cry."

"You do that, shitbag—and enjoy your grass."

Note to self—the rest of the world doesn't always have the same sense of humor, or, perhaps I'm just not always very funny. I retreated back to my seat and found another glass of wine waiting and ready to be the vehicle to dull the pain of my recent encounter. I took a sip and swished the lovely liquid around in my mouth and enjoyed the subtle flavors titillating my taste buds. I swallowed and started the entire process anew, and, by the time I had finished my wine, dinner arrived, and it looked and smelled delicious. I cut a small piece of steak, took my first bite, and nearly came in my pants. The meat was delicate, seasoned to perfection, and practically melted like butter in my mouth. In order to prolong the pleasure, I killed off the asparagus first, then took my time, eating small amounts of the potato in combination with the steak until every last morsel was gone from my plate. Properly sated, I leaned back in my seat and felt that my excellent dinner was pushing on my bladder, and it was time for a well-deserved horse piss.

I got up and started migrating aft towards one of the six bathrooms of the first class compartment. As typical on every flight I'd ever experienced, the bathrooms were having their after dinner rush, and the majority of first class was currently in line. I reached the front of the line, and a lavatory opened up, and I stepped in to find a spacious room adorned with faux wood finish, a granite sink, scented soaps, and even a glass enclosed shower. Fuck me a river! Was this how the other half lived? It was a lot fancier than any public restroom I had ever seen and was easily as opulent as the ones on the Vandenberg jet. I had always wondered what lay beyond that curtain at the end of coach, but now I knew firsthand that the amenities of first class included amazing wine, amazing food, and even more amazing bathrooms. Part of me almost wished I had to dump, but the thought of people waiting on the other side of the door would have robbed me of any actual pleasure. I lifted the seat with my foot and felt sweet relief as urine poured from my flesh faucet and filled the clean white commode with brilliant yellow liquid. I had almost forgotten about the asparagus when the dank, almost flatulent smell hit my nose, though I was fairly confident that it would be nothing more than a trifle for the ventilation system.

I kicked the seat back down, flushed, then washed my hands and opened the door, only to find my beautiful fellow steak eater standing in front of me. Fuck, she was even more spectacular now that I had a more complete view of her statuesque figure. Thank God I hadn't dumped.

"Hello, steak eater, you'll be happy to know that there's no poo in there, just asparagus pee—I promise," I said.

"And you're telling me this because?"

"Um, because I…"

Before I could answer she pushed past me and closed the door abruptly in my face. I guess there was no winning with this woman. I headed back to my seat, vowing to avoid the other side of the plane if at all possible. As I arrived back at my seat, I had a look around at my spacious surroundings. According to my ticket, it was a suite, though the fact that the walls didn't go all the way to the ceiling made it more of a cubicle in my mind, but, either way, it had more amenities than a person could ever ask for on an airplane. There was the obligatory large flat screen television with access to movies, television, and video games, and beneath it was a table for my laptop or other electronic devices. Beside that was a power plug, a shelf, and my own personal storage area. Best of all, the entire affair apparently converted into a cozy bedroom which was, for me, the only way I could get any real sleep on an airplane. All in all, it wasn't too bad for a guy used to squeezing into the economy class on Southwest.

I checked my watch and realized it was nine p.m. back home, so I decided it was time to check out the cocktail lounge. I headed up the aisle and down the stairs to the front section of the plane and found my new favorite hangout. The lounge was pretty large and filled with low slung tables and comfortable looking leather chairs, while the actual bar was circular and sat directly in the middle. Soft music was playing, and lovely subdued blue light set the mood as I made my way through the crowd and took a seat at the bar. It was tended by a decidedly attractive woman in a form fitting maroon cocktail dress, which seemed pretty risqué for the airline of a mostly Muslim country, but, I suppose the UAE was desperately trying to lure western businesses, and the strategic use of feminine wiles was probably a good start. I grabbed a seat, and the bartender immediately placed a cocktail napkin in front of me and asked what I would like to drink.

"Vodka martini, shaken not stirred," I said, doing my best Sean Connery imitation.

"Right away, Mr. Bond," she said, with a smile.

She added the vodka and vermouth to a stainless steel shaker then gave it a healthy shake, the process also making her very lovely bosoms shake as well—the entire process providing me with some excellent, although unintentional, entertainment while I waited. Finished, she poured it into a large martini glass before garnishing it with an olive and setting it in front of me. I took a sip and had to smile.

"Is it to your liking?" she asked.

"I've often said that heaven was the combination of a beautiful woman and the perfect martini, so, right now, I'm in heaven."

I wasn't kidding. She was indeed beautiful and had made the perfect Martini. While some people thought of a martini as just a glorified shot of booze, I loved the nuance and subtlety of its flavors, and that only occurred when it was made with the correct amount of vermouth—not too much, not too little. I tilted the glass to my lips yet again and relished the soft burn on my palette as the alcohol began its welcomed journey into my bloodstream, where it instantly created that brief euphoria one always felt while taking the precious first sips of a cocktail. Feeling that the world had improved ever so minutely, I turned in my chair to do a little people watching by taking stock of my fellow passengers. I liked to think of bars as zoos for humans, and, while it wasn't exactly a natural habitat, it was a convenient place to observe a wide array of interesting behaviors. I saw the couple who had been sitting a few rows behind me now sharing one of the nearby tables. I still wasn't sure if they were business associates or an actual couple until I spied his hand resting on her thigh, so it stood to reason they might be both. To their left was a group of guys in suits, probably talking business, sports, or women. The scope of the male mind often wasn't all that complicated, so it was fair to guess it had to be one of the three. I saw movement at the other end of the bar and noticed that my fellow steak eater had just arrived at the bottom of the stairs. Lovely—I wonder what I could say to offend her this time?

She took a seat at the opposite side of the bar and ordered a Vodka martini. It arrived shortly thereafter, and, as she took her first sip, she looked over and noticed that I had the same drink. I tipped my glass to her, and she raised hers in return. Progress. I ordered another then looked up to see Mr. Friendly arriving at the bar. He sat almost exactly between steak eater and myself then ordered some fifty year old highfalutin Chivas Regal and gulped it down before ordering another. You'd think the pig would at least sip a scotch of that quality. Fifty years is a long time in a cask to be chugged like a forty-ounce malt liquor. He gulped the second one as well but thankfully slowed down on his third. He obviously had a lot of money and enjoyed drinking it away—which would essentially be the same as pissing it away after it all made its way into his bladder. Oh well—to each his own, I suppose.

My second martini arrived, and I decided that I'd better make it last, or I was going to be thoroughly trashed. Steak eater had also ordered another, but, this time, she held her glass up to me. I smiled and tilted my glass towards her and took only the smallest of sips. Mr. Friendly, meanwhile, had quite a glow on and was soon looking around the room at all the available females, where I suspect he was perhaps hoping to find some new potentials for his harem. It didn't take long for his libidinous eyes to fall on steak eater, who was by far the most beautiful woman in the room. He picked up his drink and headed around the bar then sat down beside her and whispered something indiscernible in her ear. Her expression quickly evolved from shock to anger, so I was guessing Mr. Friendly was about as funny as me. He leaned in and whispered something again, but this time she stood up and began to walk away, but he managed to grab hold of her by the arm and roughly pulled her back to the bar. She looked at him with an indignant stare, and he muttered something under his breath that made her reach out and push him away—the move sending him stumbling before he recovered and stood menacingly with his teeth bared in an angry grimace. He moved towards her, his eyes ablaze with drunken fury as he slapped her across her face and knocked her back a step. She recovered quickly and stood her ground, raising her fists, obviously ready to face off against her drunken bearded nemesis.

The bartender, seeing the exchange, quickly spoke into the onboard intercom, and, a second later, Asma came hurrying down the stairs and stepped in-between Steak eater and Mr. Friendly, who were now squared off and looking at each other as though they were standing in a proper boxing ring rather than a lounge. It was giving me the obvious feeling that the extremely drunk Mr. Friendly was about to drastically up the violence level, so it was time to politely intervene. Asma was doing her best to deescalate the situation, but he was inconsolable and temporarily directed his rage against her by giving her a push that sent her sprawling onto a nearby table. Steak eater had experienced enough of Mr. Friendly and stepped in and front kicked him in the chest and sent him flying back onto his ass. It was a damn good kick and gave me the impression that she had done some martial arts or, least of all, some kickboxing classes. Good for her. I liked a woman who could some kick ass.

Mr. Friendly was now in a pure blind rage as he stood

up and pulled a gold ceremonial dagger from under his suit jacket. How in the flying fuck did he get that past airport security? Clearly, it was good to be a local when you flew Emirates Air. Now, however, it was imperative that I intervene before anyone got seriously hurt—most likely him. He suddenly made an angry lunge with the dagger, but I stepped in and managed to grab a hold of his right wrist and brought it up and around then barred my left forearm across the back of his elbow and pushed him all the way down to the ground. Of course, the maneuver was made a hell of a lot easier by the fact that he was heavily inebriated. Now, he was looking a bit dazed as he lay there face down, but he recovered enough that he started to fight back. I went with his energy, however, and allowed him to bend his arm, which opened him up for an even better long term hold—a figure four. I slipped my left arm over his forearm and grabbed my own wrist, creating with our arms what more or less, looked like a number four. From there it was a matter of lifting him onto his side and applying a little hand twist to force him to drop the dagger, thus allowing me to keep Mr. Friendly adequately supplicated until official help arrived.

Still, the curmudgeonly fucker continued to struggle, snarling, and hurling off-color insults until the Sky Marshal arrived, cuffed him, and dragged him kicking and screaming out of the lounge. The entire room was now particularly quiet as everyone calmly watched the action officially come to an end. The table of guys suddenly started clapping, then the rest of the lounge joined in, and applause filled the room.

"Next show is at eleven," I said, raising my hand and directing the praise to steak eater.

She reluctantly gave a polite nod then turned back to the bar and downed the remnants of her martini before following it up with a long sigh of relief. The bar scene quickly returned to normal, and I returned to my seat to have an apologetic looking Asma arrive a moment later.

"Thank you for your help, but I am very sorry you were brought into this detestable altercation!" she said, looking concerned.

"It's kind of making me miss flying coach," I joked.

"Believe me, this was the exception rather than the rule, so I can assure you the rest of your flight will continue without incident," she said.

"Don't worry about it. I just see it as a little extra in-flight entertainment."

Asma smiled solemnly and left only to be replaced by steak eater.

"Thanks for your help, but, just so you know, I think I could have taken him," she said.

"Without a doubt. I only stepped in to make sure you didn't kill him and get sent to prison, where I doubt they'll have grass-fed filet mignon."

She smiled.

"I'm Olivia, by the way," she said.

"I'm Tag, nice to meet you."

"So, Tag, what do you do for a living?"

"I'm a comedian."

She finally smiled.

"Now that's funny."

CHAPTER FOURTEEN
Flying the Friendlier Skies

I spent the next two hours talking, drinking, and learning all about Olivia, the woman formerly designated as steak eater. It turned out that she had a good sense of humor, but I had caught her at the end of a long and stressful day. She, as I already guessed, was a high powered attorney, and she was toiling away in the very final stages of a difficult and turbulent contract negotiation between a Silicone Valley computer company and the government of the UAE. Unfortunately, being a woman with Olivia's obvious beauty was more of a curse than a blessing in the business world, and the majority of her peers spent their time admiring her looks rather than her mind. Now, I was fortunate to experience the true Olivia, and she was smart, funny, and, like me, a native Californian. Her firm was in San Francisco, but she lived in Marin County and had a pug, a BMW M3, and took kickboxing classes at the Bay Club in Corte Madera. She was also unmarried, though in a serious relationship with an attorney from her firm, who had stupidly not gotten off his ass to propose. In my opinion, the fact that he hadn't already done so showed that he was clearly not intelligent enough to have a woman like Olivia.

"So, Tag, I have to ask. Were you really in a plane crash this morning, or was that a cheap sympathy ploy to make up for your creepy comment?"

"It wasn't a ploy, the private jet I was flying in lost power in both engines and had to make an emergency landing."

"Holy shit! That's insane!"

"Yeah, it was, but the overly tan pilot at the controls managed to restart one engine, and we landed safely back at SFO."

"Wow, so I owe you an apology for calling you a shitbag."

"Nah, I probably would have said the same shitbag comment regardless of the plane crash, but I am curious if I really did make that bad of a first impression," I said.

"Oh yeah, you did."

"So you pretty much hated me right from the start?"

"No, I didn't hate you, but I definitely didn't like you, in spite of the fact that I found you somewhat attractive."

"Wow, I must be quite the ladies man if you thought of me as a somewhat attractive, though unlikable, shitbag. Clearly that'll go down as one of my top five best first impressions."

"Hey, don't feel too bad. I deal with a lot of shitbags in

my daily life, so, when a new shitbag, even one I find mildly attractive, makes a weak felatio innuendo, my default reaction is scorn and loathing."

We sipped our drinks for a few quiet moments, then she turned to me—all the while using her left hand to play with a lock of her hair.

"So, Tag, I'm curious—what did you think of me when we first met?"

"Honestly, I thought you were somewhat attractive as well."

She playfully punched me in the arm.

"Fuck you. That's my line. What were you really thinking?"

I looked into her beautiful eyes and felt the answer coming out before I could stop it.

"That you were strikingly beautiful."

"Really?" she asked.

"Yeah, but strikingly beautiful and a little cold."

She smiled.

"Fair enough."

She took a sip of her drink then eyed me curiously.

"You've been a hell of a listener, but I still don't know anything about you. Why don't you tell me a little about yourself. I assume that you're not actually a comedian?"

"Not officially. My true occupation is private investigation."

"So you're a private dick?"

"Yeah, and a public one on airplanes, apparently."

She let out a little chuckle.

"Is it an exciting job?"

"Actually, it's surprisingly boring a lot of the time."

"So boring that you happen to be an expert martial artist?"

"Meh—that was just a little kitten play. It's easy when you're opponent is completely drunk."

"Hardly! You stepped right into the fray when that asshole pulled out that dagger. Any man who can handle that doesn't live a boring life."

I laughed to myself.

"OK, maybe it's not entirely boring."

We took a moment to sip our drinks, then Olivia turned back to me with her eyes sparkling with interest.

"I'm getting intrigued. Tell me more," she said.

"Well, I hate to say it, but a lot of my cases are divorces and lost pets."

"I know divorce isn't fun, but lost pets seem as though they could be kind of interesting."

I thought about my most recent lost pet case that involved the infamous obese feline Mr. Pickles and realized she was correct.

"On occasion, that's true."

We both took another sip of our martinis.

"And how about your personal life? I don't see a wedding ring, but I can't imagine that you're single," she said, as she scooped the olive out of her glass with her tongue, the subtly suggestive nature of it distracting me from answering her question.

"Well?" she asked.

"Sorry, I wasn't entirely sure how to answer your last question, as it's—um—well—it's complicated."

I smiled at my use of the words *it's complicated*. I used to loathe them, because every fucking client that ever walked through my door would start with those two words—regardless of how complicated or, in most cases, uncomplicated their problems might be. Now, however, it was my go-to response for any time that I didn't have an adequate answer to a question.

"Meaning?"

"Meaning I'm technically single, but there recently was a special woman, and she's very likely marrying another man this coming weekend."

"Sorry, that can't be fun."

"No, though it's probably for the best, as we're not exactly at the same place in our lives at the moment," I said, taking a sip of my martini.

"Yeah, I know how it is. I'm in a similar predicament with my boyfriend, and, honestly, I don't even know why I'm still in the relationship. We're totally incompatible, but the thought of being single is a little daunting at the moment. The minute we broke up, there would be an elite cadre of jackasses at my firm more than willing to try and take his place."

"With good reason."

She smiled.

"Unfortunately, none of those jackasses are as charming as you," she said.

"Or mildly attractive and, more importantly, grass-fed," I added.

"True," she said, as she smiled, placed her hand on my forearm, and looked into my eyes.

It was likely an innocent touch, but some body language experts might interpret it as a subtle come-on. All I knew was that it was making my heart race and my loins swell. Our brief moment of potential intimacy came to an end, however, when the bartender came by and asked if we would like anything else. We both abstained, as we had already had plenty of alcohol.

"Oh well, it's getting late, so I—ugh—guess it's probably about time to call it a night," she said.

"Yeah—good idea, as I'm pretty sure I'm going to have a busy day tomorrow."

We exchanged contact information via our iPhones then headed upstairs and paused at the opening to the first class compartment.

"I really enjoyed talking with you tonight," I said.

"Yeah, me too. We should do it again sometime."

A silence ensued, and we stood there awkwardly with neither of us apparently sure what to say.

"Well—uh—good night," I said.

"Yeah, I'll see you in the morning, and maybe we can do breakfast."

We parted ways, and I returned to my seat only to be

joined by Asma, who thankfully helped me convert my little cubicle into a sleeping chamber. It turned out to be surprisingly comfortable, though it wasn't quite the king sized mattress that I was used to on the Vandenberg jet. I laid my head back on the pillow, closed my eyes, and tried to relax, but memories of the day kept playing in my mind—everything from Estelle's sad departure to the averted plane crash, bar ruckus, and my unexpected evening with the beautiful Olivia. Fuck. I rolled over and tried to get more comfortable by using the extra pillow as a kind of surrogate sleeping partner, but, again, I couldn't sleep. Just as I was about to shift and try sleeping on my stomach, I heard a chime from my phone, and I looked over at it and saw that Olivia had just texted.

"You awake?" she had written.

I sat up and grabbed it.

"Yes," I replied.

"Can't sleep," came back a moment later.

"Me neither," I wrote.

"Do you have any special technique for falling asleep when you're traveling?" she asked.

I was still under the influence of my martini buzz and wrote a rather cheeky response.

"I find that really good sex usually helps," I wrote, before hitting send and instantly regretting it.

Shit, my buzz was making me act like an idiot, and I was left sitting in the darkness staring at my iPhone, my heart racing as I anxiously waited for the next text. It beeped, and I looked down at the screen.

"Interesting. Perhaps we should 'investigate' this further. Meet me in lavatory two, and we'll see if your pet detective skills are up to finding my beaver."

I laughed out loud as I responded.

"I'll see you shortly. XXOO, Ace," I wrote, which was an obvious reference to Jim Carrey's classic character from *Ace Ventura, Pet Detective*.

"PS, Ace, please don't mention asparagus this time!" she wrote.

"Roger that, no asparagus."

Sweet mother of infidelity! Had I somehow initiated a late night tryst? I slid out of bed, opened my door, and peered down the aisle to see if anyone was stirring. Most of the passengers were sleeping, and Asma and the other flight attendants were nowhere in sight, so I put on my shoes then quietly walked up the aisle past the now empty compartment of Mr. Friendly and stopped in front of lavatory number two. I knocked then opened the door and looked inside to see a pile of clothes on the floor and a person, hopefully Olivia, on the other side of the frosted glass wall of the shower. I stepped inside, and Olivia peaked her head out from behind the door.

"Hello, Ace—I'm relieved to see that you actually came," she said.

"Are you kidding? I practically came the second I got your invite."

"Well good, then hopefully, you'll be—up—for a little

fun."

"Oh, I'll be—up—for it all right, so, why don't you tell me more about this lost beaver, such as whether or not it has any distinguishing features."

"Well, it's wet and lonely and obviously needs some attention."

"Then it's critical I find it as soon as possible."

We shared a laugh, but then a moment of silence ensued as we now faced the awkwardness of our unusual late night meeting.

"Do you think it's weird that our second date is in a shower?" she asked, breaking the tension.

"Yeah, but it's a good weird."

"It'll of course be less weird when I'm not the only naked person in the room."

"Good point," I said, as I started undressing.

I finally got down to my boxer briefs, and, as I slid them off and dropped them on the floor, I noticed that Olivia was gazing down at my growing excitement.

"Wow, you really are happy to see me," she said.

"Yeah, unfortunately this always happens whenever I see a beautiful naked woman in a shower."

"Well, I wouldn't call it unfortunate."

We shared a laugh then entered our next official awkward moment of silence.

"So, I—um—think I should clarify that I don't generally hop into showers with strangers I only just met," she said.

"Don't worry, you're not going to get any judgement

from this creepy shitbag, because I understand that you've just finished up a stressful negotiation and could certainly use a little fun."

"And I'm also celebrating meeting an actual nice guy while also simultaneously lamenting the existence of a lame-ass non-committal boyfriend," she said, as she held up her bare ring finger.

"True, and that combined with the eight thousand mile rule means we should proceed without any guilt."

"Damn straight."

I stepped into the shower and realized it was surprisingly spacious for a plane, but small enough that we couldn't stand without our naked bodies touching. I slid under the water and felt her lovely breasts pressing against my chest as she took hold of the soap and started washing me from the shoulders down. She made slow circles, her hands drawing ever closer to my gentleman region, where Tag Junior was quietly filling with bravado and beginning to press upward and between her slippery thighs.

"Sorry about that, but sometimes it has a mind of its own and likes to say hello," I said.

"It's OK. It seems friendly enough," Olivia said, as she took hold of my penis and thoroughly applied soap from tip to balls.

Now that I was at full mast, I felt as though I should return the favor and grabbed the soap and began to wash my shower buddy. I started with her back then worked my way around to her front, where I realized there was just nothing as fun as a holding a couple of slippery bosoms. Of course, our orientation had our lips hovering only inches apart, and I felt the very real need to cross the void and kiss her.

"Would it be too forward if I kissed you?" I asked.

"Shouldn't be a problem, considering you're holding my tits, and I've got your dick in my hand."

"That sounds like probable cause to me, counselor," I said.

We closed the short distance and kissed, gently at first, but the heat of the moment grew into a frenzied bout of passion when our mouths opened, and our tongues, the most intimate and powerful muscles in the human body, met like two fencer's foils. Dodge, parry, attack—one moment I had the advantage, the next it was Olivia. It was a battle of will, swiftness, and detente until I at last broke free and made my way to her neck, where I ran my lips over her wet skin until finding her earlobe and giving it a playful nibble. I returned to her lips, and we kissed yet again before I set off on another glorious journey. This one took me south to her breasts, where I traced the outline of her areolas with my tongue then gave each nipple the gentlest of nibbles, before moving down and kissing her just above her belly button—the last move eliciting a subtle gasp of anticipation. Her demeanor abruptly changed, however, and she reached down and took hold of my head.

"Wait—stop," she said, sounding concerned

"Why? Are you going to fart?" I asked, looking up at her.

"No, you fucker, but if you ever ask me that again, I will fart."

"So, if not gas, then what's the problem?"

"I'm not sure I can handle oral sex at the moment, because my dickhead boyfriend hasn't gone down on me in a long time."

"Long time meaning?"

"I'd estimate about two years."

"Seriously? Two fucking years? That asshole hasn't gone downtown in two years?"

"Nope."

"Do you give him felatio?"

"Yeah."

"And you don't see the inequity? Come on you're a lawyer for fuck's sake."

She shrugged.

"I got used to being neglected."

"Well, not any longer."

"OK, but be gentle," she said.

It was hard to believe this was the same woman who had just knocked a guy on his ass, but I suppose everyone had their Achilles heel. Olivia's was apparently cunnilingus.

"I will, but perhaps we should come up with a safe word such as — fart — and you can say it if you're in any way uncomfortable," I said.

"Or, how about I just fart?"

"Or, how about we skip all that, and you just tap me on the head. Now, you might want to take a few deep breaths, because I'm about to bring your lost beaver back home," I said.

"Oh, sweet Jesus," she said, nervously, her heart pounding and her breasts rising and falling with each nervous breath of anticipation.

She reached out with her hands to brace herself against the sides of the shower then gritted her teeth and closed her eyes.

"You're going to be feel a lot better. I promise," I said, looking up at her.

I leaned in, kissed her stomach, then ran my hands up her thighs and to her breasts, where I gently played my fingertips over her nipples. She shivered ever so slightly, and I couldn't help but admire their beautiful form. Alas, I needed to move on, for I had been to her majestic peaks, and it was time to go unto the valley and fulfill the holy trinity. Her clitoris, a veritable pope who reigned over a neat and tidy Vatican, was now in need of some oral enlightenment. I approached St. Peter's Cathedral slowly and could feel Olivia's entire body tense as I slipped ever closer. I reached her womanly alter and pressed my tongue into her essence then slid it up over her clitoris, and she let out an audible gasp. I applied gradually more pressure, and she went from soft moans to loud cries, her legs shaking as she threw her head back against the wall of the shower. In order to prolong her pleasure, I took an occasional detour to the center of her lady fruit then started anew, all the while pushing her closer to release. I repeated this cycle several times then paused to conduct a welfare check on my shower buddy and received a scornful gaze.

"Is there a reason you stopped?"

"I just wanted to make sure you were OK. You seemed a little tense."

"Yeah, because I was about to cum, you fucker."

"So, you're apparently adapting pretty quickly to this brave new world of cunnilingus."

"Yeah, I am, so feel free to get back to it."

I took hold of her backside with both hands and pulled her essence to my mouth, doubling the pressure, and, in turn, the pleasure. Her entire body went rigid, and her back arched as her eyes glazed over with lustful abandon. Hardly a moment passed before a great cry erupted from her lips, and she set forth into glorious release. I kept my mouth firmly against her essence and used my tongue to extract every last bit of orgasmic energy from her body until I relented, and she collapsed into my arms. After recovering, she kissed me then leaned back against the shower and let out a long sigh of contentment.

"Sweet mother of God! I seriously needed that!" she exclaimed.

"Apparently."

"No, I mean it! I seriously needed that. I haven't cum that hard in a long time."

"I'm glad I could be of service."

"Yeah, and now it's time I returned the favor," she said, as she knelt down and took hold of my member.

"Believe me, I'd love to experience some of your oral pleasure and bring my whole grass-fed comment to fruition, but I think you've been giving more than your fair share for the last few years, so tonight should be all about you receiving."

"Are you sure, because I really would like to suck your dick right now, and I don't like to brag, but I'm really really fucking good at it," she said, before circling her tongue around the tip and finishing off with a devilish smile.

"Ummm—well—shit—maybe. Wait, no, I'm standing firm on this."

"I'd say firm might be an understatement," she said, as she gave my member a squeeze.

"Well that's probably true, but, alas it's time for you to prepare to make sweet hard love m'lady."

"And to think I cruelly called you a somewhat attractive shitbag," she said, as she stood up and steered my manhood into her happy place.

I slid in to full mount, and we both let out a glorious moan of pleasure, but she suddenly paused and looked a bit pensive.

"Um—I think you should know that I can't—well, I don't usually climax from intercourse, so don't feel too bad if it doesn't happen."

"Wait. Don't or can't. It's different."

"Well—don't, I guess."

"So, if you're not getting any oral stimulation, and you don't usually climax from intercourse—then you're obviously not receiving your fair share of the pleasure."

"Afraid not," she said, a little sadly.

"Well then, I have a theory I'd like to try out."

"Theory? So now you're some kind of sex scientist?"

"Yeah, and I'm going to experiment on your beaver, so I hope you don't have a problem with animal testing."

I lifted her up and braced her back against the wall of the shower then took a moment to explain what I had in mind.

"Now, having an orgasm from intercourse can often be a matter of the proximity of the clitoris to the vaginal opening."

"Excuse me?"

"Technically it's called secondary orgasmic dysfunction, and it can be resolved during intercourse by utilizing the hips to deliver more friction and, in turn, stimulation to the clitoris."

"You're starting to sound like my gynecologist."

"If that's the case, then your gynecologist is a pervert."

"Well, he did ask me out once during a visit."

"I suggest you get a new doctor. Now, I'm going to let my hips do the talking from here on out."

Many women suffered from some kind of orgasmic dysfunction, whether it was primary, which meant not being able to climax at all, or secondary, which meant only being able to climax from oral or manual stimulation. In either case, I found it generally to be the result of an inexperienced, or selfish partner—Olivia's lawyer boyfriend, for instance. I decided it would be easier to just show her what I was trying to explain, and it started with proper technique. So, rather than just move in and out like a jackhammer, I incorporated a circular motion at the apex of each thrust. This put the clitoris in the middle of a veritable flesh sandwich and made sure it received adequate stimulation. I think she at last understood my point about a second later when she dug her nails into my back and started moaning again. Jackpot.

"See—what I was trying to say is that…"

"Shut up and keep doing what you were doing," she said, as she continued to grind against me with a determined urgency.

Looking at Olivia writhing in my arms was becoming too much to bear, and I had to summon every ounce of staying power in my loins to keep from emptying my seed. Thankfully, she was on a collision course with climax and started calling out more urgently as she approached an impending release. I poured on the last burst of speed that I always kept in reserve, and, soon, we were both entwined in the divine ecstasy of a mutually assured orgasm. I powered on until my legs were spent and shaking then lowered her to the floor of the shower, where she leaned in and kissed me, holding tightly to my lips as though I were the only source of oxygen in the universe. After a long, quiet moment, she pulled back and stared at me, her intense blue eyes appearing to delve into my soul.

"You are indeed, a gifted sex scientist when it comes to

unlocking the secrets of the vagina," she said.

"Every man needs a hobby."

"I think you've found yours."

"I'd like to think so."

"How are you at cuddling?"

"I can cuddle like a motherfucker."

We cleaned up, got dressed, and left the bathroom but paused just outside the door.

"My place or yours?" I asked.

"Yours."

We walked back to my cubicle, climbed into bed, and the place was already feeling a bit more cozy now that I had company. She rolled onto her side, pulled my arm over her chest, and we spooned as though we'd been doing it for a lifetime. I gave her nipple a final gentle caress, kissed her neck, and soon drifted off to sleep, bringing to an end a day that started with a bang and ended with bang.

CHAPTER FIFTEEN
A Room with a View

A little late night calisthenics made for a wonderful night's sleep, and I awoke refreshed and ready for the day ahead. The plane was coming alive, and I could hear murmurings of conversations and already smelled breakfast cooking away in the first class kitchen. I felt Olivia stir, and I looked over in time to see her open her eyes and smile.

"Oh good, it wasn't just a dream," she said.

"Definitely not."

We slid out of bed and got dressed, and I felt a bit like a teenager who had snuck a girl into his room. I would imagine that airline policy preferred passengers to stay in their assigned seats, but there was no telling what happened in the nether world of first class.

"I heard a tray rolling down the aisle followed by Asma's voice a second later.

"Are you two ready for coffee?" she asked from the other side of the divider curtain.

I looked at Olivia, and she nodded.

"Absolutely!" I said, opening the curtain.

Asma was outside with her cart, and on it was a tray with a pot of coffee, cream, two cups, and two menus.

"I guess you know I had a sleepover last night," I said.

"The lavatory walls aren't all that soundproof, and, when I discovered her seat was empty this morning, I figured she was here."

"Sorry, I hope we didn't break any official laws or airline policy," Olivia said.

"Perhaps in coach, but not in first class," Asma said, placing the tray beside the bed.

She gave us a sassy smile as she closed the curtain and left us alone to partake of our coffee. I poured us each a cup, added cream, and handed one to Olivia. We clinked mugs then sipped the elixir of life while we perused the breakfast menu. Asma came back a few minutes later, and we both chose omelets, toast, and potatoes, although Olivia went the chick route by adding veggies and avocado while I went man-style by ordering the same with chicken apple sausages. At that point, we dressed and converted the bed back into its chair form, then slid out the table and shared the large seat. Asma appeared a moment later with her cart and placed our two plates, glasses, and a small carafe of orange juice on the table.

"*Bon appetite*," she said, before rolling her cart on to the next seat.

We enjoyed an excellent breakfast and replenished the

many calories we had burned in the shower. Employing a standing position brought the legs, especially the quads and glutes, much more into the picture and, therefore, burned a shitload more calories than your average missionary style position. Now, each bite of omelet was hopefully finding a new home rebuilding the muscle fibers we had torn down last night.

"So, Tag, I never asked—what is it that takes you to Dubai?"

"My latest case."

"Is it an exciting one?"

"Yeah, though I'd prefer if it got a little boring. What will you be doing now that your deal is mostly done?" I asked.

"Celebrating, actually. With the contract negotiations complete, there's going to be a big party at the Royal Palace in Dubai."

"Sounds like fun."

"Maybe you could be my date."

"I'd love to if my schedule allows."

We finished breakfast, then Olivia went back to her seat to get fresh clothes and shower while I did the same. I headed to the lavatories but this time had to use number four, which was the exact mirror image of two. I put my clothes on the bench, stripped down and hit the porcelain, or, in this case, plastic with faux wood trim. It was pretty comfortable for a plane and had plenty of legroom, but, best of all, it afforded adequate privacy. At last, a peaceful dump. I skipped my book and, instead, monkeyed around on my iPhone, perusing emails before bringing the session to a glorious finish. I washed my hands then shaved and stepped into the shower, which was not nearly as exciting without the beautiful Olivia. Fresh and clean, I toweled off, put on deodorant and cologne, then, feeling completely refreshed, went back to my seat. Asma swung by a minute later, and I ordered a sparkling mineral water to help re-hydrate after the previous night's martini binge. She reappeared with the water a moment later.

"Thank you," I said.

"You're welcome. Do you need anything else?"

"Perhaps a massage and a manicure," I said, joking.

"Shall I call the masseuse and the manicurist?"

"Umm—what?"

"Did you want a massage and a manicure?"

"No, I was kidding. Do you really have them on staff?"

"Of course."

"Sweet Santa's gift sack! Where the hell am I?"

"Emirates Air first class, obviously."

"First class indeed."

She departed, and I decided instead to open up my laptop and glance over Farid's file one last time. I had another look at his daily schedule, hopeful I might have missed something, but such was not the case. I groaned as I realized it was going to be a hell of a challenge just making contact, let alone having any time for a meaningful conversation. In spite of outward appearances, the United

Arab Emirates was still basically a closed society that was controlled by the wealthy Arab families who had lived there for generations. Many a foreigner had been lured to this desert paradise under false pretenses and promises of great wealth only to become an indentured servant to the powers that be, so God only knew what life was actually like for Farid.

The last page detailed my contact in Dubai. His name was Bill Reigns, and he allegedly worked for the State Department but, in truth, worked for the CIA. I wasn't exactly sure what his connection to the Topless Agenda might be or how much he knew about this operation, but I was happy to have some help from someone who knew this part of the world. Even better was the fact that he would be picking me up at the airport, and, thankfully, they had included a photo, which showed him to be around fifty, with a full head of grey hair and the weary look in his eyes of a clandestine existence. A lifetime of keeping the secrets of your country was hard on the soul and would always show in the fine worry lines around the eyes.

A beep sounded, then the pilot's voice came over the intercom, informing us that we would be landing at Dubai International Airport in thirty minutes, which would put us on the ground at 11:35 a.m. local time. I deleted the PDF file on my desktop, closed my laptop and dropped the flash drive into the remaining liquid in my glass, making sure it was thoroughly inundated with water and unlikely to ever divulge its secrets again. Of course, I would burn it once

I reached my hotel just to be safe. As I pulled it from the water, Asma appeared to take my empty bottle and trash.

"So, I'm curious—what happened with the asshole in the bar?" I asked.

"He's being held in isolation at the back of the plane."

"Good, he was a real prick."

"Yeah, but unfortunately he is a powerful prick and happens to be related to the royal family of Dubai."

"Seriously?"

"Afraid so, which means we'll likely face some kind of official reprimand or fine for the incident."

"That sucks quite a few royal dicks if you ask me."

"It does—welcome to the United Arab Emirates."

Thirty minutes later I was on the ground and waiting in line with Olivia at customs. In front of us was the business couple who had been sitting behind me on the plane. They got their passports stamped and moved on, allowing us to approach the counter to meet the stern-faced immigration officer. He looked at my passport for a moment, then me, scrutinizing my face before speaking.

"What is the purpose of your trip to the United Arab Emirates?"

"Business and a little sightseeing on the side."

He scowled, stamped my passport, and waved me through. A moment later, Olivia joined me and we walked into what was by all accounts, a pretty fucking spectacular airport—but this being a wealthy oil producing nation, I would have expected nothing less. It was large and felt more like a mall with its open central plaza that stretched up at least five stories and bustled with people from all over the world. In the course of walking twenty feet, we passed Europeans, Asians, Indians and Africans. In a challenging world economy, people followed the jobs, and right now there were apparently plenty in the United Arab Emirates to keep them coming.

Olivia, a veteran traveler to the Emirates, led me to baggage claim, where we grabbed a spot next to the conveyor. It began to spin and baggage started sliding down to the edges. My bag was second in line, which was a little surprising. In twenty years of airline travel, my bag had never come out in the first fifty, let alone five, and I realized that traveling first class meant that even your luggage was treated better. No sooner had I picked it up, than a man called out my name, and I turned to see my contact, Bill Reigns, standing a few feet away and looking every bit like the man I had seen in the picture. He walked over and held out his hand.

"I'm Bill Reigns, nice to meet you."

"I'm Finn, Tag Finn, and this is my friend Olivia, who I met on the plane."

"Nice to meet you," Bill said, appearing to like what he saw.

"I've got a car waiting right outside as soon as you're ready."

I turned to Olivia, and we exchanged a brief hug and a fairly long, interesting kiss, which elicited a smile from Bill.

"You've got my information, so give me a call if you think you can make it to the party," she said.

"I'll try."

I turned and followed Bill outside into the pleasantly warm midday sun. It was easily in the high seventies and would climb into the eighties later in the afternoon, and it felt good to at last breathe actual fresh air after having been on a plane for the last fifteen hours. At the curb in front of us was a large white four-door Mercedes sedan, and the driver, a clean shaven and fit looking man likely in his middle twenties, stepped out and took my suitcase while Bill and I sat in the back. The driver placed it in the trunk then slid in behind the wheel and pulled the car out into the bustling airport traffic.

"Can we speak freely in front of your rookie biatch?" I asked.

"Absolutely, though you might have to explain some of the bigger words."

The driver shook his head slowly side to side.

"That joke just keeps getting better and better," he said.

"Don't mind young Ted. He's just a little insecure about his Yale education."

"I'm not, actually," he said.

"Having to say you aren't is a sure sign you are," I responded.

Bill and I shared a little laugh at my quip.

"Perfect, now I'm getting shit in stereo."

"Afraid so, my young smuggle. So, Bill, what's the plan?"

"I assume you've already read your mission brief, so now it's just a matter of figuring out a way to get you close to Farid."

"Yeah, it doesn't look all that easy from what I've read."

Bill thought for a moment, a wrinkle forming across his brow.

"What was that party that your lady friend was talking about?"

"Oh, it's some kind of celebration at the royal palace. Her law firm negotiated a major contract to upgrade the computers here."

"Interesting."

"Why is that?"

"State affairs are a big deal, and everybody who is anybody is usually there. If your friend Farid happens to be going, it could end up being your best opportunity to meet with him."

"And least of all, I'm always up for a party."

"I'll look into it and see what I can find out. Meanwhile, let's check you into your hotel, get some lunch, and then go on a tour of the city."

"Sounds good. Am I staying at a hotel with decent accommodations? Because, it'll be pretty hard to compare to Emirates Air's first class."

"Oh—I think you're going to be reasonably comfortable," he said, with a knowing smile.

We left the Dubai International Airport and merged onto a large freeway heading southeast, where we passed a resort and golf course to our right and soon crossed a bridge that spanned the Dubai Creek. In my opinion it was easily big enough to be called a river or even an inland waterway but maybe people who built islands in the shape of the world's continents thought differently. We continued on past endless skyscrapers, some of which were finished, while others were still under construction. It was crazy to see such an enormous amount of development, and I had to wonder if they had enough people to actually fill all those buildings. The native population was only around eight million, so they had to be counting on a lot of foreign interest. But, with the oil drying up, I suppose they didn't have any choice. Real estate, commerce, tourism, and, theoretically, cold fusion were their last hope of keeping this dry desert nation alive and kicking.

About thirty minutes later, we exited the freeway and headed northwest towards the water then turned left and followed the shore. A little less than a mile later, I could see the illustrious Burj Al Arab Hotel resting on its man-made island just off the beach. It was quite a sight to see in person, as it stood 1053 feet tall and was designed to resemble a billowing sail with its third and most prominent side arching forward towards the shoreline like a massive spinnaker from a yacht's mast.

"I wouldn't happen to be staying there would I?"

"Of course. You're here on business, and this is where any respectable businessman would stay."

"Honestly, I'm not that respectable."

"Well, then hopefully you can pretend."

We pulled up to the hotel, and a young man, likely Indian, opened my door and welcomed me to the Burj Al Arab. I stepped out and joined Bill in the main foyer, and I could only describe the experience as equal to that of the first time that I walked into Disneyland as a child. This was a magical kingdom all right, and it was adorned in a cornucopia of bold primary hues of blue, gold, and red, and it was certainly a far cry from the rather plain hotels in the United States and Europe. But, what really set it apart was the sheer opulence of its architectural style and interior design. Every inch of wall had texture and color, and even accessing the main level required boarding an escalator that traveled up past a massive fountain bordered on either side by floor to ceiling aquariums.

We stepped off the escalator and live piano music filled the sir as we entered a great cavernous space that stretched up for several hundred feet and was reminiscent of the inside of the great cathedrals of Europe. This place, however, was bright and cheery, and, instead of having endless rows of wooden pews, had white rounded walls, sparkling gold pillars, and a polished yellow and blue marble floor that was filled with brightly colored leather furniture. We continued across to the front desk to find it occupied by a very beautiful woman with smooth olive skin, twinkling dark brown eyes, and black hair cut in an A-line bob. She immediately looked up from her computer screen and greeted us with a welcoming smile.

"Welcome to the Burj Al Arab, how may I help you?" she asked in English with only the slightest hint of an accent.

"I believe I have a reservation. The name's Finn, Tag Finn."

"Just a moment, Mr. Finn while I look up your information."

She typed into her keyboard then looked up at me with an approving smile.

"Ah, I see you're in one of our panoramic suites, so I believe you should enjoy your stay with us. And please feel free to call me if you need anything," she said, as she handed me an electronic key before signaling for a bellman.

A young man appeared, picked up my bags, and led the way to elevator, which we rode up to the sixteenth floor before exiting to find my room along the southwest side. The bellman opened the door and stepped aside, patiently waiting while I walked in first. I only made it a few steps before my breath was taken away by the sheer grandeur. I was in a large foyer open all the way up to the second floor, and there was a staircase circling up to my right, while directly before me was an entrance to a massive window lined living room. The bellman took my things upstairs while I continued straight ahead to the living room to see that the hotel's rooms were as unique and spectacular as the entrance and lobby. The floor was covered in tan carpet that matched the walls while the couches and chairs were done in royal blue. There was a desk and bar, and on the far wall was a massive gold entertainment center that I would bet was actually plated with real gold. Sweet lord of interior design! I'd never seen a hotel with so much glitz. Western and European hotels were generally a bit on the understated side, but this fucking place was like something from the Arabian Nights. I wasn't sure why the Topless Agenda had gotten me the luxurious panoramic suite, but I fully intended to enjoy it to the fullest.

"So, I'm the only one staying here?"

"Yep, and you'll be happy to know we've already swept it for bugs — the electronic kind, obviously," Bill said.

The bellman returned from upstairs and stood quietly at the periphery of the room.

"I don't think this will be big enough," I said, to him.

"Then I shall make immediate arrangements for a larger room, sir," the bellman said, pulling his phone from his pocket.

I held up my hand.

"Wait, I'm just kidding."

"Yes, sir," he said, with the faintest of smiles.

I guess I had to remember that this place attracted the kind of wealthy people who probably would have made such an asinine comment but actually meant it. I went to the window and looked out at the spectacular view, and the most prominent feature in sight was the Palm Jumeirah Artificial Island Development, which resided just southwest of the hotel. Seeing it in person, it was hard to fathom the amount of money and power it would take to create something of that magnitude. Back home in Sausalito, you practically needed a permit from the city if you wanted to change your mind. Here, they could uproot millions of tons of sand and create new neighborhoods virtually from thin air—or technically water and sand.

It was officially time to tip the bellman, but I had forgotten to exchange my money at the airport. Bill, thankfully intervened and tipped the young man, and, once he left, we took a seat on one of the luxurious couches.

"Do you have any additional information that's not contained in my brief?" I asked.

"Yeah, and it's major. Our latest intelligence says that Farid is less than a week away from beginning construction of his prototype reactor, so needless to say, we're on a very strict timeline."

"Nothing new there."

"So, today, we'll get the lay of the land, show you all of Farid's haunts, then take it from there."

"Sounds good. Mind if I freshen up?"

"Not at all. I think I can make myself comfortable here," he said, with a smile.

I went upstairs to my room and grabbed my toothbrush and entered the bathroom and, again, wasn't disappointed. It was easily as large as my living room back home and contained all the necessities even the most scrutinizing guest could possibly want or need. It had granite countertops, marble floors, toilet, bidet, glass-enclosed shower with five showerheads, and of course a Jacuzzi tub with enough room for a family of five. My next dump or shower would quite possibly be the greatest of my life, but, for the moment, all I did was pee, brush my teeth, and rejoin Bill back in the living room.

We left my heavenly panoramic suite and descended back to earth to join the mortals in the lobby before exiting back into the dry heat of Dubai. Our smug Yale man Ted pulled up to the curb, and we took a seat in the car and began heading southwest, with the goal being for me to personally recon all of Farid's daily haunts. A normal person had plenty of casual places he or she visited in a day—the grocery store or perhaps Starbucks, but someone as important as Farid would have assistants for such menial tasks. That meant the only time he was potentially ever alone was at work, home, or perhaps the bathroom at his gym. I was therefore going to survey all three, and first on the list was his gym, a modern facility called Fitness First. He would usually be there from noon to one then get lunch, return to work, and eventually head home around six—assuming he didn't go out to dinner or a nightclub.

The gym was in the middle of its noon rush, and the parking lot was nearly at capacity with people coming and going with great frequency through the front door. I suppose it made sense, as the desert heat made most outdoor activity unbearable, so people had no choice but to flock to the gym if they hoped to get any exercise.

"Can we circle around the entire building? I'd like to get a feel for the layout and see what kind of security they have in place," I said.

Ted headed off on a complete circuit, and we saw white Mercedes sedans parked strategically at every exit of the gym. Annoyingly, each and every one was occupied by stern faced men wearing sunglasses, so they were obviously part of Farid's security contingent.

"Coincidentally, I originally met Farid at his gym in Iran, and, unlike that place, this doesn't look too promising," I said.

Ted pulled around and double parked in front of the entrance, and I stepped out and took a quick look around and spied Farid's black Bentley GT Continental parked two cars away. Directly behind it was yet another Mercedes filled with more security guys. Lovely, he had more protection than the fucking president of the United States. I went inside the gym to the front desk and was immediately greeted at the front desk by a young sales woman in her early twenties. She looked European and was extremely fit, very attractive, and eager to get her hooks into a potential new customer, as gyms everywhere survived by signing up as many people as possible for yearlong contracts that less than five percent would ever utilize. It was a grim system, but keeping the fat from getting fit guaranteed their customer base for years to come.

"Hello! Welcome to Fitness First," she said, merrily, with a British accent that was a bit on the posh side of the spectrum.

"Hello."

"I'm Jeanette, the membership services coordinator

here. How can I help you today?"

"Well, Jeanette, my name's Finn, and I'm looking for a gym while I'm over here, so is there any chance you could give me a quick tour?"

"Absolutely, but, if you don't mind, I'd like to first meet in my office and answer any questions you might have," she said.

"Oh, you don't have to bother. I know my way around the gym, as I've spent half my life in these places."

"Yeah, I can see that," she said, as she eyed me from head to toe and gave me an appraising smile.

"And you obviously have as well," I said, returning the compliment.

She smiled.

"Well, thank you, Finn, but, unfortunately, corporate management likes us to always start with a little Q and A, so if you don't mind, could we do at least a minute before going on the tour?"

"Yeah, sure, assuming I can last a full minute."

She laughed.

"I imagine you can, now, please—come this way," she said, with a smile as she pointed towards a glass walled office.

She walked ahead, and my eyes unconsciously fell upon her seriously pert and well rounded backside, which was made all the more obvious by her tight body hugging exercise pants. Sweet firing glutes! Her posterior was a piece of artwork and showed all the telltale signs of some serious time on the squat rack. Before I could bring my eyes back up to her face, however, she abruptly turned around, but, oddly, smiled when she caught me enjoying the view. That made me wonder if perhaps her outfit and this whole office part were merely a purposeful ploy to help lure in male members—so to speak. It was certainly making Mr. Happy pretty happy to be here.

"Please, have a seat," she said, as she sat down on the other side of the desk.

I did as instructed, and she asked if I would like some water. I said yes, so she reached into a small refrigerator that sat beside the desk and pulled out two waters and handed me one.

"Cheers," she said, as she clinked her bottle to mine.

"Cheers," I responded.

At that point she proceeded to ask me all the obligatory questions, then gave me her practiced sales pitch about how their gym would be able to fulfill all my fitness goals. When she was done, it was finally time to go on the tour, and I once again fell in line behind her very fit backside. We ventured out onto the main floor, and I did a quick sweep of the crowd in the hope that I might find Farid. It was imperative that I spotted him before he spotted me, as I didn't want to spook him or have a very unplanned public reunion before I was ready to conduct my official meeting.

First up on the tour was the busy machine section, which was bustling with plenty of people, many of whom had pale skin, and were therefore likely expats from Europe or the

United States. Next up were the free weights, and this area attracted a more diverse crowd, with the majority looking beefy, sweaty, and pushing some pretty serious weight on the various benches and equipment. So far, there was no sign of Farid.

Last on the itinerary was the cardio area, where they had state of the art tread mills, elliptical trainers, and bikes, all occupied by busy looking professionals with earbuds in their ears and iPads and magazines in their hands. In this section, I could literally feel the increased heat and humidity permeating the air due to the excessive amount of sweaty people.

"Last, we have the locker rooms," she said, proudly.

It was apparently a major selling point, but I doubted anything could possibly compare to my room back at the hotel. She led me to the door and said she'd be waiting for me while I went in for a look. Needless to say, I had to proceed with caution, as Farid was very likely in here. I walked inside, and my fears were immediately justified when I saw a security man standing just beyond the door. I nodded at him, but he just stared ominously, so I moved on to the steam room and shower area. There, I came upon two men with the usual sunglasses, earpieces, and dour lifeless expressions of bodyguards. It was a purposeful look meant to dissuade would-be attackers, and it had been proven to be effective by numerous studies conducted by the United States Secret Service. The idea was that the bad guys never knew where the good guys were looking—which meant that they might be looking at the bad guys.

The steam room door abruptly opened, and the two men assumed alert postures as Farid stepped out wearing a towel around his waist. He strolled over to the showers, and he looked fit and apparently hadn't fallen prey to the laziness of sudden wealth and early middle age. Of course, the same could not be said for his ridiculous facial hair, which was more than stubble but less than a beard and reminiscent of those embarrassing scenesters that populated every urban locale. What had the UAE done to my friend?

He suddenly paused, stopped in mid stride, and turned back in my direction. Shit! It appeared he might have seen me, and, worse still, recognized me, so I brought my hand up to rub my head and slowly looked away in an attempt to subtly conceal my face. It apparently worked, because he turned back and continued towards the shower. It was definitely time to leave the gym, as this was clearly not going to work as a meeting place. I went out and joined Jeanette, and we returned to the front desk.

"So, are you ready to sign up?" she asked.

"I enjoyed the tour and meeting you, but I have to think about it."

"Would it help if I gave you my number?"

"It might."

"Good, then feel free to call me—even if you don't end up joining the gym," she said, as she wrote her private cell number on the back of her business card.

"If I manage to stay in town long enough, I will definitely

be in touch," I said, as I pocketed her card and headed back out into the heat.

The car was still double parked in the same place, and I was soon back in the temperate air-conditioned environment.

"Well—is there any chance it'll be a good place to stage a meeting with Farid?" Bill asked.

"No fucking way, but I did like the membership coordinator," I said.

"Yeah, Jeanette is seriously attractive."

"Oh, so you know who she is?"

"Of course, every guy in Dubai is secretly lusting after her."

"So, does she give out her number to all the potential members?"

"No, so if you really did manage to get it, you should hold onto it, or, better still, call her."

"Good to know."

"Alrighty then, let's go get some lunch, then afterward we'll check out his house."

CHAPTER SIXTEEN

Dead Men don't Wear Jogging Shorts

Bill took me to a new upscale restaurant called Toro Toro, and it was Latin American theme with three main categories: from the land, from the sea, and from the garden. I already knew I'd be going with land and garden, as I had never developed much of a taste for seafood outside of tuna fish, crab cakes, and the occasional sushi when I was incredibly drunk. So, after gazing at the menu, I ordered steak and potato tostones with poblano chilli and bell peppers—all of it topped with a hearty and delicious rich truffle, chimichurri, and parmesan marinade. The waiter left, and a short time later our lunch arrived, and we dined and talked, and it allowed me to learn about Bill's daily existence in the UAE. Officially, he was a cultural attaché for the embassy, but unofficially he was a CIA officer monitoring terrorist financiers, and that required a lot of networking and liaising at official functions. So, he pretty much knew everybody who was anybody, and it would surely make him an invaluable asset in getting to Farid.

I was, of course, also curious about his connection to the Topless Agenda, but, as it was a secret society, I had to broach the subject carefully. After a number of cleverly worded questions, I learned that Bill was a close personal friend of Senator Matheson. The two of them had met as youngsters while serving in the Navy JAG corps and remained close friends to this day. Needless to say, neither of us actually mentioned the Topless Agenda by name, but his knowing smile was enough for me to be pretty sure he was some kind of affiliate or junior member.

Lunch eventually came to an end, and, with Bill generously picking up the check, I needed to thank my host, for my mother had always taught me to be gracious whenever someone bothered to deliver, cook, or buy me a meal.

"Thanks for an excellent lunch," I said.

"No need to thank me. This one was on Uncle Sam."

"Then make sure you thank him for me."

"I will."

"So, I guess now we go see Farid's house?"

"Yeah, and it's out on the Palm Jumeirah Island, though calling it a house is an understatement. Mansion would be more accurate."

"So Farid has a mansion, a Bentley, and a life of leisure

that any rational person would kill for—yet somehow, I'm supposed to talk him into giving it all up."

"I guess that's why you get the big bucks."

"Then the Notorious B.I.G. was right—mo' money, mo' problems, though I can't help thinking mo' money problems is better than no money problems," I said.

Bill laughed.

"Alrighty then, I'm going to hit the bathroom," I said, as I stood up and placed my napkin on the table.

I walked past the various diners and found the bathroom back near the hostess station. It was empty, but I still chose one of the stalls instead of the urinals, as I preferred the privacy, roominess, and lack of spray back that you often experienced in the latter. Just as I started emptying my bladder, another customer entered the bathroom, but he decided on one of the urinals. I heard his zipper, then he uttered a low groan and began peeing and soon let loose a long slow growling fart. As usual, I instantly had a case of the giggles, but I managed to keep it locked down until finishing up and giving Tag Junior the obligatory shake. I zipped up and headed over to wash my hands at the sinks, which sat opposite the urinals. I soaped up my hands, and, as I vigorously rubbed them together, I used the mirror to glance at the farter and nearly shit my pants. It was Farid, and I instantly realized I should have already discerned it was my old friend purely by the unmistakable tone of his fucking fart. Now, I had to think fast and wondered if perhaps I should use this brief window of opportunity to make contact, but, before I could act, the door opened, and I saw that our newest arrival was one of Farid's security goons that had been at the gym. He stepped inside but remained at the entrance and proceeded to look particularly irritated.

"Farid, I've told you a hundred times not to go into a public bathroom alone," he said.

"For fuck's sake. Can't a man get a little privacy?" he asked.

"No."

The security goon turned his attention to me, and I nodded only to receive a menacing glare in return. This was definitely not the time to talk to Farid, and I desperately hoped that he didn't turn around and recognize me. I grabbed a towel, dried my hands, and moved swiftly towards the door. The guy moved over and blocked my path and stared for a moment, and I wondered if he recognized me from the gym. His expression softened ever so slightly, and he stepped aside, allowing me to continue out through the door, where I soon found Bill waiting next to the hostess stand.

"We've got to get the fuck out of here. Farid and one of his goons are in the bathroom," I said.

"Shit! I probably should have already warned you."

"You knew he was here?"

"No, but I discovered this place following him. It's his favorite restaurant."

"Well, then we'd best be going."

We hurried out and took a seat in the waiting car, and Ted

drove us out of the parking lot and merged into the bustling traffic, heading north towards the nearby Palm Jumeirah Island. We turned left and crossed a small bridge and officially left mainland Dubai and continued past the various buildings before making a right turn onto Al Fardh Street, which was the first branch of the palm shaped Island. It looped around then headed out past endless luxury condos and McMansions before at last reaching Farid's esteemed residence. It sat on the coveted last spot at the end of the spit and was by far the largest and most luxurious home I had thus far seen in the Palm Jumeirah development. We parked three houses away, then Bill explained the various security measures we were up against.

"The house has all the latest security, including infrared, sonic, laser, and motion sensors. There are cameras on every point of access and sixteen full time security people working two shifts, twenty-four hours a day. The two nearest houses are where the majority of the security people live while a select few live in the main compound."

"Jesus, how did you find out all that?" I asked.

"We bribed a tech from the security company."

"So, I take it that it's kind of a waste of time to even come out here."

"I'll let you be the judge of that."

We stepped out of the car and walked towards the compound but headed off the main street to a beach access path. There, we headed up the shoreline and pretended to be tourists enjoying the view as we walked around the sandy point that skirted Farid's property. A short distance ahead, two men stepped out of the shadow of a palm tree in order to let us know that they were there. I smiled and waved, but neither man returned the gesture.

"They're decently trained," I said.

"Why do you say that?"

"They didn't wave back, because it meant taking their hands off their triggers."

"Maybe they're just assholes."

"Maybe—but they're decently trained assholes."

We continued on to the beach access path on the other side of the spit then made our way back to the car.

"What's the security like at his work?"

"Even better."

"And when he goes to the nightclubs it's the same security assholes?"

"Yep."

"So, unless I'm a blonde with big bajumbos, we're mostly fucked."

"Yep."

"Shit."

We drove back to the hotel, and they dropped me off to give me a little time to relax and recoup before meeting up later for dinner. Bill, meanwhile, was going to look into the guest list for the party at the Royal Palace. If Farid did indeed end up being in attendance, then I would have the distinct pleasure of spending another evening with Olivia. I went up to my room and, upon stepping inside, was once again floored by the extreme opulence. It's funny, I was philosophically opposed to the idea that money brought any kind of true happiness, but looking at my current accommodations made me wonder if that was a lie perpetrated by the wealthy to keep the poor people happily in their place. I yawned and looked at my watch then realized how out of whack my personal clock was with the actual clock on the wall of my room, and I decided I might need to take a little nap. I leaned back on the main couch and looked out at the skyline of Dubai and felt my eyes close and the world recede into the blessed respite of an afternoon nap.

I woke up and looked at the clock to see that I had been asleep for a little over two and a half hours. I was definitely feeling better, and I sat up and noticed the hotel's guest guide on the coffee table. I had some time to kill, so I scanned it and saw that they had a world class spa and gym on the eighteenth floor. Perfect! I would get a little exercise before dinner. I headed upstairs and changed into some shorts and a T-shirt then headed out to the elevator. It arrived a moment later, and I began the six floor journey up to the eighteenth. The climb was technically twelve floors, but each of these levels were comprised of two story suites identical to my own. It was probably an unnecessary waste of space, but I suppose it gave every guest the feeling, and reality, that he or she had a much bigger room than was available in the average hotel.

The elevator stopped, and, as expected, I exited to find floor to ceiling windows with yet another spectacular view of Dubai. I gave them a passing glance then headed left into the gym and came upon the cardio section to find it was a bit humid from the crowd of sweaty people. Music was blaring from the speakers in the ceiling, but nearly everyone was wearing the obligatory earbuds that came with their smartphone. They were a nice way to shut out the world and focus on your workout, but, to me, they were yet another barrier to actual human interaction.

I decided to start with the treadmills, but there were only two available, and they happened to be right next to each other. The left one was beside a particularly pretty, though slightly synthetic looking, twentysomething in a wonderfully form fitting pink Lulu Lemon outfit, while the right one resided beside a sweaty and oddly pungent smelling middle aged guy. So, my choices were either pointy or stinky. Needless to say, I hopped onto the one beside the pretty twentysomething and went through the complicated sequence of giving my age, weight, and workout preference before the treadmill started moving. A moment later, I was joined by yet another twentysomething, but sadly this one was a male, and he stepped onto the empty treadmill to my right. He was a fit looking fellow-infidel and was wearing a conspicuous pair of red satin running shorts that made me wonder if the nineteen eighties Dove shorts fad was making a comeback. I looked over and nodded, and he gave me a particularly nasty look in return, so it would appear that my new neighbor was an unfriendly asshole. He turned his attention away from me and to the screen on his machine, where he went through the same startup sequence that I had just completed. The treadmill started moving at a breakneck pace, and it was only by a miracle that he reached a full sprint quickly enough to stay aboard and not get jettisoned off the back.

I continued on at my own pace, patiently waiting until I was properly warm before turning up the speed. A few minutes later, I had a pretty good sweat on, and I turned to see my unfriendly neighbor was staring at me with the same peculiar look on his face. Just as I was about to ask him what his problem was, the pretty girl to my left slowed her pace to a fast walk, took out her earbuds, then looked over and spoke to the unfriendly asshole.

"Oh, there you are, honey," she said.

"Yeah, here I am," he said, sounding annoyed.

Now, I understood the odd visage of menace. I was in between him and his woman, and, in his mind, that was trespassing on his turf. Classic. This was just the kind of behavior that justified my theory that men had actually been devolving over the last ten thousand years, which might also explain the whole bad facial hair and beard phenomena as being a physical manifestation of our latent early caveman grooming standards. That thought was interrupted, however, when the pretty woman turned to me and smiled.

"Oh, I'm sorry, I didn't mean to talk over you," she said.

"It's OK, and, if I had to choose anyone here to talk over me, it would definitely be you," I said.

She smiled.

"Well thank you. I'm Britney, by the way."

"Nice to meet you, I'm Tag."

"And you're American, I assume?"

"Yeah, born and raised in sunny California."

"Me too! I'm from Orange County. How about you?"

"Nor Cal, but specifically Marin County."

"Oh, it's so beautiful up there! I totally want to move north, but Steve's company won't approve his transfer yet."

Probably because Steve the unfriendly asshole is just as much of an unfriendly asshole at work.

"Maybe Steve should look for a new job," I responded.

"Yeah, that's what I keep saying," she said, casting an annoyed look at Steve.

Steve the unfriendly asshole cleared his throat and glared at Britney before turning his attention to me.

"Do you mind moving?" he asked grumpily.

"I'm sorry—did you want to switch treadmills with me so that you could be closer to your fiancé?" I asked, having already noticed that Britney had an engagement ring.

Britney responded first.

"Don't be ridiculous, stay where you are."

"Are you sure? It's no problem to switch," I said.

"Ignore him. He's just being a territorial asshole."

I decided to try and be nice and take the path of least resistance.

"Hey, Steve, I'm happy to switch if it makes you more comfortable," I said.

"No need to worry about it, Nor Cal, as I imagine you're probably about to finish up and hit the showers, anyway."

"Excuse me, Steve, but does he look like the type of guy who would already be hitting the showers?" Britney asked, sounding annoyed.

"There's a difference between looking in shape and being in shape," Steve said.

"I agree, so which one are you?" I asked.

"I'm a triathlete—so, I'm both," he said, smiling pompously.

Triathlons were very trendy back home in Marin County and had become the new hip activity, but a friend and I once joked that they were for people who weren't good enough to compete at either running, biking, or swimming, and were therefore relegated to only be able to do a lesser amount of all three. Joking aside, some of them were obviously kick-ass athletes, but the rigors of my Pararescue training and current workout ethic made me think very little of the territorial and unfriendly asshole on the treadmill beside me.

"Just so you know, Steve—stamina and speed are often mutually exclusive," I said.

"Isn't that the truth," Britney responded, with a hint of irony in her tone that I suspected might be an insight into their sex life.

"I suggest you just worry about yourself," he said, turning his attention back to his workout.

It appeared as though we had an unofficial challenge on our hands, and, with that in mind, I kept my pace nice and even and settled in for a long run while Steve, at his current pace, likely wouldn't last more than another five or ten minutes at best. Honestly, I didn't care if that fucker ran all night, for I wasn't about to leave the treadmill until he quit, passed out, or died. I had survived Pararescue for fuck's sake, and, in that world, giving up meant death while fighting on meant life, both to you and the person you were trying to save. It was right up there with the eternal words of Yoda—do or do not, there is no try. I looked over at the Steve and saw that he was breathing hard, pale, and working at an anaerobic level and rapidly approaching the metaphorical wall where most people's bodies just stopped working. I, on the other hand, was feeling pretty good and decided to add a little psychological pain to his misery by sparking up a casual conversation with his fiancé. Being able to talk during exercise was a good measure of a person's cardio, and I currently had a lot to say.

"So, what brings you to Dubai," I asked.

"I'm just tagging along with Steve, who's here for a sales conference."

"That sounds a little boring for you."

"Yeah, but at least I get to stay here."

"True. What kind of room do you have?"

"We have the basic one bedroom suite."

"Oh, how do you like it, Steve?" I asked, turning to my right.

He looked over, but didn't respond, so I turned back to Britney, and she immediately answered.

"We love it! Which room did you get?"

"I've got one of the panoramic suites."

"Oh my God! It must be amazing!"

"You're welcome to see it sometime."

"I'd love that!"

I looked at Steve and noticed he didn't look good, and, had he not been young, I probably would have insisted that he stop running, but, unfortunately for him, pride cometh before the fall. He trained to run a couple miles on the weekend while I trained to run for my life—two very different motivations. I reached down and upped my speed until I was at a slightly faster pace than Steve.

"How's your conference going, Steve?"

He was exerting too much to speak and again didn't respond. We continued on for another minute or so before I sparked up yet another conversation.

"You don't look so good, you might want to slow down," I suggested.

"Fu—fu—fuck you," he gasped, before stumbling and getting violently ejected onto the floor behind the treadmill.

"Steve!" Britney called out, turning off her machine and going to his side.

I did the same, and we helped him up onto his feet, only to have him brush us off.

"I'm fine!" he said, sounding annoyed.

"Fuck, Steve! You could have killed yourself!" Britney said, angrily.

"Yeah, seriously, Steve, you need to pace yourself. It's like sex. You shouldn't just sprint for the finish."

"Fuck off, Nor Cal!" he said, as he left us, wobbling as he walked across the floor and disappeared into the locker room.

"I'm sorry, I should have just left it alone and gone into the weight room."

"Wouldn't have helped. He probably would have just followed you in there and challenged you on the bench press. He gets weirdly competitive around me."

"What's he making up for?"

"Personality."

We shared a laugh, then I decided I should give her some friendly parting advice.

"Oh well, at least you're not married yet, so there's still plenty of time to reconsider your future with Steve," I said.

"Yeah, I suppose there is," she said, with a thoughtful nod as she fidgeted with her engagement ring.

"Alrighty then, I'm off to the weights, but hopefully we'll run into each other again sometime."

"Yeah, but hopefully without Steve."

We shared another laugh, then I excused myself and went to the weight room, where I did a mini circuit that focused on all the major muscle groups. Twenty minutes later, I was ready for a swim, so I headed into the locker room, took a quick rinser, then grabbed a towel and made my way over to the pool and Jacuzzi area. They ended up being in their own dedicated room, and the thirty foot ceilings and dazzling decor made me feel as though I had wandered into some sultan's palace. The pool was rectangular and lined on two sides by rows of massive floor to ceiling columns, while the circular Jacuzzi resided just a short distance away. Filling the rest of the space were a number of plush recliners that you could take advantage of if you grew tired from all the aquatic frolicking.

I found am empty chair and left my shirt and towel on it then stepped down into the pool. The temperature was just cool enough to be refreshing, but not so cold as to be jarring. I looked down and saw a number of ripples come rolling across its perfectly smooth surface, and I looked over to see Britney swimming in my direction. She saw me and smiled and stood up.

"I didn't expect to see you again so soon," she said, her wet white two-piece bikini clinging to her tan and formidable body like a second skin.

Britney had looked pretty fit in her Lulu Lemon exercise outfit, but now that she was nearly bare, I could see that she had excellent definition in her thighs, buttocks, arms, and abdominals. Even more enticing was that she still managed to hold on to her lovely feminine curves, and her pert breasts appeared to strain against the thin fabric of her bikini top—making the dark protrusions of her pokey nipples extremely apparent.

"Yeah, and now I have to officially apologize to Steve," I said.

"Why?" she asked.

"Now that I've seen you in that bikini, I can understand why he's a little territorial. Sweet Lord, woman! You have the figure of a thousand and one boners!"

"Really? A thousand and one?"

"Yep."

"What's the one for?" she asked, with a smile.

"That one is mine, obviously."

She smiled.

"Well, I'm sure you're exaggerating, but thank you nonetheless."

"I'm not, and, as someone who goes to gym regularly, I know how much work you have to put into maintaining that level of fitness."

"Unfortunately, I live in Southern California, and staying in shape is the rule rather than the exception. It's Pilates or perish, but, I can see that you also take your fitness pretty seriously. Are you by chance a professional athlete?"

"Only if they start a professional league for masturbating."

She laughed.

"Seriously now, you must be some kind of athlete, considering the way you buried Steve on the treadmills. In the three years we've been going to the gym together, no one has ever put him in his place like that."

"Well, I used to have pretty physical job not so long ago."

"Meaning what? Fitness instructor?"

"No, military."

"Ah, I bet you were a Navy SEAL."

"No, but you're close. I was a Parajumper—the Air Force equivalent, and, like SEALs, we operated on sea, air, and land, but we specialized in rescue operations."

"I knew it had to be something badass like that. Did you see much action?"

"Enough for a lifetime."

"So, what do you do now?"

"I'm a private investigator."

"Oh, is it exciting?"

"Occasionally, but it's pretty boring a lot of the time."

"I seriously doubt that, considering the kind of shape you're in."

"Nah, exercise is just my way of trying to desperately stave off the grim slide into early middle age."

"Then whatever you're dong is working really well."

"Thank you, Britney. You're too kind."

"No, just honest."

The sound of flip flops caught our attention, and we turned to see Steve looking annoyed as he arrived at the edge of the pool.

"Were you hitting on her?" he asked testily.

"No, we were just innocently talking with very little clothing on."

"Dude, seriously now, you better not have been hitting on her!"

"Relax, Steve, because, fortunately for you, I'm a nice guy, and everyone knows that women as attractive as Britney generally only go for assholes."

"Fuck you, I'm not an asshole."

"Then stop acting like one," Britney said.

"Yeah, Steve, stop acting like one."

"That's it. I'm sick of this fucker's shit!" he said, as he started heading down the steps and into the pool.

Britney moved quickly into his path and cut him off.

"Honey, you're still dazed from the treadmill accident. Come on, let's go relax in the Jacuzzi."

"No, I'm going to go teach that fucking prick a lesson."

"Yeah, but believe me, you'll be the only one who ends up learning anything," she said.

"What's that supposed to mean?" he asked.

"It means that you're out of your league here."

"Fuck that," he said, as he barreled past her and made his way over to me.

"Look, Steve, I'm not going to fight you," I said.

"Why? Are you a pussy?"

"Yeah, I'm a total pussy, and, more importantly, I have a serious medical condition called compassion that keeps me from laying a hand on a lesser man—regardless of how much he deserves it."

"That's it," he said, as he threw a right cross straight at my face.

It was a decent punch, but I was ready and moved aside and performed a move called a block-check-counter, which entailed redirecting his fist with my right hand then grabbing it with my left. At that point it was safely away from my face and in a perfect orientation to transition to an outside hand twist that I used to maneuver his arm back and around, so that I could send Steve backwards and under the water. From there I used my other hand to grab his wrist and bring him back up and wedge his forearm in between us in a move called a California come-along. I could now see the shock on his face, but, as he recovered, he started to struggle, so I gave his wrist a little twist, and he called out in pain then stopped moving.

"Alrighty then, Steve, it's time to calm down and salvage your relationship with your fiancé, and, least of all, the continued use of your right hand. Understand?" I asked.

"Fuck you," he said, once again trying to struggle free.

I gave his wrist a little twist, and he stopped moving and looked at me.

"Fine, I understand," he said, in an annoyed tone.

"Good, because you threw a right punch, so I'm pretty sure you're right handed and therefore also masturbate with your right hand—the very same hand which could end up being your only date this evening if you don't calm the fuck down and start acting like an adult. Now, I'm going to release this very important hand of yours, so that you and I can share a gentlemanly handshake that will hopefully make you look as though you've suddenly matured. Assuming your beautiful fiancé believes this has actually occurred, you will hopefully be able to leave this embarrassing moment behind and go join her in the Jacuzzi. Sound good?"

"Yes," he said, sounding resolved though not entirely happy.

"OK, then," I said, as I released his hand.

We shook hands, and I looked over at Britney.

"It's OK now. Everything is good. Steve and I were just playing around," I said.

"It didn't look like he was playing," she said, sounding equal parts annoyed and embarrassed.

Before I released Steve's hand, I decided to deliver some parting wisdom.

"You know, Steve, if you think men are checking out your fiancé, it should make you feel good, because it means you're a very lucky man that she would choose to be with you. On the other hand, your insecurity and tendency to be reactionary is highly unattractive and will make this and any future relationships short-lived."

"Whatever," he said, as he walked towards Britney but stumbled a little, as he was still feeling a bit faint.

"Come on, let's go relax, killer" Britney said, as she guided Steve up the steps, where she looked back over her shoulder at the last minute to silently mouth the words thank you.

CHAPTER SEVENTEEN
The Linen Gorilla

Britney and Steve left, and that meant I was free to do twenty quick laps before exiting the pool to dry off. I slipped on my T-shirt, and, on my way out, happened to venture past the Jacuzzi.

"It was nice meeting you, and remember what I said, Britney—there's still plenty of time."

Britney smiled, but Steve glared and lifted his hand out of the water and gave me the finger. I gave him a departing smile and headed for the elevator, where I was joined by an unusually buff Arabic man in a white linen suit. He had the obligatory Middle Eastern beard and kept his shirt unbuttoned just enough to reveal a gold medallion and a dense thicket of chest hair. He also reeked of cologne, and, while it was annoying, it was nowhere near as annoying as his extremely annoying habit of staring at me while we waited for the elevator to arrive. I gave him a friendly smile and a nod in hopes of appeasing him, but he continued to keep his eyes glued to me. Oh well, perhaps he didn't like infidels.

The doors opened, and we joined a middle aged Japanese couple, who politely nodded and said hello. I said hello back, then we all followed the usual elevator etiquette and looked towards the door. Well, everyone except for the linen gorilla, whose eyes were still on me, and I had to wonder how I had somehow become the object of his attention. The Japanese couple exited on the fourteenth floor, and I was left alone with the gawking primate, whose presence, along with the little episode back in the gym, was starting to give me the feeling that this was going to be one of those days.

"I'm sorry, do we perhaps know each other?" I asked.

"No, but I have a message for you," he said, as his reached for the pistol he was carrying in his shoulder holster.

Fortunately, I had seen the bulge under his jacket and, having already experienced his menacing glare, was expecting trouble. To that end, I purposefully started a conversation with the gorilla, because it forced him to act before he was ready, and it allowed me to have a plan in place when he reached for his pistol. Unfortunately, he was a big guy with more muscle than me—which meant he had more muscle than he needed, but bulk wasn't always a measure of strength. In this case, it wouldn't even enter the equation. It didn't matter how many weights you lifted or how many steroids you put into your body, as certain areas remained unprotected. The most critical was the neck, and, outside of wearing a suit of armor or a carbon fiber turtle neck sweater, it was incredibly vulnerable. My first move, therefore, was to use my left hand to punch him hard in the throat while I used my right to trap his gun hand. His eyes went wide with shock as he gasped for breath, and I immediately followed it up with a right vertical palm to his face that bloodied his nose and filled his eyes with tears. His vision was now blurry, and he was having a hard time breathing, allowing me to shove him backwards into the elevator wall and bring my knee up into his groin. The force had nowhere to go except up through his balls and into his body, and it lifted him off his feet. But, if his bulk actually were the result of steroids, then his balls might be a smaller and less appealing target, which is why I then directed the next knee up into his solar plexus.

The gorilla buckled over but somehow recovered enough to throw a pretty solid right uppercut into my ribs. I exhaled at the point of impact to lessen the blow, but it was still a damn good hit. He tried another, but this time I was ready and shot both of my hands into the crux of his arm to stop the strike from reaching my stomach. Now, I had the inside line, and I twisted counterclockwise and used my entire body to drive my right elbow into his stomach. The combination of the pain and the wind being knocked from his lungs dropped him onto his knees, and I hit him with two double heel palms to his neck that left him dazed and perfectly prepped for my finishing move. I was going to use the old combat slap—an unusual technique I'd learned from a member of Britain's SAS while on a joint operation in Afghanistan. It entailed delivering a monumentally hard slap to an opponent's jaw, and, done correctly, knocked him out cold. Done incorrectly, you ended up looking like a big sissy, because you just slapped another man. I therefore went all out and put my entire body into the motion, and the blow knocked him completely unconscious. His head bounced off the wall, then he collapsed against me with his face resting against my groin region in a way that, when viewed form the right direction, might appear as though he were delivering oral pleasure. Before I could move him off of me, the elevator stopped, and the doors opened to reveal an affluent looking Arabic couple who started to step aboard but abruptly stopped when they took in the scene.

"Oh, don't mind my friend here. He just realized that it was sunset, and he needed to stop and prey," I said.

"It's not sunset yet," the woman responded.

"And Mecca is the other direction," the man added.

"Yeah, unfortunately, he's dumb as fuck."

"Um, perhaps we should wait for another elevator," the man said.

"Yeah, that's probably a good idea."

The couple continued to stare as the door closed, and soon the elevator was once again heading downward, and thankfully it only stopped at my floor, thus eliminating the potential for any more awkward encounters. I grabbed the gorilla's legs and dragged him out of the elevator and stopped once I had his head clear of the doors. Fuck, what the hell was I supposed to do now? I looked around and spied a food cart just down the hall and walked over and rolled it back to the elevator and heaved the gorilla over the top the way a cowboy might heave a body over a horse. I rolled him down the hall to my room but paused to take a minute to think. If they had a man up on the gym level, it stood to reason there might also be another in my room. The linen gorilla would be the point man to lead me back here while his partner, or partners, would be waiting inside to help finish the job—which probably entailed torturing and killing me. Had I been a quitter, this would have been an excellent time to call the Topless Agenda and tell them to fuck off because I was getting on a plane and heading back home.

Unfortunately, I wasn't a quitter, so I needed to go inside my luxurious room and deal with any unwelcome visitors. But, every decent incursion began with a little recon, and, to that end, I placed my ear against the door. There was barely a sound, but, even if my room were bustling with bad guys, they could have been disco dancing with a gaggle of strippers, and I probably wouldn't have heard a thing. This was a 'seven star' hotel after all, which meant proper soundproofing, so that guests could enjoy their stay in peace—or without peace depending on their individual preference. Oh well, I guess I would just find out when I went inside. I pulled the gorilla's pistol out of his shoulder holster and slid my card into the key lock. The light flashed green, and I opened the door just far enough to do a quick visual sweep of the room. It appeared to be empty, but there still might be someone hiding out of view behind the door, so I decided to get sneaky and dropped down to the floor and slid in on my back. There, exactly as I feared, was the gorilla's partner, but he wasn't expecting anyone to slither in like an inverted lizard, so his gaze was focused at eye level, and that meant he only saw me at the last minute, which was a minute too late.

"Freeze, goatfucker, or I'll give you a lead vasectomy," I said, pointing the pistol at his groin.

The guy wasn't as bulked up with muscle as his friend, but he was fit and had the bearing of someone with a military background, and that made me think he might be more prone to trying something. Fortunately, for the sake of any of his yet to be conceived children, he understood that I had the upper hand, and he held out his arms in a placating manner.

"Good, now slowly place your pistol on the floor."

He did as I asked, which was a smart move and told me that he was the brains of this operation while the gorilla was the brawn. As it turned out, they had both miscalculated their target and both were now officially in the dumbass category. I stood up carefully, all the while keeping Brains in my sights.

"Good, now kick it over here," I said.

He did as I asked, and I picked up his gun and slid it into my waistband.

"So far, so good—now, go out and roll your friend into the room."

I stepped aside as he moved past me, and he looked relieved to see that his companion was still alive. He pushed the cart into the room and only managed to bump his friend's head once as he cleared the doorframe. With his task done, he turned his attention back to me.

"You have no idea who you are dealing with here," he said.

"True, and considering where you're sitting—neither do you."

He begrudgingly nodded.

"Regardless, it would still be in your best interest to allow me and my companion to leave here right now," he said.

"And what exactly were my options going to be?"

"The same. We were simply here to—deliver a message," he said.

I hadn't survived this long in life without learning to read people, so I knew that this fucker was talking out of his ass.

"Yeah, the gorilla said you had a message for me, but he never managed to deliver it, so, now's your chance."

"Leave."

"Meaning, this hotel? Because that would suck, as I'm really starting to enjoy all the amenities," I said, just to fuck with him.

"No, leave, as in leave the United Arab Emirates."

"Believe me, I'll be leaving soon enough, but, for the moment, I'm afraid the UAE is stuck with me."

I pulled out my phone and called Bill, and he answered

on the third ring.

"Hey, Finn—what's up?" he asked.

"Not much. I'm having a little get together in my room here with a couple uninvited visitors who are apparently here to tell me I need to leave the UAE."

"Oh shit, are you OK?"

"Yeah, the situation is under control, but I could obviously use a little help."

"No problem, I'll make arrangements. Oh, and you'll be pleased to learn that I have some good news, but I'll wait to tell you in person."

"Excellent, I'll be eagerly awaiting your arrival."

I hung up and motioned for my unwelcome guest to take a seat on the couch while I sat directly across from him where I could keep him under close watch. He fidgeted and looked around the room nervously, obviously trying to figure out how he was going to try and escape. A groan brought both of our attention to the cart, where the gorilla was stirring. He slowly came awake and struggled off the cart and looked confused as he took in the scene.

"Good morning, sunshine. Why don't you come join your friend here on the couch," I suggested.

He soon realized that I was holding a gun, and he acquiesced and walked over to sit beside Brains. Side by side, they were quite a couple—Brains and Brawn. They looked at each other and exchanged a nod, then awkward silence descended upon the room.

"Now, as we have a little time to kill, why don't you two

fucks tell me who sent you," I said.

"There were no names, but I can assure you that he is someone to be feared"

"So, it's a he, and you know he's to be feared, yet you don't know his name. That makes you either a dumbass or a liar."

"Everything was done through an intermediary, and when dealing with these kinds of people, I find it is often safest to know as little as possible."

He had a point, which was yet more proof that he was the brains of the operation. Still, I couldn't help but wonder what powerful United Arab Emirates citizen might possibly want me to leave. There were probably a lot of people counting on Farid's new discovery, but his main boss, Sheik Hamza, would certainly be a good candidate.

"Does the name Sheikh Hamza ring any bells?" I asked.

Neither man appeared to have any reaction, so it wasn't Hamza, or else they really didn't know the identity of their employer. Regardless of who this mysterious fucker might be, I still wanted to know how in the flying fuck he could know anything about me and the Topless Agenda's plans? Shitsky, something was clearly rotten in the State of Dubai, or perhaps even the Topless Agenda itself.

"As you assholes have nothing useful to say, how about we kill some time by playing *Would You Rather*," I suggested.

"What?" Brains asked.

"Would You Rather. It's a game. I ask you a question like would you rather be able to turn invisible or have x-ray vision."

They both thought for a moment.

"I would choose x-ray vision," Brawn said.

Brains scowled at his friend before responding.

"At this moment, I would obviously choose the ability to become invisible."

"Good choice," I said, with a smile.

At least he had a sense of humor, and that would make the next twenty minutes together slightly less awkward. I moved on to my next question and decided to make it a little wackier.

"Would you rather eat a Big Mac or a Whopper?"

"Big Mac," Brains said.

"Whopper, more protein, less carbs," Brawn said.

Of course the gorilla was carb conscious, but I doubted he knew that the human brain relied on a minimum of 500 calories of carbs a day for its basic functioning, which was yet another reason he was the brawn rather than the brains. Seven equally asinine questions later there was a knock at the door, and I looked through the peephole to see it was Bill and three other guys. I opened the door, and Bill smiled.

"I believe someone called for an exterminator," he said.

"Yeah, apparently even the Burj Al Arab gets roaches, though I must say—these are some pretty big fuckers."

"No problem," Bill said, as the three men with him took hold of Brain and Brawn and ushered them efficiently out of the room.

Bill closed the door behind them then came over and took a seat on the couch.

"So, what happens to those two? A long, one way trip into the desert?" I asked.

"Nah, we'll create some kind of scenario that allows them to keep their jobs, and then we'll put them on our payroll and turn enemies into assets."

"Everybody wins."

"Yeah, pretty much. So, what did those two want?" he asked.

"Supposedly they were here just to tell me that a very powerful unnamed man wants me to leave the UAE."

"That makes it pretty clear that someone knows why you're here"

"Yeah, and now we need to get this done even sooner."

"True, but at least I have some good news to balance out the bad news."

"Do tell."

"Farid is going to be at that party at the Royal Palace."

"Oh good, but won't he still have the same contingent of security?"

"Nope, the Palace is one of the few places that the existing security is good enough that he won't have additional protection."

"When is the party?"

"Tomorrow night."

"Shit, I suppose I better call Olivia."

I pulled out my phone, dialed her number, then hit the

speaker button and patiently waited until she answered on the second ring.

"Hello, Tag, I didn't expect to hear from you so soon!" she said, sounding excited.

"Yeah, and it would appear that fate is finally working in my favor."

"Oh really—what's up?"

"My penis, because I have some good news!'

"Please tell me you're free to accompany me to my big *soirée*!"

"I am m'lady!"

"Well, fuck yeah! Now, I'll have a date to keep all my lame ass coworkers off of my ass for the night."

"And someone to cuddle with when it's all over."

"Yeah, and, as I remember, you can cuddle like a motherfucker."

"I sure can, so, we're on like Donkey Kong," I said.

"Excellent, and if you count the shower on the plane as our second date, then I guess tomorrow will officially be our third."

"Shower?" Bill mouthed, looking surprised.

I muted the phone for a second while I responded.

"Best second date ever," I told him.

"Where are you staying?" Olivia asked.

"The Burj Al Arab."

"That shithole?"

"Yeah, sadly it's all my client could afford."

"Well then, I'll send a car to come rescue you at six tomorrow evening. Dress formal."

"How formal?"

"James Bond in a tuxedo ordering a Martini at the casino in Monte Carlo formal."

"Got it."

"Good, I'll see you tomorrow evening, James," she said, before hanging up.

I put down the phone and looked at Bill.

"Fuck, then I guess we need to go Tux shopping tomorrow morning," I said.

"Martini, Mr. Bond?" Bill asked.

"Yes, but shaken not stirred," I said, once again doing my best Sean Connery.

Bill and I enjoyed our martinis then headed off to dinner at one of the hotel's premier restaurants. It was called Al Muntaha, and it resided on the top floor of the Burj Al Arab and specialized in modern European cuisine. The nighttime view of Dubai was spectacular, and we enjoyed an equally spectacular, if not affordable, dinner consisting of a Wagyu filet, shaved asparagus and gratinated parmigianino macaroni. Three martini's later we parted ways in the elevator, and I managed to make it back to my room without a single altercation. I entered my suite and heard my iPhone ringing and looked at the screen to see that Senator Matheson was calling.

"*Hola*, Douglas," I said.

"*Hola*, Finn. How's it going?"

"Good and bad, I suppose."

"Oh well, give me the good news first."

"Alrighty then, I'll start with Farid. I confirmed that the intel you gave me was accurate, and they have him under tight security pretty much everywhere he goes, so he would appear to be nearly impossible to approach."

"And this is the good news?"

"No, but I'm still getting to that part. You see, on the plane over, I met a woman who needs a date for a big soirée at the Royal Palace, and it just so happens that Farid will be in attendance, and I think it would be a perfect place to make contact."

"So, what's the bad news?"

"A couple of assholes showed up at my hotel today hoping to deliver a message that a very powerful man wants me to leave the UAE, so that very same asshole apparently knows why I'm here. Combine that with our whole emergency landing snafu back at SFO, and I'd say that it seems pretty likely this same powerful asshole has somehow penetrated the Topless Agenda."

"Fuck. I just don't see how it's possible."

"Yeah, fuck, indeed, but the evidence is pretty overwhelming."

"At least the fact that you're talking to me means you're OK," he said.

"Yeah, I'm fine. I dealt with the messengers, and then your man Bill came over and relocated them for me."

Matheson was quiet for a moment, as he was obviously still thinking about my latest update.

"So, I take it you didn't get the identity of this powerful man?" he asked.

"No, but I've been wondering about who this fucker might be, and I can't help but think Sheik Hamza is a pretty good candidate."

"Well, he does have a lot to lose, but then so does the entire United Arab Emirates."

"Yeah, and when I mentioned the his name to my two unwelcome visitors today, I didn't see any kind of reaction, so hopefully the next messengers will be a little better informed."

"Let's hope so."

We had another moment of quiet, then I decided it was only polite to ask how things were going on his end.

"So, how it's going with you and the rest of the Topless Agenda?"

"Needless to say, we're in a mild state of panic, though you're latest news is going to make things even worse."

"Yeah, I bet, and speaking of which, is there any news about my fucking German tourist? I'd sure like to know how that asshole fits into this picture."

"No, but I have contacts at Homeland Security checking all the passenger manifests from recent flights in and out of SFO, Oakland, and San Jose, so we've got to find a hit somewhere. He couldn't have magically appeared."

"What about Harold Fuchs? He's German. Any chance he's gotten a little greedy and decided to get into bed with someone in the UAE?"

"No, and he would never be so obvious as to use one of his own countrymen."

"True, I guess you don't get to the top of the food chain by being stupid."

"Definitely not. Well, I'll be in touch if I find out anything new.

"Likewise."

"Good luck, Finn."

"Thanks, and keep your head down, Douglass."

"I will, and keep yours up."

I hit end and immediately went up to the massive bathroom and took a well-deserved three martini piss. Upon finishing up, I brushed my teeth then changed into a T-shirt and some pajama bottoms and grabbed my laptop and slid into bed. I decided to start by checking my email and found that I had forty-two unread messages. Interestingly, forty-two was the magical number that answered the question of the meaning of life, the universe, and everything in Douglas Adams's *Hitchhikers Guide to the Galaxy*. In the case of my email, it represented spam, non-spam, and personal messages, among which I would have hoped included one from Estelle, but sadly that wouldn't be the case.

I closed my laptop, took a swig from a bottle of sparkling mineral water on the bedside table, then turned out the light and stared up at the ceiling, wondering what was happening back home. Was Estelle walking down the aisle at this very moment, soon to be another man's happily wedded wife? My bed was suddenly feeling very large and very empty, and it left me feeling very much alone as I lay on the decadently soft cotton sheets, but such was the life of a man-whore, I suppose. At last I rolled over, closed my eyes and fell into a deep, dark slumber, ever hopeful the companionship I lacked in real life would come to me in my dreams.

CHAPTER EIGHTEEN
Mall Rats

I awoke fifteen minutes before eight and went into the bathroom to brush my teeth before heading downstairs to make myself a latte on the Nespresso machine that resided behind the bar. Two short minutes later, I took a heavenly sip then moved to the couch to peruse the breakfast menu. I chose a veggie, cheese, and bacon omelet with potatoes, toast, and fruit on the side. A half hour later, it arrived, and I ate like a king at the large dining table, enjoying both breakfast and the view of the Palm Jumeirah, which made me think about how strange it was going to be to talk to my old friend. I wonder if he had changed and become jaded by the money and jet set lifestyle of Dubai's elite. I certainly hoped not, as he had been a pretty damn good guy back when we first met.

I finished breakfast and made myself another latte and headed back upstairs, ever careful not to spill even a drop of the holy elixir. I picked out clothes for the day, stripped, then grabbed my laptop and entered my porcelain sanctuary. There, I set my latte on the counter then placed my laptop on the convenient fold out stand. My final task was to drop my backside onto the great porcelain throne where I would lay my waste. Properly seated, I opened my laptop, brought up my browser, and typed Dubai news in the Google search bar with the intention of learning a little more about my surroundings in case I got into any conversations at the party. A moment later, a page full of hits came up with the top news story being about a member of the royal family coming under scrutiny for torturing and trying to kill a business associate. Apparently, he took him out into the desert, beat him with a stick, lit his nuts on fire, then ran him over with his Land Rover, but by some miracle the man survived to tell the tale. It was certainly an extreme way to settle a business difference, but then they also stoned men, women, and children to death in this part of the world for crimes that wouldn't even be a misdemeanor back in the States. God only knew what potential punishment I would be facing for trying to lure their golden goose out of the country.

This wasn't exactly helping with my morning movement and was, in fact, working quite the opposite, so I closed my laptop and set it on the counter. It was time to clear my mind and focus on the moment by having a good dump—always the harbinger of a good day. I took a sip of my latte, relaxed, and set in motion the great cycle of life. It was truly a perfect moment, for I was in the nicest of hotels, enjoying the greatest of bathrooms, thereby making a potentially good day—great. Suddenly, a figure appeared in the doorway, and my sphincter came down on my fecal traveler like the blade of the guillotine on the neck of the French aristocracy. A high pitched scream escaped my lips as I tried to grab a towel from the nearby rack, and the movement practically caused me to fall off the toilet. I covered my privates and looked over at the intruder only to realize it was the maid. Sweet porcelain nightmares! I suddenly remembered that I had forgotten to put the little *do not disturb* tag on the door, and I was paying for my lack of vigilance in the most awkward of ways. The maid was equally startled and apologized profusely as she raced out of the bathroom. This was not a good sign, and, quite to the contrary, was an omen of bad things to come. Whenever my special time was interrupted, bad shit happened—literally. I sat there and patiently waited for my heart rate to return to normal, so that I could complete my release. A minute would pass before I was done and quietly sitting there with great feelings of trepidation. I wiped, flushed, and stepped into the shower, where I spent my time under the five showerheads trying to get my mind back to a happy place.

Refreshed and clean, though still somewhat rattled, I dressed and headed downstairs to put the do not disturb sign on the door before settling down on the couch to wait for Bill. He arrived ten minutes later, and we headed off to go tuxedo shopping at the world famous Mall of the Emirates, which had some of the most exclusive shops outside of Beverly Hills's Rodeo Drive. Oddly, it also had one of the largest indoor ski areas in the world—that privileged title of course dependent upon the fact that there actually was another indoor ski area somewhere else.

The mall was on Sheikh Zayed Road about a mile inland from my hotel, and the first thing that came into view was the enormous slanted tube of its signature eighty-five meter high ski area. It was quite a piece of architecture, and it was hard to imagine that inside there were twenty-two thousand square meters of mountain and five runs, including one black diamond. Only a country with the wealth and imagination of Dubai could bring snow to the desert.

We pulled into the parking lot, and, even though the mall opened at ten and it was only a quarter past, there were already scores of shoppers plying its retail shores, thus making finding a space a real motherfucker. Ted, the Yale man, eventually gave up and parked in a loading zone, and we stepped out to join in the procession of people entering the world renowned Mall of the Emirates.

As expected, it was a great thriving city of retail that stood three stories tall and was open and spacious and topped by a glass ceiling that allowed in the light but shielded out the harsh heat of the Middle Eastern sun. The walls were painted off-white with tasteful touches of gold, while the floor was a polished marble incorporating a myriad of colors and patterns. It was distracting, and, combined with the crowd, made it easy to get lost in the moment and forget I was here for one reason—to buy a tuxedo. Bill said they had several store choices ranging from Burberry to Dolce & Gabbana, and I went with the latter, imagining it might make me a touch more dashing amongst Dubai's elite at the royal Palace.

We navigated the sea of shoppers, and finally entered the quiet confines of Dolce & Gabbana, where I was immediately pounced upon by a young, attractive, and incredibly well put together female sales associate who was both gracious and welcoming—not something I was expecting. I always thought it was particularly ironic that some of the most pompous people I'd met in the world were salespeople. The most snobbish of all often had nary a pot to piss in, yet scrutinized their potential clients as though they were being vetted for the Supreme Court. Perhaps their pompous demeanor was the result of a contact high with their wealthy clients, and their mutualistic relationship was similar to that of a pilot fish to its host shark. The pilot fish gained protection from its larger buddy and, in return, kept the shark free of parasites. In the retail existence, the salespeople were obviously the pilot fish and, instead of gaining protection, they gained esteem by keeping their wealthy client, the shark, looking hip and fashionable. Interestingly, there was a Porsche dealership back home that had some of the most pompous sales people on the planet, and I had gone in there with a wealthy friend who was more than ready to buy a brand new Carrera Turbo S. Apparently, his athletic attire did nothing to stir any interest from the three salesmen, and we subsequently left, and he bought the very same car about one hour down the road at a dealership in Silicon Valley.

My saleswoman was the exception, however, and treated me as though I might be one of the many royals of the United Arab Emirates. She was one of those rare breed of salespeople who knew that you couldn't judge a book by its cover and, therefore, treated everyone equally, with each new client having the potential to be that Holy Grail of commission windfalls. It was smart thinking on her part and would have made her very successful back home in Marin County, where earthy dot-com millionaires were as common as the redwood trees that dotted its many valleys and hills.

In two shakes of a very chic lamb's tail, she had me in a smart looking Tux that had been on everyone from Taylor Lautner of the Twilight movies to Matthew McConaughey. I did a few James Bond poses in the three way mirror, then stood there and quietly waited while she used some chalk to mark where the various alterations would take place. Just as she finished up, a figure walked past me and into one of the other changing rooms. I didn't see his face, but his keffiyeh hinted that he was likely a local. A moment later he emerged in a similar Tux and stood beside me, where we proceeded to look at each other in the mirror. Holy fucking small worlds! I instantly recognized the man, for it was Mr. Friendly from the plane. He held his gaze on me as he scrutinized my face, and I realized that his drunken state had probably made his memory of that incident a bit hazy.

"Excuse me, but have we met?" he asked.

"Afraid not, my friend, so it's probably just a matter of all of us infidels looking alike," I said, trying to make a little joke.

He didn't exactly smile or laugh, but he at least turned his attention back to checking himself out in the mirror. Still, he kept throwing me the occasional glance, so it was probably about time to pay for my shit and make a hasty retreat from the store before he recognized me. Asma had said he was a powerful man in the Emirates, and, considering I was already on somebody's shit list, there was no need to make any more enemies. I bid him farewell, changed out of my tuxedo, and dashed to the front counter, where I slapped my credit card down in front of my saleswoman. She smiled, ran the card, and told me she would have the alterations completed and the tux delivered to my hotel by four o'clock this afternoon. I signed the sales slip, added a nice tip, then joined Bill, who was a short distance away looking at some grey dress slacks.

"Ready to go?" he asked.

"Yeah, and the sooner the better," I said.

"What's the hurry?" he asked, looking concerned.

"Well, I had a little trouble on the plane with the Sheikh over there, but luckily he was pretty drunk, so he's having a hard time remembering me. Unfortunately, that might all change any second, so it's probably a good time to get the fuck out of here."

Bill glanced over into the dressing room area and looked alarmed.

"Oh shit! That's Sheikh Emir—first cousin to the monarch of Dubai. What the hell kind of trouble did you have with him?"

"As I said, he was drunk, but the main problem was that he ended up getting a bit inappropriate with Olivia. The two of them got into a scuffle, and he pulled out a fucking ceremonial blade, so I put him in a Jujitsu hold until the Sky Marshal arrived."

"Oh shit! We've got to get the hell out of here. He is not someone to fuck with. Guys like him can make guys like us disappear very easily in this part of the world," he said, gravely.

Shit, Asma had said he was important, but I didn't know he was actually related to the Royal family. Bill and I hurried out of the store and tried to blend in with the crowd of shoppers, but Sheikh Emir came running out behind us a second later.

"You! You son of bitch! I remember you now! I will find you and castrate you like a goat!" he yelled across the throngs of shoppers.

I smiled and waved, but it was to no avail for, even a hundred feet away, Emir's anger burned as brightly as the sun.

"You always this good at finding trouble?" Bill asked.

"Apparently, but I like to think it's the other way around. Trouble finds me."

We moved to the opposite side of the mall to find a shoe store, as I now needed new dress shoes to go with the tux. The salesperson, a middle aged portly fellow, probably of Indian decent, steered me towards the usual patent leather, but I refrained, as I preferred comfort over tradition, and that meant Ecco's — my favorite shoes. Established in 1963 by Karl Toosbuy in the small town of Bredebro in southern Denmark, Ecco was built on the philosophy that shoes must follow the foot, and indeed they did. They were also built to last, and my first pair of Ecco's were with me through college, the Air Force, and well into the current day, where their semi-retirement was a quiet life on the shoe rack in my closet. I've since added many more Ecco siblings to my little shoe family and have yet to regret a single purchase.

Today, I picked a fancier looking pair with shiny leather and a squared off toe that would offset the tux nicely and allow me the comfort and convenience of a more utilitarian rubber sole design. In my line of work, I never knew when I might need to run, jump, or operate a vehicle, so my shoes needed to man up to any occasion. I handed over my card, signed the sales slip, and we headed out and decided to go to one of the most audacious Starbucks I had ever seen. It had the customary counter and assortment of comfy chairs scattered across the floor, but the walls around it were at least a hundred feet high and culminated at a domed ceiling intricately decorated with a mosaic of blue, brown, and red tiles. I turned my attention back down to the counter and grabbed my grande coffee then added cream and sat next to Bill, who was already sipping his tall black coffee.

"Wow, quite a mall," I said.

"Yeah, everything here is like Disneyland times a hundred."

"Even the bathrooms?"

"Especially the bathrooms. Speaking of which, I need to hit the head after this coffee hits me."

"One or two?"

"Both."

"So, you don't mind using public restrooms?"

"Hell no. After my time in the service, I could shit in a shoe box."

"Well, I could shit in a shoe box—if it were in my bathroom back home, but these days, I do my very best to avoid public restrooms when I'm out and about."

Bill finished his coffee, excused himself, and headed to the restroom while I looked around the nearby tables and found a discarded tabloid magazine. Unfortunately, spoiled heiresses, actors, and reality stars were the only thing filling its sordid pages, so I decided instead to people watch. Around me flowed a great sea of shoppers, the majority of whom, I assumed were tourists, while the minority appeared to be locals. I saw one particularly large group of Arabic women and children and suspected they might all be part of the same household. I found the idea of multiple wives to be such a strange custom and wondered how women in this part of the world accepted such an inequity.

I suppose if you do anything long enough, you'll eventually accept your fate, whether it's living a mundane life in suburbia, or being with your husband, his seven other wives, and your army of children.

Fifteen more minutes and about two hundred and fifty shoppers later, I was starting to wonder what was taking Bill so long. I didn't see him grab any reading material, but it was possible he was screwing around with his smart phone. Not everyone knew that a proper dump needed to be properly timed. Too short and you left some trains in the tunnel while too long meant the risk of developing hemorrhoids. You had to find that sweet spot but, right now, Bill was just a few minutes shy of developing some painful new friends on his back door. Feeling a little concerned, I finished my coffee and decided to take a piss and check on my new friend.

I zigzagged through the tide of endless people and felt as though I was fording a human river until I at last reached the entryway to the restrooms. There were two large ornate corridors, and the one on the left led to the women's restroom while the one on the right led to the men's. I went right and followed it for about twenty feet before turning the corner and finding a stern faced, burly Arabic man standing in front of the bathroom door. As I drew closer and moved to walk around him, he stepped into my path and held up his hand.

"Restroom is closed," he said, in accented English.

"That's strange, because my friend is in there taking a

shit."

"No, you are mistaken."

I was getting a bad feeling, and suddenly my thoughts returned to the cleaning woman's untimely interruption of my morning dump. Clearly, our accidental interaction had inadvertently set in motion some very unfortunate mojo.

"Look, potty guard, I really need to pee and check on my friend."

"Go somewhere else. Bathroom is closed."

I had a closer look at the man and noticed that he was dressed in a nice suit and didn't exactly look like a janitor or bathroom attendant. Of course, this was the UAE, so it was possible they had different uniforms than we had back in the states.

"Aren't you a little overdressed for bathroom duty?" I asked.

"No, now fuck off."

"Wow, and rude too. Anybody ever tell you that you're likely the worst bathroom attendant of all time?"

As he stood there glowering at me, I heard some kind of muffled grunt, and I took it to mean that something sinister was clearly happening in the bathroom. I started to push past the potty guard, but he reached out and shoved me back.

"Leave while you still can," he growled.

I guess it was time to test his resolve.

"Honestly, you're taking this whole potty guard thing way too seriously, so I'm thinking you might need a job with less stress and more joy. Have you ever thought about working at a petting zoo?"

"No."

"Ahhh—I get it. I'm sensing a bit of a beastiality vibe from you, so you're worried you might get a little handsy with the animals."

His face flushed with color, and he grabbed a hold of my shirt and started pushing me backward, which was actually a good thing because I had his hands exactly where I wanted them.

"I could totally see you going balls deep and fucking the stuffing out of a little pink pig—which, needless to say, would be inordinately cruel to the pig."

He clenched his teeth as he looked at me, his mind lost in thought as he tried to register what the hell I had just said. It sounded like mean spirited gibberish, but it was a purposeful blend of profanity, color, and alliteration meant to send my would-be adversary's mind into a temporary holding pattern. Say a color and a person's mind instantly pictured the color. Then add a little alliteration such as pink pigs, and you doubled the effect. Finally, sprinkle on a little profanity, the word fuck for instance, and you just bought yourself a nice little window of opportunity. It was basically a more sophisticated way of telling someone that his shoelace was untied.

With his mind otherwise engaged, I used my left hand to trap both of his arms to my chest then started into a series of four consecutive strikes, which purposefully utilized both upper and lower body targets in order to discombobulate the mind of the attacker, and, more or less, drop his ass. Step one was to throw a short right punch straight into his solar plexus. He gasped and lurched forward, setting him up for a left chop to the throat, then a low right punch to his groin, and finally a final left vertical palm to his face. All four strikes were delivered in about a half of a second, and it left the potty guard so weak that he collapsed into my arms, struggling for breath and on the verge of passing out. Martial arts techniques were often about brain over brawn and learning to maximize force and pinpoint targeting. A punch or kick was useless if it didn't impact the correct spot, and my burly potty guard friend had just learned that lesson the hard way. He was big, but even big guys went down when you hit the right spots in the right order. Nerves, arteries, airways, and balls were always vulnerable, and I had just hit all four. Now, he was as docile as a lamb as I crossed my arms and reached in and grabbed the collar of his suit jacket then rolled back my fists until the material tightened and cut off the blood flow to his brain. His eyes closed and he passed out, thus allowing me to lay him on the floor to take a nice late morning nap.

I moved past him and on into the bathroom to see two guys. One was holding Bill against the wall, and the other was standing back a few feet, brandishing a pistol, and asking the questions. All of them looked as though they had been in a scuffle, but Bill looked the worst and had blood seeping from his nose and mouth. He glanced my way and a semblance of a smile formed on his lips as we exchanged a little non-verbal communication. He knew I was about to take out the gunman, which meant he was free to take care of the other asshole.

I slipped quietly across the floor to within arms reach of potty guard two and noticed that he was carrying a Beretta 92 but still had the safety engaged. Clearly, it was more of a psychological show, and that would make my job a lot easier, as I could now operate without the possibility of an accidental discharge hitting Bill—or me for that matter. Still, it was a firearm only a thumb flick away from becoming a deadly weapon, so I needed to disarm the prick. I reached around the gunman's right side, grabbed the pistol with both of my hands, and wrenched it up and back towards me. It broke his trigger finger and practically dislocated his shoulder as he was jerked backward onto his ass. At that point I easily pulled the gun free and used it as a club to hit the side of his neck, which traumatized the barrow receptors in the carotid artery and knocked him out cold. It probably seemed a bit harsh, but that's what happened when you pointed guns at my friends.

"Look out!" Bill yelled.

Potty guard number three had gotten free of Bill and was moving in my direction, so it was a matter of utilizing my longest weapon—namely, a kick—either front, side, or back. In the movies, you always saw the hero do a fancy pants high spinning kick to the bad guy's head, but that was just a bunch of flashy Hollywood horse shit. The foot should never really go any higher than your waist or you lost precious balance and put yourself in unnecessary peril. High kicks were therefore only used for practice, movies, blind people, and drunks, but my attacker met none of the aforementioned criteria. Still, I decided to get a little fancy, and, when he was only a step away, I set about performing a right spinning back kick. I sighted my target over my left shoulder to time his arrival then quickly rotated clockwise, twisting and delivering what most people would agree is the most powerful kick in the martial arts arsenal. It landed square in his midsection and stopped him cold in his tracks, likely cracking a few ribs and possibly even his sternum in the process. He dropped to his knees and stared wide-eyed in shock as he tried to breathe. It gave Bill plenty of time to walk over, grab him by the scruff of the neck, and slam him headlong into the nearest urinal. It knocked him out, and Bill hit the flush button, thus submerging the man's beard in a swirling sea of urine and pubes.

"How was your dump?" I asked.

"I'm starting to give some real thought to what you said about public restrooms."

"Welcome to my world. How's your head? I don't like the look of all that blood."

"It's OK, I think, but you don't happen to have an identical twin standing next to you, do you?"

"Nope, just me. I better check you out."

I gave Bill a quick examination and found an ugly bleeding lump on the back of his head.

"Any dizziness, nausea, or ringing in the ears?"

"Yes, yes, and yes."

"Shit. I think you have a concussion. We better get you to a hospital. Any preference?"

"Yeah, Ted knows where to go."

I helped Bill get to the car, and we bid a not too fond farewell to the Mall of the Emirates, thankfully having no more contact with the very cranky Sheikh Emir or any more of the tenacious potty guards.

"So, what exactly happened back there?" I asked.

"I had just finished up on the toilet and was washing my hands when they jumped me. It's a little hazy after that, and all I remember is that they kept asking about you."

"I didn't know I was that popular in Dubai."

"Yeah, perhaps we shouldn't be spending so much time together. It's bad for my health."

"Yeah, I'm sorry about that. I have a feeling those assholes decided to go after you when they couldn't get to me, but, on the bright side, I'll hopefully be out of your hair tonight."

Ted took Bill to an emergency care clinic for expats then dropped me back at my hotel, where I swung by the cafe in the lobby and grabbed a quick lunch before returning to my room. I relaxed on the couch, put my feet up on the coffee table, and stared out at the view, taking some quality time to reflect and think about recent events. In the course of a week, I had nearly been run off a cliff in my car, survived a crash landing in a jumbo jet, and now, seemed to bring violence and chaos to all I encountered. Fuck, regardless of what Matheson and Vandenberg believed, there was definitely something awry within the Topless Agenda and its plan. Oh well, only time would tell, so I decided to follow the age old special operations adage that you slept when you could. To that end, I closed my eyes and drifted off into an afternoon nap, ever hopeful that my subconscious might find some order in the chaos.

I awoke an hour and a half later to the sound of my room phone buzzing, and I answered it to learn that my tuxedo had been delivered to the front desk, and they would be sending it up to me shortly. I made a cappuccino while I waited, and, five minutes later, a valet was handing me a garment bag with a Dolce & Gabbana logo. I tipped the guy then walked upstairs to the bedroom for a quick dump and a shower. First, and most importantly, I took a sip of my cappuccino then settled onto the toilet, hopeful to make up for the *dumpus interruptus* I'd suffered earlier in the day. Thankfully, I spent the next several minutes alone with nothing but my thoughts to fill the void, and, not too surprisingly, I kept thinking about the Topless Agenda and whether or not one of them would be crazy or stupid enough to break free and challenge the group. None of the members were either crazy or stupid, so it stood to reason that the threat was external, but, again, who would know about them, let alone go up against people with their kind of power.

I finished my coffee, flushed, and stepped into the shower of showers, and let the five powerful showerheads pummel my body from head to toe with gloriously hot water. I applied shampoo to my hair then soaped up, all the while smiling to myself as I thought about all the awesome shower sex I'd been having as of late. Life really seemed to flow like an experiential sine wave with its various ups and downs, and, right now, I was happy to be riding the current peak of sexual activity for as long as it lasted.

Clean and alone, I dried off and put on all the amenities of civilized society before stepping into my room to get dressed. I started with undergarments then moved on to the other stuff like pants, shirt, and most important of all, my shoulder holster and pistol. A man in my position needed to be prepared, especially when he was about to steal the golden goose from the guys who had all the gold. My final step was to slip on my jacket then step in front of the mirror and pull out my gun and assume the most classic of James Bond poses. There was nothing quite as self-esteem boosting as a proper fitting tuxedo, and now I was officially dressed to kill, both literally and figuratively.

"The name's Finn, Tag Finn, and it's time to lock up your daughters," I said.

I holstered my pistol then made another turn in front of the mirror to be sure that the gun didn't show under the jacket. Satisfied, I headed downstairs to make a martini and wait for my ride. I went to the bar and added the requisite vodka and vermouth before taking a seat over by the window, where I could enjoy the scenic view of Dubai. It was reaching the end of the day, and the high-rise buildings were glowing in the remnants of the late afternoon sun. Minutes passed, and, as darkness filled the land, the lights of the city flickered on and officially brought Dubai's nightlife alive. As I finished my martini, my phone buzzed, and I picked it up to hear a woman's voice.

"Mr. Finn, your ride is here," she said.

"Thank you. I'll be right down."

I left my room and headed for the elevator feeling ever excited to see my new friend Olivia and, hopefully, my old friend Farid.

CHAPTER NINETEEN
Boys Will be Boys

The car at the entrance of the hotel was a white Mercedes Maybach 62S, and the first and only time I had ever ridden in one was last week on my way to the Topless Agenda's meeting in Majorca Spain. Maybach was a privately owned German company in the old days but now was owned by Daimler and, therefore, more of a glorified Mercedes meant to compete with Rolls Royce and Bentley in the luxury car market. Sadly, the brand was now merged into the parent company as an extreme high end edition called the Mercedes-Maybach, so this meant it might be one of the few rides I'd ever take in a pure version of this showcase of German craftsmanship.

The driver, a clean cut, well-dressed Arabic man, waited patiently at the rear of the car, and, as I approached, he nodded and opened the door at the very last minute to be sure that the rear compartment remained cool and comfortable for his passenger. I slipped inside and sat down while he closed the door and walked around to the front. For a fleeting moment, I wondered if he might be an impostor, and this was all just a very expensive trap, as this was usually the part in a James Bond movie where the car doors locked and Bond found himself imprisoned and unable to escape. To assail my fears I reached over and rolled down the window a crack, and was relieved that, for the moment at least, I could still find a way out of the car. I therefore relaxed and settled back into the luxurious seat to enjoy yet another drive through the formidable city of Dubai.

Olivia was staying at the Ritz-Carlton, which resided about fifteen miles northeast of my hotel. There was still plenty of traffic at this time of day, but riding in the cool comfort of the Maybach made it a fairly civilized and particularly pleasurable drive. About twenty minutes later, we pulled up in front of the Ritz-Carlton, and the driver, as he had with me, stepped out to open the door for Olivia. I also stepped out to properly greet my date and, upon seeing her, felt the need to reach down and adjust my penis, which was already starting to swell and strain against the fabric of my pants. Sweet burning fire in my loins! She was looking utterly stunning with her long blond hair blown out and her beautiful face accented with some sultry eye shadow and a deep red lipstick. The journey of my eyes was far from over, however, for just below, resided her ample cleavage, which bulged from the top of her tight black dress and told the tale of her curvaceous figure in the kind of exacting detail that would surely haunt my dreams for many a lonely night to come.

"You're looking so absolutely beautiful that I'm thinking I should maintain a six foot safety radius because ejaculation is a clear and present danger."

"Well, thank you, Tag, and might I say that you're also looking orgasmically divine this evening."

"You mean for a somewhat attractive, though unlikable, shitbag?" I asked.

She smiled and looked ever so slightly embarrassed.

"Yeah, pretty much, and, for the record, I only called you somewhat attractive to keep you humble."

"There's no need. That's what high school was for. Now, Cinderella, shall we enter the carriage and head to the ball?" I asked, gesturing towards the door.

She climbed inside, and I followed and took a seat beside her, and we held hands and smiled at each other like silly teenagers on their way to their first prom.

"So far, I'd say our third date is going pretty well," I said.

"Yeah, and let's hope it ends as well as the last one."

The driver returned to his seat, and soon we were heading northeast up the coast of Dubai.

"So, Tag, do you know very much about the UAE?" Olivia asked.

"Some, but I'm always eager to learn more," I said.

"Well then, let me be your tour guide for the drive, and hopefully I'll have some unusual facts for you about this place. Now, I assume you know that the Burj Khalifa is the highest building in the world?"

"I do."

"Well, did you know that it is so tall that its residents from the eightieth floor and higher need to wait longer to break their fasts during Ramadan because the sun is still visible?"

"I didn't know that, but it makes sense."

"OK, now here's a weird one. Dubai has no address system, no zip codes, no area codes, and no postal system, so mail has to go to PO boxes, and home deliveries use landmarks such as supermarkets or gas station as reference points."

"That probably doesn't do a lot for internet sales."

"Definitely not, but it would explain why they have the biggest mall in the world."

Olivia continued her talk, telling me about the various landmarks, including the theme park Dubailand which was going to be twice the size of Disneyworld in Florida, and would supposedly be the most popular tourist destination by 2020. Eventually, our journey took us inland, traveling another ten miles before passing the University of Sharjah and turning left at a roundabout onto the street that led to the official entrance of the Royal Palace. Our final turn was a right onto an opulent tree lined street that took us to a gatehouse manned by serious looking men in uniforms. The driver showed them a document, then we continued on up a gradual hill and past a towering obelisk to at last see the Royal Palace. It was a square three-story structure which demonstrated some fine Islamic architectural style with its onion domes on the roof and wrap around ledges that added texture to its upper levels. The immediate grounds were of course ornately landscaped with lush lawns and greenery, and it helped make the building stand out in stark contrast from the surrounding desert—which was obviously the point. Of course, I had to wonder why the palace was inland and away from the beautiful seaside, but I suppose they would simply reroute the ocean here should the desire for an oceanfront view ever arise. It must be nice to be a member of the Dubai Royal Family, where neither the sea nor sky could limit their dreams and aspirations. I turned my attention to the line of cars waiting to drop off their passengers and suddenly felt a moment of panic as I contemplated what kind of security they would have at the main door.

"Will they have metal detectors at the entrance to the Royal Palace?" I asked Olivia.

"Doubtful. Too many of the locals carry ceremonial daggers and all number of weapons, and it would be insulting to have them check them at the door. Why do you ask?"

I slid open my jacket and revealed my pistol.

"Don't worry your pretty little head, Mr. Bond. I think you'll be OK."

Upon hearing Olivia's words, I relaxed—a little. Our car was third in line behind a green Rolls Royce and two Bentleys, one sky blue and the other black. Their prestigious passengers disembarked, and we at last reached the front of the line, where a well-dressed man opened our door and welcomed us to the Royal Palace of Dubai. We walked up the short stairs and entered what would be my first royal ball, and, true to Olivia's prediction, there were no metal detectors. We made it past the official greeters and were soon in the palace, where the sound of classical music, clinking champagne glasses, and the low murmur of a multitude of conversations filled the air. I did a quick reconnaissance and pinpointed my first and most important stop—namely, the bar, but, before we could reach it, one of Olivia's coworkers, most likely a fellow lawyer, appeared at her side and did his best to sound suave and important as he chatted her up. He was about my height and weight and looked like your typical San Francisco professional with his purposeful hipster five o'clock shadow. He was good looking, fit, and probably seemed like a catch by all accounts, but there was no adequate facade to cover an ugly personality except perhaps silence—and he wasn't exactly the silent type. In only five words, I already had a clear picture of his over inflated sense of self and corresponding insecurity. What kind of asshole opens up a dialog with the words how good do I look? He didn't even say hello or tell her how good she looked. Not surprisingly, Mr. Charming took an instant dislike to me and smiled smugly as he put his arm around Olivia's waist. That was offensive enough, but he took it one step further by sliding his hand down until it was perched directly on her buttocks. It was a dick guy move to try and claim a woman as territory, and it made me think he might be one of the elite cadre of jackass coworkers who were eagerly awaiting their chance to bone her if, and when, she became single. Fortunately, Olivia wasn't having any of it and very politely moved his hand away. Mr. Charming tried to recover his dignity by flagging down a nearby waiter and grabbing a glass of Champagne off his tray before holding it up to toast.

"To Olivia! The hottest lawyer in the firm," he said.

He had at least complimented her in his own lame-ass way but also managed to forget the most fundamental rule of being a gentleman—namely, ladies first. I grabbed two glasses and handed one to Olivia before holding mine up to toast.

"To Olivia! Clearly the *brightest* lawyer in the firm," I said.

"Thank you, Tag. A woman likes to be appreciated for more than just her looks."

Mr. Charming didn't like that one bit and gave me a purposeful sneer, which, unfortunately for him, brought me a lovely little pang of joy. Olivia, sensing the obvious discomfort in the air decided it might help if she made some official introductions.

"Tag, this is Doug, one of my very *special* coworkers," she said, thereby confirming my earlier suspicion that he was indeed one of the elite cadre of jackasses.

"Nice to meet you. What do you do?" he asked rather curtly.

We reached out and shook hands, and as expected, he clamped down like a vice. Assholes like Doug used handshakes as a way to determine their alpha male status, and responding to it usually required applying pressure to the median nerve, but this time I used my brain instead of my brawn.

"I'm a proctologist," I said, as sincerely as I could.

I wasn't entirely sure he believed me, but he instantly loosened his grip and released my hand. Unfortunately, Olivia laughed, so it became obvious I was joking. At that point he smiled and did his best to avoid looking stupid.

"I see. It was a joke. Funny," he said.

"Yeah, Tag is actually a comedian," Olivia said, with a knowing smile before excusing us from Doug to go make some more introductions.

When we were clear she leaned in close and spoke.

"Seriously now—proctologist?" she asked with a smile.

"Well—he is an asshole."

Doug obviously held a serious torch for Olivia, which meant he probably hated me, and I was thus far doing nothing to win friends and influence people. But, next on the itinerary was Olivia's boss, and I hoped to make a better impression. He was an imposing figure, good looking, tall, and in excellent shape with the only trait belying his middle age status being his thinning hair. He appeared to accept his fate, however, by keeping the sides neatly trimmed, a fact which instantly made me respect him even more. He, unlike Doug, had real intelligence behind his discerning blue eyes, and he used them to appraise me for a fairly long, almost uncomfortable moment before smiling and offering his hand.

"I'm Tom Richards, nice to meet you."

"I'm Tag Finn, congratulations on finishing up your negotiations here."

"Thanks, it's been a long haul, but our team, especially Olivia here, finally got it done."

"Time to celebrate," I said.

"Yes, it is! So, Tag, what brings you here?" he asked.

"Oh, well—technically, Olivia."

"No, not this party. I mean Dubai," he said.

Tom seemed like a good guy and was obviously protective of Olivia, though not in the same way as Doug. His behavior was more indicative of a caring mentor, so he was just curious about the man with whom she chose to keep company.

"Work, actually. I'm a private investigator."

"Interesting, and your work brought you all the way over here?"

"Sure did."

"Is it an exciting case?"

I had to smile as I thought about all that I'd experienced thus far.

"The majority of my cases can be a little mundane, but this one might just be a little too exciting, unfortunately."

"Well—you look like the kind of guy who can handle it."

"Actually, I do my best to follow the path of least resistance."

"Tag's just trying to be modest, but, in reality, he's a bit of a badass," Olivia said.

"Oh really?" Tom asked, sounding intrigued.

"Yeah, in fact he saved me from a drunken lunatic who tried to attack me with a knife on the flight over."

"Seriously?" Tom asked, looking concerned.

"Yeah," Olivia said.

"Wait, how the hell did he get a knife onto the plane?"

"He was fairly important, so he apparently got to keep his ceremonial dagger on him."

"Jesus! And he threatened you with it?" he asked Olivia.

"Yeah, but Tag stepped in and took him down without even getting a scratch."

"I'm impressed!"

"Don't be, he was too drunk to put up much of a fight."

"Hardly! You were amazing!" Olivia said, gushing.

Tom looked at me with sincere gratitude in his eyes.

"Tag, I believe I owe you a sincere thank you for keeping one of our best attorneys alive and well."

"In reality, I was probably saving his ass, considering Olivia had already loosened him up with a brutal front kick."

He laughed.

"I've seen her hit a heavy bag, so you're probably correct," Tom said, patting her on the back.

He turned his attention back to me.

"So, do you have a law enforcement, military, or government background?"

Tom was obviously a particularly perceptive person, but then a good attorney needed that trait, especially in the courtroom or during contract negotiations, where being able to get a read on a witness or the opposing council could often determine the difference between failure or success.

"The latter two," I responded.

"Me too—well the military part, anyway, though I did it after undergrad and before law school."

"I had a similar career path, but I went college, military, and then the government before beginning my illustrious current career."

"And by government I'm assuming you worked for the Agency you can't legally acknowledge working for?" he asked.

"I could say no, but I'm guessing you'd probably figure out I was lying."

Olivia was eying me curiously.

"I should have known that you were James Bond when I saw you drinking that martini at the bar," she said, as she smiled and pinched my arm.

"Hardly, I'm obviously his less dashing American counterpart who almost never had the right opening line when meeting a beautiful stranger on a plane."

"Oh, you didn't do that bad, considering you're here now," she countered.

"I guess you've forgotten about the grass-fed comment?"

"No, but now I think it's actually funny."

We shared a little laugh, but Tom looked confused.

"Grass-fed?" he asked.

"Oh, it's a long story, so, what branch of the military were you in?" I asked Tom, hoping to change the subject.

"Army, and you?"

"Air force."

"Were you a pilot?"

"PJ."

"Oh, now I can understand how you ended up with your next employer."

"Why? What's a PJ?" Olivia asked.

"Parajumpers. They're the Air Force's elite special operations unit."

"Well, now it all makes sense," she said, with a smile.

At that moment, a man wearing a keffiyeh and a rather nicely fitting tuxedo walked up and joined us. He was around thirty, tall, good looking, and carried himself with an obvious air of authority.

"Good evening, Tom," he said, his voice belying a hint of an English accent that obviously came from having going to school in the United Kingdom.

"Good evening, Sheikh Hamza," Tom said, as they shook hands.

Sweet Lord, it was the man himself!

"How wonderful that we have finally reached an agreement in our negotiations and can finally celebrate," he said.

"Yes, and I'd like to introduce you to one of the people most responsible. This is Olivia, one of our most gifted attorneys," Tom said.

"It's nice to meet you," Olivia said.

"Oh, the pleasure is all mine," he said, as he took her hand and kissed it then gazed into her eyes.

He was definitely a ladies man.

"And this is my date, Tag Finn," she said, gesturing at me.

I stepped closer, and Hamza gazed over at me with an unusual look in his eyes that could have been surprise or disdain, or perhaps both.

"It's nice to meet you, Mr. Finn," he said, smiling, though his tone was oddly ominous as he held out his hand to shake.

"And you as well," I said, as I reached out and took his hand.

We shared a moment of eye contact as we shook hands that felt like an unspoken challenge, but it might have just meant that he was interested in my date, considering Olivia was by far the most beautiful woman at the palace this evening. We completed the gesture, and he stood back and appraised me.

"What brings you to Dubai? Business or pleasure?" he asked.

"At the moment, I'd say both."

"Well, hopefully you'll have more of the latter, now, if you'll please excuse me, I have some people that I would like Tom to meet," he said.

They moved on, and I noticed Olivia staring at me with a curious look on her face.

"What's up?" I asked.

"Is it me, or was there a little underlying tension between you two?"

"Hard to say for sure, but, if there were, it was likely because he was interested in my date."

"Maybe, but it seemed as though he might have been more interested in you."

"Well, I am a people person."

"That, you are," she said, as she led me off to the food table.

It was crowded, but we managed to work our way through the herd of grazing people to fill our plates with sliced filet mignon, steamed spinach, and a cheesy potato dish. Food in hand, we found a quiet table off on the periphery, where we could eat in relative peace.

"So, I should warn you. I'm actually on the job right now and might have to make a hasty exit if I find the person I'm looking for here," I said.

"That's too bad, as I was hoping we might have a chance to spend some more time exploring your theories on female sexual gratification."

"Believe me, I sincerely hope that's the case, as I'm already sporting an early evening semi in anticipation."

"Oh, I'm sure you're just saying that to try and make me feel better."

"No, and if you don't believe me, you can handle my ham and see for yourself."

"I will," she said.

She reached under the table and took a firm hold of my privates.

"You weren't kidding!" she said.

"Nope, that fucker is legit."

"Maybe I need to make sure you know what you'll be missing," she said, as she began running her hand over my manhood, which was starting to strain against the fabric of my pants.

Sweet mother of God. She wasn't fucking around and was pretty much delivering an over-the-pants handjob. A lustful euphoria soon overtook my senses, and I found my gaze drifting aimlessly across the nearby tables until my eyes inadvertently set upon Doug. He was watching our exchange, and his angle was such that he probably had a bird's eye view of our little indiscretion beneath the table. Lovely. Now he would surely be even more pissed off. Oh well, fuck it. I decided to ignore Mr. Charming and turned my attention back to Olivia, who actually was charming, so charming, in fact, that she was mere seconds from charming the semen right out of my balls.

"So, all that's for me?" she asked.

"Every last inch."

Both of our attention was suddenly drawn to Olivia's boss, who walked up to our table at that very moment. Olivia immediately removed her hand from my happy place and smiled innocently.

"Hi, Tom! What's up?" she asked.

I was tempted to say me, but I stayed quiet while I did some deep breathing exercises to relieve the tension in my pants.

"I'm sorry to interrupt, but I would like to introduce Olivia to some people. Do you mind, Tag?"

"No problem. Business before pleasure," I said.

She stood up and accompanied her boss across the room to a table full of distinguished looking gentleman while I used the time to finish up the delicious filet mignon and scan the crowd, curious if I could find Farid. On first glance, there was no sign of my old friend, but I did make eye contact with Doug once again and saw that he and a group of other young lawyers were now drinking shots, talking, and looking menacingly in my direction. As a keen observer of human behavior, I could tell that they saw me as a stray lion who was moving in on a member of their pride, but I decided to ignore them and turned my attention to my task. Unfortunately, I only managed about four minutes and twenty-eight seconds before Doug and two of his jackass friends were hovering over my table, where they were obviously bonding over booze, bravado, and the desire to bone Olivia.

This was very likely the entirety of the elite cadre of jackasses, and now I was all alone to enjoy their company. Doug, of course, was standing in the middle of the group with his loyal comrades spread out on either side—the three of them creating a virtual wall of jackasses. The jackass on the left was the biggest and very likely a former football player, judging by his six foot plus height and substantial body mass. His problem, however, was that he stopped playing the game a long time ago but kept eating the same amount of food, and, now, what was once muscle, was looking to be mostly fat. The jackass on the right looked to be fit but had the demeanor of those wannabe weekend warrior types who organized men's only getaways, where guys did ridiculously manly things in the company of other men. In my opinion, a truly manly vacation included women.

"OK, let's face it. I can't dance with all three of you at once, so we're going to have to take turns," I said.

"We're not here to dance, asshole."

"A boy can always dream."

"Joke's over. We need to talk."

"OK, what do you want to talk about?"

"Olivia."

"Well, unfortunately she's not here at the moment, and it doesn't seem very nice to talk about her behind her back."

"Listen up, asshole! We just happen to be good friends with Olivia's boyfriend back home, so we see it as our job to make sure that pricks like you don't go sticking your dick where it doesn't belong."

"I must say, counselor, that your line of reasoning seems a little hypocritical, considering you were just playing grab-ass with the plaintiff's girlfriend."

"Fuck you! I wasn't playing grab-ass."

"Oh, so that was your evil twin's hand on Olivia's ass. Maybe you could call him over, so we could have a talk with him instead."

Doug slammed his hand on the table causing all the dishes and silverware to make a loud clattering noise that evoked several curious looks from nearby tables. For a guy on a covert mission, I was not being very covert at the moment.

"Clearly you need to take it down a notch, so why don't we all just relax, put on our big boy pants, and play nice," I said.

Doug was turning bright red and getting more angry with each passing second.

"Dude, why don't you get the fuck out of here before we throw you out," Doug said.

"What happened to my suggestion to play nice? Clearly you and the rest of Fight Club here need to take a look around and see that this isn't the time or place for anything as stupid as engaging in a little fisticuffs. If you assholes do anything to embarrass your firm or put this deal in jeopardy, then you can all say goodbye to your jobs and cushy overprivileged lives back in San Francisco, so, as it stands, nothing is going to happen, nor am I going to leave, and, now, if you'll excuse me, I have more pressing matters to attend to."

The Champagne had made its way to my bladder, and I really needed to pee, so I stood up, parted the sea of jackasses, and made my way through the crowd and over to the bathroom. Upon opening the door and stepping inside, I had to take a moment to pause and catch my breath. Holy sweet mother of porcelain kingdoms—it was a palace unto itself! It was spacious and gaudy and even had a little seating area and lounge at the entrance. I continued past the stately leather furniture and reached the most important part, the part where shit got done—literally. Here, the floors and countertops were done in a red onyx colored marble, while the individual stall walls were constructed of rich mahogany. The fixtures were made of hand blown glass, and, as expected, the place was impeccably clean from floor to ceiling. This was a bathroom truly befitting a royal behind and begged for a regal number two in spite of its semi-public designation. Unfortunately, I only had the goods for a number one, so I saddled up to a urinal and unleashed a torrent of sweet yellow bliss. Finished, I breathed a sigh of relief then sheathed my sword and headed for the sink to wash my hands. As I finished up and grabbed some paper towels, the door opened, and in walked the elite cadre of jackasses. Doug was in the lead, and he was smiling ever so cruelly as he walked closer.

"We followed your advice and got away from the crowd, so now I bet you're feeling a like a fool," Doug said.

"I don't know. Who is more foolish? The fool, or the fool that follows the fool?"

Doug gave each of his friends a look, then all three formed up around me.

"I don't think you get it, asshole. Judgement day is here."

"Oh, but I only see the three of you. Do have some other friends coming perhaps?"

"Do I really need to lay it out for you? Todd here was a

defensive lineman for Florida State. He eats guys like you for breakfast," Doug said.

Todd even had the gall to crack his knuckles and put on his best angry game face.

"Yeah, but I see he's also been out of the game awhile, and I'm guessing by his present girth that he's eaten way too many guys like me for breakfast. Honestly, it's about time he switched back to oatmeal."

Doug ignored my joke and proceeded to introduce jackass number three.

"And this badass is Jack. He does CrossFit," he said, placing the emphasis on the final T before clenching his teeth and leering at me.

Again, my summation had been correct and Jack was indeed fit, and he could do pull-ups and dead lifts until he suffered from rhabdomyolysis and ended up in the hospital with a bunch of other CrossFit dupes, but he'd never be any better in a fight.

"That's nice. Maybe he could roll an oversized truck tire out to the bar and get me another drink."

"I don't think you get it."

"Oh, I get it. You're trying to intimidate me with all this tough talk, but the way I see it, you jackasses are three of the biggest pussies I've ever met. I've spent my life around truly dangerous people, and let me tell you one thing they all have in common. They don't talk about kicking ass. They just do it."

"So let's do this," he said.

Seeing Doug's enthusiasm almost made me feel bad for him. Clearly, he was insecure, or he wouldn't have needed his two buddies along for backup—let alone been trying to engage in the most pointless fight of all time. Sadly, he was one of those all too plentiful assholes that spent his time terrorizing playgrounds, schools, and colleges until moving on to offices, bars, and nightclubs, all the while trying to build his self esteem on the belittlement of others. At some point, Doug and those like him hopefully learned the error of their ways through self enlightenment or, worse case scenario, by running headlong into the wall of reality—with reality being a bigger or tougher person just looking to give some asshole a beatdown. Right now, I was that wall.

"You, CrossFit. How much can you dead lift?"

"Two fifty—two sixty. Why?"

"I just wanted to make sure you could carry your friends here back to your hotel."

"Shut the fuck up and throw down," Doug said, angrily, before squaring off, moving back and forth on his feet, his hands up in front of him, obviously trying to look like a cage fighter.

"Honestly, I think saying throw down implies it's a fight, but a fight implies that more than one opponent is engaged in conflict, and the way I see it, neither you nor the other two jackasses are going to land a single punch. So, let's call it what it is. An exchange of knowledge—a learning exercise."

"Hey, asshole, I did a year of mixed martial arts in college," Doug said.

"Yeah, and Doug's never lost a fight. He's seriously gonna fuck you up. You should have left when you could," Jack, the CrossFit guy, said.

"Fucking A," Todd the football player added.

"So, I'm assuming all those lovely esteem building encounters were against smaller, weaker opponents who weren't even looking for a fight, yet you, being the consummate asshole, gave it to them. What a sad way to live, and, worse still, it's stupid, because you never know who is going to be your wall—your insurmountable obstacle that beats some desperately needed wisdom into your thick head. And what if I turned out to be that wall. I might be a lifelong martial artist and an ex-special operations soldier turned elite CIA operative who's just looking to teach three assholes a lesson. Of course, if you're lucky, I might just be a humble fragrance model, but the problem is you'll never know until it's too late."

All three took a moment to quietly appraise me.

"Yeah, I know. I can see in your eyes that you're starting to think about it, but the fact that I smell so good probably has you favoring the idea that I'm a fragrance model. Still, I should warn you, boys, that smells can be deceiving."

"Oh shut the fuck up! You're not going to talk your way out of this with a bunch of bullshit!"

"So, no guess as to my actual background?"

"I don't need to guess, because I know you're a fucking faggot."

"Interesting, have we taken it all the way down to disparaging remarks about sexual preference? And, if I'm indeed a faggot, then why are you three haters here to teach me a lesson for hanging out with your female friend? That would mean I was a fag-hag and, therefore, no threat. Honestly, this lack of reasoning on your part doesn't bode well for my faith in your abilities as attorneys."

"We're done talking, motherfucker!" Doug bellowed.

He came at me with an adequate, if not particularly powerful, right punch. By adequate, I mean it wasn't a big drunken roundhouse, and, instead, was a fairly straight jab. Doug had obviously done his year in MMA, and it made him feel pretty confident about his fighting abilities, so, the main life lesson tonight was going to be about philosophy as well as humility. I considered real martial arts to be about self defense and protecting you and your loved ones from actual harm. That meant fighting was about life and death, not sport or drunken party antics with your asshole friends. Doug, in walking into this bathroom, was seeking out conflict and, worse still, hoping to inflict bodily pain and injury on another person, and, needless to say, it didn't exactly paint a flowery picture of his deep inner psychological workings. Of course, the irony in all of this was that I was generally opposed to violence, yet had spent a fair portion of my life embroiled in conflict and had even had taken lives when the occasion arose, but I had only done so with the belief that my actions would save those around me, or, in some way, make the world a better place. Doug, on the other hand, used violence as a means to achieve respect and self esteem and, worse still, didn't even have the courage to do it alone.

So, as his drunken punch came in, I moved out of its path and extended my right hand to redirect his fist into my left hand so that I could transition into a fairly uncomfortable take down utilizing a variation of the figure four I had used on Sheikh Emir. With my right hand now free, I used it to lightly slap his face just for shock value, then moved it under his arm and shot it backward into his elbow joint in order to bend his forearm. From there, I took hold of his wrist with my right hand and leveraged it back until his shoulder reached its maximum stretch, thus allowing me to slip my foot behind his legs and take him down to the floor.

I decided to reposition him and barred his elbow across my knee to force him to roll over onto his stomach. He groused and groaned and obviously missed the deeper underlying reality that at any point I could have broken or dislocated a joint, but I was in teaching mode, and, therefore, being as gentle as a lamb. I stepped on his shoulder to pin his body to the floor while I kept his elbow firmly resting against my knee, all the while continuously varying the amount of pressure, so that his body wouldn't produce endorphins to counteract the pain. It was an experience I knew firsthand to be painful and demoralizing, and even more so in Doug's case, as he was experiencing it in front of his friends who thought he was a badass. Now, we were onto the humility part of the lesson.

"OK, boys and girls, I need everyone to just stand down, chill out, and relax. I'm serious. No one makes a single move. If either of you dumb fucks so much as farts, I'll break your friend Doug's arm, then come over there and break one of your arms. Questions?"

Both shook their head, relaying a unanimous no, but, as I was about to continue speaking, a tiny little high pitched fart squeaked out of someone's apparently tense butthole, and I immediately scrutinized Jack and Todd.

"It wasn't me!" they both responded at the exact same time.

"Then who was it?" I asked.

"Mew," I heard Doug mumble.

"Excuse me?" I asked.

"Mew!" Doug mumbled even louder, making me realize he couldn't properly say the word me with his face pressed against the marble floor.

"Ah, got it. All right then, Jack and Todd have been exonerated for the moment. Now, where was I?"

"Threatening to brake our arms," Jack said.

"Thanks. Now then, assuming there aren't any more fucking farts, I'd like to take a moment to impart some valuable wisdom before letting Doug go free."

Suddenly the door burst open, and Tom, Olivia's boss, walked in looking concerned.

"Is everyone OK?" he asked excitedly.

"Yeah, everyone's fine. What's up?" I asked innocently,

still holding Doug firmly in place.

"Olivia and I saw these three follow you in here, so she wanted me to make sure you didn't hurt them."

"No worry there, Tom. I was just giving the boys here a quick lesson in martial arts."

I applied a subtle twist to Doug's elbow and told him to tap when it hurt. He started tapping frantically, and I quickly released the pressure.

"Good job, next time we'll work on defending against combinations," I said, helping him up off the floor, where he stood with his bravado now replaced by embarrassment.

"It's awfully nice of you to work with these youngsters, Tag," Tom said.

"What can I say. I love helping the youth of today find their way."

"I can see that," he said, gazing at Doug.

Doug remained cowed, his eyes never looking any higher than his shoes. He was definitely embarrassed—as he should be. Fighting was incredibly immature and even more so at a work function that just happened to be at the Royal Palace where your company just made a lot of money. Tom was clearly not very pleased with his three young employees and addressed them in a rather stern tone.

"Now, I believe we all know the real reason you were in here, so let me speak frankly when I say that Tag was being unusually nice for a man with his background. You see, he was a member of one of the most elite special operations units in the United States Military and after that worked for another government agency which he can't legally mention—so, what you three all got tonight was a valuable life lesson to stop acting like a bunch of assholes, and, needless to say, we'll be talking about this later. Right now, I want all three of you to apologize to Mr. Finn," he said.

"Sorry," all three mumbled, sounding more like scolded children than adults.

"Good. Now leave and pray that you have a job in the morning."

The three filed out, but CrossFit, who was last in line, suddenly stopped and turned back to me, looking curious.

"Dude, is it true? Were you really in special operations and the CIA?" he asked.

"If I told you, I'd have to kill you, so let's just say I was a fragrance model."

Tom waited until they were gone before speaking.

"I'm very sorry, Tag. Obviously they're young and dumb."

"We all were at one time. It's not a problem, and what's a party without a little mischief?"

"Indeed."

We exited the restroom and found Olivia waiting nervously outside the door.

"Everything OK?" she asked.

"Fine, I was just engaging in a little harmless kitten play with your elite cadre of jackasses."

We parted ways with her boss and walked to the bar and ordered two martinis—Olivia's with an olive and mine with a twist. Two minutes later, we were sipping our delicious alcoholic beverages, but we opted to stay at the bar, because it afforded a better view of the party. We enjoyed our drinks and talked, and, a short time later, movement on the other side of the room caught my eye, and I looked over to see Farid talking to a pretty blond woman.

"Do you know him?" Olivia asked, having seen where I was looking.

"Yeah, he's an old friend and one of the side reasons for my visit here tonight."

"Well then, should we go say hello?"

"Unfortunately, it's something I should probably do alone, as I suspect he's going to shit his pants when he sees me, and it's unfair to make a lady witness such an indignity."

We continued to sip our drinks, and I watched and waited patiently for my opening to approach Farid. He finally said goodbye to the woman and headed up the stairs to the second level, so I excused myself from Olivia and followed him. As I arrived at the second floor, I saw him talking to a security man who was guarding the entrance to a private hallway. Farid flashed his ID then walked through the checkpoint and down the hall before disappearing around a corner. I tried to follow, but the guard put up his hand to block my way.

"VIP only," he said.

"Yeah, I know, my friend, Dr. Suleiman Zuhair, who just walked through here, told me to come meet him, as he had something he wanted to show me," I said, referring to Farid by his new alias.

"Oh, well do you have a palace VIP ID?"

"No, but I'm here for the party."

"Yes, and the party is out there. This area is VIP only," he said, curtly.

He wasn't much of a talker, so I realized it would be futile to continue the conversation. Instead, I took a moment to look around and noticed that there was a bathroom nearby that might provide access to the ledge that skirted the outside of the second floor of the palace. Assuming I could reach it, it would serve as an excellent alternative route around the stubborn doorman. I went inside the bathroom and was happy to find that it was comparable in size and amenities to its downstairs brethren and, more importantly, had an openable window. Perfect! I slid it open, but, as I was about to climb out, I heard the door open, so I played it cool and pretended to be enjoying the fresh air. As my visitor approached, I turned to see that he was wearing a keffiyeh, so he was probably local. He also had bronzed olive skin and the obligatory Middle Eastern beard, and, judging by his kind eyes and smile, was hopefully not going to cause any trouble.

"These parties can get a little stuffy. Sometimes even the hot air of the desert is relief from the hot air of our fellow guests," he said, taking up residence at one of the urinals.

Apparently, my summation was correct, and the man was indeed friendly and actually quite charming.

"I agree," I said, with a laugh.

"What brings you to the Palace tonight? Are you with

the American company?"

"No, I'm just accompanying someone from the company."

"So, you're here mostly for pleasure?"

"Mostly."

"Well, I'm not sure how long you're in the Emirates, but if you can, you should get out and visit the Liwa Oasis. It is a beautiful place and where I spend most of my time."

"Where is it?"

"Down on the southern end of the Emirates along the border with Saudi Arabia."

"Well, if I have time, I'll try and get down there."

"You won't regret it. The glamour of our coastal cities is exciting in a Disneyland kind of way, but we are a desert people at heart, and that is where you will find the true spirit of the Emirates."

"Thank you for the recommendation."

"You're welcome."

He finished up, washed his hands, and gave me a friendly nod as he exited the bathroom, finally allowing me the privacy to climb out the window and onto the ledge. I instinctively looked down and felt a brief twinge of vertigo. I wasn't exactly on a skyscraper, but a fall from this height was enough to break a few bones and perhaps even my neck. I was also a bit exposed, but I was fortunate that there wasn't a lot of lighting on this part of the building, thus allowing me to move along the ledge unseen. I was also particularly happy to have the grip of my rubber soled

Eccos to keep me from slipping and falling to my potential early demise. Thus, I continued safely on past the windows of dark empty rooms until reaching the corner, where I paused when I spied two security men on the ground level below me chatting as they made their rounds. Once they were out of sight, I continued around the corner to see light pouring out from of a window just a few rooms ahead.

I approached it cautiously, stopping before the edge of the frame, so I could lean in just enough to conduct a brief visual survey of the room. First into my field of view was Farid, who was standing on the right side of the room and appeared to be having some kind of casual conversation. To the left of him was a blond woman, but she was facing away from me, so all I could see, besides the back of her head, was her hand resting on the top of the sofa, and it stood out like a sore thumb because it was adorned with an extremely gaudy diamond encrusted bracelet. I leaned over a little more and realized that the next person was none other than Sheikh Hamza, and his presence made me suspect the woman was likely his latest model or actress girlfriend, and the bracelet was very likely a gift from the man himself. I slipped ever so slightly farther along the ledge and saw the final person in the room and nearly shit my pants.

To the left of Hamza was the Goddamn German fuck-ing tourist who'd tried to kill me back in California, which would imply that he was some kind of associate or employ-ee. At least now I knew why Hamza looked so surprised at our earlier meeting and also why he'd had such a challenging tone in his voice. I was the enemy, and now he had a real life face to go with the name. Shit, it was nice to finally have some clarity and start connecting the dots between the various bad guys, but it was a little unsettling to find out that we were up against such a powerful and influential asshole. Still, I had to wonder how this fucker even knew about the Topless Agenda and its latest plans, and, in turn, if one or even several of the members had turned against the others and joined forces with Hamza. If not, then that clever bastard had somehow found another way to penetrate the group. Now, I desperately needed to contact Matheson and tell him about this latest development, but that would have to wait, as I needed to get to Farid.

I leaned over and glanced back inside as I waited for them to finish their conversation, all the while desperately wishing I knew how to read lips. Unfortunately, the only word I had ever managed to recognize was fuck, and that was because it utilized the extremely obvious facial movement of having the top teeth practically bite the lower lip in order to form the hard F sound. None of the people happened to say fuck, so that left me sitting in the dark, both literally and figuratively, as to the content of the conversation on the other side of the glass.

The meeting finally came to an end, and Hamza, the kraut, and the woman left while Farid headed into the next room over. I continued along the ledge and saw the light turn on in the next room, and I stepped closer and peered inside to discover that it was an enormous private bathroom—and my old friend was sliding down his pants and dropping onto the toilet for a deuce. As I remembered, Farid was also not a big fan of public restrooms, which explained why he hung back to use this private commode. Lovely, that would make our meeting a little less pleasant, if not more personal, but at least he didn't have any compelling reading material, so he would hopefully keep the dump short and to the point. A few minutes passed, and he stood up, flushed, then went to the sink to wash his hands. With the sound of the running water masking my entrance, I climbed through the open window and waited for him to finish up before I spoke.

"Jesus, Farid, the years certainly haven't made your shit smell any better," I said.

He was so startled that he jumped backward and banged against the wall with his expression wavering somewhere between anger and shock, but, as recognition dawned, the hint of a smile formed on his lips.

"Tag Finn, you son of a bitch! I can't believe my eyes! What the hell are you doing here?"

"Well, actually..."

"Hey, wait a minute! That was you at the gym, wasn't it?" he asked, starting to walk towards me before suddenly stopping, his expression turning from excitement to fear.

"Oh no—fuck," he said, as he started to back towards the door.

"Farid! Wait! Relax! We need to talk!"

Suddenly it dawned on me why he was having such

an odd reaction. It was my final words to him that were now coming back to haunt me at this particular moment. That night on the Aegean Sea, before he stepped off the Gordita, I had warned him that if he ever saw me again, it meant that something had gone horribly wrong, and he needed to flee for his life.

"Wait! It's not what you think!" I said.

He opened the door and bolted from the room. Shit. Nothing in life is ever easy.

CHAPTER TWENTY
Are You There, God, it's Me, Tag

I chased after Farid, desperately hoping to reach him before he did anything crazy such as alerting the palace security, but, fortunately for me, he was running deeper into the private area of the palace and away from the checkpoint with the overly vigilant guard. I poured on the speed, but Farid was an athletic guy and maintained an even lead until coming across a set of locked double doors. With nowhere else to go, he went to the right through a different door and into a side room that turned out to be an access stairway for the help, and it descended into the kitchen, where I discovered scores of people cooking and cleaning like a hive of worker bees. There was no sign of Farid, but I looked down at a section of floor that had just been mopped and saw footprints. Bingo! I followed them until they ended at another door which accessed yet another stairway. I followed it down and emerged onto what was the basement floor of the palace. This level was inhabited entirely by what appeared to be off-work staff who milled about mostly uninterested in my presence. I suspected that my tuxedo gave me a certain degree of authority, and it was a clear indicator of the very real class structure that existed in the Emirates. Oddly, Arabs and native Emirates only made up about 39% of the population, which meant that the vast majority of the people working here, and this palace in particular, were poor immigrants and, therefore, basically indentured servants. I continued on and looked for any sign of Farid as I moved past offices, storage rooms, and walk-in freezers before arriving at what appeared to be an employee lounge. A young woman in traditional dress and a head scarf saw me and approached, all the while keeping her gaze downward and subservient as she spoke.

"Excuse me, sir. Can I help you?" she asked.

"I'm looking for my friend who just came down here a second ago."

She looked uncomfortable as though I had asked an indelicate question.

"Is there a problem?" I asked.

"No, sir."

"Well—have you seen my friend?"

I was experienced enough at reading people to know that she definitely knew who I was talking about and also probably knew exactly where he had gone.

"It's important that I find him."

She stared at me, looking conflicted. Obviously, she lived the life of an employee or, worse still, a servant and, therefore, took orders for a living, but, for some reason, perhaps the location of our conversation, she continued to remain silent.

My educational background was social psychology, so I was familiar with the fact that people had an innate tendency to become very attached and possessive of places or things that they visited or used regularly. One of the first examples of this was the desk you sat in at school. From the first day of class on, you would guard your little piece of real estate with your life, as its humble wood and steel structure were your home away from home. As adults it might become your parking space at work or a particular table at your local restaurant. For the woman in front of me, it was the basement of a palace. These people were at the beck and call of the upstairs elite, but down here I imagine they felt they had dominion, and now I was on their turf and therefore had to behave according to their rules.

"I promise you. He's a very dear old friend, and I desperately need to talk to him," I said.

The girl wasn't buying my story, so I decided I needed to throw in some interesting factoids for credibility.

"The man's name is Dr. Suleiman Zuhair, but his real name is Farid Ardeshir, and he's from Iran and would have arrived about five years ago. He's a brilliant nuclear physicist, and he has a thing for blond women with big boobs, but, more importantly, he gets terrible gas when he eats falafels."

The girl smiled.

"Everyone gets terrible gas when they eat falafels."

"Not like Farid."

"All right then. I'm going to trust that what you say is true, so come this way."

She looked around nervously then turned and led me to the back of the room, where she pulled aside a gold colored curtain to reveal a plain white steel door. She stepped aside and motioned me towards it, and I was suddenly feeling like Neo from The Matrix about to take the red pill and see how deep the rabbit hole goes. I opened it and stepped inside to find a dark hallway, and I could hear and smell more than I could see. I started walking, and exotic music and the scent of spicy Middle Eastern food was filling the air as I emerged into a large dimly lit chamber with people sitting, talking, playing games, and enjoying life. The wealthy people above must have forgotten about this lower area, and the help moved in to create a world free of their overlords.

I moved deeper into the vast room to find it was lit by small lamps that revealed a warren of life—a virtual hidden city beneath the palace above. Everywhere I looked, humanity in its purest form thrived, and the people here appeared content to enjoy each other's company and live solely in the simple pleasures of the moment. On my right sat a group of men playing cards while next to them a woman tended to her children. Past them was a group of young girls eating and talking amongst themselves. This place certainly felt far removed from the party upstairs but also—more comfortable, more real. The joys in life were often the simple things, the big three for most being food, folks, and fornication. These people, in spite of a life of servitude, had managed to create their own bubble of freedom, and it was a testament to the human spirit and stoicism in its most literal sense.

I continued on and looked for Farid amongst the many faces until I at last reached the far wall and found an open doorway with two men standing sentry. They were thin, olive skinned, and likely Indian, considering that Indians constituted about a third of the UAE's population. Both men stepped forward and blocked my path until a familiar voice called out from the room ahead.

"Let him pass, but keep an eye on him."

They stepped aside, and I walked through the doorway into a large, fairly crowded room to find Farid, who was thankfully looking a bit calmer.

"Goddammit, Farid! I know what I said five years ago, but I'm not here to kill you."

"Then why are you here?"

"Well, you're probably going to laugh, or possibly even cry, but the simple answer is that I'm here with an offer to bring you to America."

Farid laughed out loud.

"Oh really? And does the CIA have another old fishing boat waiting for us in a nearby harbor?"

"Definitely not."

"Then, I must say I'm feeling a little bit confused."

"I understand, as this time it's a little bit confusing, because I don't work for the CIA anymore. I followed your advice and got out."

"To do what?"

"I'm a private investigator."

"Seriously? Like *Magnum P.I.*?"

I laughed.

"When the hell did you watch that show?"

"Over the last few years, I've become addicted to watching classic nineteen eighties television shows online, and *Magnum P.I.* is one of my favorites, though now, I must say, I really want to go to Hawaii."

"I completely understand and get the same feeling every time I watch it, but, unfortunately, my life isn't quite so glamorous."

"So, no Ferrari?"

"No, I have a Subaru, and I live in Northern California, and, in case you're wondering, I don't reside on a wealthy writer's estate where I'm tormented by a British major-domo and his two Doberman pinschers. Instead, I live on a houseboat, and the only animal that torments me is my neighbor's morbidly obese cat Mr. Pickles."

"So, how in the hell did you end up here?"

"That's a hell of a question, and it has a hell of an answer. You see, I was living a nice quiet life until about a month ago when a very unique job brought me into the fold of an extremely powerful group of people. As it turned out, it was all a lead-up to yet another job—namely trying to persuade you to come to America."

"So, these people obviously want cold fusion," he said.

"Well, yeah, unless you've discovered something more exciting—like reusable toilet paper."

"That already exists—it's called your hand."

"Ahh—you've still got your sense of humor I see."

"Yeah, it's one of the few things I've managed to keep, thank God. So, who exactly are these powerful people?"

"Well, needless to say, they have nothing to do with the CIA or that debacle back in Istanbul, but they have serious wealth, power, and influence, so, this time, it's a completely different situation, because they don't just want cold fusion, they actually would like for you to join their little group."

"But why would I risk giving up the life I have here?"

"Excellent question, and, judging by what I'm seeing around me right now, I'd say the reason would be freedom. Real freedom."

"I see you haven't lost your keen intuition, because you are correct. I'm not free. Sure, I have expensive cars, a house, and money, but basically I am no different from the people you see around you right now—except perhaps that they actually stand a better chance of leaving this country," he said, sadly.

"And this place down here is a kind of sanctuary?"

"Exactly, and only one of a few places where we can

gather out of sight of the powers that be. Unfortunately, thousands of people are lured to the UAE every day with the belief that they will have a good job and a better life but end up as virtual slaves."

"So, it's a lot like America?"

He laughed.

"Not exactly. Here, only a rare few find prosperity or a better life. The vast majority end up like the people you see around you, but down here we have created a place where we can gather and create some degree of organization."

"And help each other return to your home countries?"

Farid smiled.

"Yes—but it's not easy. When the opportunity arises, we get the person, or persons tickets, passports, and some-times even help pay their debt—whatever's necessary to get them home. It's very much like your country's Underground Railroad with all of us being a contemporary multi-person version of Harriet Tubman."

"Except that you're stuck here—thanks to a few idiots in the CIA."

"Indeed. I'm afraid this is now my home."

I should have known that Farid would be doing some-thing like this. He was too good of a guy to live the life he did here without somehow giving back to those who were less fortunate. It was just like that car accident back in Iran, only these people didn't need to get pulled out of a burning car, they needed help getting out of a burning life.

"I'm happy to see you haven't changed," I said.

"And neither have you. Still playing the hero obviously—out rescuing people and bringing them safely home."

"All the more reason for you to come with me. I'm your ticket to freedom, my friend, so are you ready to trust me and finally come to America?"

"I trust you—I'm just not sure I can trust your friends."

"I understand, but I wouldn't be here if I didn't think it was legitimate."

"What about all the people I would leave behind?"

"You could still help them—maybe more in absentia. The people that hired me have some serious power. I'm talking politicians, industrialists, royalty—you name it."

"Yeah, so why would they help me?"

"Well, aside from the fact that you have cold fusion as a bargaining chip, they're actually pretty decent altruistic people."

"How long do I have to decide?"

I looked at my watch.

"Thirty seconds enough time?"

Farid closed his eyes and rubbed his head. I actually felt bad, as this was the second time I had come to usher him into a new life, and I damn well hoped the Topless Agenda didn't fuck it up.

"I'm sorry, but I'm not sure I can go with you. These people need me."

A woman who was sitting nearby came over and held Farid's hands as she spoke.

"You have already done so much for so many that you

deserve the right to be free."

"But there is still so much work to be done."

"And we will do it."

"But…"

"Please, you have done enough," the woman said, as she gazed into his eyes.

He looked at her then around the room before eventually turning his gaze back to me.

"OK, I'm in. I will go with you," he said, solemnly.

He stood up then came over and hugged me.

"It's good to see you, old friend."

"It's good to see you too! Dude, not a day has gone by that I haven't wondered how you were doing, and I still can't tell you how sorry I am about how things went down."

"I know, but it wasn't you're fault, and, believe me, I appreciate what you did for me, but the important thing now is that you're here, and we're going to complete the journey we started five years ago."

He led me back the way we had come, all the while explaining how he and the others had created this strange hidden world. The space we were in had originally been designed as a bomb shelter, but the royal family had never had any reason to use it, and it was locked up and forgotten. Several years ago it was discovered by palace servants, and Farid and the others took it over and converted it into a secret domicile where people could take temporary refuge from their lives of servitude. It also was the organizational center and meeting place for their underground railroad, which was fairly ironic, considering it literally existed under the noses of their captors.

We reached the exit hallway, and Farid turned to address the crowd that had gathered to see him off.

"My friends, I am sad to leave you, but once I am on the outside, I promise to continue the work we have begun here."

Everyone cheered, and he went around and exchanged a number of sad goodbyes, and it was a pretty emotional moment with hardly a dry eye left in the room. Upon finishing, my saintly friend and I walked out to the staff lounge, and we stopped to talk.

"Well, that was pretty fucking emotional," I said.

"Yeah, I hate saying goodbye."

"We all do," I said, as I patted him on the back.

"OK then, what's the plan?" he asked.

"We need to get the hell out of this country. Originally we were going to fly via private jet, but, as there have been a few setbacks, we now need a new plan, and, as you helped create an underground railroad, I'm hoping you might have some ideas."

"Well, there are many potential ways, but crossing into Saudi Arabia via the southern desert would be the fastest and easiest way to get out of the country."

"Through the Liwa Oasis?"

"Yes. You know of it?"

"Of course. While most of the UAE's population may live near the water, deep in their hearts they are still a desert people."

He looked at me skeptically.

"Do you mind if I ask how long you've been here?"

"Three days, but I suck up new cultures like a sponge."

"Apparently."

We walked back through the storage level and up the stairs into the kitchen, where everyone we passed watched us closely, probably wondering who in the hell was keeping company with their beloved benefactor.

"Should we just head out into the party from here?" I asked.

"They will be expecting me to come back through the checkpoint, so you go out here and then come up and meet me on the second level."

Farid headed up the stairs while I walked across the kitchen and followed a waiter with a tray until I was back out in the party. I made my way through the crowd and up to the second floor, where I waited for Farid at the security checkpoint. The stone faced guard was still there, and, when we made eye contact, I smiled and nodded, but it did nothing to elicit a friendly response. At last, Farid appeared, but he was talking over his shoulder to another party guest who was also walking out of the private area. The man came around from behind Farid and into view, and I suddenly felt pangs of discomfort that one might expect when giving birth to a porcupine.

"Oh, hello, Tag, I'd like to introduce you to a colleague. This is..."

"Sheikh Emir," I said.

Farid looked confused.

"Oh, you two know each other?" he asked.

"Sort of—we happened to be on the same flight recently and also like to shop at the Dolce and Gabbana store at the Mall of the Emirates."

"You!" Sheikh Emir yelled angrily, his face reddening as he pointed his finger directly between my eyes as though he wished it were the barrel of a loaded pistol.

Suddenly he was moving towards me, waving his arms and calling for security, so I grabbed Farid and headed for the stairs, as we needed to blend into the crowd and get as much space between us and Emir as possible if we hoped to stand any chance of getting out of the palace. Moving briskly, we darted in and out, dodging people, plates, and cocktails at every step. We reached the stairs and took them two at a time, then slowed up upon reaching the bottom. Two men running in a crowded room stuck out like sore thumbs but two politely mingling guests could blend in quite easily. Halfway to the front door, I spied Olivia and made a beeline. Only a few steps away, she noticed me and smiled, though her expression changed to concern when she saw the look on my face.

"Everything OK?" she asked.

"Yeah, I found my friend. This is Farid."

"Nice to meet you," she said.

"Very nice to meet you," he said, kissing her hand.

Farid, the consummate ladies man, immediately zoned

in on Olivia, drawn like a moth to a flame that was her beautiful blond locks. Having not thought about Olivia's hair color, I now had real worry about getting him to leave her side let alone the building. Suddenly there was shouting from over by the stairs, and I saw Emir and three security men all gazing in our direction.

"Shit! I'm really sorry, but I have to leave early."

"Too bad. I had a very special after dinner treat for you."

"Rain check?"

"Sure."

"Good, I'll give you a call when I get back to the Bay Area. Assuming I make it back alive, that is," I said.

I kissed her goodbye, then Farid and I continued on towards the front door.

"That woman is beautiful. Who is she?" Farid asked, as we walked.

"A friend."

"The kind of friend you have sex with?"

"A gentleman never tells."

"I'll take that as a yes, which means you are indeed a lucky man."

"Yes, but tonight I have you instead."

"Then you are doubly lucky."

"Or, as I see it, half as lucky."

Just before we exited, we both looked back inside and saw the Sheikh and his entourage of security men heading in our direction.

"Oh shit, we made it out just in time," I said.

"Yeah, so where's your car?" Farid asked.

"I don't have one. I got a ride with Olivia. What about you?"

"I have my Bentley here."

"No can do. They most certainly have a tracking chip hidden on it somewhere, so we're going to need to borrow a car. Any thoughts?"

"Yes, I'm sure we can find one down in the royal garage."

"Royal garage, eh? That seems like an overly pompous description for a place they park cars."

"Normally I'd agree, but you'll soon see what I mean."

I followed Farid farther along the roundabout, and we headed down a ramp and into a large well-lit subterranean space that seemed to stretch on for miles, and it kind of reminded me of the government warehouse at the end of *Raiders of the Lost Ark*. The immediate area was filled with all manner of luxury vehicles—everything from Bentleys and Rolls Royces to Ferraris and Porsches, but Farid inexplicably led me over to a shiny gold plated Rolls Royce golf cart. I imagine it was just one of those rare items that every oil sheikh needed to complete his collection, regardless of his proximity to a golf course or the actual desire to play golf.

"OK, I get it now. This is indeed a royal fucking garage, but how far do you think we can get in that Goddamn golf cart?"

"Far enough, get in," he said.

"Seriously?"

"Yes, it will be a lot faster than walking."

I took a seat, and we headed off deeper into the space and passed expensive car after expensive car until coming upon a lone valet standing at a little kiosk with a wall full of various car keys.

"Are you going to distract him while I find us a car?" I asked.

"No, I have a better idea. Wait here."

Farid casually walked up to the valet and spoke quietly for a moment before calling me over.

"What kind of car do we need?" Farid asked me.

"An SUV would be nice in case we have to go across any open desert, and it would be even better if it had some balls."

"I've got just what you're looking for," the valet said, his accent likely Indonesian.

"So, I take it he's part of your railroad," I said.

"Yes indeed."

"Nice."

"Very, and, contrary to that old saying that it's good to have friends in high places, I often find it more useful to have friends in low places."

"At this particular moment I would have to agree."

A second later, a great beastly roar came from the other end of the garage, followed by the appearance of an ominous black Lamborghini Cheetah. It was, in my humble opinion, the most exciting and exotic of all off-road cars and familiar to only the most stalwart of gearheads. Originally designed for military use in 1970, the Cheetah was later given the Countach's badass twelve cylinder engine and sold to civilians. Unlike its sleek brethren, it had plenty of ground clearance and carried boxy looks similar to the modern Humvee, which made sense as it was its progenitor. Lamborghini even went so far as to have Pirelli design specialized tires called Scorpions that could endure intense desert heat and high off-road speeds. I had never had the opportunity to drive one, and standing before it now was currently enough excitement to give me a semi, and I had to reach down and make some extra room in my pants for Tag Junior. The valet pulled up in front of us, rolled down the window, and smiled.

"Will this suit your needs?" he asked.

"Does a Dubai oil sheikh wipe his ass with fourteen karat gold toilet paper?" I responded.

He laughed at my response as he stepped down out of the car, because the answer was yes, as they did indeed have fourteen karat gold toilet paper in this part of the world. I climbed up and slid into the drivers seat and smiled giddily.

"It even has a full tank of gas and a brand new top of the line GPS," he said, as he patted the front fender.

"Sweet mother of internal combustion. It doesn't get any better than this."

This was for me a life dream come true and one of those rare moments where fate actually threw me a bone. I looked around the car and did my best not to ejaculate, as this was an Italian supercar, and I was a man. To that end I took some deep breaths to try and relax, but the Cheetah unfortunately smelled as though it had just come from the showroom, and the fine factory fresh scent of leather traveled deep into my olfactory receptors and awakened my deeply buried inner manchild and tickled my willy. Farid, meanwhile, climbed up into the passenger seat and immediately noticed the peculiar look of wanting on my face.

"You OK?" he asked.

"Yeah, I'm fine, except for the fact that I'm trying not cum in my pants."

"I take it you like the car?"

"Perhaps a little too much."

Farid smiled then turned to his friend.

"I believe this car was a good choice. Now, are you sure you won't get into any trouble?" he asked.

"The family hasn't used this car in years. They don't even remember that it exists."

"Thanks again and don't worry. Everything is set for you and your brother to leave next month."

"I will never forget what you've done for us, Farid," he said, choking up on his words and wiping a tear from the corner of his eye.

"Jesus, Farid, you're motherfucking Teresa around here."

"I do what I can."

"You're obviously doing a lot more than that."

"It's nothing."

"It's everything. Most people are selfish, self-centered assholes who would have taken the Bentley and the house and been perfectly satisfied."

"Eh, you've just grown cynical, my friend."

"Or realistic."

"Maybe they're one and the same, but I certainly hope not."

I turned my attention back to the vehicle to get acquainted with the controls. It could be a little tricky driving a new car and even trickier when it was Italian. I gave the engine a small rev then put the monster in gear. The Cheetah's clutch was a little heavy, so I let it out slowly, resisting the urge to pop it and spin the tires, and we headed up the ramp and out towards the turnabout of the Royal Palace.

"It's smooth sailing from here on out!" I said, with a smile.

CHAPTER TWENTY-ONE
Smokey and the Bandit

Smooth sailing turned out to be a less than accurate description of the situation that we discovered upon emerging from the garage. Sailing directly into a the path of a typhoon might have been more accurate, considering we were approaching no less than seven security vehicles waiting at the other end of the open courtyard. Seven is usually considered a lucky number, but, in this case, it represented a big steaming pile of dog shit blocking our path to freedom. So much for a nice quiet exfiltration from the palace.

"Jesus! What the fuck did you do to piss off Sheikh Emir?" Farid asked.

"Not much, other than use him to demonstrate a jujitsu hold after he got drunk and unruly and attacked Olivia on the plane ride over here. In reality, it really wasn't a big deal."

"Wasn't a big deal? You put your hands on a fucking royal for fuck's sake! We're dead men," he said, looking grave.

"Only if they catch us."

"The odds are looking particularly favorable for them at the moment."

"Never tell me the odds!" I yelled, quoting the immortal Han Solo, one of my three favorite childhood heroes—the other two of course being Indiana Jones and James Bond.

I stopped the Cheetah and looked across at the line of cars to see, standing at the front, a lone figure smiling smugly with his hands on his hips. It was Emir, and for once he actually looked happy. I realized that I preferred him angry, so it was time to wipe the smile off his face and get the fuck out of Dubai. I looked at Farid, and he looked back at me nervously—beads of sweat forming on his furrowed brow.

"What do we do now?" he asked.

"Hyperdrive."

"What?"

"Hyperdrive. You know, we make the jump to light speed."

"I'm serious now. No more Star Wars bullshit. I really want to know what the fuck we are going to do."

"As I said, hyperdrive."

I gunned the car, and the engine literally roared as we accelerated with all four wheels putting the horsepower to the ground and pushing the beast well past fifty miles per hour in mere seconds. We were only a short distance away from the wall of cars when Emir's smile was replaced by a look of panic. At the last moment, I cut the wheel hard left and bumped up onto the lawn, where the Cheetah's tires churned up a rooster tail of grass and dirt until we cleared the roadblock and swerved back onto the driveway. I hazarded a quick glance in the rearview mirror and watched as the security people all scrambled into their cars and began setting off after our charging Cheetah. Oddly, the entire spectacle brought on a thought that made me smile.

"What's so funny?" Farid asked.

"Did you ever see the movie *Smokey and the Bandit*?"

"Yeah, back during my time at Stanford. Why do you ask?"

"Well, I just realized that we're living our own modern reimagining, and I'm the Bandit, you're Frog, and Sheikh Emir is of course, Sheriff Buford T. Justice."

"Why do I have to be Frog? Why can't I be Cledus?" he asked.

"Because you're my passenger, and that means you're the Sally Field to my Burt Reynolds."

"Fair enough," he said, as he smiled and started singing.

"We've got a long way to go, and a short time to get there."

At that point I joined in.

"And we gonna do what they say can't be done," we both sang together, completing the chorus of Jerry Reed's classic East Bound and Down.

We tore out through the main gate, and two sharp left

turns later, I was hitting the gas and moving through the gears, all the while savoring every moment behind the wheel of the Italian beast. We hit the open road heading southwest, and I looked in the rearview mirror to discover the first in a line of what was obviously the seven vehicles we just avoided. I hit the accelerator and pushed the Cheetah well up over a hundred miles per hour, but our pursuers were still gaining on us, and soon they were right on our back bumper.

"They're right behind us. What are we going to do?" Farid asked nervously.

"We do what we were meant to do."

"Which is?"

"Go off-road, so make sure you're buckled in, farm boy, as it's about to get interesting."

The goal now was to utilize the Cheetah's strong points, which meant finding some serious off-road terrain. I turned the wheel hard to the left, and the tires squealed as we crossed over the highway and hit the berm on the other side and literally went airborne as we flew out into the desert. The Cheetah was built for this kind of driving, so its suspension absorbed the impact as though it were nothing more than the gentle caress of a midnight lover. The surrounding land here was basically miles upon miles of open dirt roads and desert, which meant the Cheetah would roll through it like a hot knife through butter. Our pursuers, however, were in luxury sedans, likely Mercedes judging by the headlights, which meant it would only be a matter of time before we left them far behind—or so I hoped.

The detour off the road took out the first car, whose lights temporarily disappeared as its front end embedded into the soft sand berm. The remaining drivers were smarter and avoided the same fate by taking the berm slowly and at an angle. It was now six to one, so our odds were already improving. Up ahead came a fork in the road with three tines, and I took the middle route while the cars behind me fanned out left and right probably hoping to flank us. This was going to be tricky, but I had thankfully mastered escape and evasion driving as part of my training in both special operations and the Agency. Of course, it also didn't hurt that I had spent a good portion of my young adult life off-roading, and had driven everything from two cylinder race bikes to quads and dune buggies, so, while the people of the Emirates may have been from the desert, in my mind, they were now playing on my turf.

The roads were coming back together up ahead, and I could see cars closing in on me from both sides, as they were obviously hoping to form a roadblock and trap us in the middle. I gunned the accelerator to make them think I was trying to get ahead, and they followed suit, coming up fast on their parallel courses. Just before the roads came together, I hit the brakes, and the two lead cars on each side raced forward and slammed into each other before bouncing apart and careening off into the deep sand on the sides of the road. It was a silly trick, but it worked, and now we had two more down and only four more to go.

I gunned the Cheetah, and we continued on until I saw that the road split into two directions with one going to the left and the other going slightly right and over a small hill. Perfect. I veered to the right and headed up the rise with the hope that our superior traction would allow us to gain some distance and possibly lose some, if not all, of the less capable cars. Of course, I was also praying to God that it didn't lead to a steep drop off on the other side that would potentially put all of us in a ditch. We crested the hill and thankfully came down the other side onto a nice smooth section of road, and the detour slowed our pursuers and forced them to amble over the crest well behind.

"Farid, can you look at the GPS and tell me what kind of terrain we have up ahead?"

"Yeah, as long as you can deal with a little puke. I get car sick if I try to read in a moving car."

"OK, then make it fast, as I'm a sympathetic puker, and then we'll both be riding around puking in a car full of puke, and that is no way to pick up chicks."

Farid did his best to study the small screen as the car pitched sideways and bumped along on the road.

"If we take a left at the next fork, the road gets pretty curvy and skirts a riverbed, which is probably dry at this time of year," he said, happy to turn his attention away from the little screen and back to the road.

"Wet or dry, it'll work for our purposes."

I followed his directions, then, about a half mile down the road, started purposefully steering the car onto the soft dirt on the sides with the goal being to stir up as much of a dust cloud as possible. This would create a massive visual barrier, and my efforts appeared to be working, as the pursuing cars headlights were becoming less visible. Up ahead, I saw the dry riverbed as well as the fact that the road made a hard right turn in order to avoid it. Perfect! I shut off the lights then made the turn and continued for another fifty feet then stopped to watch, wait, and hope that the dust cloud I created obscured their vision enough that they missed the turn. A second later, the cars came racing along, and all four went flying off of the edge and plowed into the soft sand below. Our last four obstacles had finally been removed, so I turned on the lights and hit the gas and continued down the road.

"Nice moves, Bandit," Farid said.

"Thanks, Frog, and I'd sure like to see the look on Sheikh Buford T. Emir's face when he finds out we escaped," I responded.

"Honestly, I'd prefer to be as far away as possible."

Our brief reprieve from the excitement of the chase was suddenly interrupted when headlights appeared down in the riverbed to our left, and I looked over and saw a fucking car matching our speed. Somehow, one of the four had survived, so it was likely an all wheel drive vehicle such as an Audi or Volvo.

"Oh well, at least they're down there, and we're up here," I said.

"Yeah, but for how long?" Farid countered.

"Not long enough. Look."

Just up ahead, there was a short connecting road, and our pursuer used it to get free of the riverbed and right back on our ass. Now that I could see the car's unusual LED headlights, it was obvious it was an Audi. Shit monkeys. Our only real advantage would be the longer travel of the Cheetah's suspension and the balls to see how hard I could push it.

Up ahead, the road moved into a series of tight curves which skirted the riverbed, and the Cheetah went into a full drift as I navigated the turns—a rooster tale of dust shooting from all four wheels as they dug into the soft soil. The Audi slowed and fell back a bit, but it managed to catch up once we were back on a straight section of road.

"What if they start shooting?" Farid asked nervously.

"They won't start shooting—not as long as the golden goose is in the car."

Suddenly, at that very moment, fate decided to make me look like an asshole, as, sure enough, gun shots started coming from the Audi. Clearly, these idiots were acting exclusively on Sheikh Emir's orders, and had no idea Farid was the UAE's golden goose. Of course, if anything happened to Farid, at least I knew Sheikh Hamza would enact some brutal retribution on his uncle. At that moment a lucky shot embedded into the vertical post behind my door, and it encouraged me to begin driving in a serpentine pattern with the hope that it would throw off their aim. The back end swung left and right as more shots rang out, but thankfully none of them managed to hit either me or Farid.

"We need to get a little more proactive," I said.

"Meaning?"

I opened my jacket and pulled out my pistol.

"This!"

"Dude, you're such a typical American."

"Yeah, but it's also the reason you're going to survive to hump another day."

"Let's hope so."

Yet another lucky shot pinged off the roof on Farid's side of the car, and we both instinctively ducked then popped back up and looked at each other.

"Time to get American on their ass!" Farid said.

"Fucking A! Nobody fucks with my Goose!" I responded.

"Wait, if I'm Goose, then that means you're Maverick. *Top Gun*! Get it?" Farid asked.

"Of course I get it, but that would mean operating under the guise of an entirely different movie metaphor. Sure, I appreciate the homoerotic undertones of *Top Gun*, but let's try and stay in one decade here, so let's take it back from the eighties to the seventies. I'm Bandit and you're Frog."

"Oh well, I suppose I'm the second banana either way."

"Yeah, but you're my second banana. Now, when I slow down and let them come up alongside, I'm going to need you to take the wheel for a second."

"Got it, Bandit."

I eased back on the throttle and favored the right side of the road, hopeful they'd take the bate. We hit a large open section, and they raced up alongside, and I leaned out the window with my gun aimed directly across at the men in the Audi. The man in the passenger seat looked particularly terrified as he tried to reload his pistol on the bumpy road, for he knew I had him dead to rights.

"Nobody hurts my Frog!" I yelled.

Still, I didn't feel as though he, or the other man in the car, deserved to die, but they did need a little motivation to get the hell off our ass. I smiled then moved my aim to their front right tire and pulled the trigger. The bullet penetrated the rubber, and it blew out, causing the driver to lose control of the car, which had turned and was now headed directly towards the ledge that overlooked the river. Judging by the brake lights, he tried to stop, but it was too late, and they flew off the embankment and landed front first, plowing through the soft sand until coming to a stop with the high speed creating enough momentum to lift the rear of the car and make it appear as though it were doing a handstand. It stayed perched on its front end for an ever so brief moment then flopped back down onto the ground, where its headlights illuminated the cloud of dust that now swirled around its final resting place.

"I know I told you not to mix movie metaphors, but I can't help feeling like we're Han Solo and Chewbacca, and we just outran the Imperial Cruisers in the trusty old Millennium Falcon," I said, patting the dashboard.

Farid did his best Chewbacca howl, but it sounded more like a Panda passing a kidney stone. Still, I had to give him credit for showing car spirit.

"We've evaded Sheikh Vader for the moment, so it's time to stop and call the Rebel Alliance."

We continued on for another five miles before turning onto a dirt road which headed in the direction of the main highway. Another mile later, we hit asphalt, and I pulled off the road and up onto a slight rise which afforded us a commanding three hundred and sixty degree view of the entire area. I turned off the car, and the quiet sounds of the desert night filled the air.

"Time to check in, but, before I do, I have a question for you."

"Sure, do you want me to explain to you where babies come from?"

"Yeah, but I'd also like to know what you, Hamza, the German, and that blond woman were talking about back at the palace."

He thought a moment.

"Oh, nothing really. I ran into them on my way to the bathroom, and we exchanged the usual party banter bullshit."

"So, nothing was spoken about a secret society he's trying to undermine?"

Farid laughed.

"No, but we did talk about the *Pâté* tasting a little off."

"Good thing I didn't have any. Do you know anything

about the German who was with him?"

"Only that his name is Klaus, and he's Hamza's right hand man and head of security, and the two are practically inseparable. Why do you ask?"

"Well, that fucker has tried to kill me at least twice—once in a car and once in a plane, and each time he came pretty close to success."

"I'm not surprised. There are rumors he used to be a soldier in the German special forces before coming to work for Hamza, and now he takes care of all of his dirty business."

"Then I guess I must be pretty dirty to get so much attention. How about the woman? Do you know anything about her?"

"I wish. As you obviously saw she's blond and beautiful."

"I couldn't see her face, so I'll just have to take your word for it."

"Yeah, and unfortunately she's completely off limits, as she's Hamza's girlfriend, but I don't know much about her, as they keep their relationship mostly on the down-low."

"Oh, well, she's probably just an innocent bystander anyway, so I'll just relay all the other shit I've learned thus far."

I looked at my watch, did some quick calculations to estimate the time back home, then pulled out my iPhone and dialed Matheson. It was late morning, so I hopefully wouldn't be catching him off guard at some ungodly hour when he might be sleeping, eating breakfast, or taking a shit.

"Finn, how's it going over there?" he asked, after picking up on the second ring.

"Good, mostly."

"Have you managed to meet up with Farid?"

"Yep, he's right here, but I have some more news for you, and you're not going to like it."

"I'm listening."

"The German guy who tried to run me off the road back home and most likely tampered with the Vandenberg jet is Sheikh Hamza's right hand man and head of security."

Matheson was quiet for a moment as he pondered the implications of that statement.

"Shit! How did you find that out?"

"I saw them together about an hour ago at the Royal Palace of Dubai."

"So, Hamza is definitely our bad guy, but how could he possibly know anything about us and our plans?"

"There has to be a leak inside the Topless Agenda."

"There can't be. It's just not possible."

"Anything's possible, apparently."

"So, how do you want to exfiltrate the UAE?" he asked.

"I'm thinking we leave the country via the southern desert by crossing the border into Saudi Arabia and maybe fly out from Riyadh."

"That could be difficult, as Saudi Arabia is pretty locked down. The only people who go there are usually invited, so let me make a few calls and see what I can work out then get back to you."

"OK, we'll be heading south until further notice."

"Good luck, Finn. Stay safe. I mean it."

"Thanks, I will," I said, before hitting the end button and looking over to see Farid eying me curiously.

"What is it?"

"Dude, wait a minute, is this mysterious group of yours seriously called the Topless Agenda?"

"Yeah, and before you say anything, I know, it's a little silly."

"Silly? It's fucking awesome!"

"I'm glad you think so, as you're about to become one of its prestigious members."

"This night just keeps getting better and better."

"Yeah, and I've also got some more good news."

"Let me guess. Road trip?" he exclaimed excitedly.

"Yeah, so it's just like old times, which reminds me— what have you eaten in the last twelve hours?"

"Falafels," he said, with a shit eating grin.

I started the Cheetah, and its twelve throaty Italian cylinders roared to life, their gurgling din a direct challenge to any road that lay ahead. I put the beast in gear, released the clutch, and hit the gas, and it sent us flying down the rise and onto the open highway. Next stop, the Liwa Oasis.

CHAPTER TWENTY-TWO
The Oddest Couple

The desert had been dark and devoid of life until we came over a rise and saw the first lights of the Liwa Oasis. It was a cluster of dwellings that stretched along the only source of water in this part of the desert, and it was hard to imagine that this remote place was the historical home of the Nahyan family, who were the founders and leaders of the UAE. Now, it was mostly inhabited by Bedouin tribes, especially the Bani Yas, who used the area to cultivate date palms.

The oasis certainly wasn't a metropolis, and up ahead I spied what I suspect was its only gas station. It would be our first stop, as Farid and I were going into the open desert, and we needed some supplies, with the most important being food, water, and fuel. I pulled into the gas station and was happy to see it also had a twenty-four hour minimart. God bless America and its influence on the rest of the world. I parked beside the center island, connected the pump up to the Cheetah's nozzle, and ended up pumping about 280 dirhams worth of fuel. It sounded like a lot of money, but, with the exchange rate being about four to one in favor of the US dollar and gas costing about two dollars a gallon, it was only about seventy dollars to top off the massive tank. That meant we had plenty of money left over to get all the bottled water and food we could fit in the Lambo. We went inside and pooled our cash then returned to the beast to stow our goodies in the trunk and have a quick look at the GPS. The main road into the Liwa Oasis ended at a three way intersection just up ahead, and our only options were to go either left or right. Right eventually looped to the border station, but it probably wasn't prudent to use any official entry or exit points, so we would go in the opposite direction. We turned left at the intersection and headed along the main road in hopes of finding a decent place to enter the desert. It was mostly quiet at this hour, which made it all the more jarring when my phone rang. I looked down to see that Matheson was calling, so I reached down and hit the accept button.

"Las Conchitas Mexican food," I said.

"Very funny, Finn. What's going on?"

"Not much, we're in the Liwa Oasis."

"Perfect—I've got some good news for you. It turns out that we have a CIA asset in Saudi Arabia who can meet you and help arrange a private flight to get you out of the Middle East."

"Sweet hot buttered corn! Where's he located?"

"That's where you're in luck. He operates out of the southern desert of Saudi Arabia and will meet you about thirty miles across the border from your present location. Do you have some kind of GPS?"

"Yeah."

"Good. I'll text you the coordinates."

"That's it?"

"That's it. He'll meet you there as soon as he can. Oh, and one more thing, he goes by the code name Desert Fox.

"Sounds mysterious."

"He is. Don't piss him off. He's an exceptional asset."

"Any kind of code phrase?"

"No, though I suspect you'll know you have the right person when you meet him. All right then. Good luck, I'll see you soon."

"Thanks."

I pulled back onto the road and continued east for another mile, and we passed palm orchards and various buildings, with one in particular appearing to be some kind of palace based on its size and elegant architecture. The Oasis was certainly a lot bigger and more populated than it looked on the map, but we soon managed to find an open area with a large number of tracks heading out into the desert. I pulled over and had a closer look and realized I recognized the place from a brochure I'd glanced at back at my hotel. Apparently, the UAE attracted a lot of off-road enthusiasts, and sand safaris were a common tourist attraction out here in the desert. The place actually reminded me a little of Palm Springs except for the absence of windmills, golf courses, and retirees.

I heard a beep and looked down at my iPhone to see that Matheson's text had finally come through, so I plugged the numbers into the GPS then turned to Farid.

"You ready, Frog?" I asked.

"I am, Bandit."

I hit the gas, and we headed out into the desert with the warm night air flowing throughout the car. It was about eleven, and a sliver moon was just peeking over the horizon and illuminating the rolling dunes and making it all look like a barren alien planet. We traveled along at just over forty miles per hour moving up one dune and down another, plying a virtual sea of sand with the task hardly worthy of the Cheetah's vast reserves of horsepower. After fifteen minutes, we could no longer see any of the lights of Liwa, and the stars came alive and filled the night sky from one side of the horizon to the other, making it a truly a magical moment.

"This is amazing," I said, looking over at Farid, whose smile was aglow in the ambient light emanating from the dashboard gauges.

"No kidding. I don't know why I've never come out here."

"It's funny. People who live by extraordinary places like this never truly appreciate them. I grew up by the Golden Gate Bridge and never once walked across it."

"Seriously?"

"Yep, never been over it except in a car."

"Come to think of it—when I was at Stanford, I never walked across it either. Fuck it, when I get to America, I'm going to walk across the fucking Golden Gate Bridge."

"I'll walk with you. We can even hold hands."

"That would be nice," he said, with a small chuckle.

We continued on into the night, the long monotonous drive allowing me time to think, and my thoughts kept returning to Farid and one major question I was dying to ask.

"Dude, I have to know. Did you really discover the secret to cold fusion?"

"Fuck yeah, I did—and it was no small task."

"I assume you understand the implications of your discovery."

"Absolutely, which is part of why I was willing to come with you. Something this important needs to be carefully overseen. Honestly, I was always afraid of what it might bring if it were in the wrong hands."

"So you don't have any reservations about the people I'm working for?"

"Well, I trust you—so, in turn, I am willing to trust them."

"I really hope I don't let you down this time."

"Me too."

Our route was less of a road and more of a loose collection of tire tracks that wove in between massive mountains of sand, but we continued on, driving deeper into the desert. Farid called out course corrections as needed, and, after taking a closer look at the GPS, finally told me to slow down.

"Are we close to our destination?" I asked.

"Not exactly, but we're almost to the border."

Up ahead a chain link fence and a dry gravel road appeared from the darkness, and I turned left and followed it in hopes of finding an opening. Of course, I also chose that direction because it avoided the border patrol station that resided a few miles away in the opposite direction. After about fifteen minutes, we found an area of fence that had been damaged and subsequently repaired. They had used wire to mend the tear, similar to the way a fisherman might use twine to mend his net. All I had to do was cut a few wires and voila, we would be in Saudi Arabia!

Off-road vehicles traditionally carried some tools, and, after stopping in front of the fence, I stepped out and rustled around through the Cheetah's various compartments. My final stop was the trunk, and there I finally found a tool box, which I imagine was probably an essential asset to carry in an older Italian car. Luckily, there were wire cutters, and I headed over to the fence and started at the bottom of the mend then worked my way up, cutting and yanking out the sections of wire a couple feet at a time until I had the beginnings of a decently sized opening that looked a little like a massive metal vagina. All of a sudden, Farid looked at me nervously.

"Do you hear that?" he asked.

I cupped my hands behind my ears to make miniature

parabolic reflectors and listened carefully.

"Yeah, shit. It must be the border patrol. Help me put this back."

The noise of the engine was growing louder, and Farid looked at me nervously as we did our best to close up the opening and make the fence a veritable virgin yet again.

"What do we say to them?" he asked.

"Nothing, just act like we're a couple of assholes out here enjoying some off-roading."

A vehicle came over the rise, and its headlights and four roof-mounted high powered off-road lights illuminated us like a movie set. It continued closer then idled for a moment before the engine turned off, and we were left in complete silence with the only sound being my breathing and the loud thumping of my racing heart. The lights were still on, and we looked at each other nervously before returning our attention back to the vehicle. The driver side door opened, and a man stepped out, but the details of his features were indiscernible under the direct assault of their bevy of lights. I tried to shield my eyes, but nothing could cut through the extreme glare, so the only sense I had left functioning was my hearing, which wasn't exactly comforting at the moment. I heard a familiar metallic sound that was reminiscent of the unique acoustic signature of someone chambering a round in an assault rifle. Shit, we were toast.

Suddenly, there was a large belch followed by the sound of a zipper then what I was pretty sure was urine trickling onto the sand. What the hell? The peeing sound soon stopped, then I heard the zipper again. The figure walked slightly closer then paused just beyond the front of his vehicle. Jesus, this guy was one cool customer if he could whip it out and take a piss so easily in front of a couple of strangers.

"How's it going, motherfuckers!" he said, sounding more like a San Francisco hipster.

"Excuse me?" I asked.

"I said. How's it going, motherfuckers!" he said, with even more gusto.

I was suddenly experiencing a great deal of confusion and was wondering if we had just run into the coolest border guard of all time. Farid and I stood silently staring at the stranger, still unsure how to respond when he spoke again.

"Oh fuck! Sorry, man, I forgot about the lights. Muti, kill the fucking lights! They can't see shit," he yelled.

The lights turned off, and my vision slowly adjusted, so that I could at last see that the man before me was probably close to thirty, clean shaven, and wearing jeans and a button down shirt. The vehicle behind him, instead of being the border patrol, was a tricked out dune buggy, and the rifle sound I heard, had in fact been the guy opening up his beer can.

"Dude! I'm Jawad, and my friend is Muti," he said, merrily.

"I'm John, and my sidekick over there is Yoko."

He was looking at me curiously, and it made me wonder if he had caught on to my silly fake names.

"What's up with the tuxedos?" he asked, apparently more interested in our unusual state of dress.

"We just came from a party. Nice dune buggy, by the way."

"Fuck me—nice Cheetah. How is the power on that son of a bitch?"

"Fucking awesome."

"Oh man, she is beautiful."

"Yes, she is."

"Beer?" Jawad asked, looking at us.

I looked at Farid, and he gave me a nod of approval.

"Why not."

Jawad went to his car and returned a moment later with his friend Muti and two beers. He handed over cans of Heineken then introduced his friend, who was about the same age as Jawad but shorter, heavier, and sporting a well trimmed beard.

"What brings you two out here?" Jawad asked.

"Just doing a little off-roading," I said.

"Same here."

We all stood there and quietly sipped our beers, until Jawad glanced towards the fence.

"I see you're planning on going across the border."

Farid and I looked at each other, both unsure what to say.

"Oh, that? We were only thinking about it—but it's obviously illegal, considering they have a fence."

"Hello, it's just a bunch of fucking wire. Who do you think cut it open in the first place." Jawad said, before finishing his beer and tossing the empty can into the sand.

"I take it that it was you and Muti."

"Hell yeah! All the best off-roading is on that side of the fence. Now, the border patrol will be coming along here any minute, so if you two really want to go, then we have to go now."

"Well, if you insist," I said, nodding my head.

Jawad motioned to Muti, and the two of them walked over to the fence and finished what Farid and I had started. After a brief moment, they had expanded the opening, and we were ready to roll.

"Follow us," Jawad said, as he and Muti walked back to their dune buggy.

I grabbed Jawad's can off the sand and threw it in the back seat of the Cheetah. There was no reason to be a litter bug, even in the middle of nowhere. Having done my little bit for the environment, I started the Cheetah and followed them through the fence into Saudi Arabia. We stopped and everyone got out and worked together to replace the fence before mounting up and heading off into the desert night. Our new friends had obviously been this way before, as their speed was never less than fifty miles per hour and at times reached well over seventy. It wasn't anywhere near the Cheetah's top end, but driving in this kind of terrain required a really good map or personal experience, and currently we had neither. We did, however, fortunately have a dune buggy version of Rudolph the Red Nosed Reindeer driving like a maniac just ahead.

"How's our direction? Are we still heading towards the coordinates?" I asked Farid.

"Yeah, perfect. Right on course."

For the moment, we followed our new friends, continuing on into the desert for another half an hour until reaching a wide open, moonlit sandy bowl where they turned around and pulled up beside us.

"This is it! The sweet spot. There are awesome jumps in every direction with this bowl making for a perfect landing spot."

Farid looked down at the GPS then smiled as he looked over at me.

"Guess what?" he asked excitedly.

"What?"

"This is our rendezvous spot."

"No fucking way."

Our revelry was suddenly interrupted when Jawad hit the gas and sent a fifty foot rooster tail of sand behind their dune buggy before disappearing over the edge of the bowl. A moment later they came flying off the edge and easily traveled a good thirty feet through the air before coming down into the sand. We watched as they did it two more times before Farid looked over at me.

"Well?"

"Fuck it. When will I ever get to drive one of these

again?"

I hit the gas and followed Jawad and Muti over the berm then returned a moment later and caught massive air. It was more fucking fun than I'd had in a car in a long time, and we did it again and again, following our new friends throughout this adult version of a skate park. Eventually we stopped, had another beer and switched vehicles. The next stop, we had yet another beer and switched drivers. The following stop was just for beer, and I was starting to wonder how our new friends managed to carry, let alone drink so much fucking beer. An hour later, Jawad and Muti were thankfully ready to head home, as it was clear that none of us should be operating any kind of motorized vehicle. They gave us their remaining four beers then said goodbye and headed off back towards the border. The sound of their engine faded until the serenity of the desert night returned, and Farid and I grabbed a beer then climbed up and sat on the hood of the Cheetah.

"This wasn't exactly how I saw this night turning out," I said.

"No shit. This has been awesome."

"Indeed."

"So, tell me about your exciting life as a private investigator. Do you meet lots of beautiful women?"

"Lately I'd have to say yes, but before that there were hardly any women, and my cases were all shitty divorces and lost pets, with the most recent one entailing me finding the fat cat I mentioned back at the palace."

"Surely you must be joking!"

"Afraid not, but, as I said, everything has taken a dramatic turn for the better since I came into the fold of the Topless Agenda."

"So, has there been anyone special among these recent beautiful women?"

"They were all special in their own way, but two stand out."

"Tell me about them."

I had to laugh as I thought about how tragic it turned out with both.

"Well, the first one was the original love of my life, and, when we reconnected recently, I unfortunately learned that she had married my close friend from the Air Force. The second one I had met while reconnecting with the first one, and she's very likely getting married to another man as we speak."

"One puts the knife in your heart and the other twists the blade. Bitches man," he said, clinking cans with me.

We finished our beers, then I went back into the Cheetah and grabbed the last two and handed one to Farid.

"How about you, player? I read in your file that you've become quite the ladies man."

"That's probably an exaggeration, though I have been dating. Unfortunately, no one special yet, but I hope that will change in America."

"I don't mean to question your dream, but there are incredible women everywhere."

"True, but America is special for me. You know—back at Stanford, I fell in love with the most beautiful girl."

"Blonde?"

"Of course, where do you think it all started?"

I nodded, and he continued with his story.

"And she was brilliant—also working on her PhD in nuclear physics. We ended up moving in together, and, honestly, it was the happiest I've ever been in my life. She was *the one*," he said, holding up his index finger.

"So what the hell happened?"

"We graduated, and I went back to Iran."

"That was it? You didn't keep in touch?"

"I tried. A few phone calls, some emails, but then we just lost track of each other. It was inevitable while we were a world apart."

I knew how he felt, as it had been basically the same story with Lux, and I too had dropped the ball and let my *one* get away.

"I did get in touch with her briefly—five years ago," he said.

"Let me guess—you called her because I was coming to take you to America."

"Yep."

"Oh man am I sorry."

"It was your government not you."

"Still sucks. Have you looked for her online?"

"Of course, and I found her on facebook and Instagram—but because I have been living under a false identity,

I couldn't friend her or make contact."

"Shit. I never thought about that. It must suck giving up your identity."

"It does, but I wonder if I will be able to be me again?"

"That's a good question, and I can't imagine why not."

"It would be nice. They say there is power in your own name. You know I took a Tai Chi class back at Stanford, and we did an exercise where you would hold up your arm and say your name while the instructor would try and push it down. If you said a false name, he could easily push it down, but if you said your own name, he couldn't. It was an interesting exercise and one I've never forgotten."

"There is some amazing shit out there in the universe."

"As a scientist, I'm on the cutting edge of all the latest shit, but I'll tell you what—we don't know shit about shit."

"No shit and that includes women. We don't know shit about them either, but I think that makes me love them all the more."

"Amen, brother," he said clinking cans with me before finishing his beer.

I finished mine, belched, and felt a very healthy buzz.

"When we get back to America and you get this whole cold fusion thing rolling, I'm going to fucking find your lost love and bring you two back together," I said.

"You're totally drunk."

"I totally am, but I'm also feeling sentimental."

"Yeah, and probably horny as well."

"Yeah, that too, so I'm really missing my *one* about now."

"Which *one?* You mentioned two."

"At the moment, it's the one who is about to get married."

"And all you have in this lonely empty desert is me."

"Do you want to cuddle—for old times sake?"

We started laughing like drunken idiots then continued to talk well into the night, the years melting away as we caught up with each other's lives. It was an amazingly bonding moment and the best I'd had in a long time. The desert was truly a magical place, and, after a final epic pee, we retired to the Lambo, tilting back our seats to sleep and await contact with the mysterious man code named the Desert Fox.

CHAPTER TWENTY-THREE
The Desert Fox

At 6:40 a.m. the sun rudely rose above the dunes to the east and cast the interior of the Cheetah aglow in warm morning light. I rolled onto my left side and buried my head in the door to hide from the obnoxious glare in hopes of gaining a few more precious hours of sleep. Thankfully I put aside the feelings of a swollen bladder and decidedly uncomfortable sleeping position and managed to doze off. I awoke sometime later and looked at the dashboard clock to discover that two hours had passed, and it was now eight eighteen. I could hold my pee no longer and pulled the door handle and practically spilled out onto the sand. I straightened up and stood on wobbly feet and turned slightly north to get the sun out of my eyes, then unzipped my fly and brought rain to the desert. It flowed like a great yellow river and soaked the sand and created a tiny little oasis of urine. I finished up with a quick shake and decided to conduct a quick three hundred and sixty degree survey of the horizon in the hope that I might find a trace of our mysterious contact, but the desert was not yet ready to reveal its secrets.

Behind me, Farid stirred and groaned as he came awake and stepped out of the Cheetah, where he staggered a few feet from the door before proceeding to pee. Like me, he had chosen to look away from the glaring sun and was more or less pointing in my direction apparently oblivious to my presence. Just as I was about to say something to my hungover friend, I looked past him and saw, to my amazement, a line of Bedouins sitting on their camels about fifty feet in front of the car. They had inexplicably appeared out of nowhere and, more alarmingly, were holding HK G36 assault rifles. Worse still, their faces were hidden behind their keffiyehs, so I was unable to discern any kind of expression that might help determine if they were friend or foe. All in all this was a potentially shitty way to start the day.

"Um, dude," I said, to Farid, pointing at the strangers.

He looked up groggily and realized I was in front of him and quickly twisted away, his pee tracing an arc across the sand as he unknowingly ended up facing the only other people within a hundred miles of our present location. Seeing them, he panicked yet again and turned back towards me but stopped about halfway, where he finally found a neutral direction in which to direct his urine.

"Um—you might want to put that away," I said.

"I can't stop mid pee," he said, nervously.

"Then don't blame me if someone takes a shot at your

dick."

"You're not helping."

I walked around Farid and closer to the Bedouins and noticed that they were all dressed in light colored thawbs, a loose fitting robe-like garment common to the people of the desert. It protected them from the sun and allowed air to circulate more freely around their bodies when they were out in the intense heat, and it was a shitload more practical than the Dolce & Gabbana tuxedo I was currently wearing. Still, I wasn't the only one in black, for the person at the center of their group was wearing a black thawb and keffiyeh, and I suspected that his different color scheme meant that he was most likely their leader. Farid finally finished peeing then came over and joined me.

"What the hell do we do?" he whispered in my ear.

"Fuck if I know. Bedouins are generally peaceful no-mads."

"Then why do they have assault rifles?"

"Maybe they're out hunting."

"In the desert? What could they possibly find out here?"

I shrugged.

"Oh, I don't know—a couple idiots and a Cheetah, per-haps?"

"Neither would be very edible," he said.

"Well, fuck it—I'm going to talk to them. Wait here."

I took a step forward with my arms out and my hands open to show that I was unarmed and meant no harm. My gesture seemed to be misunderstood, however, because, instead of looking reassured, they raised their weapons and pointed them directly at me. The leader, unlike his underlings, abruptly reached up and behind his back for what I feared was going to be a razor sharp scimitar—the curved swords common to this part of the world. Instead, he removed his head scarf to reveal the most unlikely visage I could have ever imagined appearing in the desert. He was in fact a she, and she was very likely one of the most beautiful women I had ever seen. Her hair was long and dark as coal, her skin smooth and olive, and her eyes were the most glorious shade of emerald green. The only thing to mar her otherwise perfect visage was a thin scar on her left cheek that ran from just below her eye to the corner of her mouth, but, instead of it taking away from her beauty, I thought it gave her face character in much the same way that a super model might have a unique freckle or birthmark. Sweet flower of the desert! She might have been armed and dangerous and in command of a rather imposing looking unit, but I was still officially smitten and remained all but lost in her eyes until she at last broke the silence and spoke.

"I am the Desert Fox," she said, with an accent that was more posh British than Arabic.

"I totally agree."

The woman's deadly serious expression softened, and she smiled.

"You must be Tag Finn."

"Indeed, but you may call me the Desert Stallion, and

this is my sidekick Little Gelding."

She laughed out loud, and it took a moment before she could respond.

"Sorry we're late, Stallion, but we had some unfinished business in the north."

"It's a ladies prerogative to make a gentleman wait."

She dismounted then walked over and held out her hand to introduce herself. It was an interesting gesture and one that gave me a little cultural insight into my beautiful new friend. The majority of people in this part of the world were Muslims, and they believed it was wrong to shake hands with the opposite sex and some even included members of the same sex in that category. Extremists even believed that touching the hand of a non believer required religious purification after such an encounter. The Desert Fox was therefore not particularly religious and perhaps more moderate and likely westernized in her beliefs.

"I am Dolunay Khalida, nice to meet you."

"The pleasure is all mine," I said, taking her hand.

Next, she addressed Farid.

"And nice to meet you, Dr. Ardeshir. I hope you don't mind if I wait to shake your hand until after you've cleaned up."

Farid laughed.

"Absolutely, and please, call me Farid," he said.

He leaned in and whispered into my ear.

"She knows my real name?" he asked.

"Apparently," I whispered back.

"All right, friends, we had best get going, as a car like this will bring unwanted attention in this part of the desert. Come, I will ride with you, and one of my ladies can take care of my camel."

Ladies? Interesting. I had a closer look at the line of Bedouins and did indeed detect the outline of some breasts beneath their thawbs. Sweet Yentl's yabbos! The Desert Fox was the leader of a badass all female military unit, which meant this day was just getting better and better! My attention was suddenly drawn back to my dashing desert beauty, when she started walking towards the Cheetah.

"I've always wanted to see one of these in person. It's beautiful," she said, as she stopped in front of it.

I headed over and stood at her side.

"Very beautiful," I said, turning my gaze to Dolunay.

She smiled bashfully, and I couldn't help but smile back, and we entered a long moment of uncomfortable smiling and silence that made me feel more like an awkward teen than an adult.

"And you're into your cars," I finally said, breaking from my stupor.

"Oh yes, and, as they say in England, I'm a petrol-head."

"Well in that case, do you want to drive?" I asked.

"Hell yes, so you and Little Gelding had best hold on."

"Shotgun!" I yelled as I climbed into the Cheetah, thereby relegating Farid to the doldrums of the back seat.

Dolunay turned the key and brought the beast's twelve powerful cylinders growling to life, their throaty cry a warning to the desert ahead. She put it in gear and expertly released the clutch, sending a spray of sand that spooked the nearby camels, who shuffled sideways to get clear of the mechanical monster. We charged up the wall of sand and caught massive air before landing on the soft dune below. Dolunay cranked the wheel hard over to the right and expertly pitched the car sideways into a full drift before steering southwest and presumably to her desert hideaway. I continued to watch as she her expertly used the throttle, brakes, and steering wheel to navigate the rolling dunes, and I realized that she was one hell of a driver, and it was making her even more attractive. She caught me staring and smiled.

"I know what you're thinking," she said.

"That your aggressive driving style has a tendency to make your breasts jiggle?" I asked.

She chuckled.

"No, I was thinking more along the lines that it must be strange to see a woman driving in Saudi Arabia."

She was, of course, referring to the obvious fact that women in Saudi Arabia were forbidden by law to drive, let alone vote or hold any kind of office. Coming from America or Europe it was hard to believe that this kind of inequality still existed in the supposedly civilized world, but the Women's Suffrage Movement, which had started well over a hundred years ago, had apparently missed the Middle East.

"Well, honestly, I wasn't even thinking about the fact

that you're driving, but rather how impressively you're driving."

"So, not the jiggling?"

"The jiggling is merely a side benefit to watching you handle this beast."

She smiled.

"Believe it or not, I used to do some rally and club car racing during my time at university in England, but, sadly, I don't have much time for it these days."

"Well you definitely haven't lost any of your driving skills, so, between that and the jiggling, you shouldn't be surprised to find me sporting a pretty serious chub."

She looked at me curiously.

"Chub?" she asked.

"It's a slang for boner."

She smiled.

"Ah, yes, boner. Now, there's a word I haven't heard in a while."

"Well, maybe not heard, but I'm sure you've caused more than a few of them."

She blushed, and her full sensuous lips parted into a glowing smile.

"Sorry—as you can obviously see, it's been a long time since a man paid me a compliment or used such colorful language," she said.

"Then you probably need to get out of the desert more often."

We continued on for about twenty minutes, and the

large dunes gave way to smaller ones, and soon a beautiful green oasis appeared out of the desert. The road went over a small rise, and, as we came over the top, I could see a large ancient fortress nestled amongst the palm trees. It was made from a terra cotta colored stone and, along with the surrounding grounds, was easily the size of a small city. A short distance ahead, we passed through a large gate and continued on beyond the walls to the courtyard that resided in front of the main structure. Dolunay stopped the vehicle, and we climbed out and were greeted by a small contingent of armed women. The one in front was probably in her early thirties, pretty, and appeared to be in formidable physical shape.

"I see you've found our latest visitors, Dolunay."

"Yes, and would you please check and make sure their rooms are ready?"

"Of course," the woman said, as she gave Farid and me a nice long look then smiled, apparently having liked what she'd seen.

She and the other women left shortly thereafter, and I had a look around before returning my attention to our hostess.

"So what exactly is this place?" I asked.

"It's an old fortress from the Ottoman period that I've converted into our primary base of operations."

"I imagine there's a lot of history in these walls."

"Yeah, some bad, some good, but we're doing a lot more of the latter these days."

"Speaking of which—what exactly is it you do here?"

"Come inside, and I'll tell you."

We followed Dolunay through an archway and into a grand foyer that, in turn, opened into a large living room furnished with palm plants and comfortable looking leather couches and chairs. She motioned for us to take a seat, and, a moment later, three women came in carrying trays with small bowls of fruit, bread, jelly, sparkling water, and coffee.

"I assume you're hungry," she said, taking a seat beside me.

"Yes, I am," I said, as I filled three cups of coffee then handed the first to Dolunay.

She smiled and looked a little taken aback.

"Did I do something strange?" I asked.

"No, but it's very refreshing to have a man wait on me," she said.

"I hate to sound like a broken record, but you really need to get out of the desert more often."

I clinked my cup to hers, then she proceeded to make both Farid and me a little plate of food. I thanked her then decided to start with the chocolate filled bread. It was still warm from the oven, and when I took a bite it was utterly delicious and melted in my mouth—reminding me of the chocolate croissants I enjoyed at my local French Bakery back home. I continued eating, all the while alternating bites with sips of coffee, and, combined with my lovely hostess, was making this a perfect morning.

"So, what exactly is it you do with all this," I asked.

"I'm afraid that it's kind of a long story."

"I've got all the time in the world."

She smiled.

"Well then, as you know, this and the surrounding countries are primarily Muslim, and some of them are subject to very strict and antiquated laws, the majority of which are particularly unfair to women. Every day, women of all ages, are whipped, tortured, and stoned to death for crimes that don't even exist in America or Europe. A woman can actually be imprisoned for being raped, because she is seen as having had impure relations with a man who is not her husband."

"It's absolutely idiotic and adds credence to my theory that men are actually devolving back into their primordial selves."

"Thankfully not all men, but there are enough of them out there that terrible incidents continue to occur."

"Yeah, like the one in Afghanistan where a couple of Taliban idiots executed a twenty-two year old woman because they couldn't decide which of them should have her."

"What I wouldn't have given to have been able to rescue her."

"Yeah, and kill the two idiots who caused it as well as those who watched and cheered as it happened. Each and every one of those fuckers deserves a bullet."

"Indeed, so, after my own bit of trouble, I decided to use my substantial inheritance to start a foundation that rescues these women and places them in new lives in western countries. We have contacts, supply routes, and safe houses all throughout the Middle East, North Africa, and Asia. It's grown so successful, in fact, that intelligence agencies, such as your CIA and the Mossad amongst others, pay us a lot of money to utilize our assets to move agents and resources in and out of the places we operate. We help them, and they help us."

"Everybody wins," I said.

"Exactly."

"So, who are the women here?"

"These are the ones that chose to remain with me so that they could help others the same way I helped them."

"Pretty incredible," Farid said.

"We do what we can."

"Which is more than most. I'm curious though—if it's not too personal, do you mind me asking what you meant when you said you had your own bit of trouble?" I asked.

"My parents were very wealthy Sauds, but they were progressive thinkers and had me schooled in England and America. After Oxford, I went to graduate school at Columbia University in New York, and met and fell deeply in love with a fellow student. He happened to be the son of a very powerful Emir from Yemen, and everything was like a storybook romance until we finished school and moved back to his home country to get married. At that point, things suddenly changed, and I was expected to become a proper Muslim wife, but, having been raised mostly in the

West, I didn't adapt very well, and I ended up getting this scar on my second wedding anniversary."

"I take it that it wasn't very romantic."

"No it was not. Quite the opposite in fact, because my husband wanted me to watch while he raped one of our maids."

"Where in the hell did that idea come from?"

"Things were already cooling off between us, so I think he did it as a show of force to make it clear that I was his wife and therefore had to obey him in all ways."

"And you obviously didn't go along."

"No, in fact I tried to stop him, but he attacked me with a knife and left me with this," she said, pointing to the scar on her face.

"Jesus, I'm sorry," I said.

"Don't be. This blemish on my face reminds me every day of the injustices that exist in the world, and I am proud to say that I managed to get a hold of the knife, and my husband ended up looking a lot worse than me. This of course caused his father to put out an edict for my death, but I managed to escape back across the border to Saudi Arabia and, soon thereafter, began building the organization that you see here."

"It's an amazing story, and even more so because you utilized that same courage it took to survive to now save other people in similar situations. Of course, I can't help but wonder if spending all your energy helping others never allows you to think about your own needs."

"Perhaps," she said, a little sadly.

We finished breakfast, and I took a cup of coffee to go as Dolunay led us upstairs to our rooms so that we could freshen up. I always thought that the term freshen up was kind of strange and assumed, at least in the case of women, that they were touching up their makeup or applying perfume when they said those words. After all, fresh usually implied a good smell, but Estelle, my recent love interest from the Soft Taco Island adventure, assured me that women were, in truth, actually sneaking off to take a shit. That didn't seem very fresh, so perhaps that statement was intended to be ironic. Regardless of the gender differentiation of freshening up, for me at this very moment it was going to be the combination of several things—namely shitting, showering, and brushing my teeth, so, in reality, I was only going to be sixty-six point six seven percent fresh, but that was about as good as it got after a night of drinking out in the desert.

My room turned out to be quite nice and had a king sized bed and full bathroom complete with a western style toilet, sink, shower, as well as all the necessary toiletries with the most important being toothpaste and a brand new toothbrush. There wasn't a fan unit, but ventilation would be provided by two open windows that both faced out over the lovely oasis below. I set my coffee on the sink and dropped onto the seat, shifting slightly to find that sweet spot where my bunghole was perfectly aligned over the deepest part of the bowl. Properly situated, I grabbed my coffee and took a long glorious sip then relaxed and made a horn sound, thus signaling the beginning of the great exodus of waste that was beginning its southerly migration to the humble porcelain kingdom of *Toiletistan*.

Sitting there upon that glorious seat, I was particularly relieved to be in a real bathroom after having thought that I was going to have to do my morning business au naturale behind a sand dune. Dropping a deuce in the open desert was not exactly a comforting thought, least of all when you considered the options for toilet paper. Sand? Hell no. The butthole was generally the last place you wanted sand, so I was currently feeling pretty relieved. I sensed a few more refugees coming through customs and decided to pull out my iPhone and was surprised to see that I had Wi-Fi. This truly was an oasis. I checked my email then glanced at my homepage, curious to see if the world had drastically changed in the last twenty-four hours. All was the same, which meant there was an abundance of news stories about either horrible or useless events—the former being people hurting each other, and the latter being young celebrities and spoiled children of the one percent changing sexual partners or getting into trouble. One article in particular detailed the affairs of the world's various royals, and, coincidentally, on the second page, there was a bit about Sheikh Hamza and how he had supposedly been seen cavorting with a new unnamed society gal pal—probably the one I'd seen at the palace.

I finished up, shaved, and stepped into the shower and

enjoyed washing away the remnants of the previous night's festivities. Off-roading threw up a lot of dust and sand, and the tiny particles managed to find their way into every crevice of the human body. Finally feeling fresh and clean as a baby, I wrapped my towel around my waist only to realize that I had no clothes to wear. I hadn't expected to leave the UAE on such short notice last night, and wondered if I could have my things in Dubai sent home. Of course, that wouldn't be much help at the moment, and I feared I might just be relegated to wearing my filthy Dolce & Gabbana tuxedo. As if by divine intervention, there was a knock at the door, and I opened it to find a young woman standing there with a stack of garments. She saw that I was mostly naked except for the towel and gave me a thorough once over before smiling demurely and averting her eyes.

"I'm sorry to intrude, but Dolunay saw that you had no baggage and had me bring you these clothes."

"Really? Where in the hell did you find them?" I asked.

"Many of us have skills from our former lives. Some sew, farm, or cook and the extra items that we manufacture or grow are sold to help fund our efforts."

"Pretty enterprising," I said, taking the pants off the top of the stack.

I unfolded them and draped them down across my body.

"Holy shit, these look like they'll be a perfect fit."

"Dolunay has a good eye."

"Two, in fact."

She laughed.

"Now, if you could give me your dirty clothes, I'll have them cleaned and returned later today."

I grabbed my suit and undergarments and handed them to her in a large rolled up ball.

"All right, now please come downstairs whenever you're ready, as Dolunay would like to give you a tour of our little oasis."

"Thank you, and please tell her I'll be down shortly."

I closed the door and laid the rest of the clothes out on the bed. There was a pair of baggy, loose fitting pants, a shirt, and a thawb, with the last item being the long customary robe-like garment that Dolunay and her people had been wearing in the desert. Interestingly, it was generally worn by Arabic men as their outside layer of clothing, so I assume Dolunay used it in order for her and her girls to blend more easily into the male dominated society of Saudi Arabia. There weren't any underwear, which meant that I was going full commando, though, of course, there wasn't much need for any western style undergarments around my privates in this kind of heat, and the more airflow I had around my ham and eggs, the better they, and in turn I, would feel.

I put on my new clothes then looked in the mirror, and three words instantly came to mind—Lawrence of Arabia. Perhaps it would be my destiny to unite the women of this part of the world into one giant all-powerful nation that would at last bring peace and harmony to the turbulent cradle of civilization. I went back to the bathroom, brushed my teeth, and headed downstairs to find Farid already there, chatting away with Dolunay, who smiled and waved when she saw me.

"Ah, hello, Tag. I assume you are feeling much better having been able to freshen up?"

"I am, thank you, but I hope I didn't keep you waiting too long."

"Not at all, as Farid was just filling the time by telling me the incredible story of your first meeting."

"Yeah, and it sure had a hell of a surprise ending."

"It sure did, but I imagine this one will be much happier."

"I certainly hope so."

"Well then. Are you ready for your tour?"

"Absolutely."

We all stood then followed Dolunay into a large wood paneled hallway, where the walls were adorned with art and ancient weaponry. Along the way we passed a series of rooms including the kitchen, formal dining room, library, and the laundry room before stepping down into an open garden about half the size of a football field. It consisted of vegetables and fruits and was lovingly tended to by a number of young women who all smiled bashfully as we walked past.

"The girls here don't get to see men too often—particularly ones as handsome as yourselves."

Farid and I smiled dumbly at each other, as it was always nice to get a compliment, even more so from a beautiful woman like Dolunay. We continued on into another section that opened up into a large pasture containing livestock. Here they had cows, goats, sheep, and chickens, but fortunately this area was downwind of the main building, so the particularly unpleasant smell of animal dung drifted out towards the desert rather than into the main fortress.

Moving on, the next building was dedicated to textiles and the manufacture of clothing, rugs, and furniture. Again, the only workers were women, and again they smiled and gushed at our arrival. If only high school had been like this, I might have enjoyed it more. The next room was a long rectangular indoor firing range, and a group of women were expertly shooting Heckler and Koch G36 assault rifles. Their groupings were tight, and I hoped never be on the wrong end of their barrels. The young woman in the closest firing lane finished shooting and glanced at us through the glass barrier as she slid in a fresh clip. She smiled shyly then chambered a round and continued shooting, with her first shot a perfect bullseye. We moved on, and the following rooms included a pistol range and close quarters assault course, and both were crowded with Dolunay's particularly capable soldiers.

"The girls spend half of their day training and the other half doing support jobs. All on a voluntary basis of course."

"So, you basically have your own private on-call army."

"Pretty much, though it's necessary sometimes, as rescuing these girls often entails using a little force."

"So, how do you keep all this under the official Saudi

Arabian government's radar?"

"I used my father's political connections to get this piece of desert land deemed a sovereign state by the House of Saud."

"Convenient."

"Yes indeed."

I turned around and saw that directly across from the assault course was a padded floor that was used for training in hand to hand combat. There were heavy bags, pads, and a number of melee weapons on racks around the room. A tall, powerfully built woman overseeing the group noticed us and nodded in our direction.

"Care to test your skills against Adeela?" Dolunay asked with a smile.

"Hell no."

"Smart answer—she was an Olympic gold medalist in Judo, but she also trained in karate and Wing Chun."

"I have no doubt that she can kick any and all asses that stand before her."

We moved on back towards the main area, and the last stop was a gym which had state of the art fitness equipment, free weights, and even a fifty foot climbing wall and obstacle course off to the side. Clearly, Dolunay and her ladies did some serious training, and any enemy they faced was in for a world of hurt.

"This is quite an operation you've got here," I said.

"Yes, and we even have a hangar and airfield big enough to accommodate commercial jets."

"No shit?"

"Yes, it was originally built on the north end of the fortress by the Allies during World War II, but we have made substantial improvements so it can accommodate our customized Airbus A380.

"That's quite a plane."

"Yes, and it functions as a mobile command center and assault platform that can reach pretty much anywhere in the world in a matter of hours."

"Is that how we're flying out?" I asked.

"No, your people have made their own arrangements."

"Any idea what they are?"

"Only that some local air service will be coming tomorrow morning. If my clients prefer to make their own travel arrangements, I don't ask for any details. I provide complete discretion, which is why your government likes using my services. Well—that's the end of the tour. Any questions?"

"Yeah, what are you doing for dinner?"

"I'm glad you asked," she said, gazing at me with a mischievous smile.

CHAPTER TWENTY-FOUR
The Oasis in the Oasis

About four hours later, I donned my tuxedo and was brushing my teeth when there was a knock at my door. I opened it to discover Farid looking equally sharp with his suit cleaned and pressed, and I joined him, and we walked downstairs to find the dimmed lighting and soft shadows were making the fortress look even more exotic. We reached the dining room to find a fire burning in its stately fireplace, and soft music with a Middle Eastern flare was emanating from some unseen speakers. The table was already set, and its enormous size combined with the room's ambiance made it feel as though we were dining at Hogwarts. Farid and I walked over to the windows on the other side, so that we could admire the view of the setting sun, though our quiet moment of reverie was interrupted soon thereafter by a lovely young woman in a particularly flattering blue evening dress.

"Good evening, gentleman. Dolunay has asked me to tell you to feel free to partake of the wine. She and the others will be along shortly."

Farid and I walked to the table, and each of us picked up a glass of wine.

"Here's to America," he said.

"And to you actually making it there this time," I added.

We clinked our glasses together then took a sip. It was delicious, and I had to wonder how they managed to get such excellent wine in a dry country, but I imagine it must be easier when you ran your own secret desert oasis with a private army and air force at your beck and call.

"Good evening," a voice said, from behind us.

We both turned to see Dolunay looking sinfully delicious in a long body hugging silk fuchsia colored dress. Her hair was now up, and a necklace of large bold rubies and sapphires was hanging above the forbidden fruit that was her bulging cleavage. I had thus far only seen our hostess in loose fitting desert garb, but now I could truly see the full extent of her spectacular figure—everything from her long legs to her curvaceous backside and supple breasts. If there were any air left in the room, I couldn't feel it, for I was desperately trying to catch my breath.

"Fuck me!" I said, unable to control myself.

"What was that?" she asked.

I smiled.

"An unintentional request. Sorry, I was overcome by

shock, as I didn't think it was possible for you to look even more beautiful."

"Surely you're exaggerating."

"Have you ever heard the term blue balls?"

Farid giggled and mumbled *blue balls* under his breath.

"No, but it sounds like a children's game," she said.

"More like a man's curse, and I can tell you right now that I've got them in a big way."

"So, that's a compliment?" she asked, looking confused.

"Absolutely."

I stepped forward and handed Dolunay a glass of wine.

"Here's to Dolunay Khalida, the Desert Fox," I said.

"And the Desert Stallion and his Little Gelding," she added.

I laughed, then we clinked our glasses together and had a sip of wine.

"Please, have a seat," she said, motioning at the table.

We sat down, and more women started flowing in until every seat was full, then Dolunay stood to address the room.

"Everyone, please welcome our guests Tag and Farid."

The room of lovely ladies lifted their glasses and nodded in our direction, then Dolunay sat back down and leaned over to speak to me.

"I hope you don't mind the crowd, but, as I said earlier, we don't get men around here very often."

"I find crowds of women comforting."

"Me too," Farid added.

Dinner was served shortly thereafter and consisted of chicken over a spicy cardamom rice dish as well as a salad consisting of tomatoes, olives and dates. It was a perfect evening with a full compliment of food, females, and fantastic wine, and I felt like the luckiest man on earth to be in the presence of so much charming female company. Only a few bites into dinner, my attention was drawn to the other side of the table when a pretty woman with long dark hair and inquisitive brown eyes asked me a question.

"What is it do you do back in America?" she asked

"He's a private investigator," Farid interjected.

"Does that mean you are like James Bond?" she asked.

"No, he's more like *Magnum P.I.*," he said.

"*Magnum P.I.*? I don't understand," she said, looking confused.

Dolunay laughed.

"The women here haven't seen much western television and won't know about *Magnum P.I.*," she said.

"What does this Magnum person do?" the girl asked.

"He loafs around like a bum on the beach all day," Farid said, with a giggle.

"I help people," I said, jabbing Farid with my elbow.

"So, how is it that you are out here with us?"

"I'm helping this dingleberry get to a new life in America."

The girl looked confused.

"What is a dingleberry? Is it like a raspberry or blueberry?"

"Not exactly. They're not sweet, and no one would eat one."

"Oh, that's too bad."

Farid looked over at me and shook his head side to side to silently chastise me for corrupting these women with terrible American slang.

"Well, either way, it is wonderful that you are helping this dingleberry get to freedom," she said.

"I suppose, but what you all do here is far more meaningful than what I do."

"Thanks a lot," Farid said.

"Oh don't fret, Little Gelding. Helping you is also meaningful, just not as meaningful."

The final course arrived and consisted of homemade ice cream with fresh strawberries, and I had to wonder where they could find such an un-desert like dessert. We finished the delectable treat and officially came to the end of dinner, and Dolunay invited everyone into the living room for a drink and some quiet conversation. She rose from the table and led the way—her swaying hips and backside providing a most formidable beacon as we navigated the darkened hallways. We arrived in the candle-lit living room and settled into the comfortable furniture to find bottles of port and glasses already sitting on the various coffee tables. Farid sat on the opposite couch with two of the other women while Dolunay sat next to me with her legs crossed in such a way that her foot was touching my shin. I looked down and traced the length of her long tanned thigh with my eyes, and the thought of where it led caused a flutter in my heart and a gentle stirring in my pants. I took a sip of port then returned my gaze back up to her beautiful green eyes.

"You have an amazing life here," I said.

"I suppose—but it can get a little lonely at times."

"Anywhere can be lonely—believe me. I live in the Bay Area with seven million other people, and I still feel very much alone at times."

"At least you have lots of potential company."

"I suppose, but meaningful connections aren't easy to find."

She smiled and innocently placed her hand on my leg, and it caused my pulse rate to double.

"You know about my life, so why don't you tell me a little about yours," she suggested.

"Where should I start?"

"You choose."

"OK, I'll start at the beginning, but I'll try and keep it short and sweet, so you don't get too bored. Now, I was born and raised in Northern California, where I did a lot of swimming, martial arts, and masturbating—pretty much in that order."

Dolunay laughed.

"Which of the three were you best at?" she asked.

"The last one, of course—proof that practice makes perfect."

"And how about the second one?"

"Ah, martial arts—well, I was pretty good at that too, though I had an exceptional teacher—a real life kind of Mr. Miyagi."

"So, he was like the wise old man from *The Karate Kid* movie?"

"Kind of, though he wasn't an old gardener, but rather a wealthy and mysterious twenty-nine year old business-man from Japan, who I met while he was teaching a self defense class at the local community center. He was some kind of big time investment banker, but his true love was martial arts, and for some reason he took an interest in me and began teaching me privately on the side until I left for college."

"What style?" she asked.

"Kenpo karate, but it was his own unique system that incorporated a number of other things he'd liked in other systems. It was pretty eclectic, and I felt more as though he were training me to be some kind of warrior monk."

"Sounds interesting. Perhaps you should have tested your skills against Adeela."

"Fuck no! I can tell a good martial artist when I see one, and there was no need to prove that she could kick my ass."

Adeela, who was sitting just across from me, smiled and spoke.

"You flatter me, Tag, but I suspect you are pretty good with your hands and feet, as well as other appendages," she said.

"Now, you flatter me."

Dolunay gave my thigh a little squeeze to get my attention.

"Well, Tag, I must say—I'm enjoying your life story, so please go on."

"So, for college I went to Stanford and studied social psychology and, of course, continued masturbating until I graduated and joined the military. There, I managed to make it into Pararescue and headed off to various places in the world, with the last being Afghanistan, which came to an abrupt end when I got wounded rescuing a downed pilot."

"You obviously survived, but did you also manage to save the pilot?"

"Yeah, I did, and, believe it or not, that asshole is now the vice president of the United States."

"How fortuitous!"

"Yeah, but only if he manages to do something meaningful while he's in office."

"Regardless, it shows that you also have the desire to help those in need. Now, what did you do after that?"

"I was shipped home and got recruited by the CIA shortly thereafter, and worked for them for about five more exciting years. That ended badly, as Farid already told you, and I decided to get out and become a private investigator. Life pretty much slowed down at that point until I was hired for the job that led into this one, and voila—here I am in the desert with you!"

"Interesting, and you say your life slowed down when

you became a private investigator?"

"Yeah, it was all divorce cases and lost pets."

"You went from the CIA to finding lost pets? You must be joking."

"Afraid not, and the most recent one was a morbidly obese house cat," I said, pulling out my iPhone and bringing up a picture of Mr. Pickles in which he appeared to be in my neighbor Joyce's arms.

Dolunay stared in disbelief.

"How can she possibly be strong enough to hold him up?"

"She's not—the little fucker is actually perched on a stool that you can't see in the photo."

She laughed out loud then took a sip of her wine, all the while stifling another giggle as she once again placed her hand on my leg, but this time she looked at me with the predatory zeal of a hunting tigris.

"What do you think about a midnight swim?" she asked.

"I think the less clothes we wear, the better this evening will be."

"The feeling is mutual."

Dolunay clapped her hands and stood.

"Ladies! Let us all adjourn to the pool!"

The women all stood and started milling out of the living room with Farid and me joining in the procession. I glanced at Farid and noticed that he looked as confused as I was feeling. We made a left down a hallway that I hadn't yet seen and arrived at a massive outdoor patio lit only by a waning moon high above the desert. Even in the minimal light I could see there was a massive swimming pool and smooth tiled patio bordered on the far side by dense green shrubbery and palm trees that created a veritable oasis within the oasis. In the left back corner was a raised area with a waterfall that cascaded down into the pool, and, while I couldn't tell from here, I had a sneaking suspicion it was the location of a Jacuzzi. The women all fanned out around the massive pool, and I leaned in to whisper in Dolunay's ear.

"Farid and I don't have swim suits."

"That's OK, neither do we," she said, kicking off her shoes and reaching for the zipper of her dress.

My heart suddenly skipped a beat as I looked around and saw that every woman in view was following Dolunay's lead and undressing. I turned my attention back to my lovely hostess to see that she was now nude from the waist up with more flesh soon appearing as her dress fell to the ground. Unabashedly naked, she and her army of women all jumped into the pool, then Dolunay surfaced a moment later and brushed her long hair off of her face and looked at me with the most inviting of smiles.

"We're waiting," she said.

I looked at Farid, and he shrugged.

"When in Rome," he said.

"Easy for you to say. Most of them already saw your penis back in the desert."

I suddenly felt like a male stripper as I gazed around at

the see of curious faces watching me undress. When Farid and I at last dropped our underwear, we walked over to the edge of the pool and instinctively held our hands in front our privates. This was now one of those moments in life where you had to say what the fuck and grab the bull by the balls—or in our case, forget about the bull and let go of our balls.

"Ladies, I'd like to thank you all for allowing us into your beautiful sanctuary. I'd also like to apologize for any intentional or unintentional swelling that may occur in my gentleman region in the presence of so many beautiful naked women."

I lifted my arms wide and proud, and the crowd of women all clapped and cheered. I then took a half step forward and did a nice shallow dive off the edge of the pool and surfaced just a foot from Dolunay, whose breasts were bobbing up and down in the small waves created by my watery intrusion.

"Follow me," she said, as she slipped under the shimmering surface, and swam towards the other end of the pool.

I dove down and followed, zigzagging between the endless spectacle of naked bodies until at last surfacing in the deep waters in front of the waterfall. Dolunay had somehow disappeared, but I soon heard her voice call out from beyond the cascade of water. I ventured through it and found myself inside a dimly lit cavern that resided beneath the rocky structure. The water was shallower in here, and I was able to stand and walk over to join Dolunay.

"This way," she said, leading me up a short stairway out of the water.

The path continued out the other side and then up the small rock promontory until reaching what was, indeed, the Jacuzzi. We stepped down into it until we were up to our waists then paused to allow our bodies to adjust to the heat before dropping all the way in to our necks. I heard giggling from below, and, a moment later, Farid and two women came charging up the steps and joined us in the tub.

"Cocktails?" Dolunay asked.

"Absolutely," I responded.

"Any preference?"

"How about a long slow comfortable screw against a wall?"

"Excuse me?"

"I was only joking, but it actually is a real cocktail."

"Hmmm—sounds pretty good."

"Yeah, though anything you make will be lovely."

She stood, and my eyes were drawn to her pert round backside as she moved to a mini bar built into the far side of the Jacuzzi. A moment later she was back with a pitcher and several glasses.

"I hope you like vodka and cucumber," she said.

"Sounds refreshing and delicious."

She filled the glasses then handed one to everyone in the Jacuzzi.

"To our guests," she said.

We all clinked glasses, then I took a sip of the cocktail

to discover it was light and delicious with only the faintest hint of cucumber, and the unusual concoction was especially welcome in the heat of the Jacuzzi. I leaned back and took a moment to cast my gaze up at the sky full of stars and realized this was one of those rare moments in life where you took a mental snapshot and filed it away with your most precious memories. Suddenly, there was a disturbance in the water, and I looked over to see Farid coming across the tub to join me.

"Dude, it's awesome to be hanging out with you again," he said.

"I know, and I wish I could promise it would always be this good."

Farid chugged his drink and stepped up out of the Jacuzzi and onto the edge where it overlooked the deep end of the pool. The two women joined him, then he looked back at us and smiled.

"I am a golden God," he said, opening his arms.

He was quoting the Russell character from the movie *Almost Famous*, but sadly only I was likely to understand the reference. Farid and his two lady friends then jumped off and screamed with delight until they splashed into the pool below. Dolunay and I were now alone in the turbulent waters, and she slipped in between my legs and placed her hands on my thighs.

"Does my scar bother you?"

"No—I think it makes you beautiful."

"Surely you're not serious," she said, as she brought her

hand up and ran her finger down its length.

Dolunay was a beautiful woman, yet somehow still carried a great deal of insecurity about something as insignificant as a scar, though I suppose all of us were prone to some kind of insecurity that allowed the most minuscule of physical or psychological details to hinder our lives. Even more peculiar was that she could comfortably disrobe before a virtual stranger yet still be wary of an inch and a half of physical history on her face.

"That scar isn't a blemish, but rather a physical testament to the courage of the bold and beautiful woman behind it," I said, as I leaned forward and kissed her scar where it extended across her cheek.

When I pulled back, I noticed her eyes were wet with tears.

"I hope I didn't upset you."

"No, you didn't. These are tears of joy, I'm afraid. Now, would you mind if I kissed you?" she asked.

"Not at all."

She leaned forward and kissed me, and her lips were soft and warm, and I lingered a long time, so that I could draw out the excitement of our first kiss. She pulled back and wiped the tears from her eyes before she spoke.

"That was the first time I have kissed a man since I left my husband five years ago."

"I know I'm sounding like a broken record and all, but you really, really, really need to get out of the desert more often."

She smiled as I ran my fingers through her wet hair and pulled her close for another kiss. Her lips were salty from tears but still just as delectable, and soon they parted, and her tongue came forward to meet mine in a glorious oral ballet—slipping, sliding, moving against each other in the most intimate of dances. Our lust grew more desperate, and she slid her hips forward and straddled me, so that she could grind her sweet essence against my manhood. I slid my hands down her back and took hold of her buttocks and joined her efforts by pulling her hips to mine, desperately wanting to be inside her. She let out a long sigh then pulled back her hips just enough to make room to run her hands down my chest and take hold of my very hard manhood. She gazed at me with a wicked smile playing on her lips as she ran her hands up and down its length.

"I guess my scar really doesn't bother you."

"Obviously not. In fact, I think it's rather sexy—more of a beauty mark."

"Well thank you, Tag. I never thought of it that way."

"Well, now you can, and might I say that you have officially given me the worlds most dire case of blue balls."

"Blue balls? What in God's name are these blue balls you keep mentioning?"

"You've really never heard that term?"

"Never."

"Technically, it's a slang term for vasal congestion, and it actually affects both sexes, and is a condition that occurs when a person becomes aroused, and their erogenous regions—namely, the penis, vagina, and breasts swell with blood for an extended period of time and become painful or, least of all, uncomfortable. And, those particular organs will remain so until achieving climax, which constricts the muscles and sends the blood back into proper circulation."

"So, perhaps we should do something about your blue balls. Come, follow me."

"I'm not sure we should proceed in that exact order."

She looked confused for a moment, then recognition of my stupid joke set in, and she smiled.

"True. So, follow me, and then you can *come* after we get where we're going."

"Well, as a gentleman, I alway believe that it should be ladies first," I said.

Dolunay and I climbed from the tub and proceeded down the steps and around the pool. I was naked, hard, and had no towel, so it was basically pointless to try and hide anything, least of all Mr. Happy. All of the women were smiling shyly as we passed, and a few even tried to be polite and avert their eyes, but the vast majority took a nice long look. We stopped upon reaching a sliding glass door, and Dolunay paused.

"Goodnight, ladies. I will see you all at breakfast," she said, before disappearing inside.

Farid appeared at that moment with a girl on each arm and a smile on his face.

"Dude, it's seriously awesome to be hanging out with you again."

"You already said that."

"I know—but I really mean it," he said, before he and his little entourage turned and headed back to the pool.

I turned and walked inside to discover a large candle lit room with a massive four poster bed, and beside it stood Dolunay, still beautifully naked as she sipped her drink in the flickering light. Alas, she set her cocktail on the adjacent dresser and slid onto the massive bed, where her tan lithe body stood out in stark contrast to the white comforter.

"How are yours balls feeling now?" she asked.

"Like a couple of swollen blueberries."

"Perhaps it's time for juicing."

"Ahhh—yes—nectar of the gods," I said, as I walked closer.

I arrived at the foot of the bed, and she rolled onto her back and beckoned me in as though I were a plane approaching her runway. I slid between her legs and ran my hands up her calves to her thighs, and her heart started beating visibly faster with each passing second that my fingers drew closer to her nether regions. Unable to wait any longer, she reached up and pulled me onto her, and my hard mantool pressed firmly against her lady parts. She kissed me, and, as we entwined our tongues, I ran my hand down her body, over her taut nipples, then south past her bellybutton to find my destination between her legs. There, I gently ran my fingers over the contours of her essence until focusing in on her clitoris, where I began making small delicate exploratory circles. Dolunay moaned in delight and thrust her hips upward as an obvious signal that I should delve deeper, and I realized it was time to transition to a better tool than my hand. I pulled my mouth free of her lips then kissed her neck and shoulder before continuing down to her breasts, where I used my tongue to encircle her substantial nipples. I finished with a playful nibble, then, with my work in the great north complete, headed south to where my hand was still busy at work. I kissed her stomach then continued on, sliding my lips down past her mons pubis, pausing only a breath away from her long neglected clitoris. Strangely, she started to squirm and tense, so I paused to conduct a welfare check.

"Everything OK?" I asked.

"Um, yeah, but I think you should know that I haven't had a man go down on me before."

"Not even in college?"

"No, neither my boyfriends nor husband were exactly into giving oral pleasure, so, at the moment, I'm feeling caught between excitement and terror."

"I think that someone who goes by the nickname the Desert Fox can handle it," I said, looking up at her.

It was interesting, yet sad, that I had discovered another woman living without the divine pleasure of oral sex. The world could indeed be a cruel place when a person was denied such simple niceties of human interaction. I smiled at Dolunay then used my hands to gently press open her legs.

"Now, shall I continue?" I asked.

"Yes," she said, as she reached out and gripped the sheets to steady herself.

The vagina was perhaps the most complicated organ in the universe and achieving an orgasm generally required proper handling and a lot of firsthand knowledge and experience. Thankfully, I had acquired both having spent the majority of my adult life exploring the opposite sex and, now, it was time to do my best to give Dolunay her great sexual re-awakening. I placed my lips on her essence then reached out with my tongue and pressed inside before sliding up to her clitoris, which I circled ever so gently to allow her to acclimate to the pleasure. This, in turn, gave me the opportunity to learn her unique sensitivity and find her natural rhythm, so that I could hopefully bring her to climax. Dolunay had, unfortunately, been living in a sexual vacuum and therefore was like a desert waiting for rain. Every twist of the tongue brought an involuntary gasp from her lips and a spasm to her hips, and it was only moments before her climax came on like a great earthquake, her entire body shaking violently as her cries of passion echoed into the desert night. At last, she came to rest and smiled as she closed her eyes and let out a long sigh. She opened them a second later, and a naughty smile formed on her lips as she rolled me onto my back and took hold of my manhood.

"I hope you don't mind if I reciprocate. As you obviously know, I haven't had the pleasure of having my way with a man's privates in a long time," she said, as she ran her hand up and down my hard shaft.

"I thought your previous boyfriends weren't into oral sex."

"Oh they were into it all right—receiving it."

"Bastards."

"Yes, but I enjoyed having my way with them nonetheless."

"Well don't let me get in the way of your enjoyment."

She eyed me lustfully as she abruptly leaned down and took my penis in her mouth and used her tongue to encircle the tip. She started using her mouth and hands in perfect concert, conducting a veritable symphony of pleasure that left me dizzy with ecstasy and teetering on the cusp of release. Fearing an early end to the evening I at last overcame the madness of lust and intervened.

"Um, I hate to interrupt, but I'm..."

She paused and smiled wickedly.

"Oh, did you want me to stop?"

"Of course I don't want you to stop, but, I think it's important not to finish just when we're getting started."

I sat up and pulled free of Dolunay's formidable grip and sat up.

"Oh, well what did you have in mind?" she asked.

"I'll leave it up to you, my sweet desert minx."

"Well, there are some silk sashes in the top drawer of my dresser, and I wouldn't mind if you tied me to the bed and had your way with me all night long."

I smiled as I contemplated her suggestion.

"I like your thinking, but I don't want to waste even a second away from you, which means, I'll just have to make due with this," I said, sliding forward until the tip of my manhood was resting against her opening.

I slid it up over her clitoris then back down, and it elicited a soft moan of pleasure as she pressed her hips forward in an attempt to steer me inside. I pulled back ever so slightly and smiled.

"Now you're just being cruel," she said.

"No, just taking it nice and slow. It has been five years."

"Five—long—years, so I'm pretty sure it's time for you to—how do they say it in America? Ah, yes—fuck my brains out."

"Only if you promise that we can squeeze them back into your head afterwards, as I like an intelligent woman."

She smiled and gave me a playful hit that was the signal that small talk was over, and it was time to get down to business. I moved forward, sliding my knees under her legs until my mantool was once again lined up and resting at her opening. It was a position only meant for an agile man, but it allowed an excellent view of a woman's treasures. It also afforded a good angle at hitting the mythological and hotly contested Gräfenberg spot, which resided about an inch or so inside and on the top of the vagina. Dolunay looked up expectantly then reached around and took hold of my buttocks and pulled me in towards her forgotten realms, thus forcing my manhood to slide into the wet heat of her womanhood until we were touching at the hips.

"Oh sweet Lord! This feels so good that I now realize I've had blue balls for the last five years," she said.

"Well, then don't worry, my beautiful Smurf, as we're just getting started."

"What the hell is a Smurf?"

"The bluest of creatures—but not for long."

I kissed her and started moving my manhood in and out, gently testing the waters and using the time to admire every beautiful inch of her body. It was a visual feast, and each second of contact was flooding my mind with lust and forcing me to subtly increase my speed until we were at a breakneck pace that sent her breasts bouncing hypnotically in accordance with every harsh meeting of our hips. It became too much to bear, and I was soon approaching critical mass and, therefore, had to slow down in order to sustain the pleasure. With the subtle slowing of the action, I decided to transition to missionary position, the proximity allowing me to lean down and kiss her. The second our lips touched she reached out and pulled me tight to her body, allowing me to press deep inside, only now I could add a little grinding motion. It increased her clitoral stimulation and thus evoked a loud series of moans that brought forth yet another climax. She cried out as her entire body spasmed and shook, and it was all I could do to hold back the rising tide of my own release. After she relaxed and caught her breath, she kissed me then smiled.

"Can we try another position as well?"

"Of course. What did you have in mind?" I asked.

"Will you take me from behind?"

"Ahhh—doggie style."

"Doggie style?"

"Yeah, it's not the greatest name, but I suppose it presents the right imagery."

Dolunay turned over onto her hands and knees, and it brought her curvaceous rear end up into prominence to create a tantalizing visual treat. I saddled up yet again and pressed inside of her and did a few slow exploratory thrusts until she turned and smiled at me over her shoulder.

"You're right. It's not a great name, but it is an excellent position," she said.

"And it only gets better."

We settled into a robust rhythm with my pelvis pounding against her lovely backside, and every thrust was accompanied by a loud gasp of pleasure. This was a tricky orientation, however, and achieving orgasm sometimes required understanding that every woman had her own unique playbook—as had been the case with the lovely Olivia. In fact, an orgasm from intercourse alone could be as rare as seeing a chupacabra, yeti, or even the Loch Ness Monster, but generally, I found success or failure was the direct result of the effort, or lack thereof, of a sexual partner. In our current position, the fabled Gräfenberg spot received ample attention, but the clitoris was left somewhat out in the cold. To amend that, I reached around, found her little patch of sunshine, and set to work applying a little manual stimulation. It required the ability to multitask by balancing hand and hip motion, but my efforts were soon rewarded when Dolunay started into yet another thunderous climax. Her entire body shook until she at last collapsed forward onto the bed and took a moment to recover before rolling over and talking to me with the giddiness of a schoolgirl.

"Do you mind if I climb on top?" she asked, as she rolled over and shoved me backwards onto the bed.

"Feel free to climb aboard m'lady, for I am the Desert Stallion."

She laughed.

"True, and if I remember correctly, this position is called cowgirl, but I haven't done it since college," she said.

"Don't worry—it's just like riding a bike, except you don't have to worry about falling."

"Except perhaps—in love," she said, with a smile.

"True. Except for that."

She took up the cowgirl position and made me her veritable steed—the coupling causing her eyes roll into the back of her head as she let out a little moan of pleasure. She started grinding her hips ever harder against mine, focusing more on making little circles which heightened her clitoral sensation while lessening the friction on Tag junior. This, in turn, allowed me to take a moment to gather my staying power and enjoy the view of the beautiful woman before my eyes. I reached up and took hold of Dolunay's sizable breasts, and their soft contours filled my hands as I stimulated her large hard nipples with my fingertips. She was lost to the pleasure, and it caused her to moan and increase the frequency and intensity of her gyrations. She was approaching yet another orgasm, and, as she had already had three climaxes, it was time for me to man up and share in the most primal and intimate of human experiences. I took hold of her buttocks and combined my strength with hers, and it allowed us to pick up the pace and pound our hips together until we were teetering on the edge of release. She leaned down and kissed me, and it became the spark for us to at last achieve an earth shattering mutual climax. Our cries became an ear crushing crescendo as we continued on through the successive waves of pleasure until coming to rest with our skin covered in a thin veil of lover's sweat. My green eyed goddess leaned down and came in for another kiss, and her breasts felt heavy against my chest as our tongues engaged in a final slippery embrace. We soon parted to take a long well-deserved breath, and she dropped down beside me, wrapped her arm across my chest, and we lay in the quiet comfort of the night.

"I might just have to follow your advice and get out of the desert more often," she said.

"Yeah, either that, or I seriously need to get out to the desert more often," I responded.

We shared a laugh then drifted off to sleep with our bodies spent and our minds at rest.

CHAPTER TWENTY-FIVE
The Flight of the Phoenix

I awoke around seven a.m. feeling completely disoriented and desperately needing to pee. I looked around the dim room for a moment to get my bearings then took a quick peak under the covers to see the very beautiful Dolunay sleeping on her stomach beside me. I kissed her shoulder then gave her backside a brief caress before venturing off to the bathroom, where I took the grandest of morning pisses. Finished, I used a piece of toilet paper to wipe the stray droplets from the rim of the bowl before putting the seat back down and heading off to the sink to find a toothbrush. There was an extra one in the top drawer, and I used it then slid back into bed to find Dolunay awake and looking especially peaceful in the morning light.

"How did you sleep?" I asked.

"Wonderful, thanks to you."

"It's the least I could do to repay you for your hospitality."

"Oh it was a lot more than that. It was a new lease on life."

"You do a lot of good, so you should do a little good for yourself now and then."

"From this day forward, I shall. Now, are you ready for coffee and breakfast?"

"You bet your sweet desert ass."

She got up, threw on a robe, and disappeared out her bedroom door and returned ten minutes later with a tray of breakfast goodies. She set it on the bedside table then poured each of us a cup of coffee. I added cream then breathed in the heavenly aroma before taking my beloved first sip. It was strong and aromatic and made me feel warm from my toes to my chinny chin chin. Meanwhile, Dolunay tore off a piece of bread from the freshly baked loaf, covered it in jam, then hand fed me, making me feel like the sultan of a desert palace. This experience was pretty fucking pleasant, and I couldn't help but imagine waking up to this kind of luxury every day. Thirty minutes and two and a half cups of coffee later, breakfast was done, and I was ready for my morning movement.

"I guess I should go up to my room and get ready."

"Nonsense, you can use my bathroom."

"Oh, I wouldn't want to impose."

"Don't be ridiculous."

"Well—um—OK then."

I kissed Dolunay then headed for her bathroom feeling slightly uneasy at the thought of dropping a deuce so soon into our relationship. I paused at the doorway and hazarded one last look at my hostess before closing the door and seeing that it didn't have a lock. Shit, I'd just have to trust fate to see that it remained closed, thus making my dump an act of faith unto itself. I turned and gazed upon my kingdom and realized that it was glorious, spacious, and covered in fine marble—something I hadn't noticed while I was taking my early morning horse piss. I walked over to the toilet, set down my half full cup of coffee, and took a minute to admire its contoured seat before descending onto the throne of immortals. The seat was room temperature, comfortable, and would make a fine pedestal on which to lay my waste. I took yet another sip of coffee, relaxed, and brought forth the first wave of defecation. Without warning, the door opened and in walked Dolunay. I froze in terror, my sphincter tightening up as I cowered, feeling like an opossum on a lonely highway as it stares into an oncoming car's headlights. Unlike the opossum however, I couldn't pass out from fear and instead remained fully alert and staring at my nemesis. To my utter surprise, she smiled and grabbed something from the counter.

"Sorry, I just needed my toothbrush," she said, holding it up before casually exiting.

Sweet mother of God. We just had our first official bathroom crossover time with less than eight hours elapsing after intercourse. What did this mean? Was it a good or a bad omen? Fuck. Only time would tell. Still a little in shock, I finished my business then prepared for the shower by searching for a razor in Dolunay's bathroom drawers. I knew she had one because of her excellent western style grooming standards. Both her arm pits and pubic areas were nicely maintained, the latter with just enough of a tuft of hair that there was no mistaking the fact that she indeed looked like a woman and not a prepubescent girl. I'm sure every man had their preference, but in the age of the Brazilian and the Jean-Luc Picard, I found it refreshing to at least find a Charlie Chaplin—though Dolunay was by no means a *little tramp*.

The razors were in the third drawer down, and I grabbed a new one, lathered up with soap and had a pretty decent shave, considering I was using one of those double bladed ladies models. I rinsed my face off and finally got into the spacious glass walled enclosure, where I admired the fine tiles and six showerheads. I turned on the taps, wet my hair, then stepped to the side of the watery onslaught to grab some floral scented shampoo off the shelf. After rubbing it into my hair, I grabbed some soap, lathered up, then closed my eyes and stepped back under the torrent of water. A few moments passed, and I felt a tugging on my manhood and opened my eyes to find a very naked Dolunay, using her mouth and hands to manually inflate my penis.

"Funny, I was just thinking that the shower seemed a bit lonely."

She stopped and looked up at me.

"As was the bedroom, which is why I came in here."

"You are truly a humanitarian."

She went back to work on my wood and used her tongue the way Michelangelo used a brush. She was an artist all right, and, in about fifteen more seconds, I would be ready to paint the ceiling of the Sistine Chapel—in a bold although pearlescent, shade of white.

"Wait, I feel a little selfish leaving you with this as our final act."

She paused and looked up.

"I really would like to leave you with something special to remember me by on your flight."

"You've already done that," I said, as I guided her up onto her feet and kissed her.

I took hold of her buttocks, and, as I lifted her off the ground, she reached down and guided the tip of my manhood inside her essence. I slid in to full mount then braced her against the wall of the shower and began moving my hips fore and aft, all the while gently grinding at the apex of each thrust. The precarious position allowed for a plentiful amount of penile and clitoral stimulation that left both of us riding on the edge of ecstasy. Still, the sad realization that this might be our final coupling inspired us to increase our pace into a manic frenzy. Flesh met flesh, and our hearts beat in harried unison as we pounded away at full gallop towards an oncoming orgasm. It was all I could do to hold back the tide of my loins, but she abruptly dug her fingers into the flesh my back and kissed me, and like the night before, the touching of our lips became the final spark to set our union ablaze. We climaxed together and our bodies shook as we traveled through the selfish pleasure of release until at last coming to rest. I lowered her back to the floor, and we stood there lost within each other's gaze until she broke the silence.

"Honestly, I'm surprised you had anything left after last night," she said.

"Apparently, my well hasn't run dry."

"Then you are truly an oasis in the desert."

She leaned in and kissed me again, then we parted mouths, rinsed off, and exited the shower to dry off and get dressed.

"Do you know the exact time our flight is coming?" I asked, as I slid on my pants and shirt.

"I believe it's at ten a.m., but you never really know with these sketchy third world air transport services."

"I guess we better check on Farid and make sure he's getting ready."

We dressed and headed upstairs to find his door closed and his room quiet. I knocked lightly and heard a sudden stirring followed by hushed voices. I looked at Dolunay, and we exchanged a knowing smile just seconds before the door opened to reveal Farid standing there wrapped up in a towel. I looked past him and saw two women still lying in his bed with the covers drawn up to their chins.

"Did you have a good night?" I asked, bringing my attention back to Farid.

"Dude…"

"Let me guess. It's seriously awesome hanging out with me again?"

"You have no idea."

"Oh, I've got some idea, but look here, Mr Menage A Trois—our flight out is around ten, so you might want to start getting ready."

"No problem, I'll be downstairs in a few minutes."

We left Farid and headed downstairs to wait, and he arrived about twenty minutes later looking showered and fresh as a daisy.

"Where are your friends?" I asked.

"Freshening up."

Farid grabbed some coffee and breakfast, and, once he was properly fed, we headed back upstairs to grab our things before going outside to catch a ride to the air field. Dolunay and Farid's two female friends arrived in a Range Rover, and we climbed in and headed off on the drive along the palm tree lined lane that bordered the north side of the oasis. Soon, the trees gave way to a large expanse of desert, and there ahead lay a massive hangar and a runway. The hanger doors were open, and we drove in and parked in front of the massive Airbus A380, then stepped out to wait for our ride.

"I'm really going to miss you," I said, to Dolunay.

"I'm going to miss you too. Perhaps you can come for a visit, or perhaps I could come visit you."

"I would love that."

She turned and reached into the Range Rover and pulled out a small duffel bag.

"Oh, I packed you a little to-go bag for the plane ride, as these third world airlines can be a bit lacking in amenities. It's got some snacks and water, and it'll give you a place to hide your pistol," she said.

"Thank you, good thinking," I said, as I slid my pistol out of my shoulder holster and placed it in the bag.

Just then I heard the far off sound of a plane's droning engines growing gradually louder, and I looked out to see a fairly large twin engine propeller aircraft off in the distance. It began it's final approach then lumbered in and dropped the last few feet to the ground before slowing and taxiing over to the hangar. The plane in front of us appeared to be a slightly smaller version of the C-130s I'd flown on in the Air Force, though this one was more than a few years past its prime. At least its engines appeared to be in good working order and continued to run as the side door opened, and an Arabic man in a khaki flight uniform climbed out and walked over to greet us. He had a mop of dark curly hair and a welcoming smile that made him immediately likable.

"Hello, you must be Finn," he said, still smiling as he held out his hand.

"Yes, but here I am known as the Desert Stallion," I said, as I shook his hand.

He laughed.

"Excellent nickname. Who is your sidekick?"

"This scrappy fellow is Little Gelding."

He laughed yet again then took a moment to regard Farid and me in our tuxedos. We definitely didn't look like the typical Middle Eastern travelers, and he gazed at us curiously.

"Just so you know, we do not have any kind of dress code on our airline."

"In America, we take flying very seriously."

"Apparently. Well then, let me welcome you to Jibril Airlines. My name is Rafi, and I'm the closest thing you will find to a flight attendant. Please come aboard and get comfortable. There are plenty of seats still available, and we'll have you at your destination in just a few hours."

"And just where would that be?"

"Istanbul, where I believe you have a connecting flight, though you will have to sort out those details after we arrive."

I turned to Dolunay and gave her a long hug followed by a final kiss.

"It's been a real pleasure, Dolunay," I said.

"Yes it has, Tag, and I really look forward to seeing you again. Hopefully sooner than later."

"Yeah, let's make it sooner."

Farid kissed and hugged each of the women then we walked over and stepped up into the plane, but I turned back to take one last look at Dolunay the Desert Fox. Her long hair was billowing in the wind created by the airplane's prop wash, and she was looking as beautiful and exotic as ever as she blew me a final kiss. I returned the gesture and received a stoic smile. With a heavy heart I stepped aside so that Rafi could close the door, then took a moment to look around at the interior of the plane. It was a typical third world airline experience with the passenger seating in the front and a large cargo area with pallets of supplies in the back. Farid and I went right towards the seats and saw that we only had about ten fellow passengers. I couldn't see their faces, but they were presumably Arabic judging by the fact that they were all wearing keffiyehs. We found an empty row in the middle and sat down, and I placed my bag under my seat, buckled in, then glanced out the nearest window in the hopes of catching a final look at Dolunay. She was still standing there, and it made me sad to be leaving my new friend behind, but at least I was finally fulfilling my promise to my old friend by taking him to America.

We taxied back out to the runway, and were soon lifting off and climbing high above the desert until the oasis became a mere spec on the horizon. We banked north and leveled off several thousand feet above the desert, and I leaned back in my seat and looked around at what would be my home for the next several hours. It was old and creaky, and I wondered how this piece of shit managed to get off the ground let alone stay aloft. Rafi happened to be coming up the aisle, and he saw my concerned expression and stopped to talk.

"You look a little nervous. Any questions I can answer?" he asked.

"No, It's just been a long time since I've ridden on a

plane like this."

"This is a C-123 K Thunder Pig. It has been flying for forty years and hopefully will continue to fly for at least another twenty."

"So you do passengers and air cargo?" I said, motioning towards the rear of the plane.

"Yes, as a small airline, we pretty much do everything. Those crates are food supplies that we are air dropping to a remote village in Jordan. They are fairly remote and have no airport nearby, so it's the easiest way to get them supplies. Now, would either of you like some refreshments?" he asked.

"No, thank you, I'm fine."

"Good, because we don't have any," he said, laughing as he walked to the back of the plane.

The leg room was limited, so I was curious if I might be able to get comfortable enough to actually sneak in a nap. I stretched out my legs as far as they would go and accidentally bumped the seat in front of me.

"Sorry, just trying to get comfortable," I said.

"No problem," the man said, in lightly accented English.

Strangely, his voice was vaguely familiar, but I couldn't place it for the life of me and figured he probably just sounded like someone I knew or perhaps even a famous actor. I pulled my feet back a little and hazarded a glance at Farid to see how he was fairing and was surprised when he pulled a brand new issue of some tabloid magazine out of his jacket pocket.

"Where the hell did you find that?" I asked.

"At the oasis. One of the girls gave it to me for the flight. They have regular mail deliveries and get magazines and all kinds of goodies flown in every day."

"Oasis indeed," I said, leaning back in my chair, hoping to get a little shut eye.

"America, here we come," Farid said, happily as his eyes fell upon a picture of a chesty blond starlet.

Generally, I found it nearly impossible to sleep on a commercial flight, as, even with the seat in the fully leaned back position, my head inevitably rolled to one side or the other and instantly brought me awake. Even leaning against the window or tray table proved equally unsatisfying, but, somehow, at this moment, perhaps because of all the exercise I had gotten over the last twenty-four hours, I found a sweet spot, closed my eyes, and soon drifted off into a pleasant nap.

Approximately an hour later the plane hit some turbulence, and I was jostled awake and realized I needed to pee. I stood up to headed aft to ask Rafi if they had a bathroom or, worst-case scenario, a hole in the side of the plane. I found him kicking back on one of the pallets, and he was of course playing a game on his smartphone.

"What's up?" he asked.

"I'm looking for the bathroom."

"Right there," he said, pointing at an orange five gallon bucket that had an old grubby shower curtain to provide privacy—though privacy was probably way too optimistic of a term.

"Lovely," I said.

"Well, that depends on whether it is a number one or a number two," he said, with a laugh.

"Thankfully, it's a number one."

I walked to the bucket, took out Tag Junior, and saw that there was already at least an inch of urine sloshing from side to side with the motion of the plane. Before I set about adding my soup to the stew, I looked back over my shoulder and caught Rafi smiling.

"Welcome to first class in the third world," he said.

"I'd hate to see coach."

After a moment of doing my best to relax, the urine finally came, and its pungent odor rose up from the bucket and filled my nostrils. Fuckinzee—this was about as far away as you could get from the Vandenberg jet and Emirates Air's first class, but such was life. As I stood there, I unconsciously took a look around the immediate area and noticed everything from the rusty rivets in the plane's fuselage to the emergency kit whose door was dangling open because it was improperly mounted to the wall. It certainly wasn't doing a lot to instill confidence in our ride, and I had to wonder why in hell Matheson had booked us on this flying disaster.

At last I finished and put Tag Junior back in my pants,

then decided to add to my growing unease by expanding my inspection to the rest of the plane. I ventured up to the front and saw that the door to the cockpit was wide open. I guess the paranoia of 9/11 hadn't quite reached this airline yet. I glanced inside and saw that both pilots were dining on some kind of soup. The one, who I assumed was the captain, smiled and said something in Arabic that I didn't understand. The other pilot turned around and translated.

"Sorry, we don't have any food for the passengers."

"Oh, no problem, I was just stretching my legs."

They continued eating, and I realized that I had seen all there was to see, and decided to return to my seat. On the way back, I glanced around the cabin, curious about our fellow passengers, wondering who in the hell besides us would patronize such a dingy third world airline. The vast majority appeared to be the Middle Eastern version of the average Joe with their simple, light colored clothing and predilection for beards. I was nearly to my seat when my eyes fell upon a particular passenger, and my heart skipped a beat as recognition set in. Sitting in the seat directly in front of mine was none other than Sheikh Emir, and he had a great big silver plated Desert Eagle 44 caliber pistol in his hand. It was a rather shitty turn of events, though now I knew why his voice had sounded so familiar.

"Sheikh Emir, it's so nice to see you again," I said.

"Please return to your seat," he said, gesturing with his pistol.

I did as he said and sat beside Farid, who was still engrossed in his magazine and had missed the entire interaction.

"Oh, Farid," I said.

"What?" he asked, slightly annoyed.

"We have unexpected company."

"Who would that be?" he asked, finally looking up.

"The guy in that seat in front of us," I said.

At that moment, Emir stood up and pointed his ridiculously large pistol at us.

"How good to see you, Farid."

"Fuck me. What in the hell are you doing here, Sheikh Emir?" Farid asked, folding up his magazine and placing it in his suit jacket pocket.

"I'm here for you and this piece of camel dung," he said.

"But how in the hell did you find us? I don't even know where we are," Farid said, looking painfully confused.

"The Middle East can be a small place, and it just so happens that the man who owns this airline is a friend. All it took was one call to learn that two men were being picked up just a few miles inside the Saudi Arabian border. That might seem like a meaningless detail were it not for the fact that two men just happen to have gone missing from the Emirates the night before. It was therefore as though Allah himself had brought you back to me."

"Why can't we just shake hands and make up? Make a brand new start of it," I said.

"Why don't I just shoot you right now and be done with it."

Rafi walked over, but stopped in his tracks when he saw Emir holding the pistol.

"What's going on here?" he asked nervously.

"Nothing that concerns you. Just relax, do your job, and everything will be fine. We will be taking a slight detour after your delivery in Jordan."

"What kind of detour?" he asked.

"A small one—to the United Arab Emirates. But don't worry, you and your airline will be adequately compensated and free to continue on once we reach Dubai. My only concern is these two men."

Emir turned back to Farid and me with a smug look on his sour face.

"Oh, and in case you were thinking about trying another one of your stunts, I've brought a little help."

Three men, two in front and one in the seat behind me to the right, stood up and flashed their pistols in our direction.

"As you see, there is absolutely no way for you to escape this time, and, Farid, you will have a lot of explaining to do to Prince Hamza."

Farid looked over at me and scowled.

"Dude, I take it all back. It is seriously not awesome hanging out with you again."

CHAPTER TWENTY-SIX
A Walk in the Clouds

Life always had a way of biting you in the ass when you least expected it, and, right now, it was latched on to my backside as tightly as an enraged lion, and it was tugging me ever closer to my own sad demise. Yesterday, when we parted ways with Emir and his goons, I never imagined we would ever cross paths again—least of all, the next fucking day. Unfortunately, we were now reunited, and Farid and I were officially fucked, as we had four armed antagonists surrounding us in a rickety old plane that was flying along at several thousand feet above an inhospitable desert. There were not a lot of options at the moment. Sure, I still had my pistol, but it was in my bag, and, even if I could get to it, the odds of taking out four armed adversaries without getting shot myself were very small indeed—least of all without harming any of my fellow passengers or the plane's crew.

Back in my Agency days, we had been trained in escape and evasion tactics, but, unfortunately, we never covered scenarios involving four hostile gunmen in a rickety forty-year old cargo plane. Still, as long as I lived, breathed, and had intelligent thought, there was hope for survival. That meant I needed to fully assess our surroundings in the hope of making use of this oddly challenging environment. I started by thinking about the layout of the plane, the placement of Emir and his goons, the available materials and tools, and the fact that our plane would be making some kind of air drop in Jordan before continuing on to the Emirates. I let all that swirl around in my mind and then Bingo! I had the beginnings of a plan, but the final piece ironically would come about from what some might consider to be a personality flaw. In this case, however, it was a valuable asset, and, as a person afflicted with a mild case of obsessive compulsive personality disorder, I often found myself taking inventory of generally erroneous details such as the poorly mounted emergency kit just beside the toilet bucket. The door had been hanging open to reveal its contents, and I now realized that it held the final piece of the escape puzzle, though it would all still depend upon proper timing.

I therefore patiently waited for my opening, which came when Rafi checked in with the cockpit. That was the sign that we were approaching the air drop in Jordan, and he soon reappeared and headed aft to prepare the palettes.

A short time later, the copilot poked his head out of the cockpit.

"Five minutes to drop-off, Rafi," he yelled over the din of the droning engines.

It was go-time, but, as I stood up, Emir's closest goon glared and pointed his gun at me.

"Sit down," he said.

"Easy, falafel face, I'm just going to take a piss," I said.

Emir turned around and addressed his man.

"It's OK. Let him piss. We're on an airplane. Where could he possibly go?"

"You sure?" the man asked.

Emir thought for a moment before responding.

"Yeah, but just to make sure it's not a trick, see that he actually takes a piss, and, if not, shoot him."

I walked past him to the bucket, and he kept his eyes on me the entire time, and, even as I unzipped, he refused to look away.

"Do you mind? Having a dude stare at me doesn't exactly stimulate a lot of flow," I said, pulling the curtain out an extra few inches.

Perfect, I was mostly out of view, and now all I had to do to complete the facade and not get shot was to pee. I pulled out Tag junior and stared at the amber liquid sloshing back and forth in the bucket, but still the pee wouldn't come. Fuck. I looked back out at the goon, and he cocked his pistol and smiled.

"Well?" he asked.

"Can you make a sound like running water?"

"No."

"Whistle?"

"No."

"How about a menacing stare?"

Nothing broke the goon's composure, but the brief exchange fortunately brought peace to my bladder, and golden urine began filling the bucket. Meanwhile, I reached over with my right hand and rummaged through the emergency kit's contents, which were obviously intended to be used in the event of a crash landing. That meant it contained a radio, medical supplies, a utility knife, and, more importantly, a flare gun. I grabbed the gun, loaded it with a flare cartridge, and slid it into my shoulder holster before zipping up and returning to my seat, hopeful that none of the goons saw the bulge under my tuxedo jacket. I made it back safely and sat and waited for about two minutes until Rafi announced that he would be opening the rear cargo ramp, and that we should all remain in our seats with our seat belts firmly fastened. It was officially time to bring Farid in on the plan, so I lightly elbowed him, and he glanced over at me.

"Be ready to drop to the floor and crawl like a weasel," I whispered.

"Excuse me?"

"You heard me, now be ready," I said.

I glanced briefly towards the back of the plane and saw Rafi making his final preparations. It was go time, so I slid out the flare gun and noticed Farid was looking particularly nervous.

"Don't tell me you're going to shoot them with that!" he whispered nervously.

"No, but I am going to use it to create a nice distraction."

"Dude! Seriously! Don't do it! You're going to bring down this plane!"

"Too late."

I aimed the gun upward at a slight angle and pulled the trigger, and the flare shot from the barrel and bounced off the ceiling and ricocheted back and forth across the plane, hissing and filling the compartment with a massive cloud of red sparks and white smoke. Everyone panicked and ducked for cover, which meant I had a moment to drop to the floor, pull my pistol out of my bag, and start crawling towards the back of the plane. Farid followed, and we emerged from the chaos and smoke to find Rafi readying the pallets, but, due to the fact that the rear ramp was open, the noise of the rushing wind left him oblivious to all the commotion in the passenger compartment. He finished what he was doing then turned around and looked a bit startled when he noticed us.

"It is too dangerous for you to be back here with the ramp open!" he said, as he walked over to us.

"Yeah, I know, but we needed some fresh air," I said, pointing back towards the cloud of smoke that had enveloped the plane.

"What's going on up there? Is there a fire?" he asked nervously.

"No, it's just a little smoke from the flare that some idiot set off."

"But..."

"Trust me. Everything is fine, but right now my friend and I need to get the fuck off this plane, so we're going to hitch a ride on those pallets!" I said.

"You've got be fucking kidding me!" Farid protested.

"No, and believe me—it's our only hope of escaping this plane alive."

Rafi shook his head and sighed.

"No, Little Gelding is right. It is a crazy idea. These parachutes are designed for the pallet and its cargo's specific weight, and they will fall a lot faster with you on them."

"Maybe, but it's better than facing the goon squad," I said, pointing back towards the passenger compartment.

Rafi shrugged.

"Well, I suppose it is your life to risk," he conceded.

Ravi pushed the pallets right up to the edge of the ramp and had everything ready to go, but, as we prepared to make our hasty exit, Emir and his three goons unexpectedly arrived. Our situation has just become a bit of a shit fucker, and, in order to deal with the shit, this fucker was going to have to get creative. A plan came to mind, and I slipped behind Farid and placed my gun to his head.

"Dude!" he protested angrily.

"I'm sorry, it's the only way," I responded.

"Drop your gun and move away from Farid!" Emir growled.

"No chance."

"Then I will be forced to shoot you both!"

"I sincerely doubt that, Emir, as I suspect that you have at least some knowledge as to how valuable Farid here is to Prince Hamza. You harm one little hair on my friend's head and the prince will take you and your men out to the desert and roast marshmallows over your burning ball sacks."

Emir apparently believed me and, therefore, seemed unsure how to proceed. This unofficially led us into what they called a Mexican stand-off—a confrontation in which two opposing parties had no obvious advantage over the other. Emir had superior numbers, but I had the golden goose, and I made damn sure Farid stayed in between me and the goon squad.

"Put down your gun and let go of Farid! You have nowhere to go!" he bellowed again.

Apparently, Emir still hadn't figured out why we were back here, which was probably a good thing, as it gave us the advantage of surprise. I leaned in close and whispered in Farid's ear.

"When I give you the signal, we're going to each grab hold of a pallet and push ourselves off the ramp."

"Fuck you, I can't do it! I'm afraid of fucking heights!"

"Do you want to be motor boating your long lost love's bosom's or Prince Hamza's butt cheeks?"

"I won't be able to able to motorboat anything if I'm

dead."

"Exactly! So, remember to hold on tight!"

Emir cleared his throat and spoke.

"Gentleman, it is time to head back to your seats before s
one gets hurt."

The light beside the door turned green, and an alarm sound
signify it was time to drop the pallets.

"OK, Farid, when I give you the signal, I want you to…"

Before I had even finished talking, he bolted right past m
pushed his pallet off the end with his scream trailing off as he c
peared from sight. Part of me was extremely proud of how c
geously he faced his fears and leapt from the plane, but anothe
of me was pretty pissed off that I was now entirely alone and f
off against our armed antagonists. I, therefore, did the only t
could do, which was fire two shots over Emir and his goon's
to make them panic and scatter for cover. It worked, and it
me the opening I needed to slide my gun into my waistban
push the remaining pallet off the back of the ramp. I held on
rope webbing for dear life as the pallet and I went airborne,
made the unfortunate mistake of looking down at the desert
looming several thousand feet below me. A deep dark jolt o
shot through my entire body, and all I could think was what in
name had I gotten myself into?

The drag shoot uncoiled and made the pallet flop and twist
bucking bronco, and it took all my strength to bring my feet
wrap them around the rope webbing, all the while silently p
that the main chute opened and spared me from impacting in
desert floor at about two hundred miles per hour. As if I didn'

enough to worry about, I suddenly heard gunshots then felt bullets whizzing past me, with at least one imbedding into the other side of the pallet. I looked towards the plane and saw Emir's face locked in a grimace as he furiously fired his pistol at me. Five more rounds and the shooting stopped, allowing me too focus on my next task—namely, survival. Sure, I'd jumped out of plenty of airplanes in my life, but never without a parachute firmly strapped to my back, and now I had to rely on the one connected to this fucking pallet.

The drag shoot continued to flutter, but another few seconds passed, and it finally managed to pull the main shoot open. It created a massive jolt that nearly knocked me free of the pallet's rope mesh, but I managed to hold on, and was now dangling by my hands thousands of feet above the ground. With the pallet decending more slowly, the world became eerily quiet, and the only noise was the sound of the plane as it trailed off into the distance. I climbed up onto the top of the pallet's cargo crates and took a moment to see how Farid had fared on the jump. His main shoot had opened, but there was no sign of him, which made me wonder if perhaps the shock of the open-ing had knocked him free. I looked down towards the ground, but thankfully only saw a barren landscape, so I turned my attention back to his pallet and saw, as it twisted around, that he was desperately trying to climb up to the safety of the top. Thank God! The fucker was alive, though he was most likely having some extremely unpleasant thoughts about me and my escape plan. Suddenly, a gust of wind hit him, and he lost hold with his right hand and was left dangling precariously by one arm before reaching back up and getting a grip on the netting. He started climbing again and thankfully made his way up onto the top, where he wrapped his body around the parachute lines so tightly that he looked like a Rhesus monkey clinging to its mother. He eventually floated around until he was facing me, and I gave him a friendly wave, but he responded by giving me the finger. That's gratitude for you.

We drifted that way for what seemed like an eternity, but, in reality, was only a matter of minutes before the details of the ground came into view. I saw that we were indeed approaching the outskirts of a village, and down below a crowd of people were waiting. The closer I got to the ground, however, the more obvious it was how fast I was traveling, which meant I needed to prepare for a rough landing. I had done endless jumps as a PJ but hadn't been near a parachute since my little stunt back on Soft Taco Island—and that one had only entailed parasailing onto a nice soft beach. This was entirely different, so I hoped that my training would come back and be of some use when I hit the ground. Ten feet from impact, I prepared to hop off and do a roll with the idea being to distribute the force of the landing. Just before the pallet clunked down, I stepped off the edge, and, when my feet hit the ground, I bent my knees and transitioned into an aikido roll across my shoulder and continued all the way through to a crouch before standing up without so much as a scratch.

"Tadaa!" I said, holding out my hands like a gymnast who had just completed a gold medal worthy dismount off the parallel bars.

The crowd of people started clapping, so I gave them a brief bow and hand flutter before turning my attention back to Farid. Strangely, his pallet hadn't yet reached the ground, so I imagine that his load must have been a bit lighter. He was still about fifty feet off the ground, falling rapidly, and holding on for dear life with his face locked in a grimace of terror. The people around me were probably expecting an equally elegant landing, but they wouldn't get one. When the pallet slammed down, Farid bounced off the top of the crate then went flying off to the side and landed face down in the dirt. I raced over to his side to find him motionless. At first, I thought he might have been knocked unconscious, but he coughed, and a small cloud of dust shot out from the sides of his mouth. He managed to get up onto his hands and knees, and I could see his face was coated with dirt. His eyes opened, creating two windows in the layer of soot, and it was so horribly funny that I was unable to hold back a laugh.

"I just have to say one thing," he said.

"You can stop right there, as I already know what you're going to say. So, you're welcome, my friend, because I know how seriously awesome it is hanging out with me again."

"That's not exactly what I was going to say," he said, finally mustering a small smile.

I helped him up then took a moment to look at the people gathered around us. They were all staring quietly, and I could only imagine what they might be thinking, considering the unusual fact that we were wearing tuxedos and had just fallen from the sky on a couple of pallets. An older man with a grey beard, kindly eyes, and the weathered skin of a life in the desert stepped forward. He was of course wearing a white thawb and the thick red and white keffiyeh that was common to the people of Jordan. Here, however, a keffiyeh was called a shemagh, and his had large decorative cotton tassels hanging off the sides, which meant he was likely their village elder.

"I have never seen penguins this far north," he said.

It was actually a pretty funny reference to the fact that we were wearing tuxedos.

"Yes, it's a little unusual, but I believe you'll find us on the bill of lading."

The man smiled.

"I am the village elder—call me Ismail," he said, with a smile.

"You speak English, and you've apparently read Moby Dick."

Ismail was the Arabic spelling of Ishmael, the narrator's name in Herman Melville's epic novel.

"Yes—and yes, as we are near Petra, one of our country's most popular attractions, which means there are practically more tourists than locals around here, so English is the unofficial second language."

I pulled out my iPhone and saw that I had no service. Wonderful.

"Do you by chance have a phone we could use?"

"Yes, of course, but it's a land line. The cell reception is shit this far out in the desert. Come, follow me."

The crowd moved in and loaded the pallets on an old truck then ambled back towards the village. We joined in the procession and followed Ismail north towards a congregation of dwellings a couple hundred yards across the picturesque valley. As we walked I had a look around at the sun baked mountains and could see how the millions of years of wind, water, and sand had exposed the jagged lines of their strata—making it look a bit like America's Grand Canyon but on a smaller scale. It was certainly a beautiful place, but I was betting that life here was probably difficult, so these people had to be pretty fucking hearty to survive.

This point was proved shortly thereafter by Ismail, who moved like a fucking mountain goat, forcing Farid and me to struggle to stay on his heels. Clearly, his active life kept him in good shape, and, in a matter of minutes, we were already in the heart of Ismail's village and standing before his humble abode. It was a plain white single leveled structure that an American would probably describe as fifties ranch style, though it obviously lacked the manicured lawn and obligatory minivan or Volvo station wagon in the driveway. Instead, it was ringed by a wire fence that enclosed the house and formed a corral that was occupied by sheep, two horses, and several camels. We passed through the gate and entered his home, removed our shoes, and took a seat in his living room. A moment later an older woman appeared who was probably his wife, and she served us hot tea and disappeared as quickly as she had arrived.

"That was quite an entrance you made back there. Do you mind me asking how it is you ended up on those cargo pallets?" Ismail asked.

"Well, we were supposed to leave the plane while it was on the ground in Istanbul, but we ran into an old friend who was a real asshole, and we had to leave a little sooner than planned, so, needless to say, we now desperately need to get in touch with the people who we were going to meet."

"The phone is right there," he said, pointing at a small wooden table beside the couch.

I pulled out my iPhone and looked up Matheson's information before dialing the country code then his number, and it was oddly satisfying to feel the tactile sensation of the old push button phone. After a brief pause and two clicks, it started ringing, and continued to do so until the third ring when I heard a voice.

"Matheson here."

"Hello, stranger, it's Finn."

"Are you in Istanbul on the Vandenberg jet yet?"

"Not exactly."

"What does that mean?"

"It means that we're in a small village near Petra"

"Petra, as in Jordan?" he asked, sounding confused.

"That's the place."

"What the hell are you doing there? You were supposed to fly to Istanbul."

"I know, but we had to exit our flight a little early after an unexpected run-in with an old friend."

"And who might that have been?"

"Sheikh Emir—a cousin of the royal family of Dubai. He was probably hoping to kill me then take Farid back to Prince Hamza."

"What in the hell was he doing on that plane?"

"Looking for us. Apparently, the Middle East is a very small place."

"But you're OK now?"

"Yeah, except for the fact that we need to figure out how the hell to get out of Jordan—or more specifically, Petra."

"Hold on a second."

I used the moment to have another drink of the delicious tea before Matheson finally came back on the line.

"All right, can you get to King Hussein International Airport in Aqaba?"

I repeated Matheson's question to Ismail, and he nodded.

"Yeah."

"OK, good. The Vandenberg jet will be at the private terminal in two hours. Get there as soon as you can but stay safe."

"Thanks, over and out," I said, hanging up.

"So, Ismail, how do we get to Aqaba?"

"It's easy," he said, with a mischievous smile.

It turned out that the airport wasn't actually very far away, but the journey required at least two forms of transportation with the first and fastest one being a camel or horse to Petra. We could take a car, but the road around was long, slow, and a perilous journey, which gave credence to why they had supplies dropped in by air. Traveling by animal was the wiser, faster option and meant we would go straight over the hill and actually arrive in Petra sooner. From there, Ismail had arranged for his brother to take us south all the way down to Aqaba. In theory, the entire journey would take about two or three hours. In reality, however, I had no idea.

Ismail had horses and camels, but he could only spare the latter, and of those, only two—one for us, and one for our guide. Sadly, that meant that Farid and I would be sharing a camel, but I was still mildly excited because, during the course of my unusual lifetime, I had never actually been on one and was now finally going to at last ride the great ship of the desert. Of course, it would have been a lot more pleasant had I been riding solo, but you never looked a gift camel in the mouth.

Accompanying us on this journey, and acting as our guide, was Ismail's son Asaf. He was a young man of eighteen, with dark brown hair and lively eyes who seemed to find our predicament particularly funny and let out a laugh as he regarded us in our tuxedos. He briefly explained the eccentricities of mounting and riding a camel, which in some ways, seemed a lot easier than a horse. Unlike the horse, where the rider climbed up onto its back, the camel knelt down onto the ground so that the rider could easily mount up—or so Asaf claimed.

"Shotgun!" I yelled, stepping forward.

I climbed aboard and took the front spot while Farid sat directly behind me, which technically meant he was riding bitch. At that point, Asaf prompted the camel, and it stood up and managed to get up onto its feet, and it appeared to be ready and able. So far, so good—that is until a great long gurgling fart rocked the air.

"Goddammit, Farid!"

"It wasn't me, jackass. It was our ride."

Asaf laughed once again.

"Camels can be very gassy. Especially Bashir here," he said, patting Bashir's side.

A great and terrible odor filled the air, and I was suddenly very thankful I had the front spot, as it was as far as I could get from Bashir's prolifically pungent butthole. Asaf, meanwhile, climbed onto his camel, and we set off with the three of us forming one of the most ridiculous looking caravans this part of the desert would ever see. Asaf, of course, looked like a local, but the two men in tuxedos sharing a camel looked like a couple of jackasses, and anyone we passed would be guaranteed a good laugh and a fascinating story for years to come. I hazarded a brief glance over my shoulder at Farid and had a funny thought and smiled.

"What's so funny?" he asked.

"I just realized that you have become a cliché."

"I don't understand."

"You're officially a camel jockey."

"Camel jockey—that's funny!" Asaf said, laughing.

"Actually it's not. In fact, it's a disparaging description of an Arab," Farid said, rolling his eyes.

"No, no—I think you are wrong! The words camel and jockey put together sound funny," Asaf said, as another giggle escaped his lips.

"Happy now, Mr. Cultural envoy?" Farid said, to me.

"I am as long as I can continue to bring joy to those I meet."

We headed up the hill along a well-used path that snaked its way back and forth across the mountain and gained altitude with each switchback. The camels kept up a steady pace, and soon the village below was but a number of distant specks of white against the reddish hue of the landscape. At last we crested the hill, and I was surprised to see a light dusting of snow still visible from the last storm. In this part of the world, it was easy to forget that we were well over three thousand feet above sea level, and freezing temperatures were common in the wee hours of the morning. At this hour, it was quite pleasant, and the sun was feeling warm and soothing as we started our decent down towards the ancient city of Petra. A hundred yards ahead, the path opened up onto a road, and Asaf slowed his camel and came alongside.

"Only a little bit longer," Asaf said.

"Excellent. Why don't we use the time to hear a little more about your life. Do you have a girlfriend? Boyfriend? Goat? Other?" I asked.

"Girlfriend," he said, laughing.

"Is she a hot potato?"

"Hot potato?"

"Pretty. Is she pretty?"

"Oh, yes. Very pretty."

"And plentiful bosoms?" I asked, using my hands to form two large breasts in front of my chest.

Asaf laughed again, though he reddened slightly, obviously a little embarrassed.

"You don't have to answer his questions if they make you uncomfortable," Farid interjected.

"It is OK. It is nice to speak so freely about such matters. The people of my village are not so open-minded. And to answer your question—yes, they are easily more than a handful."

"Nice. Are you going to get married and make sweet love to her in the desert?"

"I hope so—but I don't have enough money yet. Not a lot of opportunities in a small village like mine."

"That sucks."

"Yes—but that is life in the desert. What about you? Where are you guys from in America?" Asaf asked.

"I'm from Northern California, but my bitch here is actually from Iran."

"Originally, but I'm moving to the States," Farid interjected.

"Yeah—so he can meet a blond woman with big breasts and do some motor boating."

"Motor boating? Such as on a lake or the ocean?"

"No, in this case it means you place your face between a woman's breasts and wiggle your head back and forth while making a sound like a motor boat."

"Perhaps I can try that with my girlfriend one day," he said, laughing.

"You won't be disappointed."

We continued down the mountain, and the midday sun was a warm and welcome companion until we at last saw the beginnings of the once great city of Petra. Asaf turned out to be an excellent tour guide, and Farid and I learned all about this ancient city. This seemingly remote area of the Fertile Crescent, which the Bible identifies as the place where Moses's brother Aaron was buried, had been occupied for thousands of years but came into real prominence around 312 BC when an Arabic tribe called the Nabataeans settled in these mountains and made it the capital of their kingdom. This allowed them to occupy the precious caravan routes between Arabia and Syria, and, during that time, they made great advances in hydraulic engineering systems that allowed them to divert and collect the winter flood waters into reservoirs, thereby storing it for the long dry summers. Having such advanced control of their environment allowed their culture to thrive and expand, and they constructed incredible monuments and buildings, some of the most spectacular of which having been carved directly from the surrounding mountains.

By 63 BC they had been conquered by the Romans, and their great city was renamed after the reigning emperor of the time, Hadrian Petra. Though Rome took tax revenue from their new acquisition, it allowed them to govern themselves, and the Nabataeans continued to thrive up through the Byzantium era when changing trade routes and a catastrophic earthquake brought it to ruin in 551 AD. It wouldn't come back into prominence for nearly fifteen hundred years when Europeans arrived in the nineteenth century and started exploring the area. Now, Petra was littered with foreigners, luxury hotels, and had become Jordan's number one tourist destination and a UNESCO Intangible Cultural Heritage Site.

"You have to admit, this adventure has been pretty fucking amazing," I said, to Farid.

"Yeah—and I suppose I should thank you. Had it not been for you spiriting me out of Dubai—I'd have spent this time living a life of luxury, driving my Bentley, and making love to scores of beautiful women. Instead, I have been used as a human shield, forced to jump out of a perfectly good airplane, and now face the indignity of riding bitch on the back of a camel for all to see."

"My friend—you are truly welcome."

We continued down onto a path that was lined with ancient columns that were crumbling and only a fraction of their original height and magnificence due to the hundreds of years of weather and human intervention. Up ahead, a crowd of tourists were busily taking pictures of the remains of a lion statue when, one by one, their attention came to focus on the two men in tuxedos riding the camel. They all watched silently until we were only a few steps away, at which point the entire group started taking pictures with their phones, engulfing us in a sea of clicks. An older woman at the front of the crowd smiled as she spoke.

"What's the occasion?" she asked.

She was clearly American and part of a church group judging by her and her friend's T-shirts, which had the words *Restored by the Lord* on the front.

"We're on our honeymoon," I responded.

"Oh..."

"Would you mind taking our picture?" I asked, handing her my iPhone.

"Um—well—sure," she said, without a lot of enthusiasm.

She held up the phone and adjusted the framing while Farid wrapped his arms tightly around me, smiled, and kissed my cheek just as she snapped the photo. It was probably a little mean but still funny, and the entire incident left her looking decidedly unsettled as she handed me back my phone.

"Thanks! This one will be a keeper for sure," I said.

Moments like this didn't happen very often and having the picture to back up the story would be priceless. We continued on and left the crowd and made our way past the various structures whose beauty and craftsmanship was a testament to the ingenuity of the people who had built and inhabited this city nearly two thousand years ago. I'd only ever seen this place in pictures, movies, and documentaries, so it was pretty exciting to be able to literally touch, feel, and smell the history—which made it like Disneyland for any history buff or closet archaeologist like myself.

Next on the tour was the Amphitheater followed by the Treasury building, the structure most often associated with Petra. It was carved directly into the rock face, and stood over a hundred feet tall, its influence primarily Greek as evidenced by the vertical columns, roofline, and general appearance. In the smaller details, however, there were references to the Egyptian goddess Isis, or al-Uzza as the Nabateans called her, as well as carvings of Zeus's sons Castor and Pollux. It was this intricate and grandiose facade, I imagine, that inspired George Lucas to choose it as the fabled resting place of the Holy Grail in *Indiana Jones and the Last Crusade*. Ironically, the building probably was a final resting place, though most likely for one of Petra's more important citizens.

Directly opposite the Treasury was the Siq, or, in English, the shaft. It was a long, narrow winding canyon, and it served as the main pathway tourists took to Petra, so a proper arrival meant you exited the sandstone walls to immediately see the Treasury. I was therefore slightly bummed that I had broken my Petra cherry by arriving from the other direction. Oh well, at least I had managed to finally see it in person.

We ventured through the Siq until it opened up onto a wide road that went on for another half mile to reach Wadi Musa, the support city that maintained all of Petra's services the way Springdale Utah serviced Zion National Park. We made our way through the bustling tourist mecca and came to a stop in front of the Grand View Hotel.

"I take it that your uncle works here," I said.

"Yeah, and he is the only one in the family with a car."

"So, you don't get to drive too often?"

"Sadly no, though my uncle takes me out and lets me drive occasionally."

"Shit, the minute I turned sixteen, I lived in my car," I said.

"You lived in your car?"

"Not literally—but every minute I wasn't sleeping, doing homework, or jacking off, I was behind the wheel."

"God bless America," Farid said.

We stopped just off to the side of the front entrance of the hotel and dismounted from the camels, and Farid and I waited while Asaf went inside. He reappeared a moment later and smiled gleefully.

"I have good news and I have great news," he said.

"Give us the good news first."

"My uncle is busy and can't drive you right now."

"That's good news? I think you've lost me here, Asaf. If that's good news then what the hell is the great news."

"He says I can borrow his car to drive you the rest of the

way to Aqaba!"

Farid and I looked at each other nervously.

"Wait, isn't that bad news?" I asked.

CHAPTER TWENTY-SEVEN
Cannonball Run 4

Asaf was standing there smiling stupidly, and I knew exactly how he was feeling, as I had experienced that very same glee as a teenager. It was the joy of getting to drive a car, any car, anywhere—just so long as you got to drive. As an adult, we grew to take this experience for granted, as driving just became a way to perform menial chores such as shopping or going to work. Of course, that all changed depending on whether or not you drove a particularly cool or fast car such as a Porsche, Ferrari, BMW or, in my case, a lightning fast Subaru. In that instance, driving went from being an inane, soulless chore to a heart pounding joyful experience. In Asaf's case, he could have been driving a stripped down piece of shit with nothing more than a lawn mower engine, four tires, and a steering wheel, and he would have been just as thrilled.

We tied the camel's leads up to a tree then walked

around to the garage, where we paused in front of a tiny red four door hatchback. Asaf hit the key fob, and the little car's lights blinked twice as the doors unlocked.

"What the hell is this thing?" Farid asked.

"The Skoda Fabia. Isn't it awesome!" Asaf said, enthusiastically.

It was strange to hear Asaf use the word awesome, but young Jordanians were using more and more English slang these days and even had a name for the practice—*Arabizi*. It was a combination of the words Arabic and *Inglizi*, which was English in Arabic, and it made me wonder if perhaps my time with Asaf would make motor boating the next big *Arabizi* phrase in Jordan.

I walked around the car and took a closer look at our pint sized ride and remembered seeing the same or similar model on an episode of *Top Gear*. Skoda was a Czech company that was now owned by Volkswagen yet, for some reason, had never made its way into the States, and the only awareness we Yanks had of them was from watching British television.

"We don't have these in America," I said.

"I thought you had everything in America," Asaf responded.

"Well—everything but Skoda, apparently. Oh, speaking of—Shotgun!" I yelled, making my way to the front passenger door.

"That's fine. I'm happy to sit in the back where there's less chance of anyone recognizing me in this little shit box," Farid said.

The first thing I did was put on my seat belt, which was something I did every time I entered an automobile, regardless of whether or not it was moving. It somehow made me feel secure, which was currently very important, as we were traveling with a rookie driver in a foreign land. He started the car, took hold of the gear shift, and put it roughly into reverse, which elicited an audible grinding noise from the transmission. He let the clutch out too quickly, and the car lurched backwards, practically hitting a brand new Mercedes parked in the space behind us. Asaf thankfully hit the brakes and screeched to a halt only inches from the other car's bumper, and, of course, killed the engine in the process. He started it up again, put it in first gear, then slowly let out the clutch, this time giving just enough gas to start moving forward. We exited the garage and made a right turn onto the road, where Asaf got to attempt another gear change. He got it into second but stayed a little too hot on the gas and chirped the tires in the process. Third and fourth were thankfully much smoother, and soon we were driving south at a decent clip on Highway 35, which was a mostly rural two lane thoroughfare.

The traffic was light, and Asaf was doing a cool 120 kilometers per hour, which was exactly ten kilometers per hour over the posted speed limit. It translated to about 75 MPH, which I would normally think of as quite comfortable. Unfortunately, our rookie driver was not doing much to instill confidence in his passengers, and first and foremost on the list of driving hazards was his liberal interpretation of lane markers. He had a tendency to drift into the oncoming lane whenever he looked down at his speedometer, and, while this would have been fine on an empty road, it was hellishly terrifying when facing oncoming cars and trucks.

Asaf, however, looked like a kid on Christmas morning, and he was smiling from ear to ear as he gripped the wheel tightly with both hands. Up ahead was a slow truck, and Asaf swerved slightly left to see ahead only to encourage the large report of an air horn from a tractor trailer truck coming from the opposite direction. He swerved back too aggressively and skirted the side of the road, sending up a great cloud of dust over the cars behind us.

"This is so awesome!" he said, looking over at me excitedly.

"Yeah—awesome," I muttered.

He swerved left again, and, seeing open road ahead, hit the gas, and the tiny car's four cylinder engine strained with all its might. We sped past the truck and thankfully re-entered our lane unscathed, but up ahead was a large family sedan packed with passengers. Asaf raced right up onto their bumper, and the people in the back seat were so close, that I could see the sweat stains on their collars.

"Uh, Asaf—it's generally a good idea to leave a safe amount of following distance."

"Yeah, I know. That's why I'm staying back this far."

"Generally you want at least three seconds of following distance between you and the car in front."

"One-two-three—that's exactly how far back I am."

"You're not even close. You need to pick a landmark and when they pass it, count how many seconds until we reach it."

He looked ahead, found an object, then silently counted to himself before looking over with a puzzled expression on his face.

"Three seconds? Seriously? That's like a mile. That can't be right."

"Believe me, it's right, and it gives you time to stop in case they slam on their brakes."

Asaf laughed and shook his head side to side.

"You Americans are crazy! You drive like old ladies!"

He went back to focusing on his driving but only fell back about a car length. Fucking kids always thought they knew everything about everything, when in reality it was a miracle if they could go ten minutes without shitting their pants or getting their dick caught in a toaster. It was therefore a miracle if they survived their first few years of driving, which was the case with young Asaf. So far, I'd say he wasn't exactly a natural, and, in spite of having both hands on the wheel and his eyes forward, his movements were twitchy, and he was always over correcting rather than letting the car just drive itself smoothly down the highway. Sweet Lord, this was going to be the longest short drive of my life!

I decided to see how Farid was fairing and hazarded a quick glance over my shoulder, and he grimaced and made the sign of the cross. I gave him a nod of understanding then turned my attention back to the road ahead to see that it was thankfully clear and straight for at least a few miles, which meant that I had a brief moment to take in a little sightseeing. Around us stretched miles of dry, craggy hills very similar in look and color to the terrain of the high desert of California, and the lack of any kind of greenery made it hard to imagine life had flourished here for thousands of years. The topography changed a bit however when the road eventually turned slightly east, and we entered a small town, where the lifeless desert was suddenly dotted with smatterings of trees, plants, and various structures. A pedestrian up ahead was just about to cross the road, but Asaf saw him and hit the horn, sending the man jumping backward and nearly tumbling to the ground.

"You know, in America, pedestrians have the right of way," I said.

"Here too—but no one really cares."

"I think the guy back there might care," I said, to Asaf who thought I was joking and laughed as he turned his attention back to the road.

"I almost forgot about music," he said, reaching down to turn on the radio with his right hand.

This little distraction made him accidentally swerve off onto the shoulder, but he looked up just in time to avoid a sign. He cut back sharply onto the road, and, in typical Asaf fashion, it was a little too sharp, and now we were headed into the opposite lane. A car was coming from the other direction, and Asaf swerved back over, causing a plaintive squeal to erupt from the tires before we were finally back in our lane and going straight down the road.

"Any requests?" he asked.

"Yeah—how about two hands on the wheel and both eyes on the road."

"Is that a band or a song?" he joked, as he pressed a button on the radio.

Suddenly, popular Western style rock music filled the car, and Asaf started singing along and tapping his hands on the steering wheel. Lovely, yet another distraction. We cleared the town and were soon in a curvy section of highway and coming upon yet another large lumbering truck. Asaf swerved slightly left, saw that it was clear, and hit the accelerator and moved out into the oncoming lane. It would have been a relatively safe pass had he not attempted it before a blind curve, but, as luck would have it, a truck appeared from around the corner. Asaf swerved hard off to the left side of the road and sent us bouncing into the dirt, where he lost control and ended up skidding around in a complete one hundred and eighty degree turn. We came to a stop facing the opposite direction, and were engulfed in a great cloud of dust. When it finally cleared, Farid and I both turned to each other and shared a great sigh of relief to still be alive. I'd officially had enough and turned to Asaf.

"That's it, boy blunder. We're switching drivers. It's time for your first actual driving lesson."

"But..."

"But nothing. What I'm about to teach you will someday save your life, and today it will most certainly save ours."

Looking dejected, he exited the car, and the two of us crossed paths at the front before taking up our new positions. I started the car and looked over at Asaf.

"Rule one. The clutch is like a woman. She needs respect and proper attention. You've got to warm her up and treat her right if you want to play. No more grinding like an eighth grader at his first dance."

"I don't understand," he said, looking confused.

I put the car in reverse and hit the gas, expertly releasing the clutch and sending a spray of dirt and gravel out from under the front wheels as the car took off backwards. A second later, I spun the wheel and performed a perfect bootlegger, a well known maneuver that brought the front of the car back around a hundred and eighty degrees and transferred all the momentum into the same direction. I quickly put it in second gear and headed back onto the highway, where I made smooth efficient shifts until we were back up to speed.

"It all makes sense now!" Asaf said, as he smiled at me.

"What?"

"The way you arrived, the tuxedo, your awesome driving skills—you're a spy like James Bond!"

Farid laughed.

"Yeah, maybe if James Bond specialized in finding missing morbidly obese cats!" Farid said.

"Wait, you find lost cats?" Asaf asked.

"No, well yes, but not anymore, so just ignore the troll in the backseat and focus on your lessons, *padawan*. Now, your first and foremost thing to look at is how I hold the wheel—confident, but not overbearing. The car should feel like it's driving itself."

"But, that's how I was driving."

"You were driving like a virgin on prom night."

Again he looked confused, so I realized I needed a less abstract simile and perhaps an actual demonstration. I waited until we were on a long curve-free stretch of highway then took my hands off the wheel, showing him how the car continued straight as an arrow and needed little input to stay in its lane.

"See? It practically drives itself," I said, receiving a nod from Asaf, who appeared to understand.

The next lesson was passing, which, in my opinion, was the most common yet potentially dangerous maneuver you could perform in an automobile. Traveling out into the oncoming lane of traffic meant that you risked colliding with an object of equal size going at a comparable rate of speed. That basically doubled the relative speed, and more velocity meant more kinetic energy—a force one of my physics professors at Stanford had explained in very simple terms using the following question. Would you rather get hit in the face by a ten pound ball traveling at one mile per hour, or a one pound ball traveling at ten miles per hour? Most people chose the small ball, because they thought it would hurt less. Such was not the case, however, as the small ball, traveling faster, actually had greater kinetic energy, and that was the kind that hurt. So, two cars traveling towards each other at high velocity were equal to one car going like a motherfucker into a brick wall—and that was a scenario that generally left you seriously injured, or, more likely, dead.

"I can't express this next rule enough. Never, never, never, pass on a blind curve. I don't care how many times you've seen it in the movies—never do it. Wait until you can see far enough ahead and know that it's clear, and you'll live a much longer, more satisfying life."

Up ahead, the road opened up, and I gunned it and safely passed a truck then easily returned to my lane long before any automobiles came from the opposite direction.

"See how easy that was?"

"Yeah—but what was that cool spinning maneuver that you used to turn around after we switched places?"

Of course, in the midst of all these pearls, he focuses on the bootlegger. I probably should have refrained from any advanced driving techniques, but I had hoped that doing such a dramatic maneuver would get his attention. Back in the Agency, I was trained in all forms of high performance, combat, and evasive driving, although I had technically first perfected the bootlegger, along with many other maneuvers, back in High School in my parents tiny 1977 Honda Civic. It might have been a piece of shit, but it was my piece of shit, and, best of all, it only needed to be filled with gas about once a year.

"In time, *padawan*, but right now, we're focusing on fundamentals."

We came into another town, and the posted speed limit dropped to 50 kilometers per hour. The traffic was a little heavier, so I decided to hang back and leave a little extra room between us and the car in front.

"Why are you slowing down?" Asaf asked.

"When you're in a town, there are more people and things that might enter the roadway, so you need to slow down and be prepared. You shouldn't just hit the horn and hope for the best."

"Driving in America must be so boring."

"Actually, we have shitloads of good highways and back roads where we can get our thrills. There is a time and place to drive like a maniac—and it's not on crowded streets. Unfortunately, most of the American teens drive like you—the only difference being that they also talk on their phones and text at the same time."

"Awesome!"

"Not awesome and, in fact, quite illegal."

"Then why do they do it?"

"They don't care. Unfortunately, youngsters don't develop adequate impulse control until they are around twenty-five, where the lucky ones who survived the idiocy of youth generally go on to lead much safer adult lives."

Asaf looked skeptical, as his youthful ignorance was likely tainting all the knowledge I had been trying to impart. Oh well, you could lead a teen to wisdom but you couldn't necessarily make him wise. We eventually made a right turn onto Highway 15, a proper four lane highway that would take us to Aqaba, and, about a mile down the road, I pulled over, and let the car idle quietly on the side of the road.

"What's going on?" Asaf asked.

"Your turn to drive."

"Seriously? It was going so well that I was actually thinking about taking a nap," Farid said, from the back seat.

"The boy blunder needs some practical experience if he's going to have any chance of surviving until he's twenty-five."

I stepped out, and we again crossed paths at the front of the car before taking our seats.

"Alrighty then—how do you treat the clutch?"

"Like a woman."

"Excellent."

He put the car in gear, gave it some gas, and slowly released the clutch, this time accelerating smoothly onto the highway. Second was a little clunky but third and fourth were as smooth as butter.

"How are your hands?"

"Good, I think."

"Now, can you feel how the car almost drives itself—kind of like a Ouija board?"

"A what?"

"Never mind, just watch the road and remember to keep your focus farther ahead and not just on the area directly in front of the car. Also check your mirrors every couple of minutes. Think of yourself as the Terminator robot, always scanning the highway and area around you, looking for that elusive Sarah Connor, or, in your case, cops, pedestrians, and other motorists."

Asaf seemed to be doing better, and I wasn't sure what made the difference—my advice or the fact that I had been willing to entrust him yet again with our safety. Of course being on a two lane freeway with a concrete divider between us and the opposing traffic was certainly helping. Things were going so smoothly, in fact, that Farid actually managed to drift off and take a nap. A little less than an hour later we were on the outskirts of the city of Aqaba, and I decided it was time to take Asaf's driving skills to the next level.

"You've done so well thus far that I think you're ready for the bootlegger."

"Seriously?"

"Yeah, pull into that big open dirt parking lot up ahead on the right."

He pulled in and stopped in the middle, smiling and looking over at me as though I were about to reveal the greatest secret in the universe.

"OK, the bootlegger is actually very simple and relies upon basic physics. As you may or may not know, the majority of a car's weight is generally in the front, and this makes the maneuver easy. Just get up a decent amount of speed, spin the wheel, and inertia will carry the front of the car around. At that point, putting it into gear and continuing is a matter of practice and coordination. Also, if you're going pretty fast, it's often best to go into second, as first can be hard on the clutch. OK, give it a try."

"Are you sure this is a good idea?" Farid asked from the backseat.

"What could possibly happen?"

"Oh, I don't know—maybe he'll roll the car and get all three of us killed," Farid said.

"Don't listen to the troll—be the car, Asaf. Be the car."

He put it in reverse, let out the clutch, then started accelerating backwards.

"All right, spin the wheel," I said.

He did as I said but only made it about halfway around. Regardless, he looked happy and was dying for another go. He tried again, this time making it farther around. He tried two more times, and on the last attempt managed to get the car fully around but was too slow to get it into gear to continue.

"OK, last time. Do it!"

He hit the gas pedal hard, dirt and rocks pouring out from under the front of the car as he got up to speed. This was it, the moment of truth. He spun the wheel, and the car slid completely around, at which point he put it in second and stomped on the gas pedal, at last completing a perfect bootlegger. He slammed on the brakes and threw his arms up in triumph as he looked at me with his smile stretching from ear to ear.

"I did it!"

"Yes, you did, and it was glorious!"

Suddenly there was a knock on the window, and we all looked over to see a Jordanian policeman standing outside.

"Where the fuck did he come from?" Farid asked.

"The police station, obviously."

"Yeah, the very same place where the three of us are likely going to end up today," Farid said.

"What do we do now?" Asaf asked nervously.

"What any upstanding citizen would do when dealing with the police—play dumb and act innocent," I said.

Asaf rolled down the window, and the policeman, who was around thirty years old and sporting a neatly trimmed mustache, glared at us as he stood in the remnants of the dust cloud we had just created. He was also wearing typical cop sunglasses and had mastered the menacing stare that all police used when they wanted to intimidate people.

"Good afternoon, officer," I said, from across the car.

"Ah—American."

"Yes, sir," I said.

He turned his attention to Asaf.

"So, young man, do you know how fast you were going?"

"Um—what?"

"I said, do you know how fast you were going?"

"Perhaps thirty kilometers per hour," Asaf said.

"Twenty-three."

"But officer, is there actually a speed limit in a dirt lot?" Farid asked from the backseat.

"No, no there's not. Now, do you mind telling me what you three are up to?"

"We're helping my young nephew here learn to drive."

"Nephew?" he asked as he scrutinized me then Asaf and looked a bit skeptical.

"By marriage, obviously."

The cop stared at us, though his facial expression was hard to read behind his sunglasses. His radio crackled, and he stepped away to talk for a minute before returning to our car, where he stared at Asaf for a long tense moment before finally speaking.

"That was quite a bootlegger, young man, but perhaps you could choose a location other than the back lot of the police station to practice your high performance driving maneuvers."

We all turned and had a more thorough look at the building on the other side of the lot and realized it was indeed the local police station.

"Absolutely, officer, and I'm sorry to have taken up your time."

"No problem, and, young man—please drive safely."

Asaf drove off smoothly and pulled back onto the road and made his next four shifts perfectly as he reached highway speed.

"Wow—I can't believe that guy didn't even ask to see your license and registration," I said.

"Good thing he didn't. I don't have a license."

"Are you kidding me?" Farid asked from the back seat.

"Without a car, I haven't been able to practice enough to take the test."

"Well, if they require a bootlegger—you'll do just fine," I said.

He laughed, and we continued on towards the Red Sea, turning right onto Highway 65 and traveling the final mile or so to King Hussein International Airport. It wasn't exactly the largest place, so finding the private terminal was rather easy, and we were soon parked and checking in with customs. Luckily, Matheson had already put us into the system, and we managed to avoid any lengthy or uncomfortable body search. Once inside, I found a currency exchange office and made a quick withdrawal of 7070 Jordanian Dinars. It equaled about $10,000 U.S. and was about to be the first major expenditure I'd made since becoming a millionaire two weeks previously. Asaf was waiting with Farid in the main lounge as I handed him the envelope full of money.

"What's this?" he asked, looking confused.

"Payment for the ride."

He opened it, and his face flushed with color, and he looked as though he might faint.

"I cannot accept this!"

"Think of it as a wedding present."

"But I'm not getting married."

"I know, but now you can afford to, and I figure as long as you know you're going to have a beautiful wife in your near future that you might actually drive a little more carefully. So, take the money and go get your girl."

I wrote down my name and number on a scrap of paper and handed it over.

"If you make it to twenty-five, give me a call, and I'll double what you've got there and pay for your college."

He thanked me again, except this time he hugged me as well. We said our final goodbye, then Farid and I headed off to the other side of the terminal.

"That was nice—but if you go around giving every shitty driver you meet ten grand, you're going to end up in the poorhouse."

"What the fuck? I'm a millionaire. Where's the fun if you can't do stuff like that?"

"I drove you around Iran. How come you never gave me ten grand?"

"Simple. You may be an asshole but you don't drive like one."

CHAPTER TWENTY-EIGHT
Two Tickets to Paradise

The door leading outside was just up ahead, and Farid and I went through the final checkpoint and headed out to the tarmac, where I saw the Vandenberg Jet parked about sixty yards away. The boarding ramp was hooked up to the main door, and Brett and Tatyana were outside walking around the plane doing the usual preflight inspection when they saw us and waved. Farid abruptly paused and tapped me on the shoulder.

"Dude! That's our ride?" he asked looking legitimately surprised.

"Yeah."

"And those are our pilots?"

"Two of them anyway."

"No shit?"

"Yeah, and believe it or not, the overly tan guy with the

overly white teeth can fly."

"I'm not talking about him. I'm talking about that incredibly beautiful woman next to him."

I knew exactly who he was referring to but refused to miss an opportunity to give him a little shit.

"Oh her? That's Tatyana."

"Sweet Jesus."

"Yeah—it's too bad she's a brunette."

"That's why God invented hair dye."

Brett and Tatyana came over to meet us.

"How are you?" Tatyana asked.

Before I could utter a word, she kissed me, but, as we parted lips, I noticed Farid was standing there hoping he would get the same greeting.

"I'm good, but how are you? Our last meeting was a little—stressful," I said.

"I'm fine, and, as you can see, the plane is good too. I take it this is our special passenger?" she asked, as she turned to Farid.

"Yes, this tall, slightly dark, and handsome man is my old friend Farid Ardeshir."

"Nice to meet you, Farid. I'm Tatyana," she said, holding out her hand.

It wasn't the greeting Farid was hoping for, but he was happy to take her hand and kiss it nonetheless.

"It's nice to meet you, Tatyana, and may I say that you are the most beautiful pilot I have ever seen," he said.

"Well, thank you," she said, a little surprised by Farid's

compliment.

"I'm Brett, it's nice to meet you, and does that mean I'm the second most beautiful pilot you've ever seen?" he asked, holding out his hand.

"No, in spite of the fact that your teeth and tan are truly magnificent."

"Did you tell him to say that, Finn?"

"Of course not. Don't you remember that I said I wouldn't tease you about your tan and teeth after that excellent emergency landing you pulled off back at SFO?"

"Yeah, but I didn't believe it for a moment."

"Hey, any man who can perform an emergency landing with a jumbo jet and one working engine doesn't deserve to be teased, least of all for his artificially tan skin and freakishly white teeth."

Brett scowled.

"Couldn't resist could you?"

"No, but I really tried."

"Well then, why don't you gentlemen come aboard, and we get the fuck out of Jordan."

"Where are we headed? America?"

"Not yet. We were told to fly you to Nice first."

"Sounds like the best news I've heard anyone say all day," Farid responded.

"Yeah, assuming we don't have the same problem we had in San Francisco," I said.

"Wait, what problem? Does this have anything to do with the emergency landing you just mentioned?" Farid asked nervously.

"Don't worry, it's all fine now. We made it this far didn't we?" Tatyana said.

Farid looked at me a little nervously as we boarded the plane but relaxed after I gave him a brief tour of the Vandenberg jet. There was nothing like a little luxury to calm the nerves. We stowed our things in our respective cabins and settled into the main salon, where the other pilot Wendy came in to say hello.

"Nice to see you again, Tag, and it's nice to meet you, Dr. Ardeshir," she said, turning her attention to Farid.

"It's nice to meet you, and please call me Farid," he said, kissing her hand.

"I'm Wendy, and the pleasure is all mine. Now, if you boys don't mind, I must excuse myself and get back to the cockpit. A woman's work is never done, I'm afraid," she said, as she turned around and walked from the room.

Farid watched her go the way a dog watched a bite of steak go from his owner's plate to his owner's mouth.

"Is she close enough to blond for you?" I asked.

"Most definitely."

A moment later, I heard the plane's outer door shut, then Wendy's voice came over the intercom.

"Hello, passengers. Please fasten your seat belts and prepare for takeoff."

The big jet taxied out towards the runway, and we got in line to wait for clearance from the tower. A smaller Emirates Air flight took off first, then we were next. The massive engines spooled up to full power, and we began accelerating down the runway, quickly gaining speed before at last lifting off. The big jet climbed steeply into the sky, and Farid and I were both held firmly in place by the g forces as we headed out over the Red Sea. The jet banked left and settled into a northwesterly heading, where it continued to climb until reaching its cruising altitude and leveling off, whereupon Wendy came over the intercom.

"We have reached a cruising altitude of 35,000 feet, so feel free to move about the cabin. Our flight steward Yvonne will be visiting you shortly to take any food or drink orders. Flight time to Marseille Provence Airport should be about four hours. Please feel free to sit back, relax, and enjoy flying Vandenberg Air."

Wendy clicked off, and, shortly thereafter, Yvonne came into the room and hugged me before introducing herself to Farid. He was once again looking bedazzled as he regarded yet another beautiful Vandenberg female employee. I was now used to seeing the unusually comely staff, but Farid was still in the new and impressionable stage and probably already suffering from a terrible case of visually induced blue balls. It was entirely understandable, as Yvonne was incredibly attractive with her exquisite bone structure, long brown hair, blue eyes, and toned yet curvaceous figure. She was also a nice person and an extremely talented chef, with her only discernible flaw being the fact that she was dating Brett, who, while being a pretty decent guy most of the time, had an annoying propensity for tanning, tooth whitening, and talking about his beloved Naval Academy.

Yvonne, in her usual cheerful manner, told us our options for lunch then left to prepare what would most certainly be a lovely meal. Twenty minutes later, she was back with French dip sandwiches, salad, and mineral waters, and, after a long day in the desert, it was nice just to sit, eat, and rehydrate. We finished lunch, and Yvonne followed it up by bringing us cappuccinos and Madeleine cookies, though eating so much at one sitting had its repercussions, and, soon, I had some unexpected guests waiting to slip out the back door.

"Farid, do you still have that shitty tabloid magazine?"

"Yeah, why?"

"I have to dump, and I need something to read."

He reached into his inside jacket pocket and handed me the magazine.

"Here, keep it. I don't think I'll be wanting it back."

"Thanks," I said, getting up and swinging by the galley for more coffee before heading back to my stateroom.

I entered my home away from home and was surprised to find all my baggage sitting off to the side of the bed in its usual place. Matheson must have had it all shipped from the Burj Al Arab Hotel and delivered to the plane. Ah—the perks of being in a secret society. I grabbed my toiletries and headed into the bathroom and took a moment to look at myself in the mirror. I had some nice color on my face from a day in the sun but otherwise looked no worse for wear. I stripped completely down to my birthday suit and dropped onto the familiar seat, relishing the moment as though it were a reunion with a long lost friend. Properly seated, I thumbed the pages of the magazine and let it unfold naturally to what was probably the last story Farid had been reading. Of course it was a picture of a beautiful young blond girl, and my first horrifying thought was that Farid was probably thinking about using this picture to masturbate. That was unlikely, however, as his seminal reservoir must surely be empty having spent the previous night with not one but two women.

I took a nice long sip of coffee and then felt release as I brought my eyes down onto the page. I was looking at the girl more closely now, and my gaze fell upon a particular detail that suddenly made my insides feel as though I had just received an ice water enema. I looked below and read the caption just to be sure I was seeing what I thought I was seeing. Then, I read the entire story, and suddenly everything made sense. As crazy as it sounded, spending five minutes alone on a toilet with a tabloid magazine allowed me to be pretty damn certain that I had figured out Hamza's connection to the Topless Agenda. I needed to call Matheson, so I finished up on the pot, took an exceedingly quick shower, then re-donned my suit before taking a minute to think. Upon further reflection, I realized that I actually needed to make several calls, and that would require access to the jet's communication system. I left my room and passed through the main salon, where I spied Farid sleeping like a baby on one of the couches. I continued past sleeping beauty and found Yvonne in the galley.

"What's up, Tag?" she asked.

"I'm was facing a bit of a conundrum and need to make some phone calls. I assume the jet has some kind of phone system?" I asked.

"Of course!"

"Thank God," I said.

"Here, follow me."

She led me to a room I had never seen before, as it was Mr. Vandenberg's private mobile office. She showed me how to use the phone then left so I could have some privacy. First and foremost, I dialed Matheson, and he answered on the third ring.

"Hello, Finn, I take it from the number you called me that you're on the Vandenberg jet?"

"Yeah, safe and sound."

"Thank God!"

"Yeah, though you might also want to thank a man name Ismail and his son Asaf," I added.

"Excuse me?"

"Nothing, I'll explain later. Now, I believe that we're meeting up in southern France?"

"Yeah, we've called an emergency meeting of the Topless Agenda, so we're all gathering at Margaret Baine's villa near Aix en Provence."

"And everyone is going to be there?"

"Yeah, of course. Why?"

"Well, I'm fairly certain I've figured out how Hamza

infiltrated the Topless Agenda, but it's a little complicated, so I'll have to wait until we're in person to elaborate. It'll also give me some time to do a little more fact finding and fill in the rest of the blanks."

"But wait! How the hell did Hamza breach our security?"

"You'll know soon enough. Now, can you give me the exact address of Margaret's villa?"

"Sure, but your driver will know where to go."

"I'm afraid I need it right now, if you don't mind."

Matheson gave me the address, and, if memory served me correctly, it was in the same general area where the former power couple Brad Pitt and Angelina Jolie had lived before their split. Of course a billionaire and Hollywood royalty would all choose to live in same general area, and it made me think about the phrase that shit trickles down hill. If true then it explained how the fine smelling aristocracy made it's way up to places like Aix en Provence.

"OK, thanks. I'll see you in a few hours."

"But, wait, Finn! I still don't..."

It was too late, as I had already hung up. I had two more phone calls to make and no more time to talk to Matheson. My next call was to Bill Reigns, my man in Dubai, as he was the only person in the world who might be able to get the information I needed at this exact moment. Thankfully, he picked up on the second ring.

"Bill, it's Tag. How are you feeling?"

"Better, but I'm more interested to know if you made it out OK."

"We did, but now we have another problem, and I need your help."

"Absolutely. What do you need?"

"A little information—and, as usual, I need it fast."

I explained what I needed and Bill told me he would see what he could find out then call me back. In the meantime, I turned on Vandenberg's thirty inch iMac, opened a browser, and brought up Google. A moment later, I had a page full of hits with the third one down being the exact one I needed. I clicked on the link, brought up the web page, and five minutes later, had found all the necessary information. I was finally being proactive and feeling like an investigator again—and it felt good. The phone rang and I answered and heard Bill's voice.

"Finn here," I said.

"I've got the information you asked for, though you're not going to like it."

He relayed all the news I desperately needed—but didn't necessarily want to hear. It made things more complicated, but it explained a lot. I thanked him then hit end before making my final and most important phone call. The person answered, and, after the usual pleasantries, I relayed all the pertinent details then bid a fond farewell. The timing was going to be critical and getting everyone and everything into place would take a veritable miracle, but what was life without a few challenges? I had done all there was to do, so now it was time to sit, wait, and hope the universe was finally on my side.

I left Vandenberg's office and returned to my cabin, where I lay on the bed and closed my eyes, desperately hoping to get some rest before all hell broke loose. In spite of the churning excitement in my gut, I eventually drifted off to the welcomed relief of sleep.

I awoke two hours later when the announcement came over the intercom that we were on final approach to Marseille Provence Airport. I brushed my teeth then walked out and joined Farid, who was talking animatedly with Yvonne in the main salon.

"Did I miss anything exciting?" I asked.

"No, we were just talking about California and where Farid should consider living," Yvonne said.

"Northern or southern," I asked.

"Northern," Yvonne said.

"Good choice—although blondes are more abundant in Southern California," I added.

"Maybe I'll try both and see which I like better."

At that moment an announcement came over the intercom.

"Please fasten your seat belts and prepare for landing."

I double checked the tension on my seat belt then leaned back and looked out the window hoping to catch a glimpse of the city of Marseille. A light winter fog was stretching inland over the coast, so I could barely see a scant few buildings and roads below. Soon thereafter, I heard the thump of the landing gear deploying, and, only a minute or so later, we dropped with hardly a bump onto the runway. The plane decelerated rapidly then made a sharp turn and taxied towards the private terminal.

We came to a stop, and Wendy's voice came over the intercom announcing that we could unbuckle our seat belts and prepare to disembark. I returned to my cabin for my pistol, and, after sliding it into my shoulder holster, I joined Farid at the door. Brett, Tatyana, and Wendy appeared a moment later, and we said goodbye before exiting the jet to descend the boarding ramp and walk over to the waiting Maybach limousine.

The driver ushered us into the back of the particularly comfortable vehicle, and we made ourselves at home as he closed the door and took up residence behind the wheel. We left the airport and joined the bustling traffic of Marseille before merging onto the D9, which headed northeast towards Aix en Provence. The city eventually gave way to country, and the lush green landscape was dotted by the occasional farm house or barn. A little over thirty minutes later, we crossed through the center of Aix en Provence and merged onto the D10, which took us east and up into a scenic valley. It was the beginning of winter, so the trees were mostly bare, and any remaining leaves were turning yellow. It was sunny now that we were away from the coast, and I rolled down the window for a breath of fresh air and could smell and feel the dampness of a recent storm that had left a light dusting of snow on the surrounding peaks.

We continued on past a number of beautiful estates, which meant we were officially in the neighborhood of the rich and famous, and our destination was only a short distance away on the other side of the quaint village of Vauvenargues. It was a small French hamlet that also happened to be the one-time home of Pablo Picasso, and now, not surprisingly, also housed a member of the Topless Agenda. After passing through the town, we made a left and climbed up into the mountains on a winding road before pulling up and stopping before a massive wrought iron gate. An armed man appeared from inside a guard house and approached our vehicle to speak with the driver. They exchanged some words, then he went back inside his tiny dwelling, and the gate swung open, and we headed up the long driveway until at last coming to rest before a massive villa. Around us were parked a bevy of large prestigious automobiles with the only oddball in the bunch being a large passenger van, which was probably used by the house staff. The driver opened the door, and Farid and I exited and were soon met by a man dressed in a smart suit.

"Welcome to Château Les Mères Saintes, and, as cliché as it sounds, my name is actually Jeeves," he said, in a very proper British accent.

"The name's Finn, and I must say—this is quite a place you've got here."

"Yes indeed, now, if you'll please follow me. Everyone is eagerly awaiting your arrival in the conference room," he said, leading us up the steps and into the grand foyer.

The Château was old and regal, and its hardwood floors were covered by finely woven rugs, while its walls were adorned with classical artworks. Above us hung a massive chandelier, and the sun coming in through the front windows was refracting off the tiny crystals and sending thousands of tiny rivulets of light throughout the room. Ahead of us, in stark contrast, lay a dark hallway with the only illumination coming from the lights over the various paintings, sculptures, and suits of ancient armor that lined its walls. Farid looked at me nervously, clearly unsure about his current surroundings, which made sense, as he had yet to meet his mysterious new benefactors. I could understand his trepidation, as I too had felt it myself only a week ago when I first ventured into that topless tapas bar in Majorca.

Jeeves stopped and opened the door at the end of the hall and ushered us into a large stately room complete with a fireplace, bookshelves on all four walls, and a large oak table in the middle occupied by the members of the Topless Agenda. From left to right, we had Douglas Matheson, Harold Fuchs, Vladimir Strobodov, Margaret Baines, Charlene Chou, Anna Karlsson, Adya Chopra, Nicholas Abimbola, Daniel and William Vandenberg, and last, but not least, my favorite Frenchman Adrien Babineux—who, not surprisingly, was wearing yellow pants. Matheson, upon seeing us, immediately stood up and walked over.

"Good to see you safe and sound, Finn, and it's nice to

finally meet you, Dr. Ardeshir. I'm Douglass Matheson," he said, holding out his hand.

"You mean Senator Matheson as in the father of John Matheson, the current Vice President of the United States?" he asked, sounding a tad bit intimidated.

"The very same, but I think it's far more impressive to be meeting the father of cold fusion."

"Well, thank you, sir," Farid said, smiling bashfully.

"And please, call me Douglass. We like to keep things informal around here."

"In that case, call me Farid."

"Farid it is. Now, gentleman, please come join us."

We sat down at the two empty seats at the end of the table, and all eyes fell on me.

"All right, Finn. Do you want to update everyone?"

"Yeah, and as I told you on the phone, I've finally figured out how, or should I say who, Hamza is using to infiltrate the Topless Agenda," I said.

"You're not going to tell me it's one of us are you?" he asked.

"Yes and no. Unfortunately, it's a little complicated."

"Which means?"

Just then there was a disturbance outside, and a second later, two men decked out in assault gear came hustling through the door. I assumed they were friendlies until they turned their weapons towards the seated people.

"What's the meaning of this?" Matheson bellowed righteously.

No sooner had the words left his mouth that Prince Hamza and his ever faithful German henchman Klaus came striding into the room. Unlike the mercenaries they were dressed as though they were going to a party with Klaus wearing black slacks and a black button up shirt and Hamza sporting a grey business suit and a black keffiyah.

"Good afternoon, everyone, I am Prince Hamza, and I am here to take back my property," he said, in his usual smug and confident tone.

Farid leaned in and whispered in my ear.

"Dude, I know I've been going back and forth on this a lot, but now I'm pretty certain that it is seriously not awesome hanging out with you again."

CHAPTER TWENTY-NINE
Blond Ambition

There was nothing quite as effective as absolute privilege in childhood to form a complete asshole in adulthood, and Hamza was living proof of the truth of that hypothesis. He was a picture of smugness as he stood there gazing around the room, obviously taking great pleasure in knowing that some of the most important people in the world were all suddenly at his mercy. He finished his visual sweep then exchanged a look with Klaus, and they set off on what appeared to be a slow victory lap around the table. When they reached me, I couldn't help but throw out a comment to my favorite German tourist.

"Hello, Klaus, how was your swim the other night?" I asked, referring to sending him and his car into the estuary back in California.

"A lot more pleasant than the rest of your day is going to be."

"And they say Germans don't have a sense of humor."

Klaus moved closer and smiled, then punched me in the stomach. I was expecting the move, but it was still a good hit, and I crumpled over, embellishing a bit in order to make him believe that he had done enough damage and wouldn't need to repeat himself. I could take one punch for the team, but there was no reason to become a martyr just yet. Once I recovered, Prince Asshole decided to weigh in on our friendly little exchange.

"How nice to see you again, Mr. Finn, and, this time, I imagine it is you who are surprised to see me."

"Not really, nor is it particularly nice."

Hamza chuckled, then he and his faithful kraut continued on to the far end of the table, where he paused so that he could properly address the room.

"Now, Members of the Topless Agenda, it is about time you learned to stop meddling in the affairs of others, and starting today, your new world order is at an end, and mine is just beginning. So, now it is probably a good idea to pray to whatever God you believe in, as your time on this earth will officially be coming to an end very soon."

The people around the table may have been in a state of shock, but they were at least putting up a very convincing facade of brave composure. That was no small task, as the men with Hamza were obviously professional mercenaries and more than willing to kill for their employer. But, I had no intention of letting anyone get hurt today—at least not anyone on the home team, and, to that end, I took stock of our armed friends and found it odd that they had made no effort to search the people in the room for weapons. They were professionals, and professionals didn't overlook simple details like making sure their captives couldn't kill them. That simple fact meant that these people knew the rules of the Topless Agenda, with the first and foremost being that no firearms were permitted into their meetings. This, in turn, made it all that much clearer that my theory about the leak was correct. Luckily for us, however, the leak apparently didn't know that I had a propensity for carrying a pistol on my person. Still, I was up against four men, two of whom were wearing body armor, and that made for a tricky predicament, because it meant head shots, and head shots were a hell of a lot harder than center mass. The head was obviously smaller and bobbed around, so success would come down to timing, skill, and a shitload of luck.

"You can't just murder some of the most preeminent people in the world," Matheson said, looking agitated as he stood up from the table.

"Why? Are you bullet proof?" Hamza asked with a smile.

He had a point, and it would have almost been funny had the lives of thirteen people not been on the line.

"Obviously not, but you just can't make people this important disappear and expect to get away with it."

"There are a lot of bad people out in the world, and this will all be staged to look like a group of extremists conducting yet another attack against the decadent West. In fact, I've already got a local ISIS terror cell primed and ready to take the blame, and, by the time the authorities find them, you'll be dead, and we'll be long gone. Well now, friends, it's been nice, but the time for talk is over, and we should probably finish up here and be going."

One of the mercenaries stepped forward and spoke to Hamza, who suddenly looked troubled as he responded in an angry though hushed tone. More words were exchanged before the other mercenary spoke into his headset and held up his hands in frustration. It looked like our antagonists were having some kind of communication problem and couldn't contact the rest of their team. Perfect! I had my opportunity. I pulled out my pistol then leaned over to Margaret and whispered that she should pass on the news to the others to get ready to drop to the floor and cover their ears. She nodded then whispered to her immediate neighbor, and the news continued on until reaching Matheson, who mouthed the words too dangerous. I knew what he was worried about—collateral damage. It would be hard to avoid someone getting caught in the crossfire in such a small space, but the problem, however, was that we were all going to die unless we did something about our situation. Reports of people who survived life and death encounters always shared the same common denominator. Those who acted lived, and those who didn't—died. It was, therefore, time to act.

I hazarded a glance at Hamza and his small contingent of men and noticed they were all still busy discussing their sudden communication problem, which meant they were mostly oblivious to me and the people around the table.

Combine that with the fact they were all grouped together and I had a perfect opening to hit all of my targets without needing to drastically change my aim. First would be the two mercenaries, second would be Klaus, and third would be Hamza—who I would try to take alive if possible. A prick of his magnitude deserved a lot more pain than a bullet to the brain. I slid out of my chair and stepped away from the table in hopes of getting the others out of line of any return fire. I also kept my gun hidden behind my back and out of view in case they looked my way, as I needed to maintain every ounce of surprise. I managed to get clear off the table before Hamza turned around and noticed me.

"What are you doing? Sit back down!" he ordered angrily.

Shit, I needed to think fast and come up with some kind of distraction.

"I have to take a shit," I responded.

"I don't care."

"You will in about ten seconds when a deluge of diarrhea starts filling my pants—and that's assuming my pants even survive the first explosion. The way my stomach feels right now, I'm thinking we could be looking at a ten foot blast radius."

"Sit down and shut up!" he barked.

"Seriously now, I ate some bad lamb before leaving Jordan this morning, and I really need to use the toilet."

"Fine. Shoot him and put him out of his misery," Hamza said.

"Dude, don't you know that you never shoot a man with explosive diarrhea?"

My words had no effect, and the closest mercenary brought his submachine up to fire, but he was a second too late, and I put two quick shots straight through his goggles. His head jerked backward, and he collapsed and fell onto Hamza while the members of the Topless Agenda dropped to the floor and took cover beneath the table. The other mercenary, meanwhile, attempted to return fire, but again I was a step ahead and adjusted my aim and put two shots in the man's head. He, like his friend, was permanently out of the picture, and we were halfway to victory, but our problem had just gotten more difficult. Klaus was smart and quickly moved to a new position, something I also needed to do. A stationary shooter was an easy target and eventually got shot, so I dropped and fast crawled to a new location. There, I popped up and fired off two shots at Klaus, but he ducked and both shots missed him by a fraction of an inch. He popped back up a second later and returned fire, and the bullets barely missed my head as they embedded into the wall above me. Shit! He obviously knew what he was doing, which meant I needed to bring my A-game to the table—so to speak. I dropped back down and saw the members of the Topless Agenda cowering below the table, while beyond them Klaus, like me, was again moving into a new firing position. He popped up to shoot, but I stayed down this time, and fired through a gap between the people under the table. It was risky to shoot in such close proximity to friendlies, but I needed to get the sauer out of the kraut if I hoped to survive our encounter. The bullet caught him in the thigh, and he collapsed onto the floor, allowing me to move around the table to find him leaning against the wall, where he was using one of his hands to apply pressure to his leg wound. I closed the distance and arrived just as he tried to bring his pistol up to fire, but, fortunately for me, he was just a fraction too slow, and I had him dead to rights.

"Drop it or die, schnitzel face!"

He wavered for a moment then groaned in frustration as he dropped his gun and turned his attention to his leg wound. I kicked the pistol clear then backed up to do a quick three hundred and sixty degree threat assessment of the room, where I unfortunately discovered that Hamza was standing in front of the door and aiming a pistol at Margaret's head.

"Drop your gun, or she dies!" he screamed.

"He'll kill me anyway! Don't do it!" she said.

"Just relax, Hamza. No one else needs to die today."

"Fuck you! Drop your gun, or I'll blow her brains all over this room!"

My phone vibrated at that moment, and I was hopeful it was the signal I had been eagerly waiting to hear. I crouched down and pretended as though I was placing my gun on the floor.

"Tag, No!" Margaret yelled.

"It's going to be OK," I said, finally letting go of the gun and standing back up.

Traditionally, you never gave up your gun in a scenario like this, but I had an ace up my sleeve—hopefully anyway.

"You stupid asshole! Now I'm going to kill everyone in this room—starting with you!"

Hamza turned his gun towards me, but, before he could pull the trigger, the door behind him burst open and slammed into his back, sending him and Margaret crashing onto the ground, where his gun flew out of his hand and landed several feet away. A team of heavily armed assailants decked out head to toe in combat gear poured through the open doorway then spread out around the room to take up defensive positions. In the confusion, Hamza made a mad dash for the gun by scrambling on all fours, but I moved to intercept and stomped my foot down on his hand only inches before he reached his pistol. He screamed in agony, but I kept my foot firmly in place until I managed to reach down and pick up his gun.

"Time to give it up, camel jockey, or I'll rip that towel off your head and snap it against your chubby thighs until you cry like a little sissy!" I said.

"Dude!" I heard Farid say from nearby.

I glanced over and saw he was smiling and shaking his head at me.

"What?" I asked.

He held up eight fingers, five on his right and three on his left as he regarded me.

"I'm giving you an eight for creativity in using two disparaging remarks about Arabs, but I couldn't give you a ten, as you were still making disparaging remarks."

"That seems convoluted, but I can live with an eight," I said, as I ushered the members of the Topless Agenda out from under the table.

They formed up and appeared to be a bit apprehensive as they gazed at our new arrivals. I, however, knew exactly who our visitors were and couldn't help but smile.

"Do you mind letting us in on the joke?" Matheson asked.

"Yes, *dugland*, would you please enlighten us? Can't you see these people are terrified and need a break?" Babineux added.

Dugland translated as asshole and was a little inside joke between Babineux and me.

"But of course, my French friend. Everyone, please relax, as our late arrivals here are actually the good guys, or more accurately—good girls," I said.

"I'm not sure I understand," Matheson responded.

The lead figure pulled off her balaclava head cover, and her long dark hair fell past her shoulders, eliciting a number of gasps—mostly from the men in the room.

"Hello, everyone. I am the Desert Fox," she said.

"I totally agree," Matheson responded, as he stepped forward and offered his hand.

Dolunay was a remarkably beautiful woman, so it stood to reason that Matheson would bust out the exact same line as I had when I first met her.

"Thank you, Senator Matheson, and it's nice to meet you," she said.

"The pleasure is all mine, and call me Douglass."

"Douglass it is, and please call me Dolunay."

I walked over, and Dolunay and I shared a hug that she followed up with an unexpected kiss that lasted just long enough to get uncomfortable, considering the unusual circumstances and present company. Still, a kiss from a beautiful woman was a kiss nonetheless.

"I'm sure you're all wondering what the hell is going on," I said, turning to address the room.

"You've got that right," Matheson said.

"Well, luckily for all of us, I had the foresight to call Dolunay and have her bring one of her best teams here as fast as humanly possible."

"How could you have known that all of this was going to happen?" Matheson asked.

All the people in the room stared in rapt attention as they waited for me to begin speaking, and it was at last time for the big reveal, the moment where I got to deliver all my clever insights and be like television's Detective Columbo.

"People, I'm sorry to say it, but your organization has indeed been compromised."

There were a number of gasps and plaintive responses.

"But, you'll be happy to know that no one in this room is technically a party to the betrayal."

"Jesus, Finn, would you please get to the point?"

"All in good time. Now, in the interest of clarity, I suppose I should start with a brief recap of the last few days. So, first, you enlisted me to help you bring Farid to the west, and only a day later, the German here inexplicably showed up in Marin County and tried to kill me. The next day, he sabotaged the jet's engines and nearly killed not only me, but Matheson and Daniel Vandenberg."

"We know this part of the story," Matheson complained.

"I don't. Let him finish," Margaret said.

"So, at that point we knew we had a tenacious enemy, but the question was, how could he or she possibly know what we were up to and act on such unbelievably short notice—without, of course, some amount of insider knowledge. Daniel and Douglass were both emphatic that no one in this room would ever turn against the other members or leak any of its secrets, but the events told another tale. So, at that point, we had several potential possibilities to consider. One was whether the bad guy or girl was part of the Topless Agenda, and, if not, then who was the theoretical insider supplying this person with intelligence. Were we up against one person or perhaps a group of people? Well, I found out part of the answer when I saw Hamza and my favorite German tourist together at the royal palace. We had our primary bad guy and his henchman, but we still didn't have our connection to the Topless Agenda, and, oddly, the answer would come a week later in the least likely of places. You see, when I was at the Royal Palace in Dubai, I also happened to see a woman in the room with Hamza and the German. Unfortunately, she had her back to me, so all I could see was her very ornate, diamond encrusted bracelet—a detail that wouldn't mean anything until a day later when I was taking a dump on the Vandenberg jet."

"Do we really need that much detail, Finn?" Matheson complained.

"Probably not, but I'm a detail person. Now, I, like most people, read on the toilet, and, to that end, I borrowed Farid's shitty tabloid magazine, and you'll never guess what I learned."

Recognition dawned on Farid's face, and I had the feeling he knew exactly where I was going.

"The bracelet! Holy shit! I knew that woman looked familiar!" Farid exclaimed loudly.

"So, who is the girl and what does she have to do with all of this?" Matheson asked expectantly.

Before I could respond, there was a commotion out in the hall, and everyone turned to see two of Dolunay's soldiers bringing in a prisoner. She was blond, beautiful, and ornery as all hell as she fought her captors at every step. Eventually they were able to get her into the room, and she looked around then immediately cowed and averted her eyes. On her wrist, coincidentally, was the very same diamond encrusted bracelet.

"Everyone, I believe you all know Margaret's daughter Charlotte," I said.

"Charlotte! What are you doing here?" Margaret asked.

Charlotte didn't answer and instead continued to stare down at the floor.

"It's OK, I'll answer that question. You see, Charlotte's here with her boyfriend," I said.

"So, who is this mystery man, and where is he?" she asked.

"Right there," I said, pointing at Hamza.

"But, how could that be?" Margaret asked, looking utterly shocked.

"Well, once I learned that the mystery woman was Charlotte, I did a little online research and soon found the connection to Hamza. I'm pretty sure the two of them met while attending Oxford sometime between 2006 and 2010. Both were economics majors and both came from wealthy families, where they were living in the shadow of higher achieving older siblings. It, therefore, made perfect sense that they would meet, bond, and fall in love, and eventually put into action an insidious plot to gain independence from their respective families with the icing on this cake of betrayal being the attempted demise of the Topless Agenda.

"Charlotte, I don't understand how you could be involved in all this," Margaret said, sadly.

Charlotte stared silently at the floor, her eyes filling with tears before she finally spoke.

"I—I just wanted to finally get away from this family—away from you. I'm tired of being the black sheep—your little embarrassment you hide from the rest of your life. Hamza and I were going to start a new life together, but, as usual, you ruined it! You ruined it!"

Her voice trailed off, and she seemed to drift into her own little world as she collapsed onto the floor and hugged her knees into her chest.

"But wait, you still haven't explained how you knew that Hamza was going to move against us at the meeting today," Matheson said.

"Well, that part came down to intuition and some valuable intelligence from your man Bill Reigns in Dubai. Once I knew about the meeting, I realized it would be a perfect opportunity for Hamza and Charlotte to take all of you out in one fell swoop. So, I called Bill and had him check on Prince Hamza's travel plans. It turned out that our favorite prince had left Dubai and flown into Marseille Provence Airport along with an unusually large entourage this very morning. Not one to believe in coincidences, I immediately called Dolunay, and, thanks to her and her girls' timely arrival, we all get to live to fight another day."

There was a sound of approaching footsteps in the hallway, and, a moment later, two familiar faces were staring at me from the doorway. It was Dick and Jane, two of the Topless Agenda's key security people. The three of us had first crossed paths a couple weeks ago during the course of my European assignment. At the time, I thought they were the bad guys, but now, we were all friends, and they were obviously here to start the clean-up process. It wouldn't be an easy task, as there was a lot of shit to deal with—namely Hamza, his German lackey, his mercenaries, and last but not least, a girl desperately in need of a good spanking, therapy, and a reduction in her allowance.

"Dick, Jane! How nice to see you again!" I said.

"Nice to see you as well, Tag. I see you've got the situation mostly in hand."

"Mostly, thanks to Dolunay and her team."

"Well, thank you both for all the help," Jane said.

"My pleasure," Dolunay responded.

"I see your wardrobe hasn't changed much, Jane." I said.

"No, it hasn't—in spite of your antics, and I imagine you'll probably be unhappy to learn that there's no rain in the immediate forecast."

"You're right! That does make me a little unhappy."

Jane was wearing a white dress shirt, very similar to the one she had been wearing when we first met, only that time I had dumped a glass of ice water down the front as a distraction so I could steal her key fob. The ploy worked perfectly with the added benefit being that her shirt became mostly see-thru—something neither Dick nor I would soon forget. Now, it was our little inside joke, and remembering it brought a smile to all three of our faces. Dick, who was standing beside her, decided it was time to get the show on the road and pulled out his phone and called in a paramedic as well as more security people. I took that as my cue to check on the German and utilize some of my PJ medical training to make sure he survived to join Hamza in prison. He had a leg wound, and few people knew that they were particularly lethal, because a rupture of the femoral artery could bring death in mere seconds.

The German was lucky, however, and the bullet had just passed through his outer thigh. I used his belt and a wad of napkins to construct a makeshift tourniquet and bandage, which would hold until official help arrived. Within fifteen minutes, everything was practically back to normal, and all the bad guys were gone and everyone was seated around the table quietly mulling over the events of the last hour.

"Finn, again, you have proved yourself more valuable than any of us could have imagined, and everyone here owes you a debt that we could never be able to adequately repay," Matheson said.

"No problem—I've already been paid more than enough for my services, and what really matters is that everyone is safe and sound, and I am close to fulfilling my original promise to get my friend here to America, so that he can finally be with the big breasted blonde that he so dearly desires."

There were a number of chuckles from around the table, and it was a nice tension breaker to bring the mood of the room back from the dire events of earlier. Of course, I felt bad for Margaret and could only wonder how she would deal with her daughter. It wasn't every day that your child was involved in your potential demise, let alone the destruction of your secret society. Hamza's fate would also likely prove to be an interesting story, as his father wasn't going to be particularly happy to find out his son had lost the golden goose, and, worse still, had been using the Emirates assets for his own evil agenda. A waiter arrived a moment later with glasses and champagne then began filling and distributing them to each person at the table. Once everyone was properly outfitted with some bubbly, Matheson stood up and held his glass high in the air.

"It's been a challenging couple of weeks and an even more challenging day, so let's take a moment to raise our glasses to the man and woman who saved our asses today. To Tag and Dolunay."

"Here here!" Margaret said.

"To Dolunay and dugland!" Babineux added.

When the cheering dyed down, Farid, looking perplexed, spoke up.

"I'm sorry to interrupt, but I speak fluent French, yet I have never heard the word dugland," he said.

"It's Babs's pet name for me, and it means asshole *en français*," I responded.

"I like it!"

"I figured you would, and since we're giving out toasts and showering each other with praise, I think it's time we acknowledge the Topless Agenda's newest member and a person whose brilliance will very likely change the fate of the world. To Farid Ardeshir, the father of cold fusion, and, more importantly, a good man and a good friend," I said.

Everyone clinked glasses and sipped champagne, and soon the quiet rumble of voices filled the room. Waiters appeared with trays of tapas, and it was feeling very much like my first meeting with this group back in Majorca—minus, of course, the topless waiters and waitresses. The party was in full swing, and people talked, laughed, and eventually the great spark of human interaction overshadowed the earlier part of the day's averted tragedy. Farid and I talked, ate, and finally enjoyed a moment together where we weren't on the run, being shot at, or jumping out of an airplane. A waiter appeared and gave us both a refill, then Farid clinked his glass to mine.

"Dude, I can finally say without a doubt that it is seriously awesome hanging out with you again," he said.

"Dude, the feeling is mutual."

CHAPTER THIRTY
A Kind of Homecoming

I awoke around eight a.m., and, having visited at least ten countries in three weeks, had to take a minute to look around the room before deciding that I was indeed in my own bed. I'd arrived home a little after ten in the evening the previous night and stayed awake only long enough to down a glass of Soft Taco Island Rum before brushing my teeth and going straight to bed.

Morning was here, so it was time to face the day ahead, and I stood up and ambled across the floor with my body feeling beat and making audible creaking sounds as I entered my bathroom and brushed my teeth. Feeling minty fresh, I went downstairs and started the coffee machine, and, a minute later, I interrupted it's pour to fill my cup. Next, I used the backup carton of almond milk as creamer then had a seat at my breakfast table and took my beloved first sip of coffee. The warm liquid soothed my soul and awakened my mind as I gazed out at Richardson Bay to see that the day was beautiful, clear, and free of the usual fog. It was actually hard to believe that I was home, as my mind was still filled with images of my whirlwind trip across the Middle East and Europe. It had been a pretty fucking exciting time, but I was happy to be here at my humble breakfast table. I took another sip of coffee and suddenly felt a familiar pressure in my lower abdomen that inspired me to stand up and make my way to the bathroom, where I gazed fondly at my porcelain mistress.

"I've missed you, my dear, but I'm back," I said, dropping my pants and lowering my backside onto the cool plastic contoured seat.

I opened my book to my toilet paper bookmark, took another sip of coffee, then gave my fecal offering unto the bowl—thus losing myself to the quiet comfort of my porcelain kingdom. Sure, I was happy at the moment, but I would have been a hell of a lot happier with the right company—namely Estelle. She was a subject that I was desperately trying to avoid, and just recalling her name was enough to bring a twinge of pain to my heart. I glanced at my phone and for once actually kind of wished it would ring and interrupt my special time—assuming that call was from Estelle, but, that was a mere fantasy, for she was most likely off with her new husband. Oh well. I finished up and headed upstairs and stepped into the shower to wash away a week's worth of adventure, and, five minutes later,

I emerged clean and perhaps a little melancholy. I dressed and went back down to the kitchen to get another cup of coffee, and, just as I was adding the almond milk, heard a knock at the door. Who in the hell could that be? If I were lucky, it would be my neighbor Joyce with a tray of freshly baked chocolate chip cookies or blueberry muffins. I padded down the hall, opened the door, and there to my surprise, was Estelle, looking radiantly beautiful in the morning sun with her eyes aglow and her mouth forming one of the most welcoming smiles I had ever seen.

"Good morning. How was your wedding?" I asked.

"I wouldn't know."

"Seriously?"

"Yeah."

Well shit, this morning was suddenly looking a bit brighter.

"What brings you by?" I asked.

"I'm here to see if I need to make good on the promise I made when we last parted."

"What promise?"

"You know—the one where I promised to give you the most amazing blowjob you could ever imagine if I did indeed bring about some kind of catastrophic event when I interrupted you on the toilet."

"Oh yeah, that promise, well you'll be surprised to learn that, shortly thereafter, the jet I was flying on lost power and had to make an emergency landing, but I survived obviously," I said.

"Seriously?"

"Yep." I said, finding myself smiling uncontrollably from ear to ear as a healthy rush of blood began making its way to my happy place.

"Well, a promise is a promise."

We both stood there smiling stupidly at each other until a thought crossed my mind.

"I must say, I'm a little surprised you didn't call first," I said.

"I didn't want to ruin your special time."

"Estelle, you could never ruin my special time."

"You know, that's the sweetest thing you've ever said to me."

She stepped forward and wrapped her arms around me, and we shared a long hard, passionate kiss. This was definitely looking to be the beginning of a perfect day, and, holding Estelle, my thoughts returned to my earlier musings on the subject of happiness. It really does indeed come from the simple things in life—whether that's family, good friends, good health, or, in this instance, the woman you love showing up on your doorstep unmarried and, more importantly, after your morning movement.

TAG FINN WILL BE CONTINUING HIS ADVENTURES IN

MR. PICKLES

Tag Finn's obese feline neighbor, Mr. Pickles, has the inexplicably odd habit of attracting trouble, and Finn, having already had to rescue the portly pet three months earlier, is shocked to discover three armed Chinese men attempting a dastardly catnapping. Thwarting their efforts, he and his neighbor Joyce take the troublesome tub of love to the vet to get him microchipped, and they learn that Pickles already has a chip in his neck. But, it's not the kind found in pets, and instead, is filled with top secret guidance software originating from a Silicone Valley defense contractor.

Finn sets out to uncover Pickle's unlikely role in this web of international espionage and finds himself embroiled in a deadly game of cat and mouse with a Chinese spy ring and the very beautiful and potentially deadly Cherry Poppins. Utilizing every ounce of his keen mind and unique skills, he faces danger, intrigue, and wild erotic escapades as he unravels the very dramatic tale of Mr. Pickles.

THE MANTASY SERIES:

SOFT TACO ISLAND

TOPLESS AGENDA

GORDITA CONSPIRACY

MR PICKLES

STRIPPER BOAT

POI PREDICAMENT

CHALUPA CONUNDRUM

PROMETHEUS PROTOCOL

ACKNOWLEDGEMENTS

I suspect every writer has a large list of people who make their work possible, and mine begins with my wife, who hears every one of my idiotic ideas and gives her opinion freely and without fear that I might get offended and stop helping with the housework. Next, would be my editors, Ruth A. Bright, Chris Cooper, and Aria Pearson who have generously given their time to comb the book for mistakes and keep me grammatically, if not politically or morally correct. After editors, comes my army of proof-readers, namely Matt Zeeman, Chris Imlay, Bob Horton, Katherine Gundling, and Jason Bright. Following them is my family, especially my father Fred Christie, who has always believed in my artistic endeavors and supported them both figuratively and literally. Next would be my mother Jane Christie (Posthumously), who definitely played a roll in my odd sense of humor. Also in the family category, is my pushy sister Sheree Wilson who helped get me into a posh New York Literary Agency, as well as my less pushy sister, Shelly Hall. From there, it continues on to two special friends who helped in a very unusual way, namely securing the Macbook Pro laptop that I would use to write while incarcerated at Stanford Hospital. Those two generous souls, inadvertently responsible for the proliferation of the Mantasy Genre, are Michele and Dan Scanlon. Next is my oldest friend and layout expert Chris Imlay followed by Dianna Woods, Jimmy and Jodie Woods, Robert O'Brien, all of whom have been willing to suffer through early drafts, mistakes, inaccuracies, and a vast number of unusual sexual metaphors.

Another special thank you goes out to Greg Owens, good friend and international man of business acumen, who passed on the following advice from his mentor George Leonard—take the hit. Which means: should you ever be sidelined with something such as five years of cancer treatment, do something positive with the time—in my case writing a bunch of escapist, erotic, adventure novels.

I'd also like to thank Mike Rowe and his Dirty Jobs show, as well as Jeremy Clarkson, James May, and Richard Hammond and their show Top Gear (which is now more or less the Grand Tour on Amazon), as they helped make many, many—many hours in isolation bearable. After leaving the hospital, I had a new immune system and more or less was the equivalent of an adult toddler and therefore had to avoid the public and all of the requisite germs. To that end, I was home all day every day, and the only way to keep from going totally bonzo when I was writing was to have a show on in the background. My two favorites were Dirty Jobs on the Discovery Channel and Top Gear online, and both shows provided the prefect inspiration for me to create a wacky escapist book series. So, to both entities and all those involved—you have my gratitude!

My final word of thanks goes out to my vast martial arts community, all of whom helped keep me alive and well throughout the dark days of cancer treatment. At the top of that group, and requiring special thanks, are Matt Thomas, Rick Alemany, and Margaret Alemany whose wisdom and teaching helped inspire many of the techniques in the book. Beyond them and within our own karate community is Lauren and Rob Sandusky, Thandi Guile, Aria and Daniel Pearson, Tom Jacoby and Jennifer Solow, John Hedlund, Michele & Dan Scanlon, Katherine Gundling, Bob Horton, Sue Fox and J.T. Meade, Mark, Matt, Brad, and Jade Zeeman, Ted Hatch, James Parks, Jeremy Holt and the Holt Family, Sabrina Haechler, Jonathan Johnson, Brannon Beliso, Catherine and Eric Engelbrecht, Catherine and Ian Moore, Tamera Blake, the families and students of Christie Kenpo Karate, Michael Mason MD, Natalya Greyz MD, Sally Arai MD, and the Stanford University BMT Unit & ITA. If you don't see your name here, don't worry—there is a more comprehensive list of the karate community on the Thank You page of my website.

To all of you, I say be well—and more importantly—dump well.

ORIGIN OF THE MANTASY GENRE

In 2010, I was diagnosed with Stage 4 Non-Hodgkins T-Cell Lymphoma Cancer, and, with only weeks before my imminent demise, began rigorous dose dense chemotherapy. With an extremely low survival rate, about one in five, I was particularly lucky to achieve a full remission in just over two months. I went on to receive a stem cell, and eventual bone marrow transplant at Stanford University, the last procedure being the most effective treatment for a lifelong cure.

So, what exactly does a person do when faced with extreme isolation and the fear of a potentially premature demise? Well, I started reading Harry Potter and filled many long hours hooked up to a chemo drip, spending my time with the life and adventures of the boy who lived—hoping, in my case, to be the man who survived. There aren't many books more removed from the doldrums of cancer, so it became the perfect escape. The problem, however, was that I tore through them so quickly that I was soon on my own again—desperately in need of something to fill my long, anxiety filled days.

I tried several popular novels and authors I liked but couldn't find anything to adequately fill the endless hours of isolation. Of course, I could have wallowed in self pity, but I really didn't want the months of downtime to be meaningless. If I was forced to sit around like a piece of shit, then I wanted to do something with the time. I immediately decided that I should turn my screenplay writing skills into the ultimate, tell-all cancer book, but, five pages in, I realized the topic was too depressing and decided to instead write a novel. It was going to be the book I desperately wanted to read and would include all the things I lacked at that moment—namely sex, alcohol, adventure, travel, and privacy in the bathroom—the key elements for a truly rewarding existence.

I finished chemo at Kaiser then headed south to the Stanford University Hospital and quickly realized that I would have nothing but a window and the internet for a companion in the coming months. Worse still were the medical horrors that would soon become a part of my daily existence. My morning nurse, concerned about the debilitating physical effects of intense chemo, entered my room each day with the following words:

"What would you like me to check first? Your balls or your butt hole?"

"Um—neither?" I responded.

At that point, all I desired went into my writing, first and foremost being a little privacy in the ol' baño. The nurses had an annoying habit of always wanting to weigh my stools—something to do with keeping track of fluid and food intake and the subsequent amount of release. My bathroom contained what I called the cowboy hat, a plastic insert to catch waste entering the toilet. Peeing in the little urinal was enough indignity, so whenever possible, I woke up early and dumped before they could make their rounds. Every day that I sent a number two un-accosted down the drain was a small, though cherished victory. I felt like a prisoner—a veritable Count of Monte Cristo, though my prison was a hospital and my battles were waged over porcelain.

Continuing with the theme of writing about all I lacked meant that the book would sizzle with sex, adventure, and humor. Three months later, I would complete book one and within the year, finish two more—completing what I called at the time, The Mantasy Trilogy—the word Mantasy, being the combination of Male and Fantasy. The following year, I managed to write five more follow ups, all with the same character and eccentricities but with new and exciting storylines and locations. Now, I had a Mantasy Series. Or, if I wanted to follow in Douglas Adam's footsteps, I would say—books four, five, six, seven, and eight in the Mantasy Trilogy. I'm currently finishing books nine, ten, and eleven.

Writing has always been one of my great loves but sadly, it took a life threatening illness to bring us back together full-time. I have written a number of screenplays and had two optioned for motion pictures, but traditional writing is more complicated and requires a hell of a lot more work. It is, however, more rewarding because you have the ability to deliver your story directly to an audience, whether it's your friends, the woman at the Post Office, or the thousands of potential readers trolling the online eBooks. It doesn't need a fifty million dollar budget, a production team, distribution, and funding for it to reach an audience—and that is pretty awesome.

ABOUT THE AUTHOR

Lyle Christie was born in San Francisco, raised in Marin County, and attended the University of Kentfield, San Francisco State University, the Academy of Art College, and Dominican University, where he majored in film and social psychology, and minored in Philosophy, Anthropology, and Human Sexuality—all of which gave him the diverse educational background to become a writer and director. In addition, he holds a fifth degree black belt and teaches Kenpo Karate, Jujitsu, Arnis, and Wing Chun. During his lifetime in the martial arts, he has taught civilians as well as police and military personnel and has the unique pleasure of training with elite members of the United States and international defense and intelligence community.

(More on next page.)

He also teaches firearms, swords, sticks, and knives, though he is equally deadly with the nunchaku, machete, goat, tether ball, and skin flute — the last perhaps being his greatest skill set. Above all else, he maintains excellent, if not grey, hair and lives aboard a yacht in Sausalito with his wife, French Bulldog, and Miniature Dachshund. When he's not writing, directing, teaching martial arts, or training with the real life James Bonds of the world, you'll find him fighting injustice, cherishing a number two, working out, or riding his mountain bike through the scenic hills of Marin County.

You can learn more at www.lylechristie.com.